SHAKEDOWN
BEACH

Also by Eric Dezenhall

Money Wanders

Jackie Disaster

*Nail 'Em! Confronting High-Profile Attacks
on Celebrities and Businesses*

SHAKEDOWN BEACH

ERIC DEZENHALL

Thomas Dunne Books
St. Martin's Minotaur ⚏ New York

THOMAS DUNNE BOOKS.
An imprint of St. Martin's Press.

www.minotaurbooks.com

Library of Congress Cataloging-in-Publication Data

Dezenhall, Eric.
    Shakedown Beach / Eric Dezenhall.—1st ed.
        p.   cm.
    ISBN 0-312-30772-1
    EAN 978-0312-30772-1
    1. Political consultants—Fiction. 2. Atlantic City (N.J.)—Fiction. 3. Crisis management—Fiction. I. Title.
    PS3604.E94S53 2004
    813'.6—dc22   2004041754

First Edition: June 2004

10 9 8 7 6 5 4 3 2 1

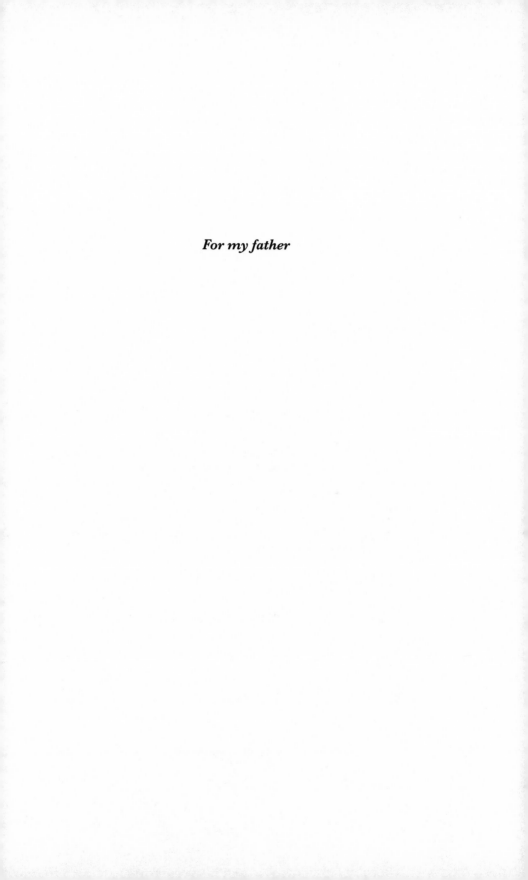

For my father

SHAKEDOWN BEACH RULES

1. Leather is not necessarily cool.

2. The other guy is scared, too.

3. Nobody has thick skin.

4. Do the right thing because it's right, not because you'll get paid back.

5. God sent certain women to destroy your life; certain others to save it.

6. There are no geniuses.

7. You're not as impressive as you think you are.

8. Sometimes you outgrow people. Sometimes they outgrow you.

9. Avoid things that piss you off.

10. You don't get stuff "out of your system."

11. When you turn the other cheek, you get bitten in the ass.

12. Happiness is relief

13. Someone knows your secret.

—JONAH EASTMAN, MARGATE, NEW JERSEY

Author's Note

Since the publication of my novels *Money Wanders* and *Jackie Disaster,* curious readers have contacted me with questions about whom my characters might be based upon. I always enjoy the indulgence, but confess at the outset of *Shakedown Beach* that all players are fabricated, just placed in familiar settings. My friend Dr. Sally Satel, an esteemed psychiatrist, believes that spinning tall tales is a pathetic device I use to convince a few girls I grew up with in South Jersey that (despite them) I've gone on to have the coolest life EVER. Perhaps, but this diagnosis should not detract from your enjoyment of either my fiction or the music I have composed and performed for decades under the stage name Bruce Springsteen and the E (for Eric) Street Band.

E.B.D.

Longport, New Jersey

"Dirt's a funny thing," the Boss said. *"Come to think of it, there ain't a thing but dirt on this green God's globe except what's under water, and that's dirt too. It's dirt makes the grass grow. A diamond ain't a thing in the world but a piece of dirt that got awful hot. And God-a-mighty picked up a handful of dirt and blew on it and made you and me and George Washington and mankind blessed in faculty and apprehension. It all depends on what you do with the dirt. That right?"*

—Robert Penn Warren, ALL THE KING'S MEN

The really great opportunities to connect with sex bombs always come along when you're already tied up with something else.

—Donald E. Westlake, THE FUGITIVE PIGEON

BOOK I

THE GRAPES OF ROTHMAN

The great convenience of superficial qualities is that, having so little meaning, they cannot be misunderstood.

—Gregg Easterbrook, THIS MAGIC MOMENT

THANKSGIVING EVE—ATLANTIC CITY, NEW JERSEY

"Secrets are like a bomb in your head."

I am the pollster who got Gardner "Rebound" Rothman elected governor of New Jersey by blaming a hurricane on his opponent. The idea hit me when I was doing sit-ups one morning while watching a press conference about the storm that blew a Wildwood motel into the Atlantic Ocean. Barri Embrey, the deceptively brittle investigative reporter for the *South Jersey Probe*, had held up a photo of the Guido Dunes Motel (motto: "We got your ocean right here") floating upside-down in the surf and asked a terrified Jersey Shore councilman, "What went wrong here?"

I thought that was beautiful: a weather system the size of Asia eats South Jersey, and Barri Embrey—known as "Barium Enema" in Jersey political circles—demands to know *who* screwed up. For media purposes, of course, that "who" would ideally be a middle-aged white guy with power. Politicians make great red meat. My racket is largely about taking credit—or blaming somebody else—for God's handiwork, so I nailed Rebound's opponent, the sitting governor, for "mishandling" the hurricane. Barium Enema went for it, and the rest of the media followed. Soon a Camden trial lawyer sued Cape May County for "meteorological negligence."

During our gubernatorial campaign, I made sure that all of Rebound Rothman's issue positions were deemed "bold"—after I polled each one carefully to make sure it pissed off as few people as possible, especially the sacred Three *I*s of New Jersey politics: Italy, Israel, and Ireland. The trick was that the word *bold*, if echoed by the right chorus, was more memorable than whatever opinion it was associated with. The only word that polled as well as *bold* was *hope*, thus Rebound's campaign slogan: **"The Boldness to Hope."**

"Yo! athlete, what's it mean?" Rebound asked with a wink that implied "Don't tell me," his South Jersey accent mixing the entire question into one syllable.

"Nothing," I said.

Rebound gave me a boyish mock punch to the jaw, buddy-style. He can be playful when you aid and abet him in not dealing with a clean truth. He flourished in obtuse realms the way palm trees flourished in the tropics. Truth withered Rebound, but he enjoyed the thespian dividends of ASKING HARD QUESTIONS if he could do it with a chop of the air or a bang on a podium.

Let me start this fable of death and subterfuge with a little candor: I am not a popular pollster; I'm just an effective one. Whereas most "communications professionals" are in the business of telling pretty lies, your narrator, Jonah Eastman, is known for telling ugly truths. People hate that. As Lenny Bruce said, "*Respectable* means under the covers." Many in my own party, Republican, won't use me. There are any number of reasons why I'm an outcast. Professional jealousy may be one of them, but it's self-serving to limit it to that. Another possible reason is because people associated with my work have been known to vanish, an eventuality not associated with conventional polling. I've come to be seen as a secret weapon, somebody who is called upon when things get nasty, but whom few admit to knowing. This is fine, provided I'm paid up front. I hate to get all Freudian, but I'm sure that some of the stuff I get caught up in can be traced to my background . . .

. . .

"See, Jonah, a secret is like a land mind," my grandfather Mickey told me when I was thirteen. "Do you know what that is?"

"I think you mean land *mine*, not *mind*, Pop-Pop," I said.

"Now don't get smart. Do you know what it is or not?" Mickey pressed.

"A land mine is like a bomb," I answered.

"It *is* a bomb," Mickey corrected. "It can be down there for so long you forget about it like a moron. Then one day you step on it and you're borscht. Secrets rip you apart like that, too."

Mickey went on and on about how dangerous secrets could be, and pressed his case that the proper term was *land mind* because "secrets are like a bomb in your head." He felt strongly about his collection of succinct life lessons, often jotting them down on playing cards and taping them to my bedroom mirror. As I got older, I came to appreciate Mickey's penchant for recording aphorisms, and I had begun to keep my own observations made during turbulent times in my own life. I jotted them down on my business cards, mostly, and tacked them to a corkboard in my study. At the moment, however, I saw no advantage in questioning Mickey further about his homicide of the English language and attendant metaphors because it only made him defensive and chide me for my "fancy talk."

I remember where Mickey and I had our talk about secrets. It was right where I was now standing, in the vault at Shekels Bank on Atlantic Avenue, which was right across the street from the Taste of the Shore saltwater taffy shop on the boardwalk, which he owned. The bank wasn't really called Shekels, but it had had so many names over the years that I found it easier to call it by the nickname Mickey gave it a lifetime ago.

Despite the passage of time, the inside of the vault at Shekels Bank remained the same—the paint on the walls was still Prozac Green, the single nervous fluorescent light buzzing above was still Panic White, the stacked steel boxes were still brushed Vertigo Silver, and stale air burped out of the rectangular morgue after I turned the key and slipped the Nausea Beige box out toward my chest. One feature was comparatively new: A wall-mounted lever reading EMERGENCY—PULL FOR AIR. I inhaled slowly to make sure I could get some oxygen into my lungs if somebody slammed the vault door shut. The sensory bombardment brought me anxiously back almost three decades, to thirteen, not long after my parents died, and Mickey and my grandmother were raising me.

I knew that Mickey was different from other grandfathers by the way tall men bowed when they bent down to shake his square golden hands. I had seen many big men shake the hands of smaller men on the boardwalk as a boy, but most small men seemed to rise desperately when they greeted bigger men. It was weird to watch giants stoop like peasants when they reached for little Mickey, who had once taken me to Wannamaker's boys' department in Philly and bought the exact sneakers for himself that he did for me, boys' size and all. Men's eyes would climb up their foreheads like caterpillars with hopes that their words would reach Mickey, as if his ears were below a sonar line of communication.

I think it was the way that Mickey stood back and spoke quietly that forced the giants to descend to him. Or maybe it was their fear that with one wag of his baby carrot finger they would be turned into a worm buffet in an impromptu Pine Barrens grave. The *Philadelphia Bulletin* had once written, "Mickey Price has sat at the apex of the American underworld longer than any mob boss in history," which was another reason why I knew that my grandfather was different from other grandfathers. One of my fourth-grade classmates had brought the article in for show-and-tell and helpfully shared with the class some of Mickey's nicknames, which were all coyly tied to the foods of his ethnic heritage: the Big Kugel, the Main Knish, Boss Bagel, the Head Hamentash of the Kosher Nostra.

That Mickey was rumored to be behind the murders of business associates who had grown inconvenient never rang true with me, not because of the grand moral implications, but because I didn't think that men who wore sneakers from Wannamaker's boys' department could actually kill people. If that were true, what would I be capable of? After all, I had the same sneakers.

Things with the law got so bad in the mid-1970s that Mickey, Deedee (my grandmother), and I had to flee the country. Between the ages of thirteen and fifteen, we lived in France. Deedee told me many things during our time on the run. None of them were important facts—such as exactly what crime Mickey had committed to trigger our flight—but they were insights that proved to be brilliant decades later. Guilt-ridden over my deprivation of a "normal boyhood," Deedee told me on the steps of the Sacré-Coeur that adolescence was "just a goddamned heartache" and I'd "make up" for it later. I took her word for it, and envisioned a future for myself filled with women named Monique St. Pierre, who was a *Playboy* playmate of that era.

Prior to our exodus, on Friday nights Mickey would walk with me from his taffy store to Shekels Bank to deposit money in full view of law enforcement, and occasionally sort out papers in his safe deposit box. Mickey's taffy store has long since been replaced by the Golden Prospect Hotel and Casino, which he built when gaming was approved in the late 1970s and quietly controlled until his death several years ago. The casino is totally corporate now, and as Mickey once growled when the FBI followed us down the beach, "Gambling will become respectable the day they run the Yids and guineas out."

As light snow whispered across Atlantic Avenue, I returned to Shekels Bank as a middle-aged man. I was wearing a wool cap, bomber jacket with the collar pulled up to obscure most of my face, and sunglasses, despite the wintry haze, to place an envelope in the safe deposit box I had inherited from Mickey. After he died, all I had found inside was his passport and certificate of naturalization, which I removed. The interior of the box was all scraped up, and I imagined all of the secrets that Mickey must have stored in there over the years: cash, guns, bound rosters of mortgaged politicians and souls, a recipe for taffy or rotgut, fake passports for an unscheduled trip.

Today, the box was empty until I dropped the thick padded envelope inside with all of the materials its new owners needed. Why had I paid $158 each year to keep an empty box? Maybe it was a superstition, a desire to sustain a connection, however hollow, between Mickey and me. Or maybe I hoped that someday I would open it up and find something inside that made my haunted life make sense.

I shut the square door and pushed the box back inside the vault, which liberated stale whispers that had been festering inside since Prohibition. An old woman in charge of the vault—she looked like pumpkin bread— waddled beside me and turned her security key to double-lock my box. I swallowed hard, feeling depressed that a matron like her was puttering around a bank on the night before Thanksgiving, but I was here, too, so what did that say about me? I wanted to pull the emergency air lever.

I walked outside into the gentle snowfall. It was getting dark. A line of magical buses snaked past me to deliver passengers to the casinos for The Jackpot that was their American due. My car, a Cadillac I recently acquired under twisted circumstances, was thirty steps away. I spied a Mercury Cruiser across the street that hadn't been there when I entered the bank. My throat began to feel tight and I could hear the thrumming of blood in my ears. None too subtly, a camera wagged like a rottweiler's tongue out the front window. I had a sickening thought that the men in the Mercury might have been dispatched by Edie, my wife, but flushed it into whatever mental receptacle stored paranoid musings. I tilted my head back and glanced skyward in an attempt to appear casual, as if I were just observing a cloud formation. I took my keys from my coat pocket, still looking up, when an elbow from a formless sidewalk mass emerged from the shadows and smashed me square on my chin.

I didn't even have the chance to reach for my revolver. I cursed myself—I was so *not* a pro. I fell against my Caddy, dropped my keys on the hood, and watched them nick the paint as they slid down to the whitening pavement. Tiny silver chips slid like tears onto me. From the street side of the Caddy, a thick gloved hand reached through the snowflakes and helped me climb back to my feet. The man who owned the hand—a ringer for John Belushi minus the quizzical expression— observed with a mouth that barely moved, "You fell?" His Russian accent was deep and rose from the back of his throat. *Hyoofeeel?* His teeth were small and unevenly spaced.

"Yes," I confirmed, glancing in the direction of whomever, whatever, had hit me and vanished.

I wondered if somehow the albino had survived . . .

Belushi's singular eyebrow made no attempt to part. There would be neither chants of "Toga!" nor riffs of "Soul Man" today, because sight-ings of fallen men were routine in his world and didn't inspire shtick. I peeled the safe deposit box key from my key ring and placed it in Belushi's leathered hand, wondering how many pollsters had been on the receiv-ing end of violence three times in two months. At least I hadn't been killed outright, like a few of the others.

Belushi ambled back to the netherworld. My assault may have just been theater, but it still hurt—another aftershock of the tragedies I had discovered at the bronze feet of my erstwhile client, Governor Roth-man, during the past election season. Perhaps the clues about him had always been there. Was it possible that I had chronically dodged his weakest points during the fresh stages of our relationship? Maybe a man doesn't spot the termites until the tree is fully rotted.

The Mercury with the zoom lens was gone, and whatever gargoyle decked me had long vanished around a side street. I thought of Mickey's little wisdoms, and made a note on a business card in my sun visor of the thirteenth and final lesson of election season:

Someone knows your secret.

A TIME TO KNEEL

"There was no misunderstanding. This was a conflict."

Labor Day—Margate, New Jersey (three months earlier)

"You didn't see Barium Enema on that goddamned program, *did* you?" the governor accused me as soon as I answered my cell phone, which I had programmed to ring to the melody of Bruce Springsteen's "Cadillac Ranch."

I was walking along the surf with my son Ricky, six, and daughter Lily, four. I promised them one last walk on the beach before we packed our cars and drove forty miles inland to where we were living in Cowtown, South Jersey.

Rebound fired his charge quickly, his voice sounding uncharacteristically high, tinny, and not at all gubernatorial. I pictured his vocal cords vibrating like the high-tension wires on the Ben Franklin Bridge. While his natural voice wasn't that deep, he usually deepened it when he was on camera. Rebound rarely called me directly, because he didn't want his words pirouetting between transmission towers from the Pine Barrens to the Hudson River and onto the ten-o'clock news. When he did call me himself, he usually opened with a fraternal "Yo, genius," then talked in code, but today he just aimed directly and fired.

"I saw the show," I said, plugging my left ear with my finger. A chestnut-colored man slathered with baby oil and wearing a toupee that resembled a dead Yorkshire terrier had just begun blasting Shirley Bassey's "History Repeating" from a boom box. A Main Line Philly Jewish young professional was attempting to extricate himself from a discussion-going-nowhere with a South Philly Irish girl. A Cherry Hill-type doctor/entrepreneur lectured a disciple on how to hide money from his avaricious wife. A crew of buff guidos fiddled with their gold chains as an excuse to flex their biceps. A gaggle of big-haired women in their forties speed-walked on the matted sand like ducks with diarrhea. A trio of mobsters sucked Havanas. A lone retiree clipped his toenails, covering the droppings with sand. Four bubbies played mah-jongg beneath an umbrella emblazoned with the Eagles logo. Two whippet-sleek Center City hotties with expressions of romantic betrayal glanced mournfully at me while I took Lily's hand.

"That's *it?* No *genius* advice?" the governor asked. The invocation of my genius was not meant as a compliment today. I sensed Rebound was smiling. Clients secretly like it when their well-paid guru fails to deliver because it validates an unconscious suspicion that they really don't need guys like me. Good work is punished because it makes you indispensable, which is resented.

I had indeed watched Barri Embrey on *Election Throb* last night. *The Throb,* as it was informally called, was the top-rated cable television program covering the midterm vote nationwide. The host frequently invited on as guests local print reporters covering hot races. Rebound was running for the U.S. Senate, which many speculated was his intended stepping-stone to the White House. Reporters such as Barium Enema loved to appear on *The Throb* because it gave them national exposure, plus it allowed them to editorialize and dish the kind of gossip that would have been considered journalistically unseemly in print. There was a direct correlation between making a witty sound bite and being invited back on *The Throb;* therefore a smart reporter like Barium Enema worked closely with the show's producer, who would set her up for the evening's zinger.

On last night's show, the subject matter was an intern program that Governor Rothman had established to help New Jersey communities that had been affected by flooding in the wake of Hurricane Mindy, the latest natural catastrophe that candidate Rothman had pledged to reverse. The intern program was entitled "A Time to Heal," and was staffed by students from New Jersey colleges, largely female. Rumors began circulating last spring that the governor had taken disproportionate interest in A Time to Heal upon meeting the nubile interns who had appeared with him at a Trenton photo op. During speculation at a nearby Starbucks about how these young women had earned their coveted internships, the wags in the press corps had informally renamed the program "A Time to Kneel."

So it came to pass that when *The Throb*'s host, Gordon Kinney, in a tsunami of sanctimony, asked Barium Enema about how young women earned their coveted A Time to Heal internships, she disclosed with a not-quite-spontaneous smirk, "Nobody knows for sure, Gordo, but the press corps calls the program 'A Time to Kneel.'"

Much studio laughter, but Barium Enema remained calm above her Chiron:

BARRI EMBREY
South Jersey Probe

The other off-site panelists broke up laughing, a courtesy that pundits afforded each other with the understanding that their quips would receive reciprocal guffaws. (I hadn't appeared as a guest on *The Throb* in a while. Gordon Kinney didn't like me, perhaps because I casually asked him in the Green Room, "What's happening with your bad self?" which Kinney, a fair-skinned black man, wrongly interpreted as a citation of his race.)

"Will you be, uh, *prob*ing this further?" Host Gordo asked Barri Embrey, satisfied with his pun.

"It's important to stress that right now it's all just rumor," Barri said with a furrowed brow. "But it's clearly something the Rothman campaign is wrestling with, given the family focus platform of his Senate race."

A solid comeback. First, kick 'em in the gonads with the vivid but unsubstantiated allegation. Second, follow up with the chin-scratching journalistic qualifier about the need for substantiation. Finally, stress the existence of the controversy (that you created) in order to justify it as legitimate news that The People demand be monitored.

I could still hear Rebound's prosecutorial breath on the phone.

"It's hard to retract gossip, Governor," I said. "You're a public figure. It's part of the job."

"Look, I needja down here now." I held the phone away from my head.

That was it. I had been summoned. Rebound was big on summoning. There was something about issuing a directive and having a nervous white guy materialize that really got him off. This time it was different. Rebound's voice wasn't the same. He was scared. To a pollster two months shy of Election Day, this meant that whatever was on the candidate's mind was my fault. As much as pollsters fancy themselves analysts of complex data, the best of us are at root instinct players whose gift is an internal radar as opposed to superior intellect. At the moment, my radar was sensing the presence of a hostile craft flying into the salt-scented airspace of Rebound Rothman. Among other things, this meant that I had to abandon my family and get over to Rebound's beach house, which was a half-mile away. I despised this ritual.

I rented a beach house in Margate during August through Labor Day. My wife, Edie, is from South Jersey, and her parents have a ranch near Cowtown. We had moved into a cottage on the Cowtown grounds from the Washington, D.C. area when my father-in-law had a hip replaced late last spring. Edie was stricken with worry about her father and wanted to be close to her parents, and I could run my business from a cell phone and laptop, so I agreed to the move. The kids would start at a private school in South Jersey in a few days. I didn't know how long we'd be staying, but it looked like it would be at least for the next school year. Prior to my father-in-law's operation, I had hoped to build a house in suburban Washington horse country on land I had owned for a few years, but I was uprooted, a familiar trend in my existence. At least I was with my family. At least I finally had a family, an enterprise I had begun in midlife.

Officially, Cowtown was named Pilesgrove; however, abutting the Morrises' property was the legendary Cowtown Rodeo. That's correct, smack-dab in the heart of South Jersey was an active rodeo that had entertained people across the Delaware Valley for decades. I had gone to countless birthday parties here as a kid.

While New Jersey was thought of by most visitors as a collection of chemical plants and concrete exit ramps, that was North Jersey. *South Jersey* was largely rural, with a thriving dairy industry, not to mention a lucrative cranberry and blueberry industry in the heart of the Pine Barrens, the vast, legend-filled woods that comprise a quarter of the state. It was in the Pine Barrens that the fabled Jersey Devil supposedly dwelled, the mutant thirteenth child of Revolutionary-era settlers.

"Okay, midgets," I told Ricky and Lily, who were shin-deep in the surf. "We need to go back up. Daddy has to see the governor."

"I hate the governor," Lily said, knowing neither who the governor was nor what *hate* meant. She just knew I had to extricate them from the beach, and that their mother was going to spray their father with a semiautomatic weapon moments after I announced that I was Rebound-bound. As we trudged off the beach, we passed a melancholy young couple talking on the seawall. Lily stared at them too long after she saw the young woman wipe her eyes.

"She is crying," Lily said. "Why is the lady sad?"

"Keep your voice down, Lil. They want to be private," I said.

"Why is she sad? Why is she crying? Did he hurt her?" Lily inquired with no less subtlety. I grinned the grin of constipation at the couple because they almost certainly heard Lily. I explained the scene to her as best I could.

Labor Day was a dangerous time of the season because everybody knew it was the end. This lead to frantic liaisons by collegiate lovers, last-ditch efforts to recover rent deposits from ornery landlords, and desperate "blowout sales" by swimwear peddlers.

I wasn't above these autumnal sentiments, which I tied to my worsening professional burnout. Most pollsters would be thrilled to be such a close confidant to a sitting governor with national ambitions, but despite Edie's resentment of my job, I, too, was tired of being in a service business where deluded clients demanded that I slave endlessly in order to achieve unattainable results. I was a pollster, not a mystic, but pixie dust was what political consultants were selling nowadays. Given my malaise, I had developed the habit of asking the same question of everybody I knew, and even some I didn't: How much money did I need to retire? The answer was usually a very unsatisfying "It depends," which threw me into a silent rage that just compounded the problem. When my head cleared, I concluded that I was a member in good standing of the middle class, but fell far short of having the kind of cash that would permit me to tell the governor where he could shove his Destiny.

As a veteran man of action who believed in tackling life's challenges with alacrity, I took responsibility for my midlife funk by doing something totally original and intrepid: I bought a silver Porsche Carrera. To Edie, a devout minimalist, this was treated as a sin on a par with adultery. To my late grandfather, Mickey, my purchase would have been considered an outrage that would cause the God of the Old Testament to descend upon me with Passover-style plagues. To Mickey, understatement with blood money was superior to flashiness with honest wealth. That the vehicle was made in Germany would have made his eyes shoot from his head the way Wile E. Coyote's did when he recognized that the Road Runner had run him off of a cliff. I believed in Old Testament wrath, and suspected that my deceased grandfather had considerable juice with the Big Guy: I operate under the principal that God is not interested in weighty issues (e.g., genocide prevention) and would prefer to devote his powers to arranging for my bank to have only one teller, a recent immigrant from Ghana who spoke no English. In the spirit of my theology, when I drove out of the Porsche dealership, I pulled the knob off the gearshift, and had to immediately turn around to have it reset. As the repair got under way, my stomach churned in the waiting room, and I began to despise my new motorized testicle. The Porsche in question now sat in the driveway of our rented beach house, the sun's reflection against the sparkling paint blinding me through my sunglasses.

The kids ran in the house and upstairs to "say good-bye" to their bunk bed. Edie stood at the doorway to their rooms. I was scared of her. I think it was because I suspected she was perfect. Now I had to break the news that I had to go to see Rebound, whom she loathed. I lingered at the bedroom door as Edie felt the kids' bathing suits to see if they were dry enough to slip right off and pack.

Edie had a stern look on her face. Her long brown hair fell around her shoulders. Her eyes were grand cocoa-covered almonds reflecting her Lenape Indian heritage on her father's side of the family, balanced on either side of a patrician nose that turned up at the end. Edie's nose reflected the ancestors on her mother's side—the ones who had arrived on the *Mayflower* and told her Dad's forebears to slide over westward. She was wearing one of my flannel shirts and an old pair of jeans. No makeup. This was Edie's standard attire, and I loved her for it.

"These bathing suits are still wet," she told Ricky and Lily. "I told you that you could get your toes in the water but not go in. Jonah, why did you let them go in? Now I have to throw them in the dryer!"

"I didn't let them go—"

"Then why are they wet?"

"They went in up to their shins. Maybe some splashed up. I don't know—"

"I know. *He* called, and you were distracted."

I had been scalped by the Indian and stung by the WASP. If you look up "futility" in the dictionary, you will find a picture of me fighting with Edie. She never found it to be in the realm of possibility that I could be anything but wrong.

"As you know, I conspire to make your life harder," I said.

"So what is it?" Edie asked without looking at me. She threw the bathing suits into the dryer.

"I'm sick of my job," I said.

"You're at that age."

"That doesn't make it any easier."

"Is it your conscience?" she asked, setting the dial.

"Not really."

"Do you see yourself retired?"

"I can't retire."

"Is this your inoculation effort justifying that Governor Narcissus summoned you?"

I was always hoping she'd be stupider. "He sounds upset."

"That's his management style. He lobs missiles to keep people on the defensive, and you fall for it every time."

This was true. Rebound rescued me from career oblivion when he hired me to handle his gubernatorial campaign after I found myself embroiled in the second ethics scandal of my career. I felt Failure snoring under my bed, and one stupid move would wake up the beast. Rebound intuited this and tweaked it mercilessly, which I permitted in order to remain employed. But the fact remained that I *had* gone through life one step ahead of disaster, something that Edie, with her oak-solid upbringing, could not process from her frame of reference.

"He's the governor," I said.

"He's a diva."

"He's up for reelection," I said.

"So, you have to go and change his diaper?"

I heard our children titter at the word *diaper*.

I searched for a snappy comeback. No dice. "This is my job, Edie."

"Then go. Do your job." Edie dragged out the word *job*.

Whenever she did this, it left me with the same feeling I had after my mother died, which was within a year or so after I lost my dad: Alone. I had learned that with Edie, "talking about it" was worthless. My business summoned, and she wanted me home packing.

I slipped down the staircase and kissed my two naked children goodbye.

WHERE THERE'S SMOKE

"Governor, is there anything I ought to know?"

I drove the half mile to Rebound's beach house and took note of the gray smoke funneling skyward from his block. I pulled up beside the state trooper's car in Rebound's driveway and surveyed the throngs at what I determined to be a Labor Day cookout or burnt offering to the God of Ambition. It was no small irony of New Jersey culture that the governor's beach house was so close to that of a hoodlum named Paul Tapio, known affectionately as "Tappo the Clown." Tappo the Clown, the host of the barbecue, was boss of the Philadelphia–South Jersey Mafia, an enterprise that was just beginning to pull out of Chapter 11 after being implicated in a variety of embarrassing scandals—such as being murderers.

Throughout the twentieth century, the marriage of respectability and, well, disrespectability had been an accepted one in South Jersey, only things were presumed to be different in the modern era, when the Mafia was supposedly dead and politicians bent themselves into Philly pretzels to show how ethical they were. The display of morality was more important than clean living because with display there was something in it for everybody.

Tappo the Clown, however, was a man of his times. What made him different from his predecessors was that he had earned his master's in Business Administration in a ten-year evening program at Lewisburg Penitentiary while on a racketeering pinch. When he emerged from prison shortly after the millennium, he formally incorporated what remained of the Mafia as a C-corporation ("LCN Ltd.", which Tappo claimed stood for Long-Caring Neighbors, as opposed to the FBI designation, La Cosa Nostra). Tappo added the "Ltd." for the British affect and filed for bankruptcy protection under the laws of New Jersey. That Tappo's activities were illegal was of no matter because we were now living in the Arthur Andersen age of full disclosure, where "trust" and "empowerment" in criminal endeavors were key to making the mob an instrument of social equity. Unlike his predecessors, who claimed to be legitimate businessmen, Tappo split the difference and promised the people of the Delaware Valley a new frontier in "socially responsible racketeering," something that the increasingly powerful Russian mob didn't view as a worthwhile marketing position. Tappo the Clown was promptly regarded as such a colossal wiseass (thus his nickname) that he was ignored by law enforcement while he successfully rebuilt a smaller, albeit more focused, gangland that emphasized the group's original core competencies such as high-interest loans, labor "conflict resolution," "intimate nurturing encounters" with "pleasure-management consultants," "substance-induced vacations," and "neighborhood insurance."

Tappo the Clown's neighborhood barbecue attracted hundreds of people who longed for the chance to tell people how Tappo had personally served them a hamburger. I could hear the chatter now: *"He's just a regular guy . . ."*

"Are you going to the barbecue?" I asked the plainclothes state trooper who stood guard at the front steps of Rebound's house.

"Wasn't invited," the guard responded. He was sandblasting fresh graffiti from the steps.

"What's the artwork?" I asked.

"Looks like some kid tried to spray-paint 'whore' or something. Musta done it last night when everybody was out."

I examined the outline of the graffiti, which was ironically made more pronounced by the attempted erasure. I could decipher what appeared to be a poorly drawn *H*, followed by an *o*, an *r*, and, perhaps, an *e* or an *a*—"Hore" or "Hora."

"All I know," the trooper said, "is that the governor went batshit when he saw it this morning and said to blast it off right away. We had to haul ass over to Pleasantville to get this contraption."

"He's in quite a mood," I echoed sympathetically, and went inside.

While Tappo the Clown's story had been chronicled down to every embellished detail, Rebound Rothman's ascent from star forward for the Philadelphia 76ers to governor of New Jersey was one vague assumption. My own theory about Rebound, while biased against him, couldn't be altogether wrong. The lonely thing about being a pollster is that you get to see your client from a perspective that no one else in the world can: that is, the unlovable side of a beloved public figure—and that side may be all you see. Sometimes I have to remind myself that it's my job to keep Rebound lovable to the public, not to love him myself.

Rebound had been at his athletic peak during the Bicentennial, which hit America at the nadir of our national mediocrity. Gerald Ford was president, *Saturday Night Live* regularly parodied his pratfalls, and Ford's challenger was an odd-duck peanut farmer from Georgia, Jimmy Carter. Inflation had blown a gaping wound in the economy, and was being valiantly fought with bumper stickers reading "WIN" (for Whip Inflation Now). Inflation didn't seem to be too frightened by the stickers, interest rates hit 20 percent a few years later, and American cars couldn't go three miles without breaking down.

In one of the most sweeping defense mechanisms in recent memory, the public wanted to believe it demanded excellence, and Rebound Rothman happened to be tall, good-looking, and vanilla-ethnic during Bicentennial fever, when all eyes were on Philadelphia, our nation's cradle. President Ford shot a basket with Rebound at the Spectrum, Jimmy Carter smiled moronically on camera beside him at the Newmarket Square waterfront, and the regulars at Studio 54—Bianca Jagger, Halston—were photographed on the dance floor doing the Hustle with him. And so, in an era of staggering underperformance, to paraphrase Shakespeare, *Some were born great, some achieved greatness, and some happened to be standing beneath the backboard when the ball dropped into his hands.* Which always seemed to surprise Rebound just a little.

Rebound wasn't a bad basketball player, but he wasn't great, either, averaging a less-than-stellar 6.7 rebounds per game. His nickname had nothing to do with this statistic. Rather, after disappointing his audience with a lazyass performance in one game, Rothman found the crowd's withdrawal of affection so distressing that whatever superhuman spirits dwelled within him fueled a comeback performance that surpassed, well, average. His capacity to contrast a subpar performance back to back with a par one left the crowd with the patina of achievement, thus the nickname Rebound. His novelty of being the only tall Jew in professional sports (with the fleeting exception of Rebound's teammate, Dr. J, Julius Irving, who was determined not to be Jewish because he wasn't an actual M.D.) only helped his standing in the Delaware Valley. At six-five, Rebound was a dwarf by NBA standards but a giant by the calibrations of the ethnic munchkins who drove New Jersey politics. With Rebound, you never looked at the statistics, you just looked at him. He seemed . . . inevitable.

I was a child in his audience when his ascent began in the early 1970s. I remember the way he glittered in perfect syncopation as the lights of the Spectrum swept across the 76ers. The song from the musical *Hair* was playing—"Aquarius"—and my giddy, unformed brain made the link between Rebound's shaggy black hair and the heavenly anthem. Even the name of the band that sung it was magical—The Fifth Dimension, as if the pulse of the music opened a portal to the most orgasmic of possibilities.

Rebound Rothman was the best that a Jewish kid from South Jersey could be. On one level, his success was impossible; on another, it was doable. I could not locate any demarcation between Rebound and the crowd; they were the same thing. I lampoon Rebound but cannot deny his genius, which was the ability to capture and project the collective hopes of big audiences, including little boys like me who were reading more and more often that their heroes were crooks (Nixon), dope addicts (Janis Joplin), or well-coiffed gigolos (Kennedy). Camelot worked because Americans needed it to work, and my trafficking in Rebound's greatness had plenty to do with my own need for a man of my own demographic to be great. In accordance with his gift, Rebound was elected to the Atlantic City council in 1980 as a Republican.

From what I could tell, Rebound had become a Republican by default. The local Democratic party was in peril due to recent prosecutions in the ABSCAM scandal, which had ruined party stalwarts from local mayors to a U.S. Senator from New Jersey. Rebound held no ideological views that I could discern. His most consistent belief was the performer's devotion to playing each scene for maximum Oscar potential. When the scene called for BOLD LEADERSHIP, he could squinch up his face BOLD LEADERLY. When the scene called for CAREFUL DELIBERATION, well, nobody could suck on the earpiece of bifocals like Rebound. After his stints as an Atlantic City councilman and mayor, Rebound later became a state assemblyman, a state senator, and, two years ago, governor.

The bond between Rebound and me adhered in several places. That both of us were South Jersey–bred political hustlers was only one factor. Rebound's awareness of public affairs, not to mention his political instincts, was immortalized when, as a state senator, he greeted Supreme Court Justice Byron White as "Your White Supremacy." Nor had it been helpful when Rebound responded to a reporter's question alleging that he was in the pocket of casino interests as "lies masturbating as truth." His press secretary insisted he had said "masquerading."

Despite his dual capacities for superficiality and denial of the obvious, Rebound's divorce from reality wasn't so complete that he didn't recognize his need for a political realist. That's where I came in.

Rebound always framed his interest in being at the shore as "family time," but the truth was more selfish and, I grudgingly admit, politically shrewd. Rebound was in extraordinary physical condition for a man in his midfifties, and he enjoyed displaying his body on the beach. A pioneer in the craft of Applied Narcissism, Rebound displayed a *People* magazine photograph of himself in his bathing suit in his Trenton office, which ultimately became the only campaign mailing in recorded political history where the candidate appeared to be nude. The magazine article featured the obligatory Kennedyesque adjectives—charisma, grace, charm, wit, grace, charisma, wit, charm . . .

The trooper opened the front door to Rebound's house and let me in. In contrast to the exterior's colonial old-shore manner, the inside of the house was decorated contemporarily. There were lots of billowy white sofas, chrome tables, and mirrored walls. An American flag snapped outside in anticipation of a president. The kitchen cabinets were mirrored. The only old item in the house was an oversized rusted gyroscope that must have been on an old ship. The gyroscope stood clumsily at the rear of the house facing the beach beside a wall of photos of: Rebound with Princess Diana. Rebound with President Ford. Rebound with President Carter. Reagan making his "I'm listening" face. Bush the First. Rebound with sports figures of his era: Dr. J, Pete Rose, Philadelphia Flyers ruffian Dave Schultz, Bjorn Borg, Billie Jean King, and Jimmy Connors. Rebound with Liza Minnelli.

The beach wall was windowed floor to ceiling, something that caused Rebound's security people endless anxiety. Gawkers frequently lined up on the seawall at night to peer inside. It would be too easy to attribute the display to Rebound's ego, but this setup wasn't unusual for the South Jersey shore, where status was determined by the extent to which the community could see what you had.

Rebound usually sat at the dining room table, but today he wasn't there. I rounded the dining room and passed through the large, modern kitchen. No Rebound. I figured I'd hit the bathroom before we met. I swung into a hallway, preoccupied with whatever gubernatorial rant awaited me, and careened into the cannonball knees of Governor Rothman, who was sitting on the toilet in his mirrored powder room with the door wide open, studying a document intensely.

"Ho!" I shouted, grabbing the doorjamb, fearing that my unchecked velocity would land me in the bowl with the rest of Rebound's waste.

It was always a surprise for the first-time Reboundite who discovered The Man evacuating himself so publicly, but I had grown accustomed to this ritual, writing it off as another indignity of being in a service business. It was dubbed by those in the governor's inner circle as the "spectator dump" because Rebound's (male) operatives would take orders from him while he was thronebound, colonic fumes a-wafting. When I foolishly asked him about *his* comfort with the ritual, Rebound mumbled something about his legs being long, and how leaving the door open gave him more room to maneuver. Truth was, he did it because he *could.*

I backed off, attempting to breathe through my mouth. I lost my own urge to use the facilities. Rebound said nothing, still boring in on his document.

"I'll be in the dining room. *Doodie* awaits," I said. *Heh.*

A cabinet door was slightly open. I decided to get a glass of water. There was a brown translucent pill bottle beside the glasses. I could make out orange pills inside with a *K* hollowed out in the middle. I heard the sound of soap and water mixing, so I closed the cabinet and darted to the opposite side of the kitchen. Rebound entered, shirtless and wearing running shorts. He opened the cabinet, shook out a K pill, stuck his mouth under the kitchen faucet, and swallowed it. "Allergies," he said.

The dining room table overlooked the beach. Rebound sat down and began picking off huge green grapes that rested grandly in a crystal bowl and popping them into his mouth. He had a white towel bearing the New Jersey state seal draped over his shoulder like a toga. It was not lost on me that the seal featured a shield being flanked by two women who appeared to be wearing bedsheets. Air from a vent above him blew his puffy silver hair. Rebound had beautiful hair, and there was something kingly about the way the sun stroked his profile, especially with the toga effect. Rebound had rolled up his running shorts an inch or two, God forbid somebody miss a sliver of him. I wore a T-shirt,

baggy khaki shorts, and a baseball cap. One time I went running with
Rebound on the beach without wearing a shirt, and he made a quip
about my showing off. It caught me off guard, but I got the message:
Only one Adonis per beach.

The governor was still lost in his damned document, and his eyes
were scanning it almost spastically. He wore platinum reading glasses,
which were startlingly bright, but aesthetically consistent with all of the
chrome surrounding him. I sat across from him and grabbed a bunch of
grapes. I always looked forward to the grapes, which Marsha Rothman
kept in perpetual abundance. There were also a few egg-shaped con-
tainers of Silly Putty on the table. Fiddling with the putty was one of
Rebound's childlike obsessive-compulsive endearments.

Finally Rebound slapped the document he was reading onto the
table. It was *US Weekly*.

"I gotta tell you, Jonah, I don't get it."

"You don't get what?"

"Friggin' Russell Crowe." Rebound pointed to the actor's photo on
the cover. "I don't think he's all that hot." Crowe was wearing a leather
aviator's jacket. Rebound flattened his putty on one of Crowe's photos
and began stretching it.

I took a look at the cover shot. "He's a stud."

"I don't see it."

"A lot of women do," I said. Mistake.

"Christ, athlete, he looks like a dirty rock star. Do you suppose he
smells, Russell Crowe?"

"Maybe of cigarettes and beer. I've never imagined him to smell,
not like Prince anyway."

"Prince Charles?"

"No, the little singer. Looks like diarrhea. I've always figured he'd
smell."

"Honest to God, I don't get what women find attractive anymore."

"Well, Governor, I guess they like bad boys."

"That's for damned sure. Makes me sick. Where have you been?"

"I was with my kids. They start school tomorrow. What's up?" I asked.

"You've got to hit Digby harder."

I looked at Rebound blankly. Digby Stahl was Rebound's Democratic opponent in the upcoming midterm election for New Jersey's open U.S. Senate seat. Digby was a former state judge from North Jersey, which had more political clout than South Jersey, our base.

"Okay, what's your thinking?"

"He's closing in on me," Rebound said vaguely.

"The last poll I ran had you fifteen points ahead."

"I just saw him on TV, Jonah. He was slamming my slogan."

Rebound's campaign slogan was FAMILY STATE. FAMILY MAN. I didn't like it, in part because I thought it provoked the media to examine any contradictions between the slogan and Rebound's personal conduct, which had been rumored about since his days with the Sixers. I also didn't like it because it was the brainchild of Abel Petz, my rival pollster, who possessed a gift for linking himself with victories and nailing other operatives with failures. Petz believed that FAMILY STATE. FAMILY MAN defused the rumors of womanizing.

"What was Digby's criticism?" I asked.

"I didn't like his tone. He repeated my slogan like I really didn't believe it."

"Governor, you have to expect your opponent will oppose. That's what opponents do."

"What about Barium Enema and the crap she blew on *The Throb?* I'd like to sue that bitch." His words contrasted with the aesthetic pose he now struck, gazing alternately between the sea and his triceps.

"You're a public figure. You're fair game for speculation."

"She libeled me, Jonah."

"No, she didn't. To win a libel suit, you'd have to prove not only that her statement was false, but that she intended to injure you with it. All she did was validate the existence of buzz. On top of that, the court would take into consideration that you are a public figure. No case."

Rebound sucked in his lips. When they emerged from his mouth they were colorless. Some politicians thrive in elections; others become angry because in their hearts they don't believe they should have to run.

Rebound wanted to grab a U.S. Senate seat the way he plucked grapes from his crystal bowl.

While his narcissism ate into his capacity for charm, Rebound did share Reagan's ability to connect with large audiences on an individual level. When I was a young aide on Reagan's staff, every encounter I had with him was about me. Reagan had a way of cocking his head toward the side as he greeted me as if surrendering to my significance. He left me with the feeling that I was locked into a private conspiracy with him. It took me years to realize that Reagan barely knew who I was.

"I want Digby on the run," Rebound snapped. "That's that."

"We have to be aware of your negatives, or we'll get creamed. We're way ahead, Governor. Besides, Americans usually vote in midterm elections to keep things balanced. With Democrats gaining ground in Congress, that may be good for you."

"I'm tired of hearing about my negatives."

"I'm just trying to get a sense of what you think is missing."

"What's missing is I'm not in the Senate." There was an uncharacteristic frantic quality about his movements. He was gripping the putty so tight his fist was red.

"It's Labor Day. The election is in two months," I said.

Rebound grabbed a handful of grapes and chewed them angrily, the sinews in his jaw flexing. I actually felt sorry for the grapes, envisioning them as roundheaded cartoon children being swallowed by the giant of their nightmares.

"Goddamn it, Jonah, just dig something up and hit him!" he said. There was a sudden rasp in his voice, which was a remarkable dub of George C. Scott's portrayal of General Patton.

I heard footsteps. "Governor," a voice said. Damn. *Him.* I looked over my shoulder and saw Lucas Currier, Rebound's chief of staff, walk in wearing khakis and a Brooks Brothers shirt. Currier was a wiry ferret of man, about thirty-five, who like all political chiefs of staff envisioned himself in Washington whispering in the ear of the president his counsel to vaporize Phlegmbagistan or some other ragged republic. Currier and Abel Petz comprised Rebound's public brain trust, even though Petz also maintained his own polling firm. I was the murkiest figure in the troika, presumably because of my "fallen" public status. I had been brought in to handle the rough stuff at the same time they kept me in the dark on day-to-day strategy. These guys needed me to play the role of "controversial pollster" in the event a goat was needed.

When Rebound hired me, his campaign staff had consisted of Currier, Petz, and a secretary. Currier tolerated me because Rebound attributed his gubernatorial victory to my strategy—something Rebound actually said aloud at an internal victory party—but Currier did not like me, and he certainly didn't want me coming to Washington with them if we won the election.

Currier began, "Just heard on the radio that Iverson hurt his knee and may be out for a month."

"Damn," Rebound said. Currier always opened up with a briefing on what was happening with the 76ers.

"What do I have this afternoon, athletes?" Rebound asked.

"Photo op with your family, then that speech at Rowan University," Currier said. "They've been lining up all day."

Rebound rubbed his temples. "We can't do the photo op."

"Why not?" Currier asked.

"For one thing, I've got a sensitive situation with the White House."

"What situation?" I asked.

"I can't discuss it." Rebound was big on references to major secret deals a-brewing with entire institutions such as "the White House." Which he never could discuss. I had been with Rebound long enough to know that if he referenced a "powwow with the Vatican," it really meant a photo op with a priest in Camden. "Besides," Rebound added, "my daughter's sick. Stomach flu or something. Now, for the Rowan speech I want to be casual."

"I'm sorry?" I asked, confused.

"Casual," he said, as if I knew what he meant. "I'm gonna wear my bomber jacket to the speech."

"Okay," Currier said. "Do you want to read your speech? I think it hits all of the messages you wanted. Real high-concept stuff, perfect for you."

"I'll look at it in the car over," Rebound said, disinterested.

"What's the speech about?" I asked.

"Learning," Currier said.

"Is my bomber jacket too casual?" Rebound asked.

"Depends on the setting," I said. "It should be all right for a college, just not on camera."

"You'll be in a classroom," Currier told the governor. "I think it's a cool look with autumn coming up."

Hey, Lucas, no need to give the governor a colonoscopy with your tongue.

"It's not that fluorescent lighting, I hope," Rebound said.

"I don't know about the lighting," Currier said nervously. "I didn't advance it myself."

"Who did?" Rebound asked.

"Platt," Currier said.

"Well, call him," the governor insisted. "See if it's recessed lighting or fluorescent."

"You want recessed lighting?" I asked.

"It makes me look tanner, it doesn't give me that damned greenish, shiny look," Rebound explained.

"Not necessarily for news crews," I qualified. "They need stronger lights."

"Just figure it out!"

"I'll call Platt," Currier said, stepping out on the deck to call the governor's chief advance man.

As soon as Currier was out the door, I leaned into Rebound and asked, "Rebound?" I only called him this when I needed his sober attention. "Is there anything I ought to know?"

"What?" he said. "You better be damned sure *you're* not hiding something."

When he pulled this shit, I always pushed back, which became easier once I realized that the guilt he attempted to transfer was equal to the vulnerability he was feeling. Normally, however, he was subtler than he was today. His current snappishness was bordering on absurdity.

"All right, you caught me," I said, hanging my head. "I embezzled New Jersey municipal bonds using your personal e-mail account to buy my Porsche."

"I didn't say that, Jonah. Sorry, I've just got so much stress lately."

"We're on the same side here. In two decades at this, I've never had a candidate so far ahead who is so anxious about losing. It makes no sense. I know it's stressful, but if you think Digby's about to spring something on us, we can try to find a way to neutralize it."

Rebound nodded, perhaps sensing that he had gone a little Nixon on me. He grabbed a handful of grapes and swallowed them without appearing to chew. He sighed. "Between that Barium Enema and Digby's comments. . . . It jabbed me somewhere raw," he said, his eyes appearing suddenly bloodshot. "Please, just think of ways we can cause Digby a little pain, okay?"

There was something truly needy about him, the way his head was bowed when he said "please." If he had done this more often, perhaps I wouldn't have the impulse to flee him, not to mention my entire profession. It wasn't all dollars and cents to me: in politics, feeling needed was almost as good as getting paid. Almost.

"You recognize, Governor, that I'll need some help. I won't bore you with details, I just wanted you to know because there will be costs."

"Don't worry about it. I don't want details."

"I'll go to . . . some of my other resources."

Rebound's eyes went dead, recognizing that I was referring to resources I had inherited from my grandfather.

"Is that necessary?"

"I don't know yet. It may be."

"Be careful, Jonah."

"You're serious about winning, so we'll need thorough people, people who don't screw around."

"Thorough, yes." Rebound nodded tentatively in the affirmative.

"A few months from now, Rebound, you'll be going for lunchtime runs around the Jefferson Memorial," I said.

Rebound sprung back to life. "With you in the cockpit, how can I lose?" With his left hand, he bequeathed big-brotherly noogies, the psychic morsel I needed. With his right hand he grabbed two grapes.

THE FIRST FAMILY

"If married people ever told the truth about that stuff—"

I walked past the state trooper in the entryway and attempted to close the door behind me when I felt it pull back open. It was Currier. He followed me onto Rebound's front steps, and we stood there like the Brady Bunch kids after they broke their mom's vase: waiting for the roulette ball of blame to fall on our number.

"Do you know what's with him, Jonah?" Currier asked.

Currier was either fishing for what I knew, or genuinely didn't know himself. We were usually able to keep our mutual hostility beneath the surface, but lately I couldn't always help myself.

"I think he wanted to see us kiss," I said.

"C'mon, Jonah."

"No, you c'mon. Gimme one." I leaned toward Currier with my eyes closed and mouth open. Currier recoiled.

"The advance team missed the objective," I said, serious again.

"Which is?"

"He's on the prowl, Lucas. He wants to look good for the coeds today, not the electorate."

Lucas flinched. "Damn. How bad do you think the problem is?"

"The prowling?"

"Uh-huh."

"The fact that we're having this talk tells you something," I said.

The matter of Rebound's philandering was something we always worked around, not through.

"Right."

"He was bizarre today, though," I said. "Did he call you about the Barium Enema thing?"

"Yeah, he started flipping out, but he's always been thin-skinned. That's why I have to engage in some foreplay with him."

"Did you find any polyps up there?" I mumbled.

"Huh?"

"*Politics* . . . I don't know Lucas," I sighed. "Rebound was more than thin-skinned. In the course of a few minutes, he went from Russell Crowe to reaming Digby Stahl to wearing a leather jacket at an education speech."

"Crowe had on a bomber jacket in that picture."

"I know, I saw," I said. "The vanity seems worse."

"What now?" Lucas asked.

I swallowed hard and met Currier's eyes. They were an intelligent blue, deep against the whites of his eyes. This blue was the color of the carpeting in the White House, the color of the globe, ambition. Keep your answer simple.

"For now, let's just light him right."

Currier nodded, and turned to go back inside.

"Nice ass, Luc," I said, my eyebrows twitching.

Currier shut the door behind him. I had made him uncomfortable. My work was done.

I stood on the steps in front of Rebound's house as a state trooper pulled into the driveway in a Chevy Suburban. The graffiti, "Hore," or whatever it was, was still visible beneath my feet.

Marsha Rothman climbed from the passenger seat carrying a grocery bag. Grapes were spilling out of the top of the bag, and she had an urgent look in her eyes, as if Rebound would hump the family pet if he didn't have more grapes right away. She was wearing a T-shirt and running tights. She had a magnificent body for a woman her age, largely because she devoted her life to its preservation. The synthetic C cups didn't hurt a bit. Her T-shirt had the letters L.U.R.P. emblazoned in fuchsia across her breasts.

Marsha was an attractive, spicy, Goldie Hawn-ish blond in her mid-fifties who looked a lot younger until you got up close and saw the strain around her eyes, which seemed to perpetually ask, "What the fuck just happened?" Her pedigree was legendary in the Delaware Valley. Her father, the late-but-aptly-named Howard Pinkus, had been chairman of the Southern New Jersey Communist Party despite having built the most successful regional collection of auto dealerships out of his flagship Chevy lot on Route 70 in Cherry Hill, near the racetrack. Chairman How, as he was called, owned Pinkus Chevrolet, Pinkus Cadillac, Pinkus Oldsmobile, Pinkus Pontiac, and, for reasons that were never clear, Pinkus Peugeot. When he died in the 1990s, Chairman How left a fortune worth more than a quarter-billion dollars (my checks came from Pinkus corporations and trusts). The acquisitive old Marxist saw no inconsistency between his political beliefs and his rajah lifestyle, a sign on his desk having read: "The workers control the means of production. Just not at Pinkus Automotive." Marsha's younger brother, Gamal Abdel Pinkus (legally, Craig), now ran the colossus, and devoted his spare time to leading other obscenely rich American Jews in the pro-Palestinian cause, for which he advocated a complete withdrawal of Jews from Israel so they could establish settlements on the grounds of the erstwhile Camp Shalom in the Pine Barrens. Ordinary Jews referred to Craig Pinkus's folly as Balsamic Jihad.

"Hey there, doll," Marsha said. "Why aren't you with your family?"

"Well, Marsha, a certain governor doesn't think I'm doing enough to stop his nemesis, Digby Stahl." I could talk to her this way. Marsha and I disagreed on most political issues, but we had an intangible sense of conspiracy when it came to her husband.

"Screwing up his plans for Camelot again, babes?"

"Yes, were it not for my incompetence, all of Mesopotamia would be under the Jerseyan Empire."

"Mesopotamia? Where was that anyway?" Marsha asked.

"Right off of Exit Four on the Turnpike. Behind Pier One Imports."

"Oh, that's right. They just opened a Loehmann's there."

"When are you gonna run for something? You're good on your feet."

"Have to be. I don't spend much time on my back."

I inhaled a beat. She was usually candid, but *yeeeah!* "If married people ever told the truth about that stuff—" I said in a jab at diplomacy.

"I know, I know."

I pointed to her shirt. "What's L.U.R.P.?"

"Oh," she said, "Lesbians United for Republican Pride."

"Has the governor seen this?"

"Shit, yeah," Marsha said, revealing very sharp eyeteeth.

"What's the group's mission?" I asked, knowing full well the truth. L.U.R.P. was all about mortifying Rebound.

"Well, women with alternative lifestyles support Republican issues, believe it or not. It couldn't hurt to throw 'em some support," she said like a seventh-grade girl who had toked a joint up in her bedroom beneath a Van Halen poster.

"Uh-huh. You recognize, Marsha, that there are plenty of hetero women who support Republican causes who might need a little shot in the arm."

"Thank you for your valuable counsel, babe." Marsha winked.

"You're a lesbian like I'm a lesbian."

Marsha cackled as the back doors of the Suburban opened. Out climbed Juliet and Dude Rothman, Rebound and Marsha's daughter and son. Juliet was a corpulent girl of roughly fourteen who, at the moment, was wearing a long black wig and a sequined dress. Not a good thing, since she was at least eighty pounds overweight despite being six feet tall—in broad daylight, no less. Dude, who had had his name legally changed from Todd, wore jeans that appeared to have been worn by the Taliban, post–U.S. bombing. He was sixteen.

"Hey, Juliet," I asked. "What's with the getup?" Juliet stopped and stared down at me. I always felt she didn't like me, because she never directly answered my questions. Today she moved her head rhythmically, curled her lips, and belted out: "Gypsies, tramps and thieves, we'd hear it from the people of the town." She then did a few jerky dance moves and approached the front door of the house. Juliet turned around before entering, whipped her fist toward her mouth like a microphone, and concluded the song somberly: "But every night, the men would come around, and lay their money down."

"Don't worry about her, Jonah," Dude assured me. "I don't know where she got that song."

"That's a thirty-year-old routine. It's by Cher."

"Who's Cher?"

"Singer-actress from a long time ago. Pretty good, actually."

"What does she do now?"

"Mostly eulogies."

"Do you like the song?"

"So-so. When I left the country with my grandfather, a news report they did on his life had that song playing. He was Rumanian. Rumania's known for gypsies, and he was known, uh . . . How's Juliet feeling?"

"She's her usual deranged self, why?"

"I thought she had a stomach flu."

"Uh, no. Where'd you get that idea?"

I stammered a few meaningless syllables and shook my head as if I had been confused. Rebound's fabrication that Juliet was sick was his elliptical language for dodging the mournful truth: he didn't want to be photographed with his kids. Move on, Jonah.

"So, what's with you, Dude? Are you still in that band?"

"You got it, homes," Dude said, with a rap-style formation of his fists.

"What's the band called again?"

"Mongoloid Sphincter."

"Whoa-ho!" I said, recoiling, which I suppose was the point.

"You like the name, Jonah?"

"How could I not?"

"You should have seen my dad's face when I told him."

"Oh, I'm sure he'll learn to love it. What kind of music is it?"

"We call it rebel-ternative."

"What are you rebelling against?"

"The way the system crushes the little guy."

Warning: It's this kind of crap that brings out my Republicanism at its most shrill. I have never seen "the little guy" as the noblest of figures. If you want to impress me, split an atom.

"You know, Dude, it occurs to me that *mongoloid* is a word used to describe people with Down's Syndrome," I said calmly.

"Yeah, retards."

"Well, they are mentally retarded, but if anybody qualifies as the little guy, as you call it, it would be people who can't help the way they are."

"You're just trying to pimp for my dad."

I had a fleeting fantasy about opening the door of the Chevy Suburban and using it to smash Dude's head repeatedly against the frame of the car until it shattered like a watermelon. I immediately suspected him of painting "whore" on his father's doorstep, but figured he was just barely bright enough to spell it right.

"That word doesn't describe the relationship I have with your father."

"Who does it then, Mucous Lucas?"

"I hear rumors like you hear rumors. I've never seen proof. Have you?"

"Whenever he's got something cooking, my mother goes gonzo trying to make sure he has everything he wants. It's like, the minute those grapes go below the bowl line, she's out restocking the stash."

"I don't know what to tell you, Dude."

"You should come and hear the band someday," Dude dodged. "We've got some shore gigs coming up."

Dude went into the Rothmans' garage and retrieved a Mongoloid Sphincter calendar of events.

"Can I bring my wife?" I asked, for the sole purpose of amusing myself.

"Hell, yeah."

Dude gave me a Power to the People fist and slipped back inside his three-million-dollar beachfront home. I lingered for a minute trying to detect movement inside the house. I didn't know what I was hoping to learn, but I hung there until a state trooper gave me one of those hard, law enforcement, you-sell-heroin-to-kindergartners faces, so I left replaying the morning's events.

It was common for troubled clients to want me to brew miracle cures without telling me the truth about their maladies. I didn't know exactly what Rebound was suffering from, but my instincts told me that the man had secrets. It was time to consult with a man who had made a career out of keeping them.

IRV THE CURVE

"There's less to Rothman than meets the eye."

Irving Aronson was in his nineties. When you're that old, it doesn't matter if you're ninety-two or ninety-eight. He had been my grandfather's business partner since Prohibition. He was a gangland legend known as Irv the Curve, because he was fabled to "see around corners." A meticulous little man who wore a tie even on the beach, Irv specialized in the political fix and intergang negotiations. While Mickey had been a brilliant strategist, he wasn't much of a talker, and I always suspected he maintained some kind of inferiority complex about his lack of education and inarticulate speech.

Irv the Curve was no Rhodes scholar, but he had been a student of politics who had taken measurable steps throughout his long life to cultivate proper speech and a knowledge of history. Accordingly, Mickey had deputized Irv to do his talking.

Irv had long since retired (whatever that meant), and had moved into the Alter Kocker Arms in Margate, a "retirement community" that faced the bay side of Absecon Island. I took him to lunch whenever I could, and Edie and my kids treated him as they would have my own grandfather.

The Alter Kocker Arms was a two-story brick building with minimal landscaping, as if to remind all visitors that its inhabitants wouldn't be staying very long. The elderly folks who staffed the front desk were hyper-vigilant about guests checking in, particularly the increasingly deaf but lethal Mrs. Pinsky, who viewed herself as America's first line of defense against bioterrorism. Whatever control the residents of the Alter Kocker Arms didn't have over their own dwindling fates, they sought to compensate for by enforcing gratuitous acts of compliance on harmless visitors.

"I'm here to see Mr. Aronson," I said to Mrs. Pinsky, who sat like Pinochet behind the desk.

"Who?" Mrs. Pinsky shouted.

"Irving Aronson."

"What's your name?"

"Lucky Luciano."

"What?"

"Tiger Woods."

"The football player?"

"Yes."

"Sign the book," she demanded. "Then print your name neatly beside it."

I complied. *T-I-G-E-R.*

"What's the purpose of your visit?" Mrs. Pinsky asked, studying my writing.

"I just wanted to say hello," I said, annoyed.

"What?"

"I'm dropping off an untraceable Beretta for a heroin run."

"Here's your visitor's badge," Mrs. Pinsky said. "It must be worn at all times."

"Thank you, Reichsführer."

I showed my badge to one of Mrs. Pinsky's Brownshirts, Rhoda "Genghis" Kahn, who was guarding B-Wing holding a can of pepper spray. Then I made my way down the narrow Corridor of Damnation. In a small alcove outside of Irv's apartment, a man sat alone beneath an air-conditioning vent nodding at a crossword puzzle. They called this man Freon Leon because of his perpetual gravitation to air-conditioning vents. Freon Leon rarely spoke; he just nodded and occasionally barked "Nixon!" I knocked on Irv's door.

"Who is it?" Irv barked.

"Jonah."

"So that's supposed to impress me?" He had become gratuitously argumentative lately, but I let it roll off.

"Do you have a broad in there?" I asked.

"Yeah, we're swinging from a chandelier. Come in, it's unlocked." Irv was wearing a starched white shirt and tie, white pants, and brown and white spectators on his feet. With his ankles crossed before him, his shoes looked like the beaks of two crows nestling side by side. Irv's thinning white hair was combed neatly across his scalp.

"Oh, look," I said, "It's George Clooney. Mr. Clooney, when did you move in?"

"It's safer here," Irv said without missing a beat. "What with the paparazzi."

Irv had reading glasses on and was holding an old book, *The Disenchanted* by Budd Schulberg. "Did we have a consultation scheduled?" he asked.

"No, Irv, this is a drop-in. I thought I'd take you to lunch and interrogate you."

"Fine, I'll get my jacket."

Irv put his book down on a coffee table. The apartment was small, with a living room, a tiny kitchen, and a bedroom. The furniture was modest, *Dick Van Dyke Show* fare. A picture my daughter drew of Irv— basically a stick figure with an oversized hat—was on the refrigerator, which made me miss my family. The most notable feature in the apartment was a huge bookshelf with hundreds of political and history books.

"You know, that novel you're reading, a lot of it's set at Dartmouth," I said. My alma mater.

"I bought it in the bookstore when your grandfather and I visited you there. I read this one on the car ride back from New Hampshire. I'm done now. Look here at this line," Irv said, picking up the book. I read it:

A second chance. That's the delusion. There never was but one.

"Why don't you borrow it, Jonah?"

"I'll pick it up from you after I'm done with this project. I remember it sitting there in Sanborn Library where I used to study. I never read it, though."

"Well, here's your second chance," Irv said.

He closed the apartment door behind us but didn't lock it. Irv waved to Freon Leon, who nodded back.

"Nixon!" Freon Leon uttered.

Irv and I nodded back as if we understood Freon Leon's point.

"Don't you want to lock the door?" I asked Irv.

"No, I'm setting a trap," Irv whispered.

"Who are you trying to catch?" I whispered back.

"Yetta Rosen down the hall. I think she comes in and snoops around. She tries to see what I read and strike up a conversation with me. It always happens to be about a subject I'm reading about before bedtime. I keep whatever the current book is on my night table in my bedroom. So I asked one of the attendants to get me a book on one of these horrible rape singers. It's on my night table now. If I go to the evening recreation tonight and Yetta Rosen starts going on and on about Snoopy Frog or whatever the hell that rape singer's name is, I'll know she's been in my place."

"They're actually called *rap* singers."

"Have you ever heard that shit? It's rape of the ears."

"Vivid. Assuming Yetta is spying, what are you going to do about it?"

"I think I'll keep getting disgusting books, put her over the edge. I have a list of horrible books. Crime scene photos. *Know Your Phlegm.* A dissertation about goiters. *Mustards of the World . . .*"

"She likes you, Irv. You should be flattered."

"Tell me, Jonah, are you flattered when a Labrador retriever sticks his nose in your crotch?"

As we made our way down the hall, different people nodded and bowed humbly at Irv. Everyone felt the need to say something to him. Irv was clearly the alpha geriatric in this joint.

"I don't see you anymore, Irv," Mrs. Abrams said. "You stay all cooped up in that apartment alone like a hermaphrodite."

"I'll tell you, Irv, I feel like I'm walking around with the president," I said.

"This place isn't like Washington. It's more like high school with a swollen prostate. What Mrs. Abrams said . . . hermaphrodite . . . Do you think she meant that?"

"Do you know what a hermaphrodite is, Irv?"

"Something bad."

"It's somebody with both sex organs. I think she meant *hermit.* Although a hermaphrodite probably wouldn't get out much either when you think about it."

Irv snickered. "What, you're going to make me get in this tin can?" Irv asked when we got to my Porsche.

"I'll help you in and out."

I helped Irv in and walked around to the driver's side.

"I feel like I'm in a blintz," Irv said when I got in.

"It's a Porsche Carrera," I said proudly. "But I haven't gotten used to the manual transmission."

"What's wrong with you? Jews don't shift."

"What do you look for in a car, Irv?"

"I'm looking to hit a telephone pole at eighty miles an hour and not feel it. You get that with the Cadillac DeVille."

Murray's was a delicatessen in a condominium tower located a few blocks from Rebound's beach house. I had been coming here for thirty years. The best thing about Murray's was that the owner never felt compelled to update the décor. I cherished sameness the way others pursued adventure, and knowing that the same graffiti would be etched into the wainscoting in the booths validated the continuity that I loved about this region. Irv and I were seated in the booth where "Linda loves Vinnie 4 Ever" had been etched in blue felt-tip marker above the Sweet'n Low since the Nixon administration. This was not to be confused with the "B-B-Bennie and the Jets" booth, which was two over, or the "Disco Blows" booth right behind me. Whenever I sat here, I was sure that Linda and Vinnie were frozen perpetually in a ballad with Springsteen's Candys and Johnnies speeding off to greasy lakes and turnpike wastelands—and rejoicing in the scent of burning rubber.

"What's on your mind?" Irv asked. I strained to hear him because there was a man sitting in the booth behind us coughing. *Could you hock up a little more phlegm?* I asked myself.

"I'm having trouble reading Rothman. He's a clever guy," I said.

"Lazy men are shrewd. There's less to Rothman than meets the eye."

"He called me over to his place today and wanted me to step up attacks on his opponent."

"So?"

"He's fifteen points ahead in the polls, and he's acting like we're getting creamed."

"He's an ambitious man."

"I felt like there was something he wasn't telling me."

"Does he have to tell you everything?"

"If he's got a problem that's making him politically vulnerable, he should tell me."

"He will when he's ready," Irv said, fiddling with Sweet'n Low packets he had no intention of opening.

"I may not be here when he's ready," I said.

"What does that mean, Jonah?"

"When you were growing up, did you see yourself doing what you ended up doing?"

"No, I went to pharmacy school."

"What happened?"

"Prohibition. There was a loophole in the law that allowed pharmacists to stockpile alcohol for medicinal purposes. I saw the opportunity and talked it over with Dutch Schultz and Longy Zwillman, who ran things in my neighborhood in Newark. I bought the alcohol with my pharmacy license and, whoops, some of it went out the back door to make booze. Go figure. Well, Dutch was crazy. He started talking about clipping a prosecutor. Dewey. Mickey, Charlie Lucky, Meyer, Longy, and Benny all got together and took Dutch out. Because we made the booze in the Pine Barrens, and Mickey controlled the pines, the shore, and Philly, I fell in with him."

"Do you ever look back and wish you had stayed a pharmacist?"

"No. Flipping a buncha pills around from one bottle to another? It was a starting point. But I still get the journals. I like looking at the pills and what they're supposed to do these days. I don't know why. What are you getting at with these questions? You restless?"

"I'm tired of doing what I do."

"Bootlegging's no longer a career option," Irv said. "What do you want to do?"

"I'm not sure."

"You don't need to be sure. You need options."

"The alcohol loophole gave you an option."

"Right. It allowed me to ease into something else. It's better to ease than to jump. Be realistic. Learning from mistakes isn't for everybody. Not everybody has to do it, just some people."

"Like who?"

"People who can't get away with things should learn from mistakes. Somebody like Rebound is a guy who gets away with things, so learning isn't economical, not worth the investment. Pretty girls don't have to learn from mistakes because more options are right around the corner. Why waste your time studying when you can just shake your ass? See, economics."

"What has Rebound gotten away with?" I repeated the question because Irv pointed to his ear after my words got lost in the coughs of the man behind me.

I remembered that I first met Rebound when I was seventeen. He was speaking with Mickey and Irv the Curve. He was about thirty and had been elected mayor of Atlantic City not long afterward. They were in the laundry room at the Golden Prospect. When Rebound first hired me, I reminded him of our initial meeting, which he claimed not to recall. Forgetfulness was a common side effect among successful people who found themselves adjacent to the name of Mickey Price, so I dropped the matter.

Irv frowned and pushed the pickle bowl away. "I'm just making a point about types of people. You raised a subject. I could not answer your question in the specific sense, only in the broad sense. You're not reckless to assume a man at the top of New Jersey politics has a secret or two. When a man wakes up sweating at three o'clock in the morning, he wonders if maybe he didn't kidnap the Lindbergh baby while he was sleepwalking. A guy like this is prone to suggestion. So suggest something."

I played with my fork.

"Irv, do you know a round orange pill that has a *K* cut out in the middle?"

"Sounds like Klonopin."

"For allergies?"

"No. Anxiety."

OTHER ISSUES

"But how had Abel Petz convinced Rebound to screw his original benefactors?"

I pulled into the dirt driveway in Cowtown at one thirty. My Porsche rumbled uncomfortably past my in-laws' tidy white split-level toward our cottage. I felt the disapproving eyes of my mother-in-law on me even though I wasn't even sure she was looking. All told, the property contained fifty acres of woods and open fields where some thirty horses grazed. Our cottage included two bedrooms, a modest living room, dining room, and kitchen, plus an attic, which functioned as the global headquarters of Jonah P. (for Price) Eastman Associates. My in-laws, the Morrises, originally intended for the cottage to serve as a guesthouse, but had it fully furnished right before I moved up with Edie and the kids.

Moving back to Jersey was far from being my first choice, and a normal husband probably would have fought it harder. Here's the thing, though: I never had a family. Sure, technically, I had my parents as a young boy and my grandparents as I got older, but we were the damned Munsters. The Morrises were the most functional family I had ever known, and I liked being in the orbit of people who didn't have corpses buried beneath their barn.

Edie looked more like her dad, whom I really adored. A ringer for

Charles Lindbergh (with the exception of his darker complexion that reflected his Lenape Indian heritage), Bob Morris had been a land-use lawyer until his retirement fifteen years ago. Like most fathers, his main criterion for a son-in-law was that whomever married his daughter must love her fiercely. He rightly saw in me such a man. Bob had always dabbled in horse trading, but admitted to me that he just liked horses and had never really made any money at it. He had spun the horses, the corral, and the barn as a "sound investment" in order to justify them to his wife, Elaine, who abhorred all excesses. Edie inherited her love of horses and the land from her dad and her sense of thrift and Puritan work ethic from her mom.

It would probably be too harsh to say that Elaine Morris disliked me, but it was something I assumed. I don't think it was my gangster lineage that bothered her. I just didn't think Elaine Morris *got* me. While I adored my kids and doted on them, I didn't provide much household utility. I sensed she thought I was lazy, and considered my business to be more mischief than actual work. My purchase of the Porsche (which one friend deemed an "act of protest" over moving back to Jersey) was validation of her notion that my work was frivolous. Seeing the way Elaine got on Bob's case whenever he took a nap or eased back to watch a ball game on television, I concluded that she didn't approve of her own husband much, which united Bob and me in a benign cabal against Elaine and Edie.

I pulled in under our lean-to and waved to Score the Helper, who was spreading fertilizer on the grass near the corral. Score was a straw-haired man in his midthirties who had earned his nickname during his roping days at the Cowtown Rodeo. He had a small apartment in the Morrises' barn.

"Look, it's an intruder," Edie said when she saw that I had come home early. "Should I call the police?" She asked this without malice in her voice, but I got the message being implied. My two biggest constituents, the professional and the personal, felt that I had abandoned them even though I was doing the best I could to balance both.

I encouraged Edie to read by herself on the porch while I took the kids for a pony ride in the corral. "When you're done with the ponies," Edie asked, "would you please check out the gutters on the cottage? I think something's blocking them." I nodded, wusslike, but seethed. I'd liberate my frustrations by behaving immaturely with the kids. A child will think you're a comic genius if you can reliably work the words "underpants" and "snot" into the same sentence.

I had thought about my lack of practical domestic skills a lot, and had come up with a rationale: having lost my parents young and been raised by grandparents who viewed organized crime as a mere bugaboo of a prejudicial society, my goal had always been respectability. Consequently, I focused obsessively on studying, reading, fitness, and worrying, all avenues I believed would lead me There. Workaday responsibilities wouldn't pay dividends.

Edie's upbringing had been inverted from my own. Her family was already respectable, therefore they focused on everyday responsibilities: cooking, cleaning, making beds, mucking horse stalls, cleaning gutters. In the Price-Eastman household, gutters were things we were trying to crawl out of, not climb back into. I had worked at the Atlantic City Racetrack for several summers, so I did have some horse-handling skills, something that had given Edie false hope about my potential during our courtship. But there were cultural differences—the kind that make people shriek about stereotypes but are, nevertheless, largely true. Jews, if they succeed, *hire* people to clean gutters. They also don't hesitate to get help with the kids if they need it. After thousands of years of wandering and abuse, something lingered in Hebrew DNA that encouraged self-preservation, which could be accomplished, in part, by the ruthless pursuit of minor conveniences. Edie would have sooner eaten our children than gotten help bathing them.

After dinner (during which my mother-in-law glared at me after Lily pointed to the corn and stated, "Please pass the underpants"), I went into my in-laws' family room and turned on GraftNet, the cable channel that pioneered the use of hidden cameras to cover New Jersey politics.

Rebound's speech at Rowan University was scheduled to run, and I was curious about what his speechwriters had him saying. I hadn't been consulted and, seeking to keep my political gunpowder dry, hadn't meddled.

Edie walked by. "The kids want to watch SpongeBob. Are you going to be long?"

"About twenty minutes. But come here, your boyfriend's on."

"Do I have to watch this?"

"Yes, just for a minute." I pulled her on the sofa beside me and put my arm around her as if this was going to be a romantic encounter. She knew that I knew how much she hated politics.

The camera crew picked up the speech after the introduction. Rebound was in an auditorium. His back was to a great wall of windows and students were pressed against them, waving. The motion was distracting, and the cameraman had the wisdom to focus closely on Rebound. He was wearing his leather bomber jacket and a white pocket T-shirt that offset his tan.

"Leather?" Edie said.

"Yes, don't you find it enticing?" I asked in a monotone.

"Tell me this wasn't your idea."

"No, it was his."

"He's in his fifties, Jonah. He looks like he's at a *Happy Days* convention. Rebound Fonzarelli."

"That's my sense, too. Like he's trying too hard."

"Am I dismissed from your focus group?"

"Yes. Pick up a stale pastry on the way out."

Edie flicked me on my scalp and departed.

Rebound's speech so far contained the garden-variety passionate references about the importance of education, as if somebody in the audience was going to protest, "Education sucks!"

Just as I began to lapse into a coma, the governor said something that snapped me awake. "But there are other issues on which we must keep an open mind . . ."

Rebound set down his notes, took a drink from a glass of water, tightened his face, and said, "So many of our state's revenues come from gaming. We've had a good run with the casinos in Atlantic City, which have contributed to our revenues for education. But I ask myself, can we expand beyond Atlantic City?

"Assemblyman Harris—one of education's most vigorous boosters—reminds us that there are waterways that surround our state, from the Delaware River to the Atlantic. And there are dozens of rivers that could house riverboats, which would undoubtedly serve as a catalyst for a great expansion of our tax base. In my term remaining as governor, I will keep an open mind about the bill my distinguished colleague has introduced . . ."

I felt a quick wave of vertigo pass through me. The wave stopped when it reached the pit of intuition that had been puzzling in my stomach ever since Rebound made his demand that I hit his opponent harder. I had just watched a major policy announcement. The Harris bill had been regarded as a joke, an anemic attempt by a Burlington County assemblyman to look good for constituents along the Delaware River waterfront who would theoretically benefit from riverboat gambling. Gambling had been a core issue in New Jersey for more than a quarter century. It had long been understood that Rebound Rothman's rise from Atlantic City councilman to governor of New Jersey was underwritten by the gaming industry, which was limited by law to a few square miles of shorefront property. It was only the power of the gaming industry that could have vaulted a politician from South Jersey (population 2.3 million) over an opponent from the vastly more powerful North Jersey (population 6.2 million). The Atlantic City casinos had long opposed efforts to establish casinos elsewhere in the region because inland locations (a proposal was once floated and defeated for Philadelphia casinos) would detract from travel to the shore. Even with casinos, Atlantic City was still Atlantic City, not Acapulco, and its natural beauty wasn't enough to keep visitors coming. No, Atlantic City casinos thrived precisely because there were no regional alternatives. Rebound supporting riverboat gambling was like a legislator from Detroit supporting more Toyota imports.

My thoughts first turned to my nemesis, Abel Petz. Had riverboat gambling been one of his campaign stunts? But how had Abel Petz convinced Rebound to screw his original benefactors? I knew my relationship with Rebound had soured, but hadn't suspected I was this deep in the doghouse. And how exactly would riverboat gambling accrue to Rebound's benefit with voters? Could this have been the catalyst for Rebound's urgent call to me, his evasive and dishonest behavior earlier in the day, his demand that I step up attacks on Digby Stahl? Why hadn't he just told me about the policy change, knowing full well I'd hear the announcement soon enough?

I had no idea about what motivated Rebound's policy switch, other than to accept that it was a seminal moment in the election and our relationship. As oblivious as I was about what lay at the root of this mystery, I decided that I had learned the first lesson of my summer as I watched Rebound step away from the podium. I retrieved a business card from my wallet and scribbled:

Leather is not necessarily cool.

WHO GAINS?

*"You have to ask yourself, how much would the riverboat
people spend to float something?"*

I called Lucas Currier on his cell phone. Currier professed shock about Rebound's announcement. "Total ad lib," he said. Currier said he hadn't yet reached Abel Petz, but promised to get back to me as soon as he heard something. I didn't hear back.

The online edition of the *South Jersey Probe* featured an article by Barri Embrey headlined RIVERBOAT SHOCKER. The opening two paragraphs read:

(Glassboro, NJ) In an announcement that stunned officials across the Delaware Valley, Governor Gardner Rothman announced in a speech at Rowan University that he would keep an "open mind" about legislation that would permit riverboat gambling in New Jersey, an enterprise that gaming operators in Rothman's hometown of Atlantic City have long bitterly opposed.

"This is news to me," said State Senator Joseph Diamond (D-Camden). Other legislators questioned what motivated what amounts to a policy change by Governor Rothman. "He's ahead in the polls in his Senate race," said Assemblywoman Janet Hart (R-Mercer), "and it's not like he desperately needed a change of course in his campaign."

I called Irv the Curve. I'd have to get with him on the riverboat caper. Irv could sit on his deck in Margate and smell a rodent taking a leak in Portugal.

The morning newspapers were filled with stories echoing the fundamental question that Barium Enema had posed in her cybercolumn last night: Why was Rothman suddenly supporting riverboat gambling? A comment from the president of the Atlantic City Chamber of Commerce was telling: "Given where the governor hails from, we find his announcement to be irrational, frankly. Perhaps he'll clarify his remarks." Barium Enema put it more bluntly in an appearance on Graft-Net's morning public affairs program. Looking pale but snarky, she said: "Either the governor is a few aces short of a full deck or the riverboat gambling industry is a lot more powerful than anybody around here knew." She went on to cite the relatively meager revenues of riverboat gaming.

I kissed Edie and the kids good-bye and began driving to the shore, my heart feeling like a barbell as I watched them shrink in the rearview mirror.

Irv the Curve rubbed his temples as he read the *Probe* story for the third time. The waitress at Murray's set our poppy bagels before us.

"I'm going over to Rebound's place after this," I said. "I'm trying to get my thoughts together. Do you have any insight?"

"Well now," Irv opened, "my Jonah's suspicious instincts are proving correct."

"So what's Rebound hiding, Irv?"

"Did you ever see *A Streetcar Named Desire?*"

"In Mr. Truitt's film class in high school twenty-five years ago."

"Okay, scholar, what was Blanche DuBois running from?"

"Her family lost her plantation."

"How respectable, but the problem ran deeper. She was a school-teacher who *shtupped* a student. In Mississippi, no less. They beat that out of her later."

"So what are you saying, Irv, that you believe the intern rumors?"

"I'm saying that sometimes one problem on the surface masks a worse one, deeper. Now, the casinos on land have already been created, so there's nothing more to create. Who gains? So what if he screws his old friends. They're *old* friends."

"They're old friends with money, Irv. The Atlantic City casinos could just give more money to Rebound's campaign than the riverboat guys. Rebound's enough of a prick to ask them, and the casino owners are businessmen enough to choke down their pride and pay—especially if it means they'll curry favor with a U.S. senator."

"Then you've got two questions: What reason would Rebound have to be sympathetic to the riverboat people? And how did the riverboat people get to Rebound without everyone knowing?"

"If I've learned anything, it's that Rebound is only sympathetic to Rebound."

"Is he capable of taking a bribe?"

"Doubtful. It's a risky move. He has his wife's money."

"You know how old Pinkus started his auto dealerships, don't you?"

"No."

"He provided the fleet that moved our booze."

"Jesus. Figures."

"So that leaves us with the possibility that the riverboat people have something on him. Now, answer this: Even if Rebound supports river-boat gambling, what are the chances it'll get approved in the statehouse?"

"A.C. will fight it with everything they've got. Passage is a long shot."

"But Jonah, we're dealing with gamblers here. Would you—personally—spend fifty grand to try to win a one-hundred-million-dollar lottery?"

"That's too much to spend on a long shot."

"Agreed. But would you spend fifty bucks to take a shot at the lot-tery?"

"Sure."

"Okay, then. You have to ask yourself, how much would the riverboat people spend to float something?"

"A half million, maybe a million to get something introduced. See how it flies, see if it's worth more investment."

"We don't believe Rebound would need the money. So to whom would—let's be generous—a million dollars be a lot of money?"

"Lots of people."

"Who would have the ability to introduce something—other than an assemblyman whose district already benefits?"

"A lobbyist."

"It's worth a look."

POP'S A TOOL

"How the hell can I help if I can't see you guys?"

As I approached Rebound's house while driving south on Atlantic Avenue, I spotted Currier's Audi darting onto the opposite side of the road. Currier was driving, and a man in a baseball cap and sunglasses was in the passenger seat. Trailing them was the navy blue Chevy Suburban that Rebound's state troopers used to ferry him around.

Neither Currier nor Rebound had returned any of my calls during the past few days, which only mounted my suspicions. I chose not to call Rebound on his mobile phone because he hated it when I did this, and because I was afraid of appearing desperate, which I was. I hung a U-turn and began tailing the caravan on Atlantic. I flipped open my cell phone and called Currier on his mobile.

"Lucas, it's Jonah. I need a hug."

"What do you want, Jonah?"

"Where are you guys going?"

"We're, ah, doing an interview with a radio station in Hammonton."

"Now?"

"Yeah, the boss just went into the studio."

"And your lips aren't clinging to his lower intestine?"

"C'mon, Jonah. What's wrong?"

The guy was lying, for one thing. Hammonton was at least a half hour's ride from here, and these bastards were a few cars in front of me in Margate. Best to play dumb and follow.

"We've got to deal with his riverboat comment, Lucas," I said.

"I hear you, Jonah, but I can't now."

"How the hell can I help you if I can't see you guys?"

"It's a complicated situation. I understand that you're frosted about it, but I can't talk right now. Sit tight. I'll be back to you soon." The line went dead.

Currier would be back to me soon. Right, and a pink kangaroo was going to jump out of my ass.

My baseball hat: on. Sunglasses: on. Visor: down. Look like a schmuck? You betcha. I lingered two or three cars back. Right lane. I got them through Margate. I got them through Ventnor. We passed Vassar Square into Atlantic City. I was behind a Ford Explorer, which was behind the Chevy Suburban, which was presumably behind Currier's Audi. I shifted into the left lane just to check. Yup, Currier was still up there ahead of the Suburban.

I slowed down. I let a few cars pass me on the right. A yuppie in a BMW behind me was pissed, and he flicked his high beams. His customized license plate read BMW 740. Lest anybody not know. I signaled back to the right-hand lane. Somebody let me pull right just past Delancey. All of a sudden, Currier shoots left and onto a side street. Vanished. The Suburban was still up there. Pick a vehicle. Currier shot away from me, but who was with him? Rebound always traveled in the Suburban. You still have the Suburban, Jonah. But Currier was always with Rebound. Two rotten choices. It was best to stick with the Suburban, so I did. Until it screeched to a halt. Whoa! I slammed on my brakes. My Porsche ground to a stop only a few feet from the Suburban. A mustachioed bodyguard climbed out of the Suburban, mounted his shoe to the rear bumper, and tied it, gazing at me in a slow burn while I pulled around him.

Okay, so they nailed me. Rebound had probably been with Currier.

Currier or the governor's boys in the Suburban caught me tailing *because I was driving a silver Porsche Carerra like a moron.* Not subtle. I sucked at this.

The move now was to find out who had gotten to Rebound. Given that Currier was almost certainly in on whatever the scheme was, I couldn't go the official route and ask his staff. I needed somebody who wanted to screw Rebound. Marsha Rothman popped into my head. Problem: Marsha wanted to screw Rebound but she probably also wanted to *screw* Rebound. All of her Lesbian Pride shit was scorn, and you don't scorn if you don't love. If you love, you can rat. No, I couldn't go to Marsha.

Dude. The bitter son. Dude might play with his irreverent Uncle Jonah. I found the flyer Dude gave me and headed down to the club that served as the headquarters for his band, Mongoloid Sphincter.

The Margate club was called Cretin's Clearwater Revival. It was located on Washington Avenue next to Maloney's restaurant. I could hear the ground vibrating from a block away. Cretin's wasn't officially open for business this early in the day, but I told the Mafia wannabe at the front door that I was a friend of Dude's who worked for his asshole father. Those were the words I used, too. This got me right in, dissin' The Man.

Dude was on guitar and gave me a chin nod when he saw me. I sat through two songs, one ballad called "You're Such a Complete Bitch" and another called "Pop's a Tool." The songs were part of the group's demo album, *Pull My Finger.* I would be sure to tell Edie to never again complain about the pain of childbirth, because I was enduring worse. Somewhere along the line, rage had become synonymous with talent, and dirtiness, combined with weak formations of facial hair, became equated with depth. But I tapped my feet to the so-called beat, very conscious of how poorly I had just fared as a sleuth in my *frigging Porsche Carerra.*

Dude took a break after "Pop's a Tool" and jumped off the stage, lighting a joint.

"Jonah, what's up?"

"Just wanted to memorize the lyrics to 'You're Such a Complete Bitch.'"

"Cool, you know any complete bitches?"

"I've been victimized by a few."

"It totally sucks."

"Yeah, it does," I agreed generically. "Look, Dude, it may not be too smart to be toking around like that."

"Why, because if I get busted with pot it'll be bad for my dad?"

"Getting busted wouldn't be good for you, either, Dude."

"Want a hit?"

"No thanks."

"You know, I've got these guys who are growing some fine flora, man. This shit here is called Trenton Mist. Say the word and I can have my guys bring it wherever you want."

"You're distributing, too?" I said, nibbling on the inside of my lip.

"I see it more as spreading enlightenment."

"Your father has opponents who are digging up dirt at this very moment, never mind what a bust would do to him. You've got decades ahead of you to make your band a success, do whatever—"

"Don't worry, Jonah," Dude said with the smirk of a kid who could not fathom life going very, very wrong for him.

"Can I get subversive with you for a second?"

"Cool."

"I could get fired for doing this."

"Cool."

"I think there's somebody out there trying to screw with your family, your dad in particular. I know you're not up on him lately, but I think something funky is going on, and every time I ask Currier about it, he ditches me."

"Mucous Lucas is a douche bag."

"That's something that I'd like the world to know someday."

"So what do you want?"

"Have you noticed anyone strange meeting with your dad lately?"

"He meets with a lot of slimebags."

"Any that stick out?"

"They all stick out."

"Your dad called me a few days ago pretty upset. He didn't say what it was about, but I think somebody set him off."

"He was probably just pissed off about that graffiti. He went apeshit."

"Over graffiti? Politicians get vandalized all the time. Anyway, I know there's a camera in back of the house that's trained on the beach for security reasons. Do you know where they keep those videotapes? I want to look over a few."

"No, the cops have that set up in the garage, and there's always a guy there who gives me looks, the dick."

"Damn."

"Did you check the Island House?" The Island House was the huge condominium tower just north of Rebound's place.

"No, why?"

"Dude," Dude said, "they've got a beach cam. A friend of mine scopes out the babes and does all this zoom stuff on their asses."

"Does he keep tapes?"

"I guess. There's one camera down low, and they've got another on top of the building that covers a bigger area."

"Would this friend do his Dude a favor?"

"For a Benjamin, I'd say he'd unload 'em on me."

"It's best that your dad's crew not see us together. Is there a way you could call ahead and tell him I'm coming by?"

"Sure, but you don't want me to glom?"

"Dude, I just don't think it's smart for you. I think you need distance. I don't know where this thing will lead."

"I'll call the guy. Name's Milo."

Milo sat in a tiny cinderblock room in the basement of the Island House condominium. It was no bigger than a walk-in closet. There were monitors all along one wall and *Playboy* centerfolds pasted on another. Milo was about eighteen, and as skinny as dental floss. He wore a baseball cap that read "Island House Security." Mrs. Pinsky could have overpowered Milo with ease. He sat on his chair and looked up at me expectantly. I remained standing next to Miss July, my line of vision at ass level.

"How long do you keep videotapes, Milo?"

"About a week."

"Can I look?"

"Can you tell me why?"

"How much do you make, Milo?"

"I make diddly. Minimum wage."

"That's about five bucks an hour times how many hours a day?"

"Ten."

"So, fifty bucks a day times, say, five times a week, is two hundred fifty dollars a week."

"You're good at math."

Truth was, I was horrible at math; I had run the numbers before I got there.

"I know. How's two hundred bucks to just let me look without asking me what I'm looking for?"

"Cool."

I paid Milo, who removed several videotapes from a drawer. "These are the past few days," he said. "You can look at them here on this VCR."

"Thanks. I'll need the one that faces south."

I was interested in the tape that would have been made the morning that Rebound had called me. While it didn't show Rebound's house, it did show the beach in front of it. There was a time code running along the right bottom of the screen. I played the appropriate tape in fast forward. From early morning until shortly before eight, I saw nothing interesting. At about eight, two uniformed policemen walked onto the beach, and I slowed the tape to real speed. Two other men that I recognized as Rebound's trooper detail greeted the two officers. The troopers carried small, tightly bound backpacks.

Rebound came into view, shirtless and wearing running shoes, accompanied by another security officer. Rebound began to jog south toward Longport, tailed by the other security men with backpacks. I pushed the fast forward button again. For a half hour in real time, the tape displayed folks milling about on the beach. I hit the regular play button when I saw a tiny Rebound and his bodyguards return at the top of the frame as they were slowing down their run.

A stocky man came into view at the bottom of the screen. He waved to Rebound, who saluted back at him. A handful of others gathered around Rebound as he veered diagonally toward his house. Rebound smiled and waved to the small gathering of gawkers, but continued drifting toward his house. The stocky man who had been at the bottom of the screen also moved toward Rebound's house.

"Milo, see this guy here?" I asked. Milo glanced up from his laptop, where he was surfing a punk-rock Web site.

"Yeah."

"Could he be coming from the Island House? It seems like he didn't come from far out on the beach, more like he came from the parking lot or something."

Milo walked over, bent down, and took a closer look at the screen.

"Oh, yeah, that's Mr. Veasey. He has a place here."

I held my breath and kept my eyes trained on the screen. The man called Veasey kept moving diagonally toward Rebound's house, while Rebound triangulated toward a collision point with Veasey that soon vanished from the camera's range.

EASY VEASEY

"You're wise to ask the opinions of others."

I knew damned well who Eddie Veasey was but saw no percentage in young Milo knowing what I knew. Veasey was, after all, more of a concept than he was a human being, but a definite creature of his environment.

Squat, ruddy-faced, with hair dyed so black it was orange, Eddie Veasey was the dark prince of New Jersey lobbying. An operator of cockfights in the Pine Barrens during his ill-spent youth, he was known as "Easy" Veasey for his confident assertions to clients that he and only he could deliver to them legislative victory. His specialty was gambling. He had represented casino companies in Trenton since the mid-1970s, when debate about the prospects for Atlantic City gambling was most ferocious. What Easy Veasey's contributions were to the ultimate passage of gaming in the state weren't clear, but everyone associated with the victory wore a halo for years afterward.

According to local lore, clients hired Easy Veasey because they were frightened of him. Unlike most lobbyists, who were amiable remember-your-wife's-name glad-handers, Veasey had no interest in lubrication; his modus operandi was the threat: Support me or you'll pay a price.

The fate of a state legislator from farm country who crossed Veasey in the late 1980s was well known to Jersey politicos. The assemblyman, named Sleck, opposed a Veasey-sponsored initiative that would give tax breaks to companies providing services to the Atlantic City casinos. Veasey's bill ultimately passed with some modifications. Smarting from Sleck's opposition, however, Veasey introduced a bill that would prohibit trucks over a certain weight from traveling on small roads in Sleck's district, thereby hampering agricultural commerce. "This is a great day for, uh, the environment," declared Veasey when the bill passed. Sleck was voted out of office in the next election cycle, and was soon replaced by a Veasey-friendly assemblyman.

I didn't know who Veasey's clients were these days, but I thought a well-choreographed "chance" meeting with him was in order. Our encounters over the years had been entirely neutral and I had no reason to believe he held me in either high or low esteem. So I looked up the address of his shore office in Ventnor, swiped my father-in-law's binoculars, and staked out the place from the parking lot of an adjacent liquor store to see what time he came in. As I gazed through the lenses, I felt a mixture of excitement and depression. For a square guy, it was a rush to spy on somebody. I felt like a kid playing cops and robbers, and never entirely outgrew the desire to shout "Freeze, scumbag!" to a perp while he melted at the sight of the aperture of my .357 Magnum.

My melancholy was the mirror image of my adrenaline rush. I was, after all, a one-time presidential pollster in his forties who was in the parking lot of a shore liquor store (off-season, no less) spying on a rutting boar of a New Jersey lobbyist. It was impossible to look through those binoculars and not prosecute myself, my opening statement being the question: Is this where your arc ends, Jonah? What if my children surveyed their father spying on Easy Veasey?

I was an early-morning guy. Veasey, like most lobbyists, was not. He got in at around ten thirty, which was practically lunchtime for me. His office was in a storefront-style office on Ventnor Avenue. I saw him climb from his Mercedes and walk. He was wearing a suit that was certainly expensive, but appeared cheap on him. Veasey's skin was piggy pink and

I could see his nostrils from a hundred yards away because they were structured more in front of his nose than at the base, like headlights. I was momentarily disappointed to see when he turned to the side for a moment that he didn't have a squiggly little tail.

I got out of my Porsche wearing a sports jacket and tie, and timed my walk so that I'd pass Veasey before he actually got to his office.

"Eddie," I said from about fifteen yards.

"Yeah, oh, hi, Jonah," Veasey said, his facial pores winking at me.

"I'm taking a few minutes off before I go get my Rebound fix for the day."

"Yeah? I saw him a few days ago. He behaving?"

"I think so. I'm a little concerned about him. You know, I'm handling his polling for the Senate race."

"Right, I know. So what's the problem?" he asked, impatient. Veasey gazed past me.

"Well, while I've got you, this whole riverboat gaming thing is causing some jitters in the polls. He'd been up about fifteen points, and that's starting to soften." (Total lie.)

"Over *that?*"

"Seems that way. What do you make of it? Are you still repping the casinos?"

"I don't do gambling the way I used to, a little consulting here and there. I think the damned media are making a molehill out of an ant," Veasey said, spittle falling from his lips onto the concrete.

"I don't know, Eddie. Even so, it's making him look irrational."

"So, that's how you're advising him?" Veasey said, tugging at his French cuffs.

"I don't know. I've got to talk to him first. I understand that you sympathize with the A.C. casinos—"

"Oh, yeah, they put a lot of food on my table over the years. The casinos sent you to college, what with your grandpop and all."

"Right. For me, it's about how I advise the governor, not my old-time loyalties. My instincts, though, are to pull him away from the riverboat bill. Now I've got the media investigating."

"Aw, they investigate everything."

"Who knows, maybe Rebound should embrace it."

"Embrace what, Jonah?"

"The press. Maybe he should brief Barri Embrey and her crowd. If they smell something, tell 'em to dig all they want, there's nothing there."

"Look, Jonah, I can't tell you how to do your job, but I think you're being naïve. If you provoke these media bastards, there's no end to what they'll do to you. You don't feed these things." Veasey put his hand on my shoulder and moved closer to me, inappropriately close. He did it in a way that suggested he thought he was being smooth, but it scared me a little.

"That's where you spin docs get it wrong. You think if you step up to the plate, it'll all go away. Sometimes if you step up, you get beaned by a ball. Learn from your grandfather," Veasey said, his nose quivering. "Too bad he's not around anymore."

"What does that mean?" I asked.

"It means you're a smart guy, but sometimes smart guys who once had White House badges can learn a thing or two by paying attention to what happens out on the streets where people have to make a living."

"So you've got a dog in this race, Eddie?"

"Not really, no. If I can be frank with you, Jonah, I thought the riverboat remark was a little strange, but politicians say strange stuff all the time. I think the governor was sucking a little ass with the assembly-man in his home district, no more, no less."

"Maybe you're right," I said, attempting respect for my elder. "You know how things get in these campaigns, Eddie. You fish around trying to take the right position on an issue. You never know if you're over-playing or underplaying. It's easy to get obsessed."

Veasey brought his hand back up to my shoulder. "I understand." *Unnerstann.* "You're wise to ask the opinions of others. A lot of hotshot consultants wouldn't. You know how I am: you ask me, I tell you."

"Thanks, Eddie. Don't hesitate to call me if you have any other thoughts about this. I'm still muddling through."

"You got it," Veasey said, his unctuous skin tightening in a hearty grin, and his fat pink hands grabbing mine as if we had reached an understanding. I felt in whatever part of my system that houses intuition that I had learned the second lesson of my election-season frolic:

The other guy is scared, too.

If only I knew for certain who that other guy was.

ELECTILE DYSFUNCTION

"It's very tribal here."

Abel Petz, with his kinky hair and his red suspenders, looked like a rodent with broccoli on his head and ketchup on his shoulders. He usually wore red Converse sneakers to solidify his Shtick = Genius persona, but I couldn't see them beneath the interview table on tonight's edition of *Election Throb*. Friends who knew how much I loathed Petz have tried to make me feel better by questioning whether his "routine" really worked. The truth? You bet it did—with clients and the press alike. And here he was on national television, declaring that Rebound's riverboat gambling proposal was a stroke of "political genius" designed to distance himself from his original Atlantic City benefactors.

Abel Petz's first move upon being retained by any client was to leak his hiring to a high-profile print reporter. In the subsequent interview, he would claim with a sigh to be "humbled that [name of prestigious client] chose to bring me aboard for my insight." What Petz failed to mention was that the main reason why the client hired him in the first place was to prevent him from going on the air and punditing that [name of prestigious client]'s problem was being "staggeringly mismanaged," thereby making negative coverage a self-fulfilling prophecy.

Of course, now that Abel Petz was on board, the problem would be "masterfully choreographed," never mind that plenty of his clients fired him within a month, something that the client never announced for fear Abel would tell the media that he had resigned their business because [name of prestigious client] had not been forthright with him; after all, "absolute candor is my trademark." Reporters could never bring themselves to expose Petz, because he housed more leaks than a stadium urinal and no journalist wanted to shut that spigot off. And so the hustle—entirely legal and with the client's complicity—continued.

"Why has Digby Stahl's campaign been so ineffective so far?" *The Throb*'s host Gordon Kinney asked.

"Well, Gordon," Petz began, antic, "the Stahl campaign is in a state of *electile dysfunction*."

The in-the-know laughter began in the studio. Abel Petz smiled his me-so-clever smile as *The Throb*'s other guests gave him his digital wet kiss.

"I'm on fire tonight," Petz said, his fingers flickering before him as if he were playing an invisible keyboard. "The Stahl campaign has botched things from the beginning. They have no message, no reason to offer the voters of New Jersey as to why they should choose him over an enormously popular governor and former sports star who is running a *champ-paign*, not a campaign."

Gordon grinned at Petz's adorable pun, but there were no titters from the other panelists this time. No, he wouldn't beat *electile dysfunction* tonight. Still, Kinney dismissed Petz with, "Abel, you were on fire tonight."

Next, Barri Embrey came on. Where Petz was a jester who spouted a whole lot of nothing, Barium Enema always ended up bearing some sliver of her soul.

"Barri, why would Governor Rothman be so pro-casino while would-be Senator Rothman has a sudden affection for riverboat gamblers?"

Barium Enema was wearing a pair of reading glasses today on camera. I found this to be an amusing affectation. *Playboy* pulled stunts like this—featured a centerfold partially dressed as a librarian for the sole purpose of making horny men imagine themselves removing those glasses and getting down to business. It was a tease, an attempt to postpone the animal inevitable or deny that the scene was all about fornication. Just say it, Barri: *I hate Rothman. I hate men. But I want them to want me, so I'll tit-illate with these props* . . .

"Well, Gordo," Barri began, "we've gone from A Time to Kneel to A Time to Deal. We just don't know what that deal consists of."

Another frigging rhymer.

"Isn't it possible, Barri," Kinney asked, "that Rothman was just do-ing what politicians do—telling a locality what it wants to hear? That doesn't make it a scandal, does it?"

"Scandal? Not necessarily, but you have to understand New Jersey politics. This is one state where you've got to know who your friends are. It's very tribal here. Rebound Rothman's roots are in Atlantic City. Even hinting at a policy switch sends signals that he's not loyal to his tribe. The public here will forgive A Time to Kneel—and all that it im-plies with young interns—before they forgive politicians who abandon constituents."

SOMEWHERE IN THE SWAMPS OF JERSEY

"How much time do you have left?"

I was determined to see Rebound and Currier even if I had to stalk them. Today they were at Morven, the governor's mansion in Princeton, which was a one-hour drive from Cowtown. I pulled my Porsche onto a nameless road off of Route 45 shortly after nine o'clock and throttled up. I determined within thirty seconds of hitting fourth gear why there were laws against speeding. My right rear tire blew without any visible catalyst. My heart skidded in my chest, and I felt my vital organs gather in my throat while I downshifted along the gravelly shoulder of the road. My steering wheel convulsed in a supernatural way. My knuckles began to pulse as whatever gelatin held my eyes in place rushed toward the back of my skull. This damned car. God wanted me out of this Porsche. That's right, God was ignoring global plagues today and focusing on screwing with Jonah-boy's wheels. A man thinks this way when the tuna fish can with a jet engine he's driving is about to hit a pine tree. In a quarter of a mile I was able to rumble to a stop. My suit was drenched as I came to believe (after more than four decades of hearing it said) that the human body really was made of water. I felt like I had shed a hundred gallons.

I climbed from the car to inspect it. The right rear tire was a flat, stringy black ooze, practically liquid. I didn't even know if the frigging Porsche had a frigging spare tire.

An old brown Ford pickup dragged down the road and appeared to be slowing. I waved to the driver. It was indeed slowing. The man behind the wheel appeared to be enormous. He wore a floppy leather hat. The current scene was a hick's fantasy—a city-bred, Ivy League–educated yuppie asshole in a $100,000 race car that he couldn't handle—struck down by the Always Just God of Resentment. I crouched down beside the tire, pretending to be evaluating the damage in order to make the repair myself. Yeah, right. I had no intention of changing the tire for a very good reason: I didn't know how. The Talmud expressly decreed that Jewish men shall pay he-of-another-faith for such work. My conviction was validated when a friend of our family's (named Greenberg) was killed as he changed a tire on the side of the road. I ran my fingers along the rim, as if this were the kind of thing that Actual Men did prior to changing a tire.

"It's ripped up good," I told the approaching Goliath. The giant was cross-eyed. His hair was thin, very blond, and lifeless. His features were small and, in a sense, unformed, the way fetuses appear in *in utero* photographs: you can tell that the nose is where a nose goes and the mouth is where a mouth goes, but the features are not defined in a way that one could describe them beyond the fact that they existed.

"A shot from a carbine'll do that," the featureless monster said, raising his hand high and striking me on the back of my head.

My face was pressed against cold, ribbed steel. I tried to press myself up using my arms, but found that I had no arms. I turned my head around in an attempt to search for them, but there wasn't enough light to make an inspection. My hands had been tied behind my back. My chest rumbled across the metal. I was in a vehicle. Oh, yeah, the pickup. We were moving all of a sudden along rougher terrain and my chin bounced against the metal. The top of my head hit a canvas tarp. Jesus, he was going to kill me and bury me somewhere. Why didn't he kill me back on the road next to my worthless six-figure car? Too public. Blood everywhere. Not smart. Drag me into the pines. Smarter.

Ricky and Lily. How would they—

NO! Your sentimentality doesn't serve you here, Jonah. Your love for your children has no utility now. You blame Rebound for your predicament, but blaming him for your death doesn't buy you anything. It's Mickey Price Time, time to think with icy precision. What's the move? Escape. Okay, how? You fancy yourself a tough guy. But you're not street-tough, and you're not Pine Barrens–tough. You're luncheon-tough, and you can't change a goddamn tire. I breathed deeply and smelled dried fruit. I tried to wriggle my hands free when—

The truck stopped and the engine croaked. So much for escape. But I couldn't fathom that this was how it ended. It. My life. Call it faith or stupidity, but this could not be the end. *Money.* I'd bribe the bastard. But how did that work? I didn't have much money on me. He could just take the cash after he killed me. All $180 or so. If I promised him more, what exactly did I propose to do, take him to my broker at Merrill Lynch and have him wait in the lobby while I liquidated my Fidelity Magellan mutual fund?

The back of the pickup opened and the tarp flew off. Brightness in the pines.

"C'mon," the monster said.

"Who are you?" I asked stupidly.

"Jersey Devil," he muttered. Made sense.

I shifted myself so that I could sit up, which took me a few tries. The hollow at the base of my head throbbed from where the Jersey Devil had hit me. There were crimson spots along the metal floor of the pickup. Blood? No, they had texture. Cranberries, of course, we were in the Pine Barrens.

"What now?" I said.

"C'mon."

"If you're going to kill me, why would I get up?"

"If I wanted you killed I woulda killed you."

"You look like a smart man," I lied. "To do it back in the street wouldn't have been smart."

"Keep on talkin', boy," the Jersey Devil said, his hands on his hips.

I looked around. I wasn't going to do much escaping sitting in back of the truck. Look cooperative, I thought. And run when you get a break. I managed to stand and hopped out of the truck.

"What's this about, Jersey Devil?" I asked.

He began to walk. Wanting to appear resigned, I stood beside him. He grabbed my arm and pulled me along with him.

"You been aggravatin' people."

"Did my wife put you up to this?"

The Jersey Devil laughed from his Adam's apple. "I don't ask questions."

"If you're not going to kill me, maybe you can tell me my mistake so I don't do it again." The best I could do was keep him talking.

"I tole you. You're aggravatin' people."

"Don't you mean *irritate?* To aggravate means to make a situation worse."

The Jersey Devil squinted and moved his lips in a way that suggested he was trying to process what I had said.

"You're just aggravatin' people is all," he finally said, after nearly blowing a circuit in his pea brain.

"Did I aggravate the governor?"

"Dunno."

"Did I aggravate Lucas Currier?"

"Never hearda him."

"Did you smile perty?" I asked.

"What're you talking 'bout?"

"I have a security camera in my car. After my team heard Eddie Veasey bragging about his farmer friend, I turned it on in case anything happened—"

The Jersey Devil swung me around. He grabbed my jaw with his giant hands. "You got a smart mouth, boy!" I saw his milky-white spit fly at me.

"It doesn't have to be murder, Jersey Devil," I squeezed out. "It doesn't have to be anything at all."

The Jersey Devil let go and dropped me against a young, sinewy pine tree. He pulled a rope from a deep pocket and wrapped it around my torso, pulling me against the tree. "You gotta learn to stop aggra-vatin' people," he said, his breath smelling like spoiled pork. I knocked my head against the tree as he tied me to it. I feigned a loss of con-sciousness. The Jersey Devil bounded away.

As soon as the Ford vanished into the pines, I began trying to break free. Where was the bastard going? Perhaps he was going to get my car, perhaps to hide it, or maybe to see if there really was a camera inside, which there wasn't. Then he'd be pissed, and he'd come back for me. He'd know he was in the clear, then he'd finish me off. On the other hand, maybe he was just going to run and hide and get as far away from the kidnapping as he could. Perhaps this exercise was just to scare me. Not a wise assumption on my part. He'd be back.

After what seemed like hours of rhythmic movements, I was able to reach my cell phone in the right pocket of my suit jacket. I spilled it out on the ground beside me and managed to slide it closer. Once the phone was inches behind me, I was able to flip it open with my right hand. Feeling around with the numbers, I dialed Irv the Curve.

"Sunset Subs," a nasal female voice answered.

"Jesus, Irv?" I shouted, praying that my voice would carry behind me.

"You must have the wrong number."

"No, listen, who is this?"

"Sunset Subs, Somers Point."

"You've got to listen, dammit!"

"Don't raise your voice to me, pal."

"You don't understand, I've been kidnapped."

"Look, asshole, making calls like this is against the law."

The phone went dead.

I dialed Irv the Curve again.

"Yellow."

"Irv, it's Jonah!"

"You sound like you're in a wind tunnel."

"Irv, I've been kidnapped. I'm in the Pine Barrens. I need help!"

"Are you shitting me?"

"Irv, I swear. Somebody shot out my tire, a great big hick in a brown Ford pickup. I think he's coming back to kill me. He got me on a road, a two-lane road, right off of Route Forty-five near Cowtown."

"How far did he take you?"

"He knocked me out and put me in the back of his truck. What time is it now?"

"Ten forty-five."

"Okay, he got me at about ten after nine. He drove me out here. I've been here I guess forty-five minutes, so I couldn't be that far away from where he got me."

"Listen to me. How much power do you have on that phone?"

"I juiced it this morning. It gives me an hour of talk time, about ten hours of standby."

"You try to get free. You call me every fifteen minutes. I have a guy who may be able to pinpoint the signal."

"What about the police?"

"Nitwits. Do what I tell you to do. Get off the line, now!"

"Who are you going to call?"

I could have sworn he said "some dames." Then the phone went dead.

Dames. I began to snicker in my desperation. What the hell could he be talking about? Maybe I heard him wrong. As I twisted my arms behind me searching for freedom, I kept thinking, dames?

I dialed 911.

"Emergency Assistance."

"Yes, can you hear me?"

"You'll have to speak louder, sir."

"Can you hear me now?"

"What seems to be the trouble?"

"Nothing *seems* to be the trouble, I've been kidnapped."

"Where are you, sir?"

"I'm somewhere out in the Pine Barrens."

"Can you be more specific?"

"No. I mean, I may still be in Salem County, that's where I was picked up."

"Technically, those aren't the Pine Barrens. Wharton and Lebanon State Forests are east of Salem."

"Look, I don't care where I am technically. I'm in the woods."

"I'm sorry, sir, you're breaking up."

We've got phones that allow us to play video games, but not make telephone calls.

"Dammit!"

"Sir?"

I began to laugh hysterically.

"Sir?"

Fearing that my battery would run out, I hung up, and tried again to break free while convincing myself—not for the first time in my life—that Bruce Springsteen had me in mind when he composed, "My tires were slashed and I almost crashed but the Lord had mercy."

What does a middle-aged man in a Brooks Brothers suit think about when he is tied to a tree in the Pine Barrens waiting to die? In the Hollywood version, he sees bright lights and the faces of his parents encircling the central point in the kaleidoscopic Cliff Notes of his life. He has a revelation. It's all very deep, sensitive, literary. I am a reflective guy, but I kept picturing my kids finding me tied up and laughing. Ricky and Lily thought everything I did was funny, so why not this? Bruce: "My machine she's a dud, I'm stuck in the mud somewhere in the swamps of Jersey."

I called Irv again. "Irv, it's me."

"They get you yet?"

"No."

"Stay on a second."

Irv covered the phone and mumbled something to somebody.

"How much time do you have left on your phone?" he asked.

"I wish I knew."

Irv mumbled something else to whoever was with him. "Okay, leave the phone on now. What the hell?"

. . .

The sun set at about eight o'clock in the evening in the late summer in South Jersey, except in the Pine Barrens, where it got dark earlier because of all of the trees. I could not see my watch, given its position behind my back, but assumed it was about eight. I hadn't eaten since early in the morning, and functioned poorly without food. I felt lightheaded and thought I could hear my blood circulating. I had difficulty swallowing, which I compounded by constantly trying to swallow to see if my swallowing had improved. The logic of anxiety.

How hard could it be to break free?

"Why are you on the ground?" I heard Lily ask, although she was not here.

"Get up," Ricky said.

"Did you do the gutters yet?" Edie asked.

I saw Score the Helper standing behind my family.

"I'll do the gutters," Score the Helper said. Son of a bitch.

"No, I'll do it, dammit," I said aloud to the trees.

Footsteps in the pines, crunching against leaves and needles. Quiet Jonah. The Jersey Devil.

"Jonah!" a voice cried.

I shook my head and shed my hallucination. God, maybe the voice that yelled my name was the Jersey Devil. But he didn't sound the same, it didn't have that inbred lilt.

"Jonah!"

I saw blue light. Was this Hell or Kmart, for God's sake?

"Keep talking, son," the voice said.

"Irv?"

"Keep talking!"

More blue light cut through the trees.

"Jonah!"

Blue lights growing white. I could have sworn I saw a headdress and a turban in the mist. Three monsters. The Knights Who Say *Nee!* from Monty Python?

"There he is," one giant silhouette said. I must have been dead, but didn't remember having been killed. Heaven or hell? Standing before me were indeed three giant ghosts from my boyhood: Chief Willie Thundercloud, Sheik Abu Heinous, and the Viking. All were wearing jeans. The Chief wore a suede garment on his torso and there was a headdress affixed to his cranium. The Sheik wore a puffy silver shirt and a turban. The Viking was topless, his bleached blond hair falling beneath his helmet.

" 'All armed prophets succeed whereas unarmed ones fail!' " said Chief Willie Thundercloud, borrowing a huge blade from Sheik Abu Heinous and cutting me loose.

"Machiavelli wrote that," I said as Chief Willie and the Viking helped me up. The Sheik stood guard with a revolver made of stainless steel that glowed against the flashlights like an angel.

Chief Willie Thundercloud patted me on the shoulder. He said, "Chief Willie say, 'You grew.' "

SANCTUARY

"What kind of monsters are you involved with?"

Long before the spectacle of professional wrestling became a global behemoth, it was a collection of local characters, and one locality where wrestling was particularly popular was the Philadelphia–South Jersey region. I remember vividly that on my tenth birthday, Mickey and Irv took me and a handful of my friends to see a match at the old Lenape Hotel on the Boardwalk. Afterward, some of the big names—Captain Lou Albano, Billy White Wolf, Buddy Rogers, and Gorilla Monsoon— came into the restaurant to share birthday cake with my awestruck gang and me. Gorilla Monsoon picked me up in the palm of his hand and held me aloft so that my head touched the ceiling. I felt like a human antenna, and marveled at my luck that a man I had seen on TV was actually touching *me*. There was something immortalizing about it, and I remember feeling as though South Jersey was the center of the universe when months later I saw Buddy Rogers and Gorilla Monsoon on television and eating lunch in Lou's restaurant in Ventnor on the *same day*.

"We don't live far from here, kiddo," Monsoon had told me, vanishing half an omelet in one sucking bite. "I'm in Willingboro, and Buddy here is in Cherry Hill." Mickey nodded as Gorilla blew my little mind.

I went home that evening wondering if I'd ever be as good a wrestler as these men to make South Jersey sufficiently proud that car washes would place my picture above the spectator windows where the people watched as their motorized trophies were accosted by soap, water, and that huge rubber octopus that licked the cars clean.

Also attending my birthday party so long ago was a trio of lesser wrestlers who billed themselves as "The Dames." The Dames were even more local than Gorilla Monsoon and Buddy Rogers. They lived in Ventnor, and I hadn't seen them since my tenth birthday party, thus Chief Willie's observation about my growth.

Dame Number One was Chief Willie Thundercloud, who was said to be "the greatest Indian warrior of the twentieth century." That very little Indian warrioring had taken place during the twentieth century was not nearly as curious as the red-haired, headdressed wrestler's real name, Marty Kramer.

Chief Willie Thundercloud was known in casino parlance as a "boomerang"—an off-the-books hybrid bounty hunter-enforcer-private investigator whose job was to bring back the ill-gotten winnings of casino cheats. Casinos couldn't always prove in the legal sense that they had been cheated, but they couldn't just ignore a suspected hustle. After all, word gets around. That's where Chief Willie came into the picture. Were boomerangs illegal? You betcha, but it was in no one's interest to discuss the activities of a boomerang, not the least the suspected grifter, who was lucky to leave the encounter with his life. For his services, Chief Willie, a stocky, bearded, rust-colored fellow (who favored his Irish mother over his Jewish father), received a percentage of the booty he returned to his sponsors.

Then there was the Viking, who wore a great helmet with horns. He also sported a bleached blond mustache and iron wrist cuffs. Prior to his wrestling debut, the Viking had played on the offensive line at Atlantic City High School under his legal, less intimidating name, Stu Moskowitz. The Viking was a substitute gym teacher.

The final Dame was Sheik Abu Heinous, who became the most famous of the three during the oil crisis of the 1970s, when he would tromp into the ring wearing a turban to frighten the amply coached, sobbing youngsters (of which I had once been one) who lined his pathway. The crowd would jeer something bloody, and Sheik Heinous would inevitably go down in the third round to a challenger such as the beefy, freckle-faced Johnny Ray Peachpie. One time a bespectacled attorney representing Arab Americans for a Philadelphia-based antidefamation group confronted the six-foot-six Sheik Heinous outside the locker room at the Palestra. "The Sheik's" essential nature shone through, and the wrestler, whose real name was Vinnie Santafurio, stuffed the lawyer in a trash bin. The Sheik was deputy chief of the Ventnor Fire Department.

It had been the most glorious time of my life, when baby Jonah was protected by mountains of muscle, maternal love, and grandparental indulgence, all of which were to end soon enough with the deaths of my parents and subsequent flights across the globe to duck subpoenas.

Chief Willie Thundercloud, Sheik Abu Heinous, and the Viking drove me back to Cowtown. They assured me that Irv had called Edie, which would result in two things: convince her that I was now safe, and that I recently hadn't been. Edie knew that I reached out for Irv when there was trouble. Regrettably, this hadn't been the first time.

Whatever misgivings I had had about moving back to New Jersey and living near my in-laws evaporated the moment I saw the familiar yellow lights on inside Edie's parents' house. When Edie heard the rumbling of Chief Willie Thundercloud's 1980 Trans Am (license plate: "CHIEF 1") over the gravel, she ran from the cottage. I could see that her mother was holding the kids back in the house. Edie stopped cold, her jaw falling slack, when she saw the Dames in semi-regalia climb out of the truck behind me. She had joked on more than one occasion that she had married a freak show, but it's academic until it administers a full nelson in your driveway.

Edie hugged me. Her face was wan and her eyes were angry.

"What happened?"

"My tire blew out."

"That damned car."

"I'm coming to the conclusion that you're right. Irv called?"

"Yes. He was vague."

"That's Irv."

"Your suit's ruined and your chin's scraped up. All of that from a blown tire? Where did it happen?"

"Right off Route Forty-five."

"That's right here. Why didn't you call?"

"The story gets worse. Somebody punctured the tire on purpose." I decided to leave out the gunshot. "A guy knocked me out and threw me in the back of a truck—"

"Oh, Jonah!" Edie covered her eyes. The muscles in her jaw rolled.

"I know. He left me tied to a tree in the Pines. I had my phone. I finally called Irv, and he sent these guys to get me."

Edie studied the men, who bowed their heads in the Yes, Ma'am style of the Old West.

Edie, usually so reserved, embraced me again and then, jerkily, backed away.

"Do you need anything?" she asked the Dames.

"No, thank you. We've got canteens," Sheik Abu Heinous said.

Ricky, Lily, and my mother-in-law, Elaine, appeared on the porch.

"Cool!" Ricky said when he saw the Dames. Lily just studied them curiously. Elaine pursed her lips to underscore her historic disapproval of me.

"Hey, guys!" I said to the kids. I introduced them to the Dames, who tossed them about to their joy, and to Elaine's horror.

"I can't thank you enough," I told them as they approached their truck.

"Chief Willie happy to help," Chief Willie said, his arms folded, presumably the way an Indian chief might. "We made arrangements to have the car towed to a dealership for repair."

"It was still there?"

"Uh-huh."

"What do I owe you?" I asked.

"You can talk it over with Irv," Chief Willie said. "In the meantime,

Chief Willie say this: 'The sum of virtue is to be sociable with them that will be sociable and formidable to them that will not.'"

"That sounds familiar," I said.

"Hobbes," Chief Willie answered.

"Do all of you study political philosophy?" I asked.

"Just the Sheik and me. The Viking reads romances. Anyhow, Chief Willie suggests you carry a friend. Do you have a friend?" He made a gun with his hand.

"I do."

"You know how to use it?"

"Believe it or not, yes."

"Good. If you need us, here's Chief Willie's card." Chief Willie handed me a business card that read, "Chief Willie Thundercloud, Lenape Warrior." A phone number was at the bottom of the card.

"What kind of monsters are you involved with?" Edie asked once we were sitting in our kitchen. "Is this about . . . *him?*"

Him was the governor.

"I was the one who was attacked. You ask that like I was an accomplice."

"Maybe in a way you were. You're repeating a lifestyle that's familiar to you. Is there any chance it was *him?*"

"No, it wasn't him."

"But was it done in his service?"

"I don't know."

"You have to stop working for Rothman, Jonah. He's going to get you killed."

"I just can't walk away—"

"This is your *life. Our* lives!"

"I have to make a living. Why do you find that so hard to understand?"

When Edie and I met, she had been a music teacher, and had been able to live modestly on her income. We didn't exactly live like Rothschilds now, but my income had grown to be many multiples of what Edie had made teaching music. That our lifestyle—living on one robust income while Edie was free to stay home to raise the kids, play guitar, and ride horses—resulted from hard labor on my part was a concept that, despite her intelligence, was truly lost on her.

"Get another client."

"Just like that? Snap my fingers and get another client? It doesn't work that way. C'mon."

"You have to find options. You're the one removed from the world. You think your adventures are real life."

"How do you think things get paid for? You are so sheltered that you don't know who pays for the shelter."

"This isn't about me. It's about trying to save your life, and that's because *I'm* sheltered? This isn't the first time your work has led to violence."

"I nearly get killed and *I'm* the villain. Why do you think I go to work, Edie? Just to show off? I know you're worried about your parents getting older, and that you've never—"

Edie turned around, went into our room, and slammed the door behind her. I was left alone in my filthy, shredded suit standing in the cottage's living room. Later, alone on the couch in the living room without a pillow or blanket, I examined the trail of my career, and where it had led me, on the panorama of the drywall above me.

Reality: Rebound was my only client, and I couldn't help but think of the scene in *The Godfather* when the *consigliere*, Tom Hagen, describes his practice as "special" because he only handles one client, the don. While I had had episodes of client diversification, at the moment I was economically bound to the Rothmans. In addition to my financial dependence, Rebound's tentacles reached into my seminal sense of who I had become. I had left Washington in disgrace several years ago when allegations surfaced that I had fabricated a poll in Arizona to make a client's opponent, a dullard named Straun, appear to be a racist. I accomplished this not through Straun's actual record, but by demonstrating through a backhanded poll that bigoted voters just happened to be supporting him. One result summarized that 63 percent of Straun supporters agreed with the statement that the Martin Luther King Jr. holiday was "another excuse not to go to work." While the poll had not been fabricated, its device made me so politically radioactive that the best of my bad options was to vanish, figuring that even radioactivity has a half-life.

After my disgrace, Mickey summoned me back to Atlantic City to take on the only client who would hire me: the Philadelphia-South Jersey Mafia boss, Mario Vanni, who wanted a legitimate casino operator's license. Mickey died—I am convinced that my involvement with a racketeer killed him—but I was able to get the New Jersey Casino Commission to grant Vanni a license after a summerlong image-building campaign whereby the public got to see a kinder, gentler sociopath functioning as a solid citizen. Vanni's ostensible softness was showcased at the same time a black, dreadlocked drug dealer I fabricated named Automatic Bart was said to be violently taking control of the region's underworld. I positioned Vanni as firmly antidrug: whenever a drug pusher turned up dead, I made sure the mob boss was seen in public tickling babies while categorically denying with his boardwalk-nurtured smirk that he had anything to do with the "cleansing" of local streets. By the end of the summer, my polling had demonstrated that the jittery citizens of the Delaware Valley were convinced that only Vanni could protect them from Automatic Bart. I executed this campaign (and others) with the help of a crew of Internet hackers, dirty journalists, loose cash, and enough morally flexible clergy and labor chiefs to convince the authorities that the Mid-Atlantic states would erupt if Vanni wasn't granted his license. Vanni got his license, and acquired my grandfather's hotel legally. He handed the Golden Prospect over to his M.B.A. daughter, Angela.

Soon Vanni was murdered, and an investigation ensued. I had not been implicated in any crime, but it became public knowledge that I had helped to engineer a public relations campaign tinged with skullduggery. My bloodline to Mickey Price became fodder for the chattering classes. Again, I was out of work.

I was also newly married to Edie. Early in a relationship, adversity can be bonding, but after a while, the person not under siege may conclude that they ended up with a loser. Edie got pregnant. I had been borrowing heavily against my retirement fund, which I never told Edie. I was down to $2,300 when I heard that Rebound was running for governor.

We moved into a one-bedroom apartment in Margate, and I began stalking Rebound when he took his daily run on the beach. I caught up to him on one run in which I regaled him with embellished stories about my years working with Ronald Reagan in the White House. The more Reagan stories I told Rebound, the more he shook his head in amazement and whispered "genius." Rebound invited me inside his beach house for some Gatorade. I ad-libbed a campaign strategy for Rebound and his wife, Marsha, that emphasized his local-hero status and suggested his potential to continue to the national stage. They hired me as a "behind-the-scenes" adviser, to use Marsha's term. Rebound, after punctuating the discussion with "genius" once more, grabbed my knee and said, "You . . . are the future of this state."

I casually dropped my hiring to Edie that evening at dinner with her parents. She casually said, "That's nice," having no clue that her Ivy League–educated husband was nearly broke. That night, I read the Book of Jonah on a dark beach with a flashlight to thank God for sending the Rothmans into my life.

BARIUM ENEMA

"Americans are tacit supporters of fornication,
but bitter opponents of hypocrisy."

The next morning I got up early and ran three miles. I used to run far-
ther, but my knees couldn't take the pounding anymore. I used to think
people who had aches, pains, and sicknesses were losers, but realized
shortly after turning forty that all people, including me, only know what
their own life experience has taught them. I tried once to pass off my
knee pain as a temporary condition until Edie rolled her eyes at me and
snapped, "You're old."

It was one of those runs where I pretended to be happy to be alive. I
even plastered on a fake grin, as if I were a film version of myself. The
problem was that I wasn't buying my own act. Rebound and I were un-
raveling. Edie and I were at a stalemate, and somebody wanted me either dead or badly hurt.

I showered and tried to shave, but the scrapes from the Jersey Devil's
truck beneath my chin hurt like hell. A couple of years ago, I had tried
out a goatee for a few days before I turned forty. I got up on the morning
of my actual birthday, studied myself in the mirror, thought of the number forty, and said aloud, "You look it." The goatee was almost all gray.

Now, the question of post–Jersey Devil security: It was a black stainless steel Ruger .357 Magnum revolver with a four-inch barrel. I kept it in a lockbox behind a hidden beam in our bedroom. I housed the hollow-point rounds separately. I usually preferred firing .38 caliber rounds, but with the Jersey Devil out there I preferred Magnum slugs because they would knock a giant on his ass in addition to leaving a crater-sized exit wound. I don't know why, but this pleased me.

I had a shoulder holster for the gun, which I had bought in West Virginia from a local tannery. I bought it because my grandfather instilled in my head the notion that it was only a matter of time before I'd have to run. Carrying around a monster like the .357 wasn't easy, but I maintained a morbid fear of being unarmed when mutant pineys were trying to kill me. I wore it beneath a loose-fitting windbreaker. Its bulk was a healthy encumbrance, I thought. I had carried a smaller piece once, years ago. The problem with a smaller gun was that after a while carrying it felt normal, and I didn't want being armed to ever feel normal. At some point, it was a greater risk to perpetually prepare for danger than it was to actually live your life.

I prepared cereal for the kids and drove them to school. Edie stayed in bed, hating me, especially after I told her that I intended to hire the Dames to conduct random visits to help guard the Cowtown property. I felt around for my gun as I drove, mourning that my children, like their father, were growing up around men with guns. My cell phone rang as I pulled out of the school.

"Jonah?"

"Yes."

"Barri."

Deep breath. And the impulse to soil myself, thus reinforcing the journalistic legend of Barium Enema. Self-control. "Hi, Barri."

"Do you have a minute for me today?"

"It's what I live for."

Barri chuckled. "What's your schedule?"

"I just dropped my kids off at school. Wanna meet somewhere?" Show openness, not guilt.

"Sure. Do you know the Short Hills Deli in Cherry Hill?"

. . .

The Short Hills Deli was a modern operation on Evesham Road on the east side of Cherry Hill. Unlike Murray's down the shore, this deli featured sleek new booths without graffiti. I saw Barri Embrey sitting in a booth near the back of the restaurant. She was roughly my age, somewhere in the first half of her forties. She was rail-thin and wore a lot of makeup, which obscured a face that was naturally pretty in a bitter way. She had a toothy smile, a dimple in her chin, which gave her a vulnerable look that she wouldn't have had otherwise, and intelligent brown eyes that shot out like howitzer barrels against her blonde hair. She was dressed in crème-colored business attire and the V in her top showed just enough freckled cleavage to make me feel as if I were doing something bad by being there. A golden cross dangled between her breasts for spite.

I felt a twinge of panic when I realized I was carrying a gun, a question that an investigative reporter would rightly want answered. I decided to preempt any potential hug with a hearty "Don't get up" and a handshake.

"The last time I saw you in person was in the green room for *Election Throb*," she said, still seated, thank God.

"That's right. What were we geniusing on that day?"

"I think it was when Torricelli withdrew from the Senate race."

"Yes. The Republicans were pissed," I said.

"They should have been. They lost."

"They don't like that."

"Neither side does. It's the one thing they've got in common. What did you do to your chin?" Barri asked.

"Oh, I, uh, was standing on a rung on our fence and slipped off, banged my chin. Do I look rugged?"

"With the gray stubble, sure. Thanks for seeing me, Jonah."

"What's up, Bar?"

"Look, I know you're capable of subterfuge, but you've always been straight with me," Barri said.

"Let me guess the subject?" I asked. "Riverboat gambling."

"Bingo. Your idea, Jonah?"

What did I tell her? That I was on the outs with Rebound? Not smart. Reporters only wanted to deal with players, and conceding that I was out of the game got me nowhere. Besides, I had every intention of using my ordeal as leverage against Rebound. He knew damned well he had been avoiding me since his bombshell, and he'd be scared to keep doing so once he found out about my adventure with the Jersey Devil.

"No. Not my idea."

"Jonah, if you told Rebound to conduct the Trenton Philharmonic with his dick, he would."

"Flattery becomes you," I said.

"C'mon, his reliance on you for hardball is the worst-kept secret in the state."

"That doesn't mean I'm the only one with influence."

"Factions?"

"There are differing points of view among his advisers," I said.

"The riverboat thing makes no sense. Rebound's either a few noodles short of a kugel or he's getting muscled from somewhere. I never thought he had much pushing his eyes, Jonah, but crazy? Nah."

"No, he's not crazy, Barri," I said.

A young waitress with a tiny face and enormous hair came by and we both ordered. She had enough gum in her mouth to dam the Nile.

"So, it's Currier and Petz," Barri said as the waitress slipped away.

"Functionaries. They have influence, not power."

"Who has power, Jonah?" Barri asked, resting her mannequin face in her willowy hands.

"Beats the shit out of me," I said.

"I always enjoyed that stark metaphor."

"Who said it was a metaphor?"

"I see. Are you available for future consultations?"

"Depends. You may ask me to betray confidences vital to my career."

"I'm a strict Catholic girl. I respect confessions. I'll protect you."

"Why, Grandmother," I said, "what big teeth you have."

"I won't eat you, Little Red Riding Hood," she winked.

"Good, so we agree that if I have something, and I share it with you, my name never sees the paper."

"Yes."

"And you realize that I may never have anything at all."

"I realize that," Barri frowned. "Any other requirement?"

"I'm curious: Why the hard-on for Rebound?"

Barri backed up. "Girls don't have hard-ons."

"Au contraire," I said, feeling like a nimrod. I had never used that phrase before in my life. "Girls can get them worse than men. Whenever I see you on TV you're talking about A Time to Kneel."

"TV chatter. The producers think the pun is funny."

"Plenty of reporters would traffic in smut if it got them on *The Throb.* I don't believe you would." This was utterly untrue. Of course she would—she *had been.* "You must have something, Barri. Puns are funny once."

"I have leads. I won't lie to you."

"I'm surprised you've never asked me about it."

"I wouldn't ask you about that. You've got a rep, Jonah."

"I know I have a rep, but what does it have to do with an intern program?"

"You're regarded as a lethal strategist, but even your worst critics don't think you're a pimp. Word is you're like your grandfather. Killer by day, family man at night. Anyway, I'm hearing lurid stuff. Interns. Drugs. Skinny-dipping."

"Jesus, Barri, you make him sound like Caligula."

"Caligula didn't run for emperor of Rome on a family values platform," Barri said. "Americans are tacit supporters of fornication, but bitter opponents of hypocrisy. It's a nuance few understand."

"I take it you've got a woman spinning yarns to you in a bar somewhere."

Barri shrugged, noncommittal.

"Honestly, Barri, I've always wanted to get embroiled in a sex scandal."

"A seasoned pimp wouldn't have such a goal. He'd be living it."

I sighed and rubbed my temples. Perhaps Barri had evidence that Caligula was alive and living it up at the Jersey Shore, perhaps she didn't. That she was digging at all in election season disturbed me because I couldn't write Barri's pursuit off to a rabid, witch-hunting media when I, too, believed there was something going on with my Klonopin-popping client. I decided to establish trust with a touch of vulnerability.

"Barri, do you think there's a tie between the intern program and the riverboat deal?"

"Dunno. But I don't have a hard-on for Rebound, Jonah. I'm a reporter. I appreciate your honesty, but resent your implication. Objective reporting requires that I ask hard questions."

Barri's sermonette was all I needed to hear. Every time in my life a reporter went virginal on me about objectivity, it meant the opposite.

Despite all of the dark thoughts I had ramming against each other like Steel Pier bumper cars, I knew virtually nothing that was of any use just yet. Whatever muck was out there, however, I knew I had to dig it up *first*. While I stood to gain very little if Rebound was elected to the Senate, I stood to lose plenty if he lost, what with Currier and Petz out there. A victory would be attributed to Currier, Petz, and Rebound's charisma, grace, charm, and wit. A loss would have been caused by my fumbling. I envisioned Petz somberly stating to Gordon Kinney on *The Throb* that he had not been able to overcome the "astonishing mishandling" of Rebound's campaign. Off-camera, Petz would whisper my name to Kinney. *The Throb* would call me to discuss *my* failed campaign. I would decline, as always, to discuss my client work. *The Throb* would end with a grainy photo of me, then the lush baritone of Gordon Kinney stating, "*The Throb* invited controversial pollster Jonah Eastman, who authored Governor Rothman's failed campaign, on our show. He declined to appear."

The waitress set a plate of fruit and a bagel before each of us. Barri plucked a red grape from a stem and bit it in half. She studied the congealed innards of the decapitated fruit and bit it yet again.

I felt uncomfortable, and thought about pinching a Klonopin from Rebound. I also didn't like the prospect of having a scar on my chin. My circumstances urgently required the assistance of a soul who was committed as a matter of principle to fighting unfairly.

BOOK II

FOX ON THE RUN

The town was a gargantuan masquerade, as visitor deceived visitor. . . . And people wanted to be deceived, to see life other than what it was, to pretend to be more then they were.

—Charles Funnell, BY THE BEAUTIFUL SEA
(on Atlantic City)

THE BOOMERANG

"He appeared to be a man who got his own joke."

Sheik Abu Heinous, in full regalia, dropped in for a random patrolling of the Cowtown property. My mother-in-law scowled from her kitchen window while my father-in-law smiled broadly, savoring her disapproval.

Edie and I dropped the kids off at school and she silently drove me to the Porsche dealership in Cherry Hill to retrieve my so-called "car." My cell phone rang soon after my rocket got comfortable in fourth gear.

"Jonah, it's Lucas. What the hell happened?"

Lucas. My buddy! I had left Currier a voice mail about my ordeal, which finally got him to call me back.

"Oh, nothing really, except Bigfoot blew me off the road with a rifle and left me tied to a tree in the Pine Barrens. Why, how've *you* been?"

"Are you all right? God."

"I'm a little shaken up, but I've dealt with rabid fans before. Usually Victoria's Secret models."

"Do you know why they did it?"

"He said I was *aggravating* somebody. Incorrect usage of the word, technically."

"The nuts out there, honest . . . When can we meet? Our man is anxious. The opponent is on TV questioning our campaign slogan and all. At some point govvy's going to have to talk off the cuff to the press. Can you get up here today?"

"No, Lucas, I can't do it today. I've got a few things going." Blow *him* off, scare *him* a little. "Why don't we do it tomorrow? I've got to see a guy now. Maybe I can media-train the boss on some of the things I've been hearing."

There was a beat of silence on the line. "Hearing what?"

"Lots of questions about the riverboat gambling announcement. Buzz about the intern program, like there's a connection."

"That's total bullshit."

"Probably, but what's out there's out there. If my little trip to the Pine Barrens gets out, who knows, maybe somebody could connect that and make a whole big conspiracy."

"You don't honestly think—"

"I don't think much these days."

"See you tomorrow, Jonah, ten-ish."

There was static on the line, which I exploited. "You betcha, Mucous."

"Huh? You're cutting out."

Chief Willie Thundercloud hadn't become the top boomerang in Atlantic City because he fought fair, and since my mortal threat with the Jersey Devil I had lost interest in ethical fighting techniques. I made an appointment to meet him at his house in Ventnor. He opened the door wearing jeans, sandals, a chamois shirt with polished silver buttons, and a beaded headband.

"Tell me, tribal wise man, why do millions of people come to Atlantic City every year and give away their money?" I asked.

"Like Chief Willie always say, Mongoose Behind the Dune, it's not the heat, it's the stupidity." This talking in the third person was going to be a treat.

"Mongoose Behind the Dune? Is that my Indian name?"

"Mongoose for short. Irv says you have a good heart, but are fast and deadly when provoked by snakes. Chief Willie senses this in you," he said, crossing his arms. The look didn't quite square with the red hair and freckles.

Chief Willie's apartment was decorated in three styles: Native American (the artwork), 1950s Irish (plastic slipcovers on the sofas), and twenty-first-century Yiddish (expensive electronics). Chief Willie gestured for me to be seated on the smaller of the two couches.

"I can't believe that bastard tied you up in Chesilhurst."

"Why?"

"Chief Willie never tied anybody up there. Too hilly."

"I'll keep that in mind."

"It was probably a scare job. If he wanted to clip you, he would have done it somewhere flat with softer ground. Throw your ass in a ditch."

"Oh. What good's a scare job if nobody told me what I'm supposed to be scared of?"

"Dunno. Maybe your camera-in-the-car ruse threw him. Maybe he was coming back and got distracted. Maybe he's a frigging chowder-head."

"Thanks for the leads."

"Chief Willie used to believe in big conspiracies where everybody did stuff for a reason. These hotel clients I've got, case in point. Everybody thinks they're badasses who control the world. Truth is, they can't conspire on lunch. You got any theories?"

I told him about Rebound, Currier, Veasey, Barium Enema, A Time to Kneel.

"I thought that riverboat thing was funky," Chief Willie said, slipping into the first person. He appeared to be a man who got his own joke, and I felt a spasm of love for the loon because of it. "The casinos made Rothman. He knew your grandpop."

"I know."

"You got a budget, Mongoose?"

"I've got a big campaign polling budget. Ever since my little incident in the woods, Rebound and Currier are taking my calls. They want me to be happy. He's letting me do a bunch of polls to head off whatever he thinks Digby's planning. I can cover you in my polling budget for a while."

"What does he think Digby's planning?"

"Rebound hasn't been straight with me, Chief, so I'm going with the worst-case scenario. Somebody's got dirt on him. The dirt's tied to something bad, maybe an intern—or seven. We could get an October surprise in the campaign."

"Then why not look into his opponent, the judge?"

"That would have been great six months ago, but I'm not sure there's much dirt there. You don't hear rumors about the guy. I may not be able to get at him dirtwise, but I think he's got some negatives I can probe in my polling."

"So what's your endgame with Chief Willie, Mongoose?"

"Find out what it is that my client's not telling me, so that I can save him and not get hung out to dry by Abel Petz if Rebound goes down in November."

"Petz? The guy from TV?"

"Yes."

"The Lenape have a word for man like that—*douchebag*."

"I never knew that was an Indian word."

"Oh, yes. Coined by the Comanche tribe to describe the railroad barons," the Chief winked. "You don't like this Petz, huh, Goose?"

I couldn't quite get used to my new nickname, but I didn't want my head crushed, so I went with it. "He's made a career out of making other consultants take falls. What do you do about something like that?"

"I had a guy who badmouthed me to a client. The guy was hitting on the client, a real thoroughbred feminist broad from Bucks County. So Chief Willie pasted up the guy's Lexus with pro-life stickers after a meeting. The two of 'em come out to the lot to go to lunch, and she loses it when she sees the stickers. No lunch for you, asshole." Chief Willie snickered like a third grader.

"So where would you start, Chief?"

Chief Willie glanced at a mirror. He threw punches at his huge reflection.

"Can't touch Barium Enema. You start looking into a reporter, that's death. Then we become the story, and that's for shit. I think we run a few courses: you keep with Rebound and Barri, and I'll look at this Veasey chucklehead. I've seen him around."

"He looks like a pig, doesn't he?" I said. I know, it was juvenile.

Chief Willie rolled his short neck around, cracking it a few times. He threw an air punch, extended his hand, and said, "Pigs are sloppy, Mongoose."

MORVEN

"Digby doesn't have an upper lip."

Morven was the name Annis Stockton, the wife of a colonial hotshot, had given to the mansion that her husband had built in Princeton in 1754. Morven had been the name of a mythical kingdom in the work of a Gaelic poet. At one point, Morven encompassed three hundred acres and was the home to black slaves and countless other servants. The mansion had been the home of a handful of New Jersey governors throughout the twentieth century, but had been converted into a museum—until Rebound decided he wanted to live in it.

Rebound worked out of a study in Morven much of the time. He now stood behind an ornate desk, the recessed lights dancing across a cabinet filled with trophies and photos of himself with famous people. He was flanked by a tab-collared Lucas Currier. Rebound had maintained his tan with a regimen of moisturizer, and he looked like one of his trophies. His silver hair glittered in the mirrored wall that backed his ME cabinet of self congratulation. On a pure optical level, he was presidential. Maybe the optics could carry him there. I didn't know anymore.

"Jonah!" he said, appearing genuinely excited to see me. "What, you've got a goatee going there, athlete?"

I felt my chin, which was indeed stubbly. "I hurt my chin a few days ago during my little adventure, and it hurts to shave it," I said.

"I like the distinguished guru look," he said. "Adds to your mystique." Rebound's eyes tensed a bit when he remembered that the catalyst of my fashion change had been my violent incident in the Pines.

Rebound shook his head knowingly, and I felt momentarily guilty about believing he was complicit in my troubles. He turned around, approached a bowl of huge green grapes (where did Marsha find them?), and popped a few into his mouth.

"Did you see Digby on *The Throb?*" Currier asked.

"No," I said.

"You guys better be damned sure you keep an eye on him," Rebound said, his stress causing him to regress from his initial charm. A blob of Silly Putty emerged in his hand and he thunked it down on this morning's photo of himself in the *Trentonian*. Once his imprint was on the putty, he began stretching it lengthwise. Dissatisfied with the resulting distortion, he crushed the putty in his hands and pinched at it angrily.

Currier tensed up. I conjured up a massively insincere smile, the kind that involves every facial muscle. Robert DeNiro does this face when he's pretending to be amused right before he jams a nail file into somebody's eye. I opted against violence for the moment and instead walked to the Table of Abundance and ripped off a small bunch of grapes.

"Gee whiz, Governor," I said softly, "I would have loved to have seen it, but being tied up in the woods by a hired goon and all sort of made it a challenge." I ate a few grapes for effect.

"Oh . . . that's right. The thing Lucas mentioned . . . Christ."

"Before you get the governor on camera," Currier interrupted, "I want both of you to see how Digby comes across."

Currier slid a videotape into a machine that was balanced on an antique table. Color bars and a hideous squeal tore through the speakers, and Rebound glared at Currier until he muted the volume. Digby appeared. He was split-screened with *Throb* host Gordon Kinney. "Freeze the frame," I barked at Currier.

Digby's long, patrician face filled the rectangle on the tube nicely.

His salt-and-pepper hair was neatly parted, his creased faced suggested a recent regatta in Cape May, and his pale-blue button-down shirt and rep tie left little doubt that his college degree had come from one of those schools that most New Jerseyans found to be both unattainable and interchangeable.

"I never noticed that before," I said, primarily to myself.

"What?" Rebound asked enthusiastically.

"Digby doesn't have an upper lip," I said.

"Really?" Rebound said. He bent down and studied the monitor. "He doesn't, Jonah. What does that mean?"

"I'm not sure," I said. "Push Play."

Rebound rolled his eyes.

Kinney's first question on that night's edition of *Election Throb* was about the relevancy of Digby's state judgeship to his political career. Digby lit up. "When I went to law school, Gordon, I remember thinking, What am I doing? I always thought of law as protecting good people and punishing bad people, and it took a while for me to see what law school had to do with that. To be honest with you, I didn't do as well as I thought I would the first year."

"Why did you stick with it?" Kinney asked.

"I thought that even if I didn't like school, maybe I'd like being an actual lawyer, which turned out to be the case. It wasn't until I prosecuted those cop killers in Newark that I realized I had made the right career choice, but there were years of self-doubt."

"Freeze the tape," I said.

"What? What?" Rebound asked.

"He's pretty good there," I said. "He comes off as being real."

"You're right, Jonah," Currier said, "He's good when he's regular, admits to some flaw."

"Let's keep it going," I said.

"You've been critical of Governor Rothman," Kinney continued. "Why, specifically, do you feel he's been a bad governor?"

"I never said he was a bad governor, Gordon," Digby continued, appearing hurt by his interrogator's lead-in. "I'm just skeptical of some of the things he claims to be standing for. He's been out hawking this slogan of his, Family State, Family Man." Digby's eyes closed for a moment, his head tilted back, and he tittered a little. Digby reminded me of that guy . . . what was his name, the participatory journalist . . . Plimpton, George Plimpton. Clever guy, but looked out of your league. "I mean, what programs does Governor Rothman propose to advance this agenda? What does it even mean?"

Kinney fired back: "Are you referring, Judge Stahl, to the innuendo about Rothman's intern program, A Time to Heal? Are you saying that his slogan is hypocritical given the rumors?"

"Oh, Gordon, of course not. Rumors like that drag a campaign down, and I personally don't believe them. The question isn't what Governor Rothman does in private, it's what he does for the public. I'm running for Senate on a platform of doing what must be done to make New Jersey recognized as the power that it is. Governor Rothman— who has refused to debate me on the subject—hides behind platitudes that have no discernable meaning. This isn't nineteen seventy-six, courtside, when crowds were cheering a layup. This is more than a quarter century later, and there are complex problems that must be addressed."

"Complex problems," I said. "Bite me."

Rebound laughed cathartically. It was right from his gut, too. I had an obsessive dislike of politicians who spoke about complex problems. While many problems were difficult, few were complex. I was convinced that "complex" was code for "let's not do anything."

Kinney: "Some people believe, Judge Stahl, that the main credential you have in your favor is that you're a squeaky-clean Democrat running for office in an environment when there have been so many Democratic scandals. I'm not just talking about New Jersey, I'm talking nationally as well. Is your main credential, Judge, that you've never been caught doing anything naughty?"

Digby's answer wasn't bad: "I've been a judge for twenty-five years. Judges see good and judges see bad. The ability to differentiate between the two should be a prerequisite but not a platform. The Senate is a lawmaking body and I've devoted my life to moving things forward through law. It's a nice match."

Very little interesting took place during the next seven minutes of the interview. It wasn't until Kinney asked Digby about his great-grandfather, Commodore Ducius Stahl, the founder of Stahl Motors, manufacturer of industrial engines, that I saw something that gave me hope.

"What do you remember about Commodore Stahl, Judge? He played an important role in New Jersey history, not to mention our national economy."

"Oh, Gordon, I was a boy when he died, but because he lived to be ninety-four, I do remember him. He had this wonderful cottage in Deal, and I would sit on his lap and we'd watch the ocean for hours. He told me about his youth in Sweden, meeting with presidents, and how he helped try to find the Lindbergh baby. Of course, Stally, as he was called, was great friends and neighbors with Lindy. When I went to church as a boy, and the priest at St. Matthew's Episcopal spoke about God, I always thought that God must have looked like Stally and been from Sweden."

"Freeze the tape," I said.

The frame memorialized Digby as a craggily handsome upper-lipless twit whose head was thrown back as if he had a polo mallet up his ass.

"What does it mean, Jonah?" Rebound asked genuinely.

"It means something, Governor, I just don't know what yet. It's a feeling I get. Give me a few days and I'll explore it."

"Do you guys think I have to debate this jackass?" Rebound asked.

"I don't," Lucas said.

Rebound asked, "If I don't, it'll look like I'm ducking him."

"You *are* ducking him," I said. "But the question is, what's in a debate for you? I only play games that I can win. He's the outsider hammering at your record. I don't want you being hammered for an hour just to make you look like a good sport."

"You don't think I can beat him in a debate, do you, Jonah?"

What I was thinking: *No, Rebound, you can't beat him. That's because he has a portfolio of beliefs, he's better on his feet, and you so deeply resent having to compete that you'll get pissed off on camera and bury yourself. So we'll duck him every way we can.*

What I said: "That's not it at all, Governor. He's the fresh outsider. You're on the defensive by virtue of your position, that's it. Look, why don't we get a feel for you on camera and we'll refine our message from there."

"I hate that training crap," Rebound said.

"I know you do. Let me just poke and prod you like it's a real interview. Where you're strong, we'll display you to the world. Where you're less comfortable, we'll do our best to duck it."

A VERY EFFECTIVE POLLSTER IN THE PAST

*"A quarter dropped into a slot machine on the Passaic River
is one less quarter for Atlantic City."*

A two-man camera crew had set up the library, which was adjacent to the governor's study. Cameras were stationed behind two chairs that were facing one another, interview-style. Rebound took a seat in one, I sat in the other to play his interrogator. A television monitor was set on the ground between us, which would allow us to play back Rebound's performance.

One of the crew boys, a bullet-headed dude in his thirties, hooked microphones to Rebound's and my ties. His partner, a guy with long hair and a prominent jaw, prepared to shoot Rebound from over my shoulder. Rebound studied the bullet-head. "You look like somebody," Rebound said.

"People say I look like Moby."

"The whale?" the governor asked.

"No, man, the singer," Moby said.

"I don't know him," Rebound said, agitated that a pop-culture reference had passed him by. "Any of you athletes know him?"

"I know who Moby is," I said. "A couple of guys beat him up after a performance or something."

"Why did they do that?" Rebound asked.

"I think he was feuding with Eminem," I explained.

"They fought over M&M's?" Rebound asked.

"No," I said. "Are we rolling?"

"Rolling," Moby said.

I decided to start off easy, then ratchet up the artillery.

"Governor," I began, "you're a popular governor. Why leave for the Senate?"

"I haven't been elected yet," Rebound said. "But if I am, I wouldn't be leaving New Jersey, I'd be representing the state in a larger forum. A national forum."

"Some say it's a stepping-stone for you—"

"Stepping-stone to what?"

"The presidency."

"If I were thinking in those terms, I'd stay on as governor if I could. I can't remember the last time a senator went straight to the Oval Office."

"Fair enough. What can you do for New Jersey in the Senate that you can't do in Trenton?"

"It's no secret that the economy both in New Jersey and in the U.S. has been in recession. New Jersey has been hit less than other states."

"And getting hit less badly is an achievement of your administration?"

"You're missing the point. I think that some of the things we've done to attract businesses to this state, incentives and all, have been responsible for how well we've fared here."

"Stop speed," I said to Moby, who stopped rolling tape. "Now, Governor—"

"You're nailing me one after the other," Rebound complained.

"You're doing fine. You're not letting me get away with the putdowns, which is good. But when you tell me I've missed the point, you look defensive. Remember, you're the king who is descending to meet with an inquiring reporter. A king would rise above my barking, rather than being threatened by it. When I hit you like that, gently gloss over my hostility and talk about what you want to talk about."

"Did you do this with Reagan?" Rebound asked.

"Yes, speed, please," I said. Moby flipped a switch and responded, "Speed."

"Much of the economic success of New Jersey is skewed," I began, "as a result of the casino gaming industry. It's not really honest, is it, to say that New Jersey fared well economically across all industries—"

"Well, in any economic report it's not unusual to have a few players doing the heavy lifting. That's what happened with tech in the nineties. Cycles come and go, but every state is known for having some industries that are stronger than others."

"Okay," I continued, "but that begs a big question. You suggested in a speech at Rowan that you'd be open to riverboat gambling. Given that casino gambling has done well for the state—and your own career—why would you open the door to a proposal that would hurt New Jersey, not to mention some of your career's greatest supporters?"

Rebound glanced around for Currier, who was invisible behind Moby.

"You're putting words in my mouth," Rebound said.

"Governor, did you or did you not open the door to riverboat gambling?"

"There's a big difference between opening a door and mandating a whole new policy."

"Again, did you open the door to riverboat gambling?"

Rebound's lips disappeared, and tiny ringlets of sweat surfaced below his hairline. He made a squeezing gesture with his hand, then appeared lost when he realized that it held no putty to distort. "Given the budgeting challenges we have, we just can't go around slamming doors."

"You're treating my question, Governor, as if it's mean-spirited, when I think it's quite logical. The fact is, your roots are in Atlantic City; Atlantic City is still on the map because of casino gambling; the casino gambling industry has historically been the biggest benefactor of your campaigns; and now you're denying that a proposal to compete with that industry is a threat. A quarter dropped into a slot machine on the Passaic River is one less quarter for Atlantic City. If you were that concerned about the state's revenues why not propose bringing the Olympics here, or convincing more New York– and Philly-based companies to come to New Jersey—"

"That's enough!" Rebound said. "Turn off that camera."

An anxious Moby complied.

"This isn't helpful, it's downright abusive," Rebound said. "Not to mention a waste of my time. I've got some of my boys at the Pentagon waiting for a signal from me, and I'm caught up with this shit. Television shouldn't be used as a political tool!" he concluded, his voice sounding like shredded brake pads on an oversized truck.

I couldn't help laughing out loud, which I knew was wrong. It was visceral. "That's like saying colonoscopes shouldn't be shoved up anybody's ass."

"Just what I need right now, a metaphor," Rebound said.

"What's up with the Pentagon?" I asked in counterfeit awe.

Currier stepped in. "Can I ask you gentlemen to leave for a moment?" he said to Moby and his partner, who slipped out the door. "I have to agree, Jonah, you're hectoring him, not training him."

"It's not constructive," Rebound barked.

"Then what's the answer, gents? What's the answer?" I snapped back. "You can sit here and tell me that I'm hectoring the governor, but every reporter has a right to an answer to the question about riverboat gambling, and it's not an answer you seem to want to give."

"The answer's simple," Currier said. Rebound glanced up at Currier.

"What's the answer then, Lucas?" I asked.

"The answer, Jonah, as you well know, is that politicians send up trial balloons—"

"Fine. Then my next question is: Is this a trial balloon aimed at winning votes in Burlington County in election season, or do you intend to follow through and support riverboat gambling?"

Currier answered, "We're looking at a variety of revenue-generating options. This one is no more special than the others."

Rebound nodded his approval.

"Fine," I continued, "what are these other options? And why are you so worried about votes in Burlington County, where Governor Rothman is already very strong?"

"This is enough, Jonah," Currier said.

"You need an answer, gentlemen."

"We've got one," Rebound said.

"It'll have to be better than what I just heard."

"Don't you think I know what's happening here?" the Governor accused.

"Let me tell you exactly what will happen," I said, flushing tact completely down the toilet. "You will go on TV and tank against Digby. Despite your miserable performance, Currier and Petz will tell you that you hit a home run. That'll be the phrase they use—home run. The next day, when the *Probe,* the *Inquirer,* the *Times,* the *Star-Ledger,* and the *Bulletin* cornhole you, a new PR consultant will tell you that the coverage was a lot better than they expected. And you will feel better. Christ, some of your people," I said without looking at Currier, "are like an intravenous opiate drip, and they'll drip at you until Digby is elected. That's why I'm here. I know where you're strong and where you're weak, and I'm trying to navigate you through this minefield."

Rebound held his hands out in a slow-down gesture. He didn't like being disapproved of by anyone, even me.

"Look," Currier attempted to conclude. "You've been a very effective pollster for the governor in the past, Jonah."

In the past.

"But" Currier continued, "I just don't think this is the best use for you right now, for us. You're a key . . . knowledge partner." *Knowledge partner?* A comic notion of being seventeen at prom time: *Jonah, please don't try to unhook my bra, I see you as more of a knowledge partner.* My God, I was being spun. Me!

"So I roughed up the governor in media training and I'm out."

"You're not out," Rebound said, eager to deliver better news. "We need you to go after Digby like we talked about."

Currier added, "It's just that we're more comfortable with Abel's style for message, training and all."

"That's not necessary, Lucas," Rebound said, statesmanlike. But I knew that Rebound was a coward and that Currier's lips conveyed Rebound's wishes.

I recognized my crimes and had scribbled lesson number three on my notepad, which had to do with the mythology of taking criticism well:

Nobody has thick skin.

"Okay," I said, throwing up my hands in surrender. "I'll stay on Digby."

With that, a skittish Rebound attempted to have things both ways by leaning forward and asking, "Where are you going to be the next few days, Jonah, I may need you?"

"I'll be around. I cancelled my powwow with The Hague," I said, ramming Rebound's favorite defense mechanism up his ass. Currier's eyes flickered. He caught it. Rebound remained staring at the floor, seemingly oblivious to my mock. "I'm taking my uncle to services tomorrow."

"Services?" Rebound said.

"Yom Kippur's tomorrow."

"Tomorrow?" Rebound said.

"You may want to release a happy holidays sentiment or something. Jews vote in serious numbers."

"Right, but not Republican," he said.

I was in no position to admonish Rebound for his position. I had, after all, married a Methodist who was one-quarter Lenape Indian, and had brought up my children in that cowboy faith of America, a place that many sane people suspect, but would not dare utter, is the new Jerusalem. I rationalized a difference between Rebound's spirituality and my own: where I was inclined to lash out against my assigned faith, Rebound didn't seem to know one was there.

WHITEY?

"Not right in the head."

However much I hated doing it, I had dropped by Score the Helper's little apartment and given him a few hundred bucks to keep his eyes open for the Jersey Devil. I told him to coordinate rounds with the Dames, one of whom would be by later in the day. Score accepted the money, but gave me a look as if I were a paranoid psycho. I had the feeling that somebody, maybe Edie or her mother, had told him bad things about me.

My father-in-law waved me over as I walked across the gravel drive. He was standing on the porch holding onto a post. He was actually walking well despite his hip problems, but I sensed he was afraid of falling down, so I went to him. His brown eyes reflected the wisdom of a peaceful Lenape elder.

I leaned against the same post as Bob. "Do you have a chore for me?" I asked.

"Chore? Nah," he said. "Just wondering about something. Edie said this man who came at you in the woods was a big towheaded guy."

"That's right."

"Mmm," was all Bob Morris said, poking a finger in his ear for a quick scratch.

"Does he sound familiar?"

"He may."

"Bob, you're like your daughter. You make me work for every morsel."

Bob Morris chuckled, but it was strained. "Well, we'd best be careful. You know there's all kinds of stories in the Pine Barrens."

"Like the Jersey Devil?"

"Like that, sure. But Jonah, some of these stories are true. Like things from your grandpop's day. There really were liquor stills."

"I know. What does that have to do with the albino?"

"There was a family of pig farmers out near Ong's Hat years ago. Leeds was their name. Simple pineys, kept to themselves. They had a son. Late 1950s, early 1960s or thereabouts. Kid had no pigment, called him Whitey. Obvious reasons. Not right in the head. Haven't seen him since he was a boy, but from time to time I hear stories. If you follow events, he probably runs the family's farm now. What do you know about pigs, Jonah?"

"They're not kosher."

"That's true. They also eat a lot. They can eat through bone if you give them enough time."

I swallowed hard and strained to make sure my bladder was under control.

"Okay," I said, hoping to tease out Bob Morris's thinking.

"When we have a horse carcass, we carry if off somewhere for disposal. I don't deal with that end of things myself. I know that some of the horsemen around here in years past have taken their carcasses to a pig farm, although they're not supposed to."

"Is your worry that maybe he wanted to take me to that pig farm, Bob?"

"What if whomever it is you ticked off knows about Whitey Leeds and his pig farm, knows he can make horses disappear? If he can make horses disappear, he can make humans disappear. That type of thing."

I pulled back my sports jacket and showed Bob my .357. Bob nodded approvingly. "Between this and the Dames we should be okay."

"Okay," Bob said. "Then you should be able to handle this." Bob pulled an index card from his pocket and handed it to me. "I found it in the barn this morning tacked to your horse's stall. I don't think it was meant for me." The typewritten note read:

The wicked flee when no man pursueth: but the righteous are bold as a lion.
—Proverbs 28:1

GOOD DOG, BAD DOG

"Where does loyalty end and being a schmuck begin?"

"I'm not getting in that little space capsule you drive," Irv said the moment I stepped in his apartment. "It's bad luck. We'll drive my Caddy to the synagogue." Irv handed me the keys to his Cadillac Deville, which was a soft gold color.

I held the passenger door of the Cadillac for Irv, and he fell into the seat with an "oy." I started the Caddy up and glided through the lot. I liked the feel of this car, I thought, immediately wondering what was wrong with me. Old men drove Cadillacs.

"You could steer it with your finger," Irv said, extending his finger.

"I bet you could."

"So," Irv said, immediately after I pulled onto Jerome Avenue, "let's discuss this Veasey bastard. You think he put you on the spot?"

"He's a prime suspect. What do you know about him?"

"I know he's an animal. That scare you, Jonah?"

"A little."

"Good. That's healthy. Of course, fear only gets you so far."

"I know," I said.

"No, you don't."

I laughed. "I don't? Irv, you still talk to me like I'm ten years old."

"What are you now?"

"Comfortably over forty."

"Okay, so I'm thirty years off—nothing in the scheme of things."

"You were saying that fear only gets you so far—"

"Right. Everybody was scared of my old boss, the Dutchman, but we got him. Albert Anastasia . . . they called him the Lord High Executioner of Murder Incorporated. Very extravagant name. He wasn't so tough after Junior Persico popped him a few in that barber's chair. Then came Vito Genovese, who was shut down on a drug frame-up. Point is, sooner or later, someone comes along whose incentive overwhelms his fear, and he'll piss in your kasha."

"I've never liked kasha, and now I never will."

"Does your incentive to get to the bottom of this overwhelm your fear?"

"Not yet."

"All right, let me know when it does."

"And what, Irv, you'll beat Veasey up for me?"

"No, but you've got me interested in this caper. I've been bored. How much *Who Wants to Be a Millionaire?* can a guy watch?"

The synagogue wasn't a synagogue. It was a collection of folding chairs under the boardwalk near Buffalo Avenue in Ventnor. A makeshift sign at the entrance read "Vilda Chaya Reform." *Vilda* (pronounced *VILL*-duh) meant *wild* in Yiddish, and *Chaya* (roughly pronounced *HIGH*-ya) meant *animal.* Together the term was the equivalent of "bad seed," "rotten apple," with a strong hint of violence. This was a temple for Jewish gangsters and other assorted thieves.

Folding chairs for about twenty were set up facing a broken refrigerator, which was used as an ark, presumably containing a low-rent Torah. The rabbi was an old friend of Mickey's named Wald. He had once been convicted of assault after he cold-cocked his understudy, who referred to the Palestinians as "our cousins." I thought his combination *yarmulke, tallis,* and Tony Lama cowboy boots was a nice look, especially with sand on them. Rabbi Wald had married Edie and me, which may have explained why Edie's mother cried at the service.

"Rabbi," Irv said. "Where did you get all of those fancy prayer books?"

The rabbi took a furtive glance at a folding table where the books were piled up, and proceeded to whisper to Irv: "I swiped 'em from Temple Emanuel in Cherry Hill."

Irv nodded as if this were to be expected. "It's been a while since I've seen you repent, Jonah," the rabbi reminded me.

"I repent in installments," I said.

"It all adds up," the rabbi concluded and moved onto other congregants.

Irv and I took our seats near an algae-covered support beam. I could hear sparse footsteps on the boardwalk above us. A pale and stocky man in his late forties ambled in and nodded to Irv. He was wearing a burnt-orange leisure suit, a lime-green tie against a brown shirt, and white shoes. He had a gold cap on one of his eyeteeth, and was carrying a newspaper. Irv rose and extended his hand, so I rose beside him.

"Jonah," he said to me, "I'd like you to meet Vadim Pokolov."

"Good to meet you."

"Good as well," Vadim said. *Gutuzzveal.*

Vadim sat in front of us. I studied his getup, but restrained a strong impulse to fall onto the sand laughing.

Vadim turned around and pointed to the headline of the *Philadelphia Daily News* for Irv to read:

KORSHENKO DEPORTED

"You see what they do to honest businessman?" Vadim sighed. "They send him back to Russia. A simple vending machine repairman."

"I understand, Vadim," Irv said. "Many of my old associates had to leave this country one way or the other. Joey Adonis. Charlie Lucky. Meyer."

"I know, Irv," Vadim said. "I know stories."

After Vadim turned around again, Irv whispered, "These ones from Russia make our old gang look like the Keystone Kops. They look like peasants, but they've got minds like diamonds."

"You're shitting me," I said.

"I shit you not," Irv countered. "Don't let the sartorial tragedy throw you—back during Prohibition, the WASPs looked at the Jews and Italians that way. Only this crowd is much more ruthless and farsighted. Korshenko was the financial brains of their endeavor." This wasn't the first time I had heard such respect conveyed about the Russian mob, but to look at Vadim . . .

"They had almost a century of living like dogs in the gulag," Irv continued, "all the while seeing our wealth in America and pretending they disapproved of it. They want it all and they want it right now. They don't care how they look."

"What about Tappo the Clown?"

"No dummy. But Tappo doesn't have the international backing that a man like Vadim has."

"Does Vadim have a specialty?"

"Call it business development," Irv said with a chuckle.

Rabbi Wald took us through a handful of prayers. He knew the type of men he was dealing with—men who wanted to pay their respects, but not too many respects—so he closed his prayer book after about thirty minutes and folded his hands together on top of the highest box on his podium of boxes. He began his sermon:

"On Yom Kippur, God asks us to think about right and wrong, good and evil. We're supposed to think about these things all the time, but we don't because we don't want to. We want to do what we want to do, am I right? Ah, we figure, we'll worry about it later. Yom Kippur is later. That's the whole idea. Later's right now, today.

"So here we are. Now what? A student I had years ago before I got pinched for that thing . . . the student asked me about good and evil. I told him that we all have good and evil inside of us. Good and evil fight like dogs. There's the *kelev tov*, as we say in Hebrew, the good dog. Then there's the *kelev raah,* the evil dog. They're both inside," the rabbi said, stepping from behind the boxes and bouncing his fingers off his belly.

"So this kid asked me, 'If the good dog and the bad dog are fighting, which dog wins?'

"'The one that I feed,' I told my student.

"In order to do good, we must acknowledge the *kelev tov* and *kelev raah* inside of each of us, and then take real steps to do good, not just yammer about it once a year. The reason why God spared Ninevah in the book of Jonah is because the king repented. He knew there was a force larger than himself, a requirement greater than his own needs. The Bible does not say, 'God saw their sackcloth and fasting,' but 'God saw their *deeds*'—that they had turned back from their evil ways.

"If you want the good dog to win, you feed the good dog. You don't just come here and apologize on Yom Kippur for what the bad dog did."

I drove Irv home. The Alter Kocker Arms was practically empty, Mrs. Pinsky presumably concluding that Al Qaeda guerrillas would not be storming the place today. An aqua-haired woman I didn't recognize urged me to close the front door more swiftly, mumbling something about "air escaping."

Freon Leon sat in his alcove appearing forlorn. He wasn't nodding or shouting about Nixon today. A copy of the facility's newsletter, *Play Nice,* was in his hand. "This happens with him when the weather gets cold," Irv explained. "He gets upset when they turn the air conditioner off. He thinks he's going to hell."

"Doesn't he know it's autumn, and there's no need for air conditioning?"

"It's not a temperature thing with him," Irv explained as I sat him back in his favorite seat inside his apartment. "It's like the cold air from the vents is his friend or something. You worried about Freon Leon?"

"No. Rebound," I said. "There are few things sadder than watching what happens to a man when his bag of tricks runs out."

"But, Jonah, you *are* his bag of tricks."

"I'm not sure, Irv. I always hoped that he'd appreciate me more."

"That's the orphan in you talking. You want a father, a brother. What you've got is a client."

"I understand that."

"You most certainly do not. You want him to see you as a partner."

I felt as if I had been kicked in the stomach by a giant wearing construction boots. "At some level, he must," I said.

"He is not capable of that, Jonah," Irv shouted. Irv was not a shouter. "The truth is, son, he believes *he* made *you*."

"*He* made *me?*" I said. I covered my mouth because I was afraid it was turning down in a facial precursor to an out-and-out cry.

"Of course!" Irv said, his eyes hard. "Of course!"

"I mean, he did give me a break after I had my troubles, but how could he look at the things I've done that have nothing to do with—"

"Jonah!" Irv punched the air. He took a deep breath, and for a moment I worried that he might be having a heart attack. He wasn't. "Stop trying to examine the evidence," he said softly. "Don't you see, Rothman must see himself with a special type of . . . lens in order to climb out of bed in the morning, and that that lens does not—*cannot*—include you in the picture?"

"I always thought my debt was paid back a long time ago."

"You are wrong there, boy. That debt can never be paid back. A man like Rothman will never see another man's success as authentic. If your success is authentic, Rothman disappears."

"I never like letting people down," I said, disgusted with myself, but not sure why.

"Rothman knows that about you, which is why he has you and treats you the way he does. It's quite a little shakedown. If you cease to sit in the can with him when he voids his bowels, *you're* disloyal. The central question here is: *Where does loyalty end and being a schmuck begin?* Given your background, you have a great need to be attached to people. See, Rothman is entitled to his view, Jonah. He's entitled to whatever version of events he wants." Irv leaned forward, rubbed his hands together, and whispered, "The question is, what will that view cost him?"

"You know, you were with Rebound when I first met him." Now was as good a time as any to bring up the brief but haunting gathering in the Golden Prospect's laundry room so long ago. "Spring. 1980. At the Prospect."

Irv closed his eyes as if straining to think. "May have been one of those promotional things he did."

"Maybe. It was in the laundry room downstairs."

"Laundry? What the hell are you talking about, laundry? So, why do you take an old man to services?" Irv asked, putting his feet up on the coffee table. I sensed he was uncomfortable with the topic. Knowing when to drop a subject was a minitalent I had learned from Mickey. "Do you think there's a payoff?"

"Of course not."

"Then why do you cart me around?"

"Because it feels right," I said.

Irv smiled broadly, and patted my knee with his fist.

"You're on the right track," Irv said, rubbing his eyes and his cheeks curiously, as if he were trying to make himself red to mask tears. "Veasey . . . rattle his cage, Jonah. This *momzer* isn't Superman. You're on the right track."

When the engine of my Porsche turned over without event, I chose to interpret the day's events optimistically. I felt a warm sensation like heated pool water drift through me as I made a note of the fourth lesson of my adventure:

Do the right thing because it's right, not because you'll get paid back.

IS ANYTHING MISSING?

"Chief Willie say, 'Hog not loyal to farmer who does not feed him.'"

"You know what it's about. Yes, you do. It's about the soul." So spoketh the Geater with the Heater, Philadelphia's eternally reigning Prince of the Night, Jerry Blavat. To label Blavat a deejay was like classifying the 1963 Corvette a car. Blavat had ruled the Delaware Valley airwaves since the 1960s, when he wasn't long out of high school. The Geater's wisdom echoed along the boardwalk until his gospel was overpowered by the *blinging* of pinball machines.

Chief Willie met me at an arcade on the boardwalk that smelled like a clogged artery. It was a few doors down from the Golden Prospect, a place I had passed every day for the first eighteen years of my life but cannot recall having ever entered. Chief Willie was play-boxing with the elderly attendant, who had a tangerine-colored face and looked like Popeye, which is what everybody called him. Chief Willie solemnly imparted a "How" of greeting as soon as he saw me. I remembered Popeye as a boardwalk fixture from my Mickey days.

"Long time," Popeye said, clearly recognizing me, not because of my own achievements, but because of my bond to Mickey. I could tell he was studying my eyes. Mickey and I had the same green eyes.

"Yes, sir," I said, "I'm Jonah."

"Right, I know," Popeye said as Chief Willie lingered. "I had a roller chair down by Million Dollar Pier from the forties through the eighties. Good memory."

Chief Willie saluted Popeye and we left the arcade, which was abrasive to every human sense with its chirping shrieks, whizzing lights, and buttery smell. I turned around to get a last glimpse of Popeye, and declared a silent victory that he had remained here where God stationed him.

Chief Willie leaned against the railing facing the ocean. The light hit him in a way that made him look every bit his age—probably pushing sixty. I joined him in the pose, feeling like a cinema detective. Actually, that's not true: I felt like a pollster trying to look like a cinema detective.

"Here's the deal, Mongoose." Chief Willie began dispensing with his Native American affectations. "You know lobbyists have to register their clients with the statehouse, right?"

"Right."

"Cool. This pig-and-a-half, Veasey, is still registered as a lobbyist for a group of A.C. casinos like he's been for years. He's not repping the riverboat chuckleheads, at least not officially. They're repped by another guy who has his own shop, no link to Veasey that we know about."

"Could Veasey be repping the riverboats on the side?"

"Yeah, but it would be illegal if he didn't declare his representation. He could lose his license. Then again, if he is repping them, he's repping his client's competitor, so declaring wouldn't be cool, either."

"So, Chief, you don't think he's our guy?"

Chief Willie sucked on an eyetooth and checked out a young woman walking down the boardwalk with a pudgy middle-aged man. I could tell the scene pissed him off. "Here's the thing, Mongoose: Veasey's lobbying fees from the casinos have gone way down in the past few years. They don't need the guy. Still, his lifestyle is pretty sweet."

"What's your point, Chief?"

"Chief Willie say, 'Hog not loyal to farmer who does not feed him.'"

Veasey wouldn't be as loyal to the casinos as he was when he was getting paid big."

"So he might be inclined to switch sides."

"Uh-huh."

"But he's not registered for the riverboaters, you said."

"No, but Rebound's little bombshell is pretty recent. There's a grace period for registering."

"I don't know, Chief Willie, just bouncing from one client to their archrival doesn't strike me as a shrewd move."

"No, it doesn't."

"So where does this leave us?"

"The Kiowa warriors used to have a trick. When they wanted to see how many rangers were in a camp, they'd throw rattlesnakes into their campfire to see who ran out. I'm saying, we rattle Veasey's cage. We think he's guilty of something but we don't know what. We don't know who he's talking to, or what's up his pig ass. Here's the idea: we do something to rock his world and see where he goes, what he does, who he calls."

"Will we be breaking any laws?"

"Yeah, but they're stupid laws."

"Oh, ever hear of a guy named Whitey Leeds?"

"Chief Willie say 'no.'"

"My father-in-law says he's a pig farmer. He may be the guy who came after me."

"I'll keep my nostrils open."

"Hi there, young lady," the effeminate voice said when Veasey's secretary answered the phone. "Is Mr. Veasey there?"

"I can check," the secretary said. "May I tell him who's calling?"

"Certainly, this is Pat McGroin. I'm a field producer from KBRO-TV in Philadelphia."

A beat of silence. "Uh, um, yes. May I tell Mr., um, Veasey what this is regarding?"

"Malfeasance."

. . .

Veasey, not surprisingly, didn't take the call. The secretary took a number. The call had been placed by the Viking (with a lisp), who left his mobile phone number with Veasey's secretary.

"I've got a deal with a guy at KBRO that he'll vouch for my guys in exchange for some shit you don't need to know about," Chief Willie explained after playing back the brief conversation for me on the phone.

"So what does this accomplish?"

"It's a teaser," Chief Willie said. "I'm planting a seed is all."

"For what?"

"Hold on for a couple of days, Mongoose."

After a few days without contact, I was starting to wonder about Chief Willie, which was my own foolishness. The Chief was a results kind of guy, not a client service kind of guy—he didn't feel the consultant's need to substitute a demonstration of his worth with token hand-holding.

Finally, my cell phone rang as soon as Ricky and Lily went off to school. "There's a green van outside of Stewart's Hot Dogs in Margate. Be there at nine fifteen." Chief Willie.

I knew something funky was going down and didn't want to be tooling around in my conspicuous Porsche, so I borrowed my father-in-law's Buick.

After passing a store called Jamaican Me Crazy, I parked Bob Morris's car on Douglass Avenue in Margate. The green van was right in front of Stewart's Hot Dogs, as Chief Willie promised. I had on jeans, an Eddie Bauer autumn-weight jacket, aviator sunglasses, and an Eagles baseball cap. I knocked on the van. It slid open.

"What kind of cookies you got, little girl?" Chief Willie asked, falsetto.

"Peanut butter," I said.

"That crap sticks to your arteries," Chief Willie said as I climbed in. Chief Willie sat in the driver's seat and pointed with his chin for me to sit in the passenger seat. He pulled out, took a U-turn, and slid north toward Ventnor. My heart galloped as Chief Willie told me what had just gone down.

Chief Willie had phoned a buddy at the burglar alarm company last night, ahead of time. His contact's job was to see nothing, to make certain that if the alarm in Veasey's Ventnor office went off, the signal wouldn't register with the company or the police. The Viking bypassed the alarm using whatever techniques one uses to bypass an alarm, picked the locks, and got inside.

First, the Viking flipped on a few computers. He left tamper marks on a filing cabinet and swiped a few random files. He went through Veasey's office to see if he had a safe. He did. It was a floor safe beneath a marginata plant. The Viking made sure the marginata was turned around from its normal position. He left just enough evidence to suggest a sloppy break-in, but not enough to leave Veasey and his associates absolutely certain that they had been penetrated. Chief Willie summed it up as a "garden-variety mind-fuck."

"The Viking dropped a beacon in his office," Chief Willie told me.

"A beacon?" I asked.

"A bug. A listening device. He slipped it under a lamp so any third-rate spook'll find it."

"He *broke* in?"

"It's easier to ask for forgiveness than it is for permission."

"An old Indian saying from Montana, Chief?"

"No, my uncle Timmy Doyle from Northeast Philly."

"I like it. Where are we going, Chief?"

"We're going to have a sensory adventure. We're going to hear how Veasey reacts to his ordeal, what he says."

"We're going to his office?" I said, now scared.

"Nah, just outside."

Chief Willie opened the van's ashtray. "Have a toothpick," he said. I took one. Chief Willie took one and flipped it into his mouth. "The important thing is that you see the dividends of your resources. Besides, you get to watch my crew engage in a little assplay, which is always good." I was torn between my desire not to appear to be a wuss and the fact that I was a wuss. Chief Willie had just pulled up across and a block from Veasey's office on Ventnor Avenue.

"Bacon-ass gets in around now," Chief Willie said. "His secretary has been in for about a half hour."

"So what, Chief, we just listen and watch?"

"I don't mean to be overly reflective," Chief Willie said, "but while violence may not solve everything, it never fails to cause the enemy to regroup."

Ricky and Lily would be brought to the prison on visiting day by someone other than Edie, who never wanted to see me again after the conviction. The kids would press their hands against the thick glass windows. Their hands would be so small, and they would study my hands to see what the digits of a criminal looked like. The guard—his name would be Roscoe or something coarse— would grip me by the shoulder and pull me back to my cell, where my "husband," DeWayne, would be waiting . . .

Veasey parked his Mercedes in front of his office. He was cool, fine. Chief Willie pulled out a pair of binoculars and put them down as soon as Veasey entered his place. He turned on a radio of some kind that he had rested on the hump between the driver's and passenger seats. There was chatter inside Veasey's office, but it was inaudible. "They're in an outer office," Chief Willie said.

"Is anything missing?" I heard Veasey say, not so cool now.

"I don't know, Eddie," a woman with a cigarette-scarred voice said in a molasses-thick South Jersey accent. It was the same voice that had fielded the Viking's malfeasance inquiry. *"A few computers were on."*

"Christ, Shirley, check!" Veasey said.

There was the sound of drawers opening and shutting. I heard a grunt.

"Here, let me help you?" Shirley said, her voice muffled somewhat because she must have been turning away from the bug.

"No!" Veasey said, breathless. *"Let me do this in here."*

"Huh," Chief Willie said. "He doesn't want her in there while he looks for something. He sounds like he's bending down. Must be that floor safe the Viking mentioned."

I breathed slowly. Please, God, get me home soon. Please let this be cool.

"*Thank God,*" Veasey finally said. "*Whoo, thank God.*"

"*What? What?*" Shirley said.

"*Nothing,*" Veasey replied, audibly straining to stand up. "*Thank God. How about out there?*"

"*I don't know, Eddie. A few computers are on, there's a scratch on the file cabinet. I don't know if it was there before or not.*"

"*Thank God.*" Veasey breathed hard.

"*I'll call the police,*" Shirley said.

"*Jesus Christ, no!*" Veasey shouted.

"*We had a break-in, didn't we?*"

"*We didn't have anything, do you hear me? We didn't have anything. I'll handle this with my own people.*"

"*Are you sure?*"

"*Stop the questions! Just look around when I'm gone.*"

Chief Willie picked up his mobile phone, which had a walkie-talkie feature. "Oink-oink," he said.

An early-model Ford Explorer slowly rounded the corner south of Veasey's office and stopped. Chief Willie studied the vehicle through his binoculars and then set them down. I couldn't tell for certain, but there appeared to be two people in the truck.

"Looks like Sir Sausage wants to get something out of that office pretty quick," Chief Willie said.

Veasey waddled outside with an accordion portfolio in his chubby pink hands. He settled into his Mercedes after putting the file beside him on the passenger seat. Within seconds of the grinning grille of his Mercedes pulling onto the street, the Explorer accelerated, and clipped it hard.

Veasey began shouting something and banging his fists against the steering wheel. The Explorer's driver, a large, menacingly attractive woman, probably in her late twenties, stepped out—after blocking him in—and held her hands to her face in an "I'm-such-an-idiot" way. Veasey didn't bother to roll down his window, he just kept ranting.

"Recognize her?" Chief Willie asked.

"No," I said.

"She's not in costume. She wrestles as Oblivia Newton-John."

Oblivia just kept uttering useless hysterics. Then I noticed the Explorer's passenger. It was a man. It was the Viking. As Oblivia shrieked at her clumsiness and Veasey oinked at his terrible fortune, the Viking slipped behind Veasey's car, opened the passenger door, grabbed the accordion portfolio from the front seat, and took off back in the direction of where the Explorer had come from.

Veasey lunged toward the portfolio from the driver's seat, but failed to catch anything. He turned in the direction of Oblivia, but she had slipped away, quick as mercury. The Explorer remained.

Chief Willie popped his cheek and muttered, "We're on."

Chief Willie slowly pulled out and made his way down a side street. When he was out on Atlantic Avenue, he hooked south and picked up the Viking and Oblivia Newton-John on a corner, and drove calmly north back to Atlantic City.

PHOTOGENIC

"Cameras and beauty beat pathways to each other."

The Viking and Oblivia Newton-John changed clothing quietly in the back of the van while I tried to control my breath in the passenger seat. Chief Willie pulled onto Delancey Street and said "Nice work" to the two hustlers in the back. They nimbly exited the rear of the van, got into a little Honda, and went wherever. Chief Willie headed back to his house in Ventnor. Veasey's purloined accordion portfolio was behind the Chief.

When we got inside Chief Willie's house, he lit a long pipe and handed me Veasey's portfolio. I took it reluctantly, immediately aware that it now contained my fingerprints. I unwrapped the elastic string and pulled out three manila envelopes. Chief Willie and I sucked in our breath as I slid the images onto his dining room table. A microcassette also fell out.

It was a vile thing to behold: what we were seeing had been intentionally recorded for blackmail purposes. Furthermore, these illicit materials had been obtained through violence that I had authorized and paid for.

Chief Willie and I spread the images around the table. I stumbled back into one of the chairs, which slipped out from behind me. I landed on my ass on a woven Indian rug.

"You all right, Mongoose?" Chief Willie asked.

"Sure," I said, maneuvering onto my knees. "It's a time to kneel."

Chief Willie studied the images. "It looks like it may also be time to bark like a dog. Do you know her? She's practically performing like she's onstage."

I shook my head in the negative, not wanting to look anymore. A Time to Kneel was now more than a cute sound bite. I couldn't be sure if she was an intern or not, but she was young.

"Look at this one," Chief Willie said. "It's like she's in a cage."

I looked. Quickly. "I don't know what that is, but it looks like a jail cell."

"Well, Mongoose, we can't exactly turn these into posters and slap them on telephone polls around town with a toll-free number, can we?"

"I may have to find a way to gag her—"

"Chief Willie say, 'Girl doesn't look like she gags easy in this picture.'"

"C'mon, this is serious."

"Sorry. What would you do once you found her?"

"I'd find out what she's about. Some political tarts want notoriety because they've got nothing to lose. Others want love, and don't want to come forward, because they have lots to lose. Is this recreation for her, or is it love?"

"Ah, back to Marcus Aurelius, finding a person's essential nature. You know Rothman. What do you think the chick is for him?"

"Sport. But, Chief, most of these women nowadays are like moths to a flame once the camera goes on. That's what I worry about. If we've got the only pictures, which isn't a smart bet, denying the affair may be one option. Or we may have to admit it, but I don't like that, either. A lot of what we do will depend on what this girl is, what she wants."

I picked up one of the photos. The woman's head was thrown back and sweat beads were winking at me from a neckline that could have earned its own constellation. Each breast rested softly on either side of what appeared to be a wooden bar, as if she were allowing inmates a fleeting stroke of a nipple for a fee. I held up the photo more closely.

"Mongoose, you've been married too long," Chief Willie said.

"It's not that," I said. "Look at this."

"What about it?"

"Even though her head is back and her eyes appear to be closed, you can still see her eyes a little. It's like she's looking at us."

"Cameras and beauty beat pathways to each other," Chief Willie said poetically. "Do you think this is all it is?"

"Chief, the thing with Rebound is that there's always more. And there's always less. God. Let me know what's on Veasey's cassette, would you?"

Chief Willie nodded.

I tried to apply logic to a new question: what kind of monster merits a cage? As a detective, I was out of my depth. As a man, I had a theory.

"Chief, you have friends at the phone company, right?"

"The Lenape are a peaceful tribe. We enjoy conversation."

HARD LINE

"Are we wicked or righteous?"

Later that week, I was at home on my computer when my phone rang. Chief Willie told me that his contact at the State Police had tipped him off that Rebound's security detail had signed out. As always, they didn't specify where they were going. I called Rebound's mobile phone, which he hated.

"Hello," Rebound answered.

"It's me."

"Not now." I expected this.

"I need to ask you something right away," I said. "Call me back on a hard line. It's an emergency." I gave him my home number.

Thirty seconds later my home phone rang.

"What's up?" Rebound growled.

"Do you know Eddie Veasey?"

Hesitation. "Yeah, sure."

"Why would he be talking to Barium Enema?" Total lie on my part.

No immediate response. "I don't know. Maybe she called him to comment on something."

"But why would *he* be calling *her?*"

"I don't know, dammit."

"I know this subject makes you uncomfortable, but does Veasey have a role in this riverboat thing?"

"You'll have to talk to Lucas. I don't know."

"Rebound?"

"What, for Christ's sake?"

I read to him the biblical proverb that my father-in-law found tacked to our barn. "Are we wicked or righteous?"

"What the hell are you talking about?"

"I guess we can talk about it later."

Rebound hung up. I hung up. My mobile phone rang: Chief Willie. "Chief Willie say 'Celebrity Motel in A.C.'"

The idea had been to call Rebound, rattle him into using a hard line, and trace it to wherever the hell he was. Which was the Celebrity Motel in Atlantic City. I knew what Rebound's girl looked like, pretty much, those criminal eyes boring into the camera.

CELEBRITY

"Do you like being treated . . . bad?"

The Celebrity Motel was a downmarket two-story dive on Albany Avenue across the street from a few of the major beachfront casinos. It had been a dump since the Johnson administration (Andrew). It's most distinguishing feature was its neon logo: an oversized caricature of Marilyn Monroe with her black sunglasses tipped downward and her left eye winking gaudily, as if everyone who bunked at the Celebrity were united in one gargantuan quickie. And, yes, there was a double-mushroom cloud of cleavage just beneath "Marilyn's" neck. The Celebrity may have been quasi-respectable in the 1960s, but these days it was the kind of place where folks of humble means stayed with the understanding that when they told their friends back home they had been to Atlantic City, they would be implying they had stayed at one of the major hotels across the street. Of course, it was also a hangout for college preppies who stayed there for the slumming outré of it all, and were known to wear T-shirts and baseball caps back to school with the Marilyn logo.

A tall, flat-chested blonde woman in a leather getup walked toward me on the balcony. I averted my eyes and tried to study her at the same time. She didn't resemble the girl in Veasey's photo. The blonde stopped in front of a motel room door and said, "Hi there."

"Hello," I said like a terrified seventh grader.

"Do you like being treated . . . bad?" she asked.

"Not really, no."

"Hold on," she said, stepping inside her room. She came out with a business card and handed it to me.

"Fatima the Netherworld Hell-Bitch," I read aloud. "Huh." She listed the Celebrity as her address.

"Treating men bad is what I do," Fatima said resignedly.

"Funny, you don't look like a Fatima," I said.

"Kathy Simmons. From Pleasantville," she surrendered.

"I'm Jonah, the Extreme Ivy League Suburbanite."

"Sounds dangerous," Fatima/Kathy said.

"I got beaned with a ball at my son's Little League game last year."

"Intrepid. I'm here if you need me."

"I'll file it away, Fatima. Do you live here all the time?"

"Why, wanna move in with me already? Now, that's commitment!"

"Does anyone else live here all the time?"

"Looking for someone in particular?"

What now, bonehead? "Uh, not really."

"I'll be around," Fatima the Netherworld Hell Bitch said, shutting her door.

I walked around the balcony for a few minutes cursing myself. I knew who I was looking for but then again, I didn't. What's the move? I trolled around the motel balconies pretending to be taking in the scenery. Of a slimebag motel in Atlantic City in late September? Screw it, why not play rough? You've got the little goatee going. Act like a cop.

I walked back downstairs and into the lobby. I asked a gum-smacking tart with too much green eye shadow where I could find the maid because I needed a towel. She asked me what room I was in, and I told her 213. I winced when it occurred to me that that might be Fatima the Netherworld Hell-Bitch's room.

"I can have some towels brought up, or you can see the maid, La-Trina, in the maid's, uh, quarters," Tart-breath said. To say the Celebrity had "quarters" was like calling the homeless guys who sing at the Atlantic City Bus Terminal the Philharmonic.

"Where's that?"

"Around the corner next to the ice machine."

Off I went. I felt around to make sure my gun was there. Yup. Total badass. I found the maid's station. The door was halfway open. A dark-skinned woman in her fifties of indeterminate ethnicity sat at a beat-up card table reading the *Globe*. She had suspicious eyes and a world-weary expression on her face. I liked that.

"LaTrina," I said. "Babycakes. What's up?"

"I know you?"

I pulled out a folding chair and set it down across from her. "My name's Vic."

"I don't know no Vic."

"Well, now you do, see." I took out two twenty-dollar bills and plunked them before her. She studied them as if I had just hocked a wad of phlegm in front of her. "I'm looking for a young woman who may get visits from a tall man with silver hair, see."

"I know what I know, and that ain't much."

"What does that mean, Treeney?"

"Lots of men with silver hair come here."

"Are there any young women that are here a lot, as more than temporary guests?"

"I seen you talkin' to Fatima."

"Yeah, I talked to Fatima."

"What did she tell you?"

"I didn't ask her anything. Look, LaTrina, I'm looking for a woman who may be an intern with the state government."

"Intern. Like that Lewinsky was with Clinton?"

I peeled out two more twenty-dollar bills and held them in front of LaTrina. "Kinda like that, see. Who are you covering for, LaTrina?"

"I don't cover for nobody."

"If you're not part of this operation, see, why don't you point me in the right direction?"

"Operation?"

"You're the courier, aren't you?"

"I don't courier diddly."

"You want to inform for my squad, LaTrina? I can get you out of the mule racket, see."

"Look, man, there's a lady in two-oh-four who's got a friend like the one you're talkin' about, but I ain't part of no operation. I'm no mule."

I handed LaTrina the cash. "Thanks, LaTrina. We never met, see."

Room 204. A few down from Fatima the Netherworld Hell-Bitch. I knocked twice. As the door opened, the steady heartbeat of a bubblegum song that I remembered from my early teens invaded my senses, "Fox on the Run" by Sweet. It had been popular when I was living in exile with my grandparents, but American hits always found their way to Europe. The words of the song were lame, but the sentiments they generated were strong and reached a cul-de-sac somewhere in my anatomy that had cobwebbed with middle age. "Fox on the run / You scream and everybody comes a-runnin' / Take a run and hide yourself away . . ." Sweet wasn't a threat to Dylan, but the words fit the moment, not to mention the nocturnal emission that stood in human form before me.

She was wearing a parchment-colored bikini. As autumn slid toward winter, she was wearing a bikini. She said nothing.

"Hi there," I said. I'm good. Real good.

"Hi," she said questioningly.

"My name is Jonah Eastman."

"I'm Simone Lava," she said.

"Lava. What kind of name is that?"

"My father was from Macedonia."

Macedonia. What a magical place. Where the hell was it?

"Eastman. Eastman. Polls, right?"

"Rumanians, actually."

"No, I meant, you're the pollster."

"Oh, yes. I am Eastman the Pollster." I bowed with a slight flourish. This was not me. I didn't act like this. I was like a horny fourteen-year-old who couldn't nail the cheerleader by being the quarterback so he played the clown. I had a clear recognition of the clown going home from the dance alone, and the quarterback showing up at school Monday morning with a big-ass grin.

Simone extended her hand and I shook it. It was hot, but desert dry. Her eyes were the color of smoke, the way the Atlantic appeared after an autumn storm. Her face was heart-shaped, capped by thick chestnut hair that hinted at another time, perhaps the 1940s in Paris, even though I wasn't sure how women looked in the 1940s in Paris. Simone's nose was short and perfectly symmetrical, anchored by a criminal mouth—bow-shaped, not fully closed even in repose. Her chin was shaped like a teardrop. Pearls of perspiration dotted her upper lip, which made me curious about what could make a woman like this sweat in autumn.

Simone was no taller than five-three, but proportioned the way Playboy bunnies were in the 1960s. I know this because Mickey's associate, Carvin' Marvin, used to slip old *Playboys* to me when he was through with them. Any man of my generation will know this build: All curves, breasts that you could probably see from behind—soft, and not manufactured by conglomerates; a tummy that was flat but without a machine-cut six-pack (as if men really liked that); and legs that were lean, with natural muscle that hadn't been torn to rags by marathons.

Hers was not the look of a femme fatale—that willowy twister with icey, knifelike features like a Patrick Nagel lithograph—which is precisely what made her one.

I studied Simone's skin, pretending to see something curious, and noticed it was settled in a perpetual blush like the peach that taunts the thirteen-year-old boy in you from the windowsill of a friend's kitchen.

You instinctively know that the peach isn't yours, and the blush suggests it knows what you are thinking.

I pointed to her upper lip and said, "You look hot."

"I was doing yoga. Do you do yoga?"

"Every day."

"Really?"

"No, no yoga for me," I said.

Simone laughed. "You're funny."

"My kids think so."

"How old are they?"

"Dunno."

Simone laughed again. I shook my head like Scooby-Doo did when he saw a ghost, and corrected myself. "They're six and four. I'm just a few years older maturity-wise."

Simone's motel room was ordinary save one thing: a giant wooden birdcage in the corner of the room. It was big enough for a few cushions and blankets to be spread out. On the floor of the birdcage, there were shriveled brown grape stalks strewn about near thick cushions where I presumed Rebound and Simone did their plucking. A brochure on internships had fallen beside a cushion, entitled "Get Involved." There was also a tiny television set in there, a high-end number. Simone saw me looking at it. "Gardner got a special one for me through his connections. I watch him whenever he's on. It's how I see him most of the time, if you want to know the truth." I was stunned by her utter openness that it was what it was.

"I guess it would be hard for the two of you to get out."

"Oh, impossible. Gardner doesn't want me to go out at all."

"But you've got that nice bathing suit on."

"Are you kidding? He'd go nuts if I started walking around outside like this."

I found a spot on the wall to focus on so I could avoid studying Simone's bathing suit.

"What do you do all day?" I asked.

"I go up to Trenton and work on my Time to Heal internship. Some-times I do it from here on computer. Oh, and I work on a musical fanfare for Gardner."

"I'm sorry, a musical fanfare?"

"Well, do you know how there's 'Hail to the Chief' for the president?"

"Yes, I know it."

"Gardner and I thought there should be a fanfare for the New Jersey governor."

She handed me a lined piece of notebook paper with feminine hand-writing where the i's were dotted with hearts and smiley faces. It con-tained verses such as:

> All hail a son of Jersey
> From High Point to Cape May
> Rise now for a son of Jersey
> From the Delaware to Barnegat Bay

The fanfare was entitled "Hail a Son of Jersey."

"Can I tell you something embarrassing?" she asked.

As if the fanfare wasn't enough? I nodded yes.

"Sometimes we play 'Hail to the Chief' on a cassette, and Gardner and I walk out of the bathroom, and we pretend we're waving to the crowd at the White House."

"Huh."

Simone entered the birdcage. When she sat on a cushion in the bird-cage, I felt the brand of messianic outrage that gushes through every byway of one's masculine being when it becomes evident that someone you despise is doing precisely who you want to do. It's this notion that her not choosing you must have been a cosmic mixup, not a lucid choice of Him over You. It shouldn't take on the mantle of fire and brimstone when it's pure Darwinian competition, but the only way a civilized man can process the enzymes is to attach them to something higher. *Yes, Jonah, God wants You to have her legs wrapped around you (not Him), and it is your biblical duty to possess her so that Jerusalem may be freed of the infidels.*

I turned and inspected the room further. There was a photo of Simone in a fluffy outfit of some kind. She looked like a pie.

"I was Miss Little Egg Harbor Township," Simone said. "That was a few years ago when I was a senior at Egg Harbor High." She wanted me to think she wasn't proud of this achievement, but the portability of the picture suggested otherwise. I thought about what my grandmother had told me so long ago about my destiny to "make up" for a lost adolescence.

"Gardner says I could be an actress, but that's not where I think I'm headed. He's got people in Hollywood, you know."

"Really. Like who?"

"Oh, he guards his network closely," Simone explained. "With one phone call from him, I could have bumped Ashley Judd from a role she just got, but Rebound needs me here, and I think it's more important to be with him now."

"You know, Simone, one call from me to Murray's Delicatessen, and they'd have a plate of whitefish for you ready in ten minutes."

"Whitefish?" she said, perplexed. My humor had ceased working. I averted my eyes from her once again by feigning interest in her gubernatorial fanfare:

> Standing above the pines
> His crown reaches the sky
> Form erect like Batsto iron
> Garden State rises high

Oy.

Simone smiled in a juvenile way. It was an expression that demanded a compliment lest I suffer the penalty of withheld affection.

"You really worked in things about the state," I said.

"Oh, yes. I'm on top of things. Jonah, why are you here?"

"I guess I should explain. You've been very honest with me, Simone, so I'll be very honest with you. The governor doesn't know I'm here. He's never told me about you, but there are some people trafficking in rumors. They don't necessarily know your name, but they know you exist."

"I see what Barri Embrey writes and says on TV."

"Right. Well, Simone, I'm very protective of the governor. I'd like to see him win the Senate seat. I assume you know that your relationship would be a problem for him, especially with his family values platform."

"Yes, we've talked about that."

"What did he tell you?"

"Don't worry, Jonah, we've got that all worked out."

"Oh, that's good. What's the plan?"

"I'll keep behind the scenes until after the election. He'll introduce me in Washington in the spring, and the wedding will be in the summer."

I felt a huge geological formation take shape in my gut. How did I begin tackling this? I didn't. I couldn't say, "Listen, Miss Little Egg Harbor Township, that's just not gonna happen." I couldn't introduce Miss Little Egg Harbor Township to the Dark Prince of Reality during election season. No way. I needed a calm, delusional Miss Little Egg Harbor Township until Governor Gonad was happily sworn in as Senator Hard-on.

"Right. The summer," I said. "That makes sense. I feel better knowing the timing."

"Believe me, Jonah, I'm not stupid."

"That's why I feel better meeting you. Do you mind if I check in on you from time to time?"

"Of course."

"I've heard a lot about you."

"Gardner told me all about how much help you've been to him since he helped you get back on your feet. He says you've really started paying your debt back. I know he appreciates it."

The volcano bubbled in my chest. I was useful. After Rebound got me back on my feet. I handed her my business card.

"I try to be useful," I said, feeling as wounded as I've ever been. I shook her hot hand and let go of it quickly after imagining where it was capable of going. Then I left.

I made my way around the concrete balcony despising Rebound for taking advantage of this dazed and pouting adolescent. I spied the Celebrity's winking Marilyn Monroe receding in my rearview mirror, and Rebound and Simone, Edie and Irv the Curve, Ricky and Lily, Fatima the Netherworld Hell-Bitch and Chief Willie spun in a kaleidoscopic whirl. I jotted down the fifth lesson of my most recent damage-control campaign on a business card:

God sent certain women to destroy your life, certain others to save it.

I went to sleep that night dreaming of yoga and Macedonia. Actually, I didn't sleep at all, so I got up and looked up Macedonia on the Internet. Then I looked up yoga. One maneuver required a person to stand against the wall and bend over to stretch out the back muscles. The following morning, Edie caught me doing it downstairs. She rolled her eyes. I got in my car and drove toward Macedonia.

MICROEXPRESSIONS

"Avoid situations where he has to speak."

The green and white sign on Interstate 91 read DARTMOUTH—LAKE SUNAPEE REGION, and it always forced me to concentrate on my breath, as if my autonomic lung function were an act of precision. When we first drove to New Hampshire almost a quarter century ago to begin my freshman fall at Dartmouth, my grandfather the murderer wiped tears from his eyes when the steeple of Baker Tower flashed at us from above the pines. I hadn't even seen Mickey cry when my mother, his only child, died at such a young age years before.

My own emotional reaction to the sign and the tower in the fall of 1980 was a garden-variety response from a kid who was leaving home for college. But for Mickey, the arrival took on literary proportions. As with Gatsby's reach for Daisy Buchanan's green light or Ahab's spotting of the great whale, for Mickey the Dartmouth–Lake Sunapee sign was his scoreboard, and Baker Tower was his trophy. For the first time in his then seventy-eight-year life, the former Moses Prinzkowicz of Romania ("land of the gypsies," he called it) had become the prosperous businessman Mickey Price, with a grandson a member in good standing of the most legitimate of all American enterprises, the Ivy League.

I pulled into the covered entrance of the Hanover Inn. Several obscenely young-looking women passed me. I climbed out of the car and nodded to them, feeling half stud, half child molester. They were Simone's age, only somehow Simone was youthful and ancient at the same time. I checked myself out in the reflection of a car window and noticed how gray the stubble on my beard growth had become. Suddenly I felt 10 percent stud, 90 percent child molester.

The Inn had been remodeled and appeared far more contemporary than it had in my day. *In my day.* A term that had never popped into my head until now. Jesus. Anyhow, there used to be a breakfast restaurant with old oak tables, dark paneling, and New Englandy paintings on the wall. A group of old men, all retired alumni, would have coffee there every morning. They would argue about politics, whether admitting women to the college had been a good idea or a bad one, and if the college's Indian symbol should be retrieved from "the concentration camp of political correctness," as one of the men put it. Mickey desperately wanted to join the discussion, I could tell. On one level, he identified with the men because he was their age. On another level, despite the oracle status granted him in gangland circles, Mickey felt inferior.

"Why won't he say hello to those men?" I asked my grandmother, Deedee, one morning when Mickey ducked out for a newspaper.

Deedee sat at the corner table with her red hair, red lipstick, and red boots and said, "Because, Sweet Knees, he's a little old *gonif.*" Yiddish for thief.

While Mickey may have felt inferior to this drama at Dartmouth, Deedee did not. In fact, she was in her element among these gentry because she was an exotic, brassy former cigarette girl* who was convinced that all men who gathered in gangs were obsessed with her, which somehow ended up coming true.

"Lemme tell you what I think about this Indian symbol, sweethearts," she interrupted one morning. The cotton-haired coffee klatchers turned

---

* Deedee claimed that she had been a showgirl at one of Skinny D'Amato's nightclubs that predated his 500 Club in Atlantic City. This wasn't true. She had been a cigarette girl.

around, stunned, as she removed her cigarette from its pearl holder and ground it out on a plate of hash browns. "Anybody who doesn't want to be a symbol shouldn't have to be, baby. You want to put me on a T-shirt, hot damn, I say, go for it, dolls. You can call 'em the Dartmouth Show-girls!"

The men sat stone-faced until Deedee lit up another cigarette, and the stodgiest old man of them all, Mr. Maxwell, tilted his head slowly back and stated in curt New England cadence, "I like it." He then asked Deedee to be his date for Homecoming. She accepted.

"That gentleman who was sitting with you earlier," Mr. Maxwell crisply began, "was he your husband?"

In my mortification, I looked at Deedee, awaiting her response. "Honey," she told Mr. Maxwell, "I don't know who the hell you're talking about." Within minutes, Deedee was sitting next to Mr. Maxwell, and when Mickey ambled back into the restaurant, she loudly told him she was "breaking up" with him despite their fifty-year marriage. Mickey shrugged his shoulders, left the restaurant, fired up a cigarette, and read his *Racing Form* on the front porch of the Hanover Inn.

Professor Sully Rogers appeared very much the same to me as when I had been a student, with the exception of his Abraham Lincoln beard, which had grown whiter. I arrived at his cluttered office on the second floor of Silsby Hall feeling nervous. I had spent my time at Dartmouth anxious that the authorities were going to kick in my classroom door one day and shout (with guns drawn), "Eastman! Hands above your head! You're coming with us, you poseur!" Today I considered my out-of-place anxiety legitimate. I was here, after all, to engage a respected professor of government into helping me win a dirty political fight.

Professor Rogers spent a half hour showing me a series of graphs purportedly demonstrating a correlation between facial "microexpres-sions"—tiny facial movements that are unconsciously perceived—and a candidate's electability. He sat back in a painful-looking wooden chair and stated: "I anxiously await your thesis statement."

"Professor, I know you're not in the consulting business, but I'll be very direct about my situation. I am advising Governor Rothman in New Jersey on his Senate race. I believe he is lying."

"Why do you believe this?"

"He has no real core, no steady belief system. With him, it's all a function of what it takes to get your vote at that moment."

"That's not uncommon in his field."

"I know. But if I can isolate what he's lying about, I may be able to solve this riddle. Is there a way to can look at his microexpressions?"

"Certainly, but in a day's time, there won't be anything scientific about it."

"I'm in the instinct business. I'm not asking for a scholarly study. I'm asking you for your judgment—something that you *feel* based on your work."

Professor Rogers laughed and stroked his Abe Lincoln beard. "You were always impatient with the scientific process, Jonah."

"I know, Professor. It's not that I don't respect it, it's that I don't have the time for it. I'm a street guy."

"I imagine you see yourself this way because of that grandfather of yours. I think you think that others look at you and see him—"

"Believe me, plenty people do."

"I understand. You told me about him years ago as if you were the only young man ever to have such a ghost. Whether it's a grandfather who was a racketeer or a brother who is a drug addict, we've all got characters in our backgrounds. My wife's father kept another family on the other side of the state. What I'm saying is that having ghosts is not exotic."

Professor Rogers and I walked over to an adjacent building, a modern one named after Nelson Rockefeller, who had graduated from Dartmouth in the 1930s. The professor set up a videotape I gave him. On the videotape were two of the governor's media appearances, the speech at Rowan University and a subsequent news conference. I had also brought along the videotape of Digby Stahl's recent appearance on *The Throb*. "Now, don't tell me when you think he is lying. Let me just watch," Professor Rogers said.

We watched the two segments on Rebound's tape, which lasted for a combined forty minutes. The professor scribbled notes with a tight smile frozen on his lips as if he were writing something vulgar.

He then put the videotape in another machine, which was attached to a computer.

"What does this contraption do?" I asked.

"It makes an inventory of his facial expressions, and files them away."

I sat back and watched, fascinated by what began to appear on the computer. On the screen before me, Professor Rogers was literally creating a portfolio of Rebound's expressions, which he numbered Friendly 1, 2, 3, Hostile 1, 2, 3, Neutral 1, 2, 3, and so forth.

"Now, Jonah, tell me the subjects that you think he's lying about?"

"I think he's lying about the intern program and the riverboat gambling bill."

Professor Rogers clacked a few words onto the keyboard. "All right," he said, when a response came up. "On those subjects, he exhibits Hostile 3A. That's a code I gave this expression." Professor Rogers clicked his mouse and brought up two of Rebound's facial expressions side by side. "Here, I've slowed it down to one word every fifteen seconds. Watch what he does."

I moved up closer to the monitor. Rebound indeed did something with his face in slow motion that I had never seen in real time. He drew his lips together in a tight, prissy way. I imitated the face. "It's kind of a prune face," I said.

"Yes."

"With Hostile 3A, when he's talking about the riverboat bill . . . can the public perceive this?" I asked.

"Unconsciously, sure, but it would probably take constant exposure to cause a big problem. Rothman seems to be most at home with small talk."

"Can you reverse a microexpression?"

"Sometimes you can train someone, but that's a prolonged process. It's better to just make sure no one sees it." This reinforced what my instincts had been during media training.

"So what you're saying, Professor, is that my client's problem is not that he lies, it's that he lies poorly."

"Essentially."

"Meaning?"

"Avoid situations where he has to speak."

"The guy's running for the Senate!"

"I understand."

A slow grin began to cross my face. "What?" Professor Rogers asked.

I closed my eyes and tried to think it through. "I'll keep his TV appearances to nonspeaking engagements. I'll have him greeting crowds and let them respond to his . . . initial charisma. I won't have him filmed for big policy addresses. No TV debates. I'll try to confine his actual speeches to radio. He can still do public appearances, but I'll confine the substantive ones to radio where no one can see him lie."

"That's up to you."

"And there's something about Digby that I keep seeing that I can't put my finger on," I told the professor, tapping on one of his monitors. "Take a look and see if you see something."

Professor Rogers put the tape of Digby's recent interview with *The Throb* into the machine and began to watch. After Digby answered the third question posed to him, the professor tilted his head to the side, and he began typing something furiously. After ten minutes of points and clicks with his mouse (in which he arranged a half dozen Digbys side by side), he swiveled toward me and placed his hands on his hips. "Tell me what you think you saw when you looked at this."

"Digby does something with his upper lip when he hears a question he doesn't like."

"Not exactly. First of all, he doesn't have an upper lip. And his reaction isn't necessarily to a question he doesn't like, it's really any transition to a new subject."

Professor Rogers clicked his mouse, which elicited a rapid-fire series of backward head tilts and lip retractions effetely performed by Judge Digby Stahl.

I tugged at my evolving goatee. "So," I said, "when he begins to answer a question, or engages a new subject, Digby tilts his head back and starts to speak—"

"Once his chin is above his Adam's apple."

"Right. And what little he has of an upper lip retracts into his gum."

"Have we ever discussed illusory causation?"

"I don't believe so."

"It's a phenomenon whereby people associate something that they see with a cause or intention."

Professor Rogers clicked the mouse, which caused the series of Digbys on his computer screen to begin firing at a slower speed than they had before. In addition to Digby's nose tilting upward and his upper lip vanishing, his eyes—ever so slightly—rolled up into his head, and his eyelids closed. The multiplicity of tics, however unintentionally, conveyed snobbery. There was an unquantifiable sense of being above answering the inquiry of a prole reporter. When I had first reviewed the tape with Rebound and Currier, I hadn't been conscious of the tics; however, when Digby began speaking about his beloved grandfather, "Stally," *something* registered in my gut. All told, what I had on Digby amounted to something less than science, but I hadn't made it this far in politics because I had beakers full of proof.

MIND GAMES AT ECHELON MALL

"Smell Me, Why Don't Cha"

We had two brief campaign stops in South Jersey, one at a kindergarten class in Haddonfield, the other at a retirement home in Stratford. Because they were located close to where I was holding focus groups later in the day, I joined Rebound and Currier.

Rebound impressed the kindergartners and cameramen alike with his jump-roping skill, but his awkwardness in conversing with the children inside the classroom was palpable. The principal had selected a precocious girl named Amber to give Rebound a tour of the classroom, which was all well and good until she arrived at a table with a naked Barbie doll. The naked doll made me think of Simone in her bathing suit. Amber was hellbent on dressing Barbie.

"This Barbie is sad," Amber said.

"Why is that, Amber?" Rebound asked.

"Because she doesn't have a vagina."

The child picked up the Barbie and pointed to the smooth plastic mound between the doll's legs. "See, there's supposed to be a crack right here."

Rebound's mouth fell open. "I guess so," he said robotically until the

teacher diverted him to another part of the classroom. "Look at our autumn collage . . ."

An elderly man named Bernie (according to his name tag) weighed
in during Rebound's stop at the Stratford nursing home. The Governor
was noshing on a donut when Bernie wheeled himself over to Rebound
and said, "Governor, it's nobody's business if you're *shtupping* that intern. Believe me, if I could, I would."

The exchanges—thank God—didn't make the evening news, but a
stringer for the *Probe* reported it the following day in a box entitled,
"Thoughts from Constituents Young and Old."

I launched two types of opinion research. The first was a conventional
poll to assess basic attitudes among New Jersey's various ethnic groups
toward Rebound and Digby. The poll would quantify public opinion
with numbers: How many people approve of the job Rebound is doing?
How many think Digby could address the state's challenges better? Are
Irish men more likely to vote for Rebound than Italian women?

As an old pollster in Reagan's White House once told me, statistics
are like a bikini: what they reveal is interesting, but what they conceal is
vital. That's where focus groups come in. In a focus group, you can watch
the faces, breathe the nuances in through your eyes and ears, register the
unspeakable signs of attraction and revulsion, and distinguish between
opinions (which change) and values (which don't).

Today's focus group was in Voorhees, New Jersey, a Philadelphia
suburb. It was strategically located so that we wouldn't have a difficult
time recruiting people from the Italian, Irish, and Jewish communities,
which were our primary targets.

The Voorhees focus group was located in the Echelon Mall, the
newest of the region's indoor megamalls (Cherry Hill boasted America's first indoor megamall, built in the early 1960s). As I searched
for the offices of the research firm Voorhees Views, I passed a gaggle
of middle-aged accountants competing for their brown belts in tae
kwon do; suburban women in early middle age with frosted hair and

machine-blasted tans flirting with hairy-chested jewelers, almost certainly fantasizing about what their lives would be like with "Tony" if they just "went for it" and left their accountant husbands; teens cutting school but in pursuit of higher learning among puzzles of obese naked women in Spencer Gifts; and kindly geriatrics taking walks and squinting to protect themselves from the orgy of neon, wondering if they were in heaven or hell.

The focus group moderator was Dr. Eliza Baird, a psychologist in her midforties with a gift for drawing people out without making them feel as if they were being interrogated. I had worked with her on many campaigns over the years. My goal was to move humankind from Point A to Point B, and Eliza Baird had never let me down in that pursuit.

Today our Voorhees focus group consisted of Alessandra, a stock broker in her late thirties with a Greek-sounding surname; Ariel, a single white office manager in her twenties whose last name was Irish; Russell, a black graphic designer; Claudia, a Hispanic grandmother; Paul, a hearty contractor who looked like Paul Bunyan; Benny, an Italian optometrist; Jay, a squeaky-clean journalist for an outdoors publication; and Eva, a college student at Rutgers. I felt that the Three I's (and more) were well represented, but there would be other groups to make certain that we got everybody in. I observed the proceedings from behind a one-way mirror and could communicate with Eliza via laptop.

"Who here follows politics?" Eliza asked the group.

Jay was the first to raise his hand. "I follow environmental stuff mostly."

This prompted a round in which participants highlighted their areas of interest, which ranged broadly from abortion rights to the Middle East. I heard very little in this section that I found to be pivotal other than a sense that most of these people leaned left of center.

"Are you following the New Jersey Senate election?" Dr. Baird asked.

"I don't see what the big difference is between these two guys," Russell said. "Rothman's a moderate Republican and Stahl's a conservative-leaning Democrat. What's the diff?" he asked hiply.

Alessandra said, "They're the same on abortion. Pro-choice."

"A smart move for Rothman," Jay said.

"Why's that?" Dr. Baird asked.

"He like da ladies," Jay answered, eliciting chuckles from most of the group.

"I've got to say, the governor's smokin' hot," Ariel said.

"He knows it, too," Paul said.

"Oh, you're just jealous," Ariel said in a lighthearted way.

"The guy cheats on his wife big time," Paul responded.

"You don't know that," Eva said. "Those are rumors."

"C'mon," Benny said, "the press wouldn't take the risk of saying all that stuff if there wasn't anything there."

"They just keep attacking the man," Claudia said. "He's just a man. Men do what they do."

"If I did what he did," Jay said, "my wife would put two slugs behind my ear."

QUERY IF THEY BELIEVE DIGBY CHEATS ON HIS WIFE. I typed to Dr. Baird. The note pinged on her laptop screen.

"You say you hear these rumors about Governor Rothman," Dr. Baird said to the group. "Do you hear them about Judge Stahl?"

"I haven't paid attention to him," Alessandra said.

"Who'd want to have an affair with him?" Ariel said.

"So, it's all right for Rebound to get some strange, but it's not okay for Digby?" Benny asked.

"I wasn't saying that," Ariel said.

Oh, yes you were, honey, I thought. *Guys you dig can; guys you don't dig can't.*

"What's so bad about Digby Stahl?" Dr. Baird asked.

"He seems very judgmental," Alessandra said.

Almost every head in the room nodded. Yes, that's it.

"Well," Paul reminded the group, "he's a *judge*."

"Right," Claudia said, "but people don't like feeling like somebody's looking down on them."

"Forgive me," Dr. Baird interjected, "but would somebody explain how Stahl is looking down on them?"

There were a few seconds of silence until Paul chimed in: "Maybe it's not such a bad thing that somebody's being judgmental. Why is everybody so afraid of being judged? What are you people up to anyway?" he asked, sparking some laughter.

Still, the core question had yet to be answered. Why did people believe that Digby Stahl was judgmental?

It was time to test out Professor Rogers's theory of illusory causation. Dr. Baird played for the group a series of short video snippets of both Digby and Rebound.

"Ooh, smell me, why don't cha," Ariel said in reaction to one of Digby's snippets. Everybody chuckled.

"What does that mean? 'Smell me'?" Dr. Baird asked.

"It's like he thinks he's better than you are," Ariel answered. "I heard him interviewed about his fancy Swedish grandfather, the robber baron. I dunno, it was just . . . *smell me.*"

"In all of these clips?" Dr. Baird asked.

"No," Claudia said, "just some."

QUERY THE SWEDEN THING, I typed.

"Ariel, is there something about Swedish people that makes them different from others?"

"Yeah, they're like . . . perfect." *Smell me, why don't cha.* That was good.

Everybody laughed. The next ten minutes were spent attempting to determine which video segments of Digby were deemed most offensive.

When the focus group was completed, I returned to my Porsche, looking forward to a speedy drive back to Cowtown. This wasn't going to happen. My windshield was covered with blood, which I assumed to be from an animal, judging by a caked hunk of fur caught in the windshield wipers. I reached into my windbreaker to make certain that my revolver was there, and it was. Then I found a snowbrush in the trunk of my car and scraped off as much of the blood as I could. With my revolver in my right hand and a hose in my left, I sprayed off the car at a do-it-yourself car wash on Evesham Road. I had concluded that my grandfather had been right: there was no such thing as paranoia—everybody did want to kill you.

After several more days of focus groups, Dr. Baird and I had established general trends. Digby was more inclined to be deemed snobbish in clips where he was reacting to harsh questions, as opposed to when he was just speaking on a subject of his choosing. When under stress, Digby did something unquantifiable with his upper lip that put people off. Also, his invocation of his Swedish background evoked a reaction. The concept of his "WASPyness" was a repeated theme, even if Swedes weren't technically Anglo-Saxons. The feelings about the Swedish represented a new kind of bigotry for me. Whereas most bigotry was anchored in notions of the hated group's unworthiness, the anti-Swedish sentiment appeared to be rooted in a low-grade sense that Swedes may be technically superior to the Three I's. Yet all of these emotions fell short of the Fear Threshold, which might have been different if Stahl had been German. I'd have to spread this one around like pixie dust, not drop it like a bomb.

Folks seemed to like the *concept* of Rebound, but found him to be insincere when he was addressing sensitive topics. When Rebound was doing something social or symbolic—shaking hands, waving—participants liked him. When he was speaking to issues, they thought he was "fulla blarney," as Paul put it.

Both sexes had responded equally poorly to a month-old clip of Rebound denying that there was anything to the rumors about his involvement with interns from his A Time to Heal program.

I ran a fast quantitative survey to determine the extent to which voters saw Digby as being judgmental. The number among ethnics was around 66 percent. The figure for Rebound was under 10 percent.

I conducted another quantitative survey seeking to rank negative personality traits. Being "judgmental" polled as being a less desirable trait than being "unfaithful" to one's spouse. Adultery appeared to be situational. Judgmentalism and snobbery, however, were almost always wrong.

My vanity was that when it came to public opinion, I was never wrong, but something came out in the battery of focus groups that I never would have predicted: the women were not only *not* critical of Rebound for his philandering, they were essentially defending his right to philander! It was the men who resented Rebound's sex life, presumably because they couldn't have gotten away with what he had, which was a whole different reason from moral outrage. Still, while Digby had his share of negatives, he really didn't have many positives. Even though Rebound was a Republican, it was Democrat Digby who struck the Three Is of New Jersey as an elitist prick. That's the thing about Jersey voters—we didn't care what you called yourself, provided that you were just as fucked up as the rest of us.

ABEL PETZ STEPS OVER THE LINE

"All arcs eventually curve downward."

Yippee, it was time for another installment of *Election Throb,* a show that I despised but couldn't ignore. As the opening montage came on, I saw the turban of the ever-watchful Sheik Abu Heinous beneath the window. How was I going to pay for him, the Dames, the car repairs, everything needed to manage my life? I couldn't bill it all to Rebound's campaign. I tuned in at the show's beginning to hear Gordon Kinney confirm civilization's conspiracy against me: Abel Petz was to be the *Throb*'s guest in the show's second block.

I endured the first segment, which featured an aging Hollywood actress, Selma Nella, decrying sport utility vehicles and handguns. An intrepid conservative muckraker was brought on at the end of the segment to play The Asshole. He displayed a grainy photograph of Ms. Nella climbing into her SUV plus a receipt for a .38 special revolver that she had bought during the Los Angeles riots. Her response to being confronted with her staggering hypocrisy was to observe that "everybody in Europe hates America."

Turbo-wanker Abel Petz graced the *Throb* after the commercial break.

"Abel, are we on fire tonight, or what?" Kinney asked.

"I don't know about you, Gordon, but I sure am. You know, there's a lot of concern about how past loyalists to Governor Rothman have handled the rumors about him," Abel said.

"Isn't Jonah Eastman a longtime adviser to Rothman?" host Gordon Kinney asked.

"Yes, he is," Petz replied, "and Jonah has been a very effective adviser to the governor in the past, but the question being asked around the state-house is, 'Has Jonah been swallowed by this whale of a campaign?'"

In the past.

I didn't sleep that night. In fact, I had tremors so acute that I slept down-stairs on the sofa so I wouldn't wake up Edie. I called Petz's office the next morning. He was working out of a suite in Philadelphia. It was worth the drive. I left my jacket open just far enough so that the recep-tionist in the polling joint would see my .357 when I asked her where Abel was. She swallowed hard and told me. I know it's wrong, but there's something viscerally thrilling about frightening someone with a firearm.

Petz was sitting alone at a conference table with his broccoli head and pale kindergarten skin.

"I have the perfect strategy for Rebound," I said.

"What's that?" Petz said, startled. He began his antic playing of the air piano, that flicking of the fingers.

"He's going to have to nail every woman in New Jersey."

"That's a disgusting sexist remark."

"Now that I know you're offended, Abel, I know I've got myself a winner. It's the shit people deny the hardest that always turns out to be the truest."

"You mistake being abrasive for being honest, Jonah. You think it makes you edgy, purifies you somehow," Petz said.

"Well, you know—"

"We've got to work together, Jonah, at least until the campaign's done."

"I'll work with you, Abel. Just remember, I have children. I have to make a living. Name-calling hurts, especially on TV."

"So, this visit commences your vendetta, yes?"

"No, it's your baptism," I answered. "I don't have a vendetta mapped out for you, and it's not something I really want to spend time on. I'd rather go horseback riding with my kids and take my wife out to dinner, which we haven't done in a long time. I'm not obsessively vindictive, either. It's just that everybody has a breaking point, and everybody's career has an arc. This is your time, Abel. I can't deny it."

"Your point, please?" Petz sat up.

"My point is that all arcs eventually curve downward. You don't believe that right now, but I've slid down that slope before, and that was *after* I was the White House's boy genius. White House staff to the White House Sub Shop on Arctic Avenue." I laughed involuntarily. "I can be a neutral player in your arc, or I can be an active participant in bringing about its turn south."

"And I can be the same in yours."

"No doubt about it. I'm not immune from getting rolled, I've just been through it before. That's my only advantage over you, Abel, and you've already embarked in a certain direction—a direction that assumes that your immunity from shock is guaranteed because of your genius."

I then let Petz in on my sixth revelation:

There are no geniuses.

As he processed my wisdom, the door to his office flew open, and three firemen came in and blasted Petz off his chair with a stream from a fire hose. The physics at work were fascinating. The little man actually flew against the window, his legs flipping up over his head. I sat down in Petz's chair and watched the shock set in. Petz's mouth dropped open in an effeminate display of horror. I really hoped he would tattletale to Rebound and Currier. I did. He looked pathetic, which was nice.

I left Abel Petz on his ass, and the Dames, decked out as firemen, trailed me. Petz's receptionist froze against the wall.

"False alarm," I said. "I thought somebody was on fire."

SAME TIME NEXT YEAR

"He can charm you into thinking that you're going places, you know?"

Dude Rothman stood atop the sandblasted "Hore" graffiti on the front steps of his family's beach house smoking a cigarette. I could tell he didn't like the cigarette, but wanted to experiment with a more dudelike posture in front of someone whom he regarded as being semicool.

"Didja find my dad's wench yet?" Dude asked. Wench.

"I'm not your father's keeper."

"How about what he's got gnawing at him? You know what that's all about? You can tell me before he gets here in, like, an hour."

"Not really. I'm still digging, but your friend Milo was a real help."

Dude took a drag of his cigarette. Cool, like. "Give me the skinny when you got it," he concluded, stubbing the butt out on the imprint of the "Hore" vandalism for somebody else to clean up. He strutted off.

Marsha Rothman appeared at the door to the beach house. Marsha looked very good in an aging-Hollywood-wife kind of way. She was wearing a tight-fitting blue sweater opened to reveal maximum cleavage, white jeans, and red pointed pumps. It was hard to fathom that Dude and Juliet had emerged from such a slim woman.

I followed Marsha to the foot of the stairs and she called up for Juliet, who did not answer. She sighed and motioned for me to follow her into the living room that faced the ocean. She sat beside a pillow that displayed the Pinkus family's coat of arms—two seahorses bearing swords atop a mountain. How they got this emblem out of a bunch of Jews being chased across Poland by Cossacks was beyond me, but maybe there were more armed seahorses in Pinsk than I knew about.

"What's wrong, Marsha?" I asked.

"She sits in her room, watches TV, and eats. All damned day."

"Juliet's not in school?" I asked. Master of the Obvious.

"She took a semester off," Marsha said. "I don't know why we let her do it, but what can you do?"

"I don't know. I've never dealt with anything quite like it."

A voice bellowed down the stairs. "Half-breed, that's all I ever heard. Half-breed, how I learned to hate the word." Another Cher song. Juliet waddled through the kitchen dressed in a long black wig and an Indian headband. She grabbed two ice cream sandwiches from the freezer, contemplated putting one back, and then decided to go for a third.

"Hi, Juliet," I said.

Juliet turned to me and belted out, "Both sides were against me from the day I was born!" She then took sad rhinoceros steps up to her five-hundred-channel lair.

Marsha played with her necklace and unzipped the top of her sweater a few more inches. She fanned herself even though it wasn't hot.

"You're very close to your children, aren't you, Jonah?"

"I hate being away from them for even one night."

"Then you probably won't have this problem."

"What do you think caused it?"

"What a father and daughter can have . . . it's like a romance of sorts. A girl needs to feel she's loved. I'm not saying the relationship has to be sick, but it really can be kind of a romance. I had that with my father. Every night when he came home, he sang to me."

"He sounds like he was a very good father."

"Oh, he was. Juliet never had anything like that with Rebound.

Neither of the kids really do. He always looked at them like they were science experiments."

"Then why did you have them?"

"I thought it would be magic. I thought kids would change everything. When they were younger and Rebound started out in politics, he would prop them up on his lap for pictures. I think he liked that part."

"What changed?"

"Maybe they didn't turn out to be what he wanted. Maybe none of us did. Juliet got heavy as she got older. Todd changed his name to Dude, which really upset Rebound. Todd's never been really great at anything, and I suppose Rebound wanted an all-star son. A babe for a daughter. He got neither."

"When you grow up terrified, you don't want to be happy, you want to be in control. At least Juliet knows that when she wants to be Cher, she can be."

Marsha turned and gazed out the southern window of her living room. There was a lone tugboat in the Atlantic, which wasn't tugging anything. "Do you know who she is?"

"Who, Marsha?"

"The girl. Please, please don't be evasive with me, Jonah."

"Rebound and Lucas have frozen me out." Slippery, Mongoose.

Marsha sniffed. "Probably because they know you'd disapprove."

"Things are bad between your husband and me."

Marsha nodded, but I couldn't tell if she heard what I had said. "Do you know that play—they made it into a movie—*Same Time, Next Year?*"

"I know the gist. Two people, both married. No investment, just bed time."

"How do you feel about that?"

"I think you have to be a certain kind of person to pull that off."

"What kind of person?" she asked.

"A person who separates sex from . . . other things."

"What do you think?" Marsha tilted her head, focused on my eyes, and bit her lower lip. Jesus, I thought she had been referring to Rebound and his women.

"Um, Marsha, I'm not a great signal reader—"

Marsha repeated her question: "What do *you* think?"

"I think I wonder why this stuff didn't happen to me when I was twenty-one." I processed the proposal. Did I bang the governor's wife or his mistress? Hmm. The wife would actually be smarter because there was no chance of me actually falling for her . . . *Was I fucking nuts?*

"What stuff?" Marsha asked, knowing damned well the answer.

"Uh, opportunities."

"Some males make better men than they do adolescents."

"What about your husband?"

"Rebound's one of the great adolescents of our time."

"Not me. I was bad at youth when I had it. And I didn't have enough luck with sex to ruin my life over it."

"Your wife is lucky."

"I'm not sure. I think Edie thinks a lot about what she didn't get from me."

"What didn't she get?"

"A guy who chops wood. Marsha, did you ever think that maybe you don't love Rebound, that maybe you're just obsessed with him?"

"It's possible. But you feel what you feel regardless of what you call it. I guess what kills a marriage are the expectations."

"What did you expect when you married Rebound?"

"That the parties would continue. The engagement parties. The coronations," she said theatrically, with a desperate chuckle. "We were good at that. It was the everyday stuff that killed us."

"But Marsha, everyday stuff is . . . what it is."

"I know."

But I sensed that she *didn't* know, and may have been no less deluded than her husband. It's the money, I thought. It's the money that makes people stupid. Marsha had never had to confront reality because Chairman How made certain that his brood was shielded from the contradictions between his couture communism and his true belief system: equality for them, monarchy for us.

"When did you meet Rebound?"

"April 1980. He was doing an auto promotion at one of my dad's places. I wanted to meet him. He had a crowd around him. I acted calm, but felt insane inside."

"Why do you put up with it him, underwrite . . . all of it?"

"He can charm you into thinking that you're going places, you know?"

DOING A GREATER GOOD

"Sometimes you hate somebody because of how they make you feel,
not anything that they did."

After I had a bowl of borscht alone at Murray's, I began walking from
the restaurant back to Rebound's house. My talk with Marsha had in-
spired me to raise the matter of Simone with the governor. I changed into
a new T-shirt and zipped up my jacket over it. Showtime.

A grinning Easy Veasey appeared on the sidewalk on Atlantic Avenue near Lucy the Elephant. A lean man with hollow cheeks and sandy
hair was beside him. They were both looking at me. I sensed that they
had been waiting there, which meant they had probably followed me. I
don't know why Veasey was so happy, but I saw it as being in my best interest to act as if a mutant hadn't tried to kill me in the Pine Barrens,
and I hadn't ordered the break-in and theft at Veasey's office. I wasn't
quite sure how that "look" went.

"Hey, Eddie," I said.

"Jonah," Veasey said, and pointed with his head to the lean man,
who struck a pose that included a frozen chop of his hands. "This is my
friend, Mr. Unruh."

Unruh. I shuddered. There had been a Howard Unruh in the middle twentieth century who had murdered thirteen people in Camden.

Total psycho. It was South Jersey's worst mass murder. If Unruh were still alive, he'd be a million years old, still incarcerated in a hospital for the criminally insane. This guy wasn't him, but still, this was turning into a 1974 martial arts flick with voices dubbed over unmatching lip movements. Xing Fong Productions Presents:

Mr. Unruh:
Enter the Tool

I extended my hand to shake Mr. Unruh's. He didn't take it. "Your instincts are good, Mr. Unruh," I said. "This finger was one knuckle deep into my nose on the way here. Got a real goober, too."

"Mr. Unruh used to work outside of Washington. Northern Virginia," Veasey said with a wink. This was code for CIA. Nimrods and wannabes were forever hinting at "Northern Virginia" and "Langley," the Virginia town where the CIA was based.

"Northern Virginia. Huh. If I'm not mistaken, Ringling Brothers Circus is based there. Were you a juggler, Mr. Unruh?"

Mr. Unruh stepped back, pivoted, and punched one of the slats on the fence surrounding Lucy the Elephant until it snapped into two pieces.

"That was good, Mr. Unruh," I said as Veasey beamed. "Is there any reason I should be seeing this display?"

"No," Veasey said. "I just know you grew up seeing spectacles at the shore and might appreciate a little demo."

"I did. Splendid, my good man, splendid."

"Did you hear my office had a little break-in?"

"You broke wind?" I cupped my ear.

"My office had a break-in. Somebody stole my porn collection. Heh-heh-heh." Veasey winked at Mr. Unruh, who stared me down, stone-faced. I had my revolver. Now might be a good time to use it. Epiphany: the irony of firearms is that it's not enough to have them, one must use them. If I was so reluctant to use mine, why did I have it? Perhaps it just wasn't the time. While the shore wasn't crowded this time of year, there were enough people milling about that it was unlikely we were going to have an O.K. Corral on Atlantic Avenue. Keep the gun sheathed, boy.

"I'm sorry to hear that," I said. "I have a meeting with the governor. Would you like me to bring it up with him?"

"Not necessary," Veasey said. "If you hear anything, would you let me know? Could happen to anybody."

"You bet, Eddie," I said.

Mr. Unruh brooded. He meant it to be scary. He kind of was. Sometimes when I get nervous, I lurch reflexively into absurd humor, so I began imitating Dustin Hoffman in *Rain Man*—that nervous, observant, staccato monotone with a Midwestern twang: "You're very shadowy, very spooky," I said to Mr. Unruh without looking right at him. "Definitely very shadowy. *Ooooh!* Definitely late for the governor." I averted my eyes and walked away, my head tilted to the side like a pollster savant.

It was a Friday afternoon in mid-October. The traffic was down from peak season, but a fair number of cars were beginning to fill the streets for the weekend. I decided to show Rebound my new T-shirt. It featured the Celebrity Motel's logo, the cartoonized Marilyn Monroe. I wanted to detonate a reaction from Rebound in a manner other than conventional input, which only made him lie.

Rebound slid open the glass door at the rear of his beach house and entered the kitchen alcove shirtless. He wiped his brow with his towel and said, "I need a break, athl—"

Rebound's tan melted the moment he saw my Celebrity shirt. A scared expression fell across his face.

"Lucas!" Rebound shouted.

"Hold on," Currier said from another room, "I'm finishing up a call."

Rebound sat on one of his dining room chairs. He kept his face under his towel. Truth is ugly, that kind of thing. Lucas Currier entered from Rebound's study, closing up his cell phone. He caught my T-shirt and quickly looked away.

"I'm here to discuss Simone Lava. Let's talk about what we do."

Accepting his weak position, Currier sat down. Rebound remained beneath his towel pretending to cool off. "What do you suggest?" Currier asked.

"We have to be able to characterize the relationship," I said.

"*Relationship* is your word, Jonah." Bill Fucking Clinton.

"Look, if Barium Enema writes that Rebound is banging an intern, are you going to demand a correction on the grounds that they were only blow jobs?"

"Now hold on just a minute here," Rebound said. And added no follow-up point.

"There can be no characterization," Currier said. "There's no relationship."

"Can we at least agree that the governor shouldn't see her during the campaign?" I suggested.

"She'd go batshit," Rebound said through his towel.

"Batshit wouldn't be good," I said.

"How did you happen to be at the Celebrity?" Currier asked.

"There are rumors floating around. They were too specific for my liking. I was worried that somebody might have something firm on the Governor."

"Well, do they?" Currier asked.

"I don't know," I lied. I didn't think it was time to tell them that I had rolled Veasey and pinched the photographs. "But guys, there are enough people who know how to make it a problem, if not a nice story in the *Probe*."

Rebound peered from beneath his towel. "So, now what?"

"We step up attacks on Digby," Currier said. "We look for political diversions. And we don't comment on every political smear that the Governor's opponent attempts to plant."

I nodded. It was all we could do for now, given what we knew and what I was willing to tell them. Currier left. It was the first time I had ever seen him flash dagger eyes at the Governor, who remained beneath his towel.

"Why do you cheat on your wife, Governor?" I asked once we were alone.

"Because I hate the way she chews," he said calmly, spontaneously.

"The way she chews?"

"The way she chews. I hate hearing the sound of saliva mixing with her bagel. I don't get the science of it, but whenever I hear Marsha's teeth go through bread, I have to bang a chick in her twenties so I know I'm not in hell."

"Wow," I said, truly impressed with the poetry of Rebound's argument. While I may not have approved of it morally, his rationale was too original, his absence of self-aggrandizing spin too apparent, for this to not have been at least partially true. I even felt threatened, fearing that Rebound spoke to Simone this artfully. Speaking artfully was *my* thing.

"Even her hair makes noise, Jonah. That's what kills me, I think. I think it's the noise. I can hear her hair grow. It makes me think of death. Honestly, that's the sound I think I'll hear in hell. Marsha chewing. The same thing, day in and day out. The way she chews. The way she breathes. The way she says *draul* for *drawer.* I hate it when she says 'ointment.' When she tells you something sad, she makes a frowny face, the way you would with little kids—like your kids' ages. And, yeah, I can even *hear* her face move. It makes a fuckin' noise, Jonah. I want to make it like I hate her for something that she did, but that's not it at all. Sometimes you hate somebody because of how they make you feel, not anything that they did. So now you know. You're lucky you don't feel this way about Edie."

This was the first time in the years that I'd known Rebound that he acknowledged I had children. It was the first time I heard him use Edie's name. Maybe he was playing me, but at the moment I didn't care. His technique had worked for now, and it was my hardball tactic of digging up dirt on him and throwing it in his face that brought the situation into the light.

"I don't feel that way about Edie, no. I'm scared of her, actually. I think she disapproves of me, but it makes me want to get in her good graces, I guess."

"I don't want to get into Marsha's good graces."

"You're making me think of something my grandmother once told me, a Yiddish proverb. 'Those who marry for money end up earning it.'"

Rebound, not big on philosophy, just shrugged. "You met Simone. Wasn't there a part of you that thought, now *this* is the answer?"

"I had that thought, yes."

"You know something? For me she IS the answer. I know you're not supposed to say that. You're supposed to say, 'I realize my mistake' and shuffle back to your family. But I don't feel that way. I know it's supposed to be wrong, but when that hot piece of ass is in that birdcage, she *is* the answer."

"The problem is, Governor, she doesn't want to stay in that birdcage."

"That's where I'm fucked."

"That's where she's fucked, too . . . if she's out of that birdcage, if she's your wife—"

"That's not gonna happen."

This is why men like Rebound get women like Simone—they don't care. They feel nothing for the women, only for the way those women make them feel. "If she's out of that birdcage," I said, "she belongs to the world—"

"That can't happen, either. If she comes down to Washington with me—if I win—then those pricks down there will want her in their own birdcage."

"It's good that you recognize that. That there's competition. That outside of the birdcage there are options, and those options go beyond you. Sometimes we don't grab something, not because we don't want the object but because we can't pay the price."

"Powerful men need release," Rebound responded in one of his more memorable non sequiturs. "Sometimes we need a release. In order to do a greater good."

You're doing a greater good, all right.

Rebound's antennae had submerged by this point. My bluntness hadn't served me well lately, so I softened my counsel.

"Governor, as long as they're just allegations about Simone, you're okay. If they *see* evidence, they'll be pissed. People forgive adultery. They punish sloppiness. Adultery by a man in power is admired. Sloppiness means you're unfit to lead."

Rebound searched for an answer on the Atlantic horizon. It didn't come. He said blandly, "The voters want answers."

"No," I said, "they want to be told tales, and we've got to tell them one."

"They won't stop," Rebound said under his breath.

"Who won't stop? Veasey?"

"Who knows what he's got?" This wasn't really a question. He knew Veasey had something.

"Maybe we can find out what he's got."

"Who knows what they've got from back—" Rebound tightened his lips so no errant syllables escaped.

"*Back* what?"

"Nothing," Rebound dismissed.

I followed up on another sentence segment: "*You'd* know what they've got. So what do they have?"

"Nothing. They don't have anything," Rebound sighed. We had gone from Veasey to *they* rather quickly. Who was *they?* When was *back?*

"Somebody spray-painted 'whore' on your front steps. Could that mean anything?"

Rebound brought his arm back as if he were holding a tennis racket. He lowered himself against the dining room table and swept the Grapes of Rothman across the room until the bowl flew onto the sofa and bounced between some pillows. The grapes dripped onto the floor. Miraculously, nothing broke. But that was God enforcing Rebound's luck.

I suddenly understood why I was still on board. Rebound was definitely hiding more. He had no intention of telling his other pollster the depth of his secrets and Petz, by constitution, wouldn't press him. Part of Petz's contract was feigning ignorance. Rebound would lie to me, but he knew that I'd expect him to lie, and would, by constitution, seek to cover up his problem as if it were my own.

I left Rebound's house and pulled onto Atlantic Avenue, where the Margate bar scene had begun to percolate. It may have been folks coming south from Atlantic City, but it was more likely people from the Delaware Valley who were desperately trying to hold onto a season that had passed. Some of them even had tans, the kind of incandescent sheen that mistook charred skin for good health. An ancient song by a 1970s group called 10cc whispered from an idle Camaro, "Big boys don't cry / Big boys don't cry."

Who knows what they've got from back——? The governor said it, but what did it mean? Back. Back when? There was something else.

THE REMINDER

"We may need some help."

Why was I still working for this sonofabitch, I asked myself?

My answer came the following evening at a thousand-dollar-a-plate dinner at Woodcrest Country Club in Cherry Hill. The reception room burst into applause when Rebound entered, the light from the flashbulbs spinning like dreidels across his hair. Simone would have had an orgasm on the spot. This is what it was all about for her.

Rebound tugged my arm—"C'mere, athlete"—he wanted me beside him for some reason, and I obliged. Neither Currier nor Petz were there.

Rebound approached a fiftyish man in a gray pinstriped suit. "Hey, Bob, good to see you. Jonah, you know Andrew Lewis from Spring Pharmaceuticals, don't you?"

"No, we've never met. I know the company, though," I said.

"Good to meet you, Jonah," Lewis said.

The governor planted an antiseptic kiss on the cheek of Malinda Waughtal, the chairwoman of the New Jersey Light and Power Commission.

"You know Jonah Eastman, don't you, Malinda?"

She didn't know me, but she said, "Of course."

"Rebound!" a gregarious Mediterranean-looking man said. The Governor embraced him.

"Jonah, this is the only time you'll see this athlete without a tennis racket in his hand," Rebound joshed. "He wants people to think he runs Mid-Atlantic Wireless, but he hacks on the court all day."

"Aw, Governor, I only goof off when you're around," the man said, pleased to have his hobby acknowledged.

"Jonah, this is Peter Mirijanian," Rebound said.

"Good to meet you," we both said simultaneously, laughing as if this had been ripshit funny. My conscience yanked me somewhere down low, as I feared that I was capable of being as bad a suckass as Abel Petz.

As Rebound melted into the crowd, Peter put his arm around me and asked, "What do you do, Jonah?"

"I do polling and media strategy for the governor," I said.

"Well, we should talk," Peter said, serious all of a sudden. "Have you been reading about the legislation they're trying to pass banning mobile phones from cars?"

"It's hard to avoid the subject."

Peter reached into his pocket and pulled out a business card. "Gimme a call," he said. "This thing could get ugly if it gets to Congress, and we may need some help."

I studied the card: Peter Mirijanian. President and Chief Executive Officer. Mid-Atlantic Wireless, Inc.

"I'll call, Peter," I promised. "If our buddy Rebound lets me out of his clutches."

"I know how it is, Jonah," my new friend said.

I surveyed the room from the corner overlooking the golf course. There were hundreds of heads bobbing about, but all I saw were sacks of cash propped atop shoulders. Perhaps that's what Abel Petz saw, too. I caught my reflection in the window, and considered that maybe I hated Petz so much because I saw myself in his avarice, the desperate monkey-boy hopping around, doing tricks for a banana as the Hell Bitch of Democracy played her polka. *"I'm a player! I'm a player!"* Petz embraced his monkeyness with a full hard-on, while I fought it. I despised that a part of me missed the days when I was the big polling Petz, inflicting my gaudy brilliance on America. This drive, this inner hurricane, had been downgrading within me in the past year. Not the money, though. Just give me the money. How much? Enough. Not mansion money, freedom money.

I ground my jaw, thinking: These are the scenes that Edie never sees—the ones that remind me not to be such a smartass, that there's a dividend that comes from putting up with Rebound. It wasn't a dividend I had always spent on Porsches, either. More like food. The waiters were tossing platters of harvest chicken onto the fund-raisers' tables as if they were Frisbees. Brown rice cascaded from the center of the chicken, and I heard my stomach growl despite the noise in the room. I stole myself a place at the closest table, pretended I was somebody, and dug in.

RACE CARD STRATEGIES

"How bad is the truth?"

Chief Willie and I took a train into 30th Street Station from Atlantic City. The Chief told me what had been on Veasey's microcasette.

"Veasey's a bigger slime than I thought," I reacted.

"He thought this through good," Chief Willie said. "He wanted to be in a position to take everybody down."

"At least we know that we haven't been that far off base with the riverboat scheme."

"The cassette's pretty cool, but it doesn't nail Rebound, Mongoose. His involvement is still flimsy in the whole thing. The press would be careful about making the leap from intern-banging to the gambling proposal."

"We're only midway through the adventure, I know it. That's why I have you. I think you'll like this guy we're going to meet with."

"Friend of Mongoose become friend of Chief Willie," the Chief said with a tribal bow. "Mongoose, I don't like to get into deep discussions, but you don't sound so good. You're talking slow or something."

"Chief, do you ever see yourself in a window or a mirror and wonder how much you can take? Do you ever wonder if you'll just break down? Completely?"

"Yeah," Chief Willie said surprisingly fast. "When the wrestling business went national, us local guys were screwed. We didn't translate onto the new stage. I didn't know what the hell I would do with myself. I was driving over the causeway to Somers Point one night, and another car was coming at me fast in the other lane. I'm thinking, *If it hits me, who gives a shit?* You're not thinking about pointing that gun in the wrong direction, are you, Mongoose?"

"No, it's not that. I'm just wondering if I'm going to crash and fall straight down like a helicopter without the blades. You know that helicopters aren't even supposed to fly once you get the physics."

"You won't crash because you can't. Sitting Bull once said, 'Man with lots of buffalo shit in teepee must live in shit until he puts buffalo shit in somebody else's teepee.'"

"Sitting Bull didn't say that."

Chief Willie winked. So ended the therapy.

Ten minutes in a cab later we arrived at the offices of Race Card Strategies, the exterior door of which simply read "RCS."

Torch Wyeth was the proprietor of Race Card Strategies. He had one of those faces that made you think he was mad at you. He was an intense man of roughly thirty-five with piercing coal-black eyes, equally black hair that was slicked back, and tiny wire-rimmed glasses that focused his gaze into dual lasers.

The wall art in Torch's reception area was political. There was an oversized photograph of Martin Luther King speaking at the Mall in Washington to tens of thousands lining the Reflecting Pool. The 1960 Democratic National Convention poster of John F. Kennedy headlined "A Time for Greatness" was placed beside King. On another wall, Richard Nixon's mudslide of a profile stood against bold letters declaring "Nixon: Now More Than Ever." A musical mix playing softly over the speakers incanted a campaign song that had been used against Martin van Buren in a political campaign. I couldn't even fathom the date. A trio of bold voices asked and answered: *"Who deserves the lowest place in hell? Van Buren!"* Proof that nastiness in political campaigns was not an invention of modern consultants.

"This is my friend Chief Willie Thundercloud," I told Torch, who shook his head approvingly at the Chief's silver-laden leather vest and matching Western hat and boots.

"Good to meet you, Mr. Wyeth," Chief Willie said. "I heard you were involved in those Badlands riots they had a few years ago when Street was running for mayor."

Torch's eyes went hot in his skull like nuclear-tipped missiles in a Nebraska silo.

"That's total bullshit, man," Torch said sharply.

"You weren't involved with the riots?"

"No, man. I *started* them. Get your facts straight," Torch smirked archly.

Chief Willie snickered. "Cold, ain't he?" he said.

Torch escorted Chief Willie and me into a conference room that overlooked Independence Hall, which was teeming with schoolchildren on field trips. Torch gestured to a spot at the end of the table where I should sit. Chief Willie sat across from Torch. I was facing a photograph of an elderly man. It took me a moment to recall who he was.

"Saul Alinsky," Torch said.

"Who the hell is he?" Chief Willie asked.

"He wrote a book called *Rules for Radicals*," Torch told Chief Willie. "He organized protests against the Man years ago, mostly in Chicago."

"Looks harmless," Chief Willie said. "Which was why he raised so much hell, I guess." The Chief recorded the name of the book on a piece of paper.

"Do you gents want to tell me what you need, or do you want to know more about what I do?" Torch asked.

"Let me tell you what we've got and you can react," I said, noticing that Torch hadn't brought in a notepad to record our discussion. A pro: "I've worked for Governor Rothman for a long time. He's ahead in the polls versus Stahl, but not ahead enough to make him comfortable. We're worried about some of these rumors circulating about him and want to inoculate against trouble by raising Digby's negatives."

"These rumors, Jonah," Torch began. "How bad is the truth?"

I didn't want Torch to wade into the depths of my suspicions, but I couldn't brush off all of my fears. Torch was, after all, a man who made his living by helping clients who were motivated to have their problems resolved using unconventional means. Besides, he'd spot a lie.

"I think the rumors about women have some truth," I said.

"This guy likes the squaws, and he's not as careful as he thinks he is," Chief Willie added.

"I assume you have a strategy that considers admitting that he has been a less than perfect husband?" Torch asked.

"Our client, Torch, has a veracity disability," I explained. "I'm doing the best I can with what I have to work with, but regardless, we need to sling some shit on the judge."

"And you've done polling to this end?"

"Yes." I gave Torch the topline of what my opinion research had gleaned about New Jersey voters. The snobbery. The upper lip. The Swedish thing that seemed to stick in everybody's ass.

"Consistent with my experience," Torch chuckled. "Sometimes I wonder why you guys bother doing polls at all. I mean, don't we always know going in?"

"I poll a little differently, Torch," I said. "I'm interested in what people deny. Then I know what they're really thinking."

"Makes sense," Torch said. "I think I can help you. Can you share the data with me? So I can see what people deny."

"Sure, then what?"

"I'm foreseeing some special events," Torch said, glancing out at Independence Mall. "Something viral, just free-floating hostilities focused a little. Things that get people thinking bitter about the hijacking of the American Dream."

"Who's the hijacker, Torchy Boy?" Chief Willie asked.

"Judgie," Torch said. "Nobody likes their inheritance grabbed by an elite."

"If the judge stole something from people, Torch, won't somebody need to give them hope?" I asked.

"More than that, Jonah," Torch said. "The bringer of hope will need to be rewarded for his heroism."

"I'm pretty sure I can get funding for your program," I assured Torch.

"The governor has a rich wife, correct?" Torch said.

I spoke to Currier and got verbal approval for Torch Wyeth's program. I had to draw from my corporate money market account for twenty-five thousand dollars because Marsha Rothman was in New York and couldn't sign. I hated doing this, but Marsha had never welshed on an invoice yet, so I cut the check and sent it to Race Card Strategies.

THE CHERRY HILL INSTITUTE FOR NARCISSISTIC PERSONALITY DISORDERS

"Are you surprised when you are not recognized on the street even though you are not famous?"

The sensation of crashing that I had discussed with Chief Willie hadn't left me, so I repressed my association of psychiatry with bored suburban housewives, and decided to pay a visit to a childhood friend in the head racket to see what he had to say.

I knew that my forty-year friendship with Jerry Cohen had grown stale when he ceased finding farts funny. Jerry and I had grown up together in Atlantic City, but he went off to Amherst, Penn Medical School, and the Sorbonne to become a psychiatrist. He returned to the U.S. test-driving a British accent, while I somehow remained American. That the Sorbonne was in France didn't matter because Jerry had become British and, as everyone knows, they don't fart over there.

Jerry had earned a place in the pantheon of pranksters when in fifth grade he blasted one and shrewdly blamed it on a corpulent, pimply girl named Corna Hester, whose guilt was roundly embraced because the ferocity of the odor matched her appearance more plausibly than it did Jerry's. When I called him decades later at the offices of his thriving psychiatric clinic, he didn't respond when I asked him to pull my finger.

Jerry operated the Cherry Hill Center for Narcissistic Personality Disorders, or CHINPOD. I had checked out CHINPOD's Internet site to get the exact address. The clinic's home page asked:

- Are you preoccupied with Donald Trump?
- Do you believe you are smarter than those who are more successful than you are?
- Are you surprised when you are not recognized on the street even though you are not famous?
- Do you take karaoke seriously?

Jerry actually hugged me when I entered his spacious office overlooking the Moorestown Mall. I was surprised because hugging wasn't very British. Jerry wasn't wearing his usual ascot, which was nice, just an Oxford cloth shirt with a tie featuring a fox-hunting scene in the English countryside.

"Ah, how I miss our fox-hunting days on the boardwalk," I said.

"I thought it was more graceful than etchings of a wop rolling a Jew on the Steel Pier," Jerry said, sitting beneath a painting of polo players.

"How are your mom and dad, Jer?"

"Great, they just bought a Hummer."

"All right, Morty and Selma, goin' off-road."

"In Margate, no less."

"Intrepid."

"I heard somewhere that you're in the governor's employ?" Jerry asked.

"Funny you should ask, Jer. One of the reasons why I'm here is to ask your analysis of him. Do you have any psychiatric theories about Rothman?"

Jerry shrugged. "Even though we're not supposed to theorize about nonpatients, I've always felt Rothman's genius is in an area that psychiatry calls projective identification."

"What does it mean?" I asked, truly interested.

"I'm just warning you that I'll be grossly oversimplifying."

"Gross oversimplification pays my American Express bill every month."

"All right, then. One theory of projective identification is that certain people have a gift for sensing what others really want. They then design their personalities and behaviors to fit the other person's fantasies. In effect, such a personality is whatever others want him to be at that moment."

"A politician."

"Often, yes."

"How does a person like this . . . get made?"

"One theory has it going back to the breast—"

"Doesn't everything?"

"Well, yes. Anyhow, the theory goes that the baby will do anything to get the mother's breast back. Some children are more desperate than others, and become more savvy in manipulating the mother, whom the child believes has abandoned him. These skills evolve over time. In the case of someone like Rothman, his abilities are rendered even more potent because of his looks, his fame, his position."

"Hmm," I said. "I don't know about the origins, but the manifestation sounds spot on."

"Is that what you came to ask me about, Jonah?"

I just looked down.

"Something's on your mind, friend, and your machismo is keeping it down lest you be seen as weak by your dead gangster grandfather."

"Okay. Okay. I hate my job. I hate Rothman. Edie and I aren't getting along. I keep feeling like I'm going to crash. Like a helicopter, not an airplane. Straight down. Is that possible?"

"It's possible that you feel like you are crashing, yes. You've got a lot going on in your head and in your life. That's a burden."

"I don't sleep . . . Sometimes I watch my kids sleep at night and I cry."

"What are you thinking about when you feel that way?"

"Failing. Failing the kids. Failing Edie. Falling straight down."

"You've passed the age that your parents were when they died."

"So?"

"I would speculate that you are aware of it superficially, but also unconsciously. They failed you by dying. Your grandparents failed you by living . . . living as they did."

"What's the answer?"

"There's no one answer. You're depressed, Jonah. Medication is one course of action. You look thin. Are you eating?"

"Not so much. I'm still running."

"Good, that's part of the answer, too. Where good men get into trouble is making drastic moves: Quitting their jobs in a utopian rush. Leaving their wives. Stalking a younger woman."

"What about buying a Porsche?"

"Did you?"

"Yes."

"It's pronounced *Porsh*-eh, by the way. It's a harmless move, Jonah. Unlike quitting a good job . . . or women."

I must have betrayed some emotion, because Jerry asked, "Who is she?"

"Shit, Jerry, nothing's happened. Just erotic dreams."

"I'll put on my friend hat for a moment, Jonah. If I had to place a bet, I'd bet that you could weather your professional distress and this depression. But a man who can't bring himself to ask the girl he's adored for years to the prom is not a man who would make a competent adulterer."

"Jer, you're not right about everything, but you're right about a lot."

"Do you need medication?"

"No. I need to know that I'm not making psychiatric history here."

"An ambitious man with a train wreck of a family background working in a thankless industry—there is nothing you have told me that I find surprising."

"I appreciate this, Jer."

"And, Jonah, if I may say something that is none of my business?"

"Sure."

"Weak men pose the greatest danger to others."

"I'm sorry—"

"Rothman. He's weak."

"How do you fight a weak man?"

"If you are his adversary, you destroy him with prejudice."

"What if you're his pollster?"

"You get him out of your life."

SEEDS OF OUTRAGE

"A spate of disturbing graffiti has descended across the Garden State."

Al Just of KBRO-TV in Philly broke the story first. It had all of the right elements: an emotionally resonant occurrence combined with a phenomenon no one could explain. Al Just led with a map of New Jersey with little red dots in the locations where the vandalism took place.

"A spate of disturbing graffiti has descended across the Garden State," Al Just began in his grim baritone, the collar on his leather bomber jacket flapping in the wind. "The vandalism contains the ambiguous word 'Judge,' followed by an explanation point."

The camera panned the St. Inga Swedish Church in Flemington. Al Just continued, "The perplexing graffiti, so far, has appeared exclusively on facilities that appear to have some tie to Sweden. A Volvo dealership was vandalized in Audubon, and a cinder block was hurled through an Ikea store's window in New Brunswick."

Good. After the broadcast I retreated to my attic study to map out where else seeds of outrage needed dissemination. My mobile phone rang as the first symptoms of my thinking limped along my notepad. I answered it. I heard feminine hysterics. My heart stopped. "Edie?" I said, momentarily forgetting that she was downstairs.

"No, it's Simone."

"Simone?"

"I think he's leaving me, Jonah," she sobbed.

I recalled my discussion with Rebound and Currier about Simone. Rebound was afraid she'd go batshit at any suggestion of separation, even temporary. A batshit mistress was not a good thing.

"Where are you, Simone?" I asked.

"In my room," she cried.

"Do you know the White House Sub Shop in A.C.?"

"Yeah."

"Meet me there in an hour."

"Okay."

"Calm down, kiddo," I said, feeling self-confident in a testosterone-laden way.

"Okay."

"I'll be there. I promise."

I called Chief Willie. I had read somewhere that the Chinese symbol for crisis meant danger *and* opportunity. An opportunity was upon me.

BOOK III

MOON OVER PARAMUS

"Who's gonna get the girl is an American metaphor. The girl is America—that's what the election is all about—who's gonna get the girl."

—Mort Sahl

WHITE HOUSE, TAKE II

"Simone Lava was an unknown woman traveling incognito."

The door to room 204 of the Celebrity Motel was locked, but that was no problem for Chief Willie, who was concealing a special set of little tools. His Shore Heating baseball cap was pulled down to his brow, and his ponytail was obscured beneath it. A random mook walked by, which prompted Chief Willie to crouch and pretend to inspect a vent. The mook bopped down the steps, Chief Willie duckwalked over to the door, and with a few deft clicks with his tools he was inside Simone's lair.

Look at that fuckin' birdcage, Chief Willie thought. *Weird-ass bastard, that governor.* He skulked around the birdcage shaking his head. Chief Willie stepped into the birdcage and scanned the walls searching for the God of Electronic Surveillance to give him a sign. Nothing. He knelt down and scanned the room from a lower perch. Hmm. Interesting.

Chief Willie stepped out of the cage and perused a flap in the wallpaper about a foot above the alarm clock. Even though it was light enough to see around the room clearly, he pulled out a flashlight and inspected the strips of wallpaper. The strip above the alarm clock appeared fresher than the ones beside it. With a razor, the Chief cut along the edge of the seam and gently pulled back the piece of paper. There was a crevasse about a centimeter in diameter. He stuck his finger in it and pulled it out. Putty.

Chief Willie crawled around the base of the floor and tugged at the carpet, which was where he found the wire. That was all he needed.

He approached the window and peeled back the curtain to see if anyone was milling around outside. Clear. He went outside, shut the door behind him, and proceeded down the balcony. A dark-skinned woman rounded the corner and cocked her head at Chief Willie, who did not meet her eyes. He just borrowed a tune from West Side Story and sang chillingly, *"LaTrina—I just saw a girl named LaTrina . . ."*

The expressionless woman decocked her head back to its vertical position and focused a point out on the horizon in order to underscore the message of her body language: *Didn't see nuthin.'*

I parked on Arctic Avenue outside the White House Sub Shop. I was abundantly aware that I had once worked in a very different White House, one that wasn't sweet on neon and linoleum. Yes, God, I know—Lost Promise.

I checked myself out in the rearview mirror as if I were getting ready for the junior prom. I thought I looked rugged. Yeah, that was the word I'd choose. With my graying goatee and thinning hair, I didn't think *gorgeous* or *really cute* worked. But I wanted gorgeous and really cute. I wanted Simone to meet her friends at the Shore Mall in Pleasantville and tell them she met a "gorgeous, really cute guy—Jonah." There is little I could tell you about my current state of mind that is more embarrassing than that.

I stepped out of my Porsche posing rugged and walked into the White House Sub Shop. Johnny Cash's baritone was taunting me with "Personal Jesus." The White House hadn't changed in decades—the way things should be. The walls were adorned with local customers intermingling with Atlantic City royalty like Vic Damone. Everyone in these photos knew who they were, unlike Simone, who was sitting at a booth in the back. She was wearing sunglasses and a scarf. It was an early-1960s

movie star look, but no particular star popped into my head. Simone
Lava was an unknown woman traveling incognito. Despite Simone's
farce, she still possessed evidence of God. That's what beauty is, I decided. Even beneath the abrasive fluorescent lights, her skin looked like
buttermilk. I wanted to shrink down to about a quarter of an inch in
height and walk around on her face just to feel her skin between my toes.
I imagined myself sinking in a little, but springing back; it was that kind of
skin—soft but taut. *Johnny Cash: "Reach out and touch faith."*

Simone waved me over, as if I might have mistaken her for the un-
shaven gambler with the heinous combover who was oozing mustard
from his crooked teeth onto his book, *Black Jack and Retire.*

"Do you hear this song, Jonah? I love Johnny Cash," she said tepidly
as I slid into the narrow booth with the orange vinyl upholstery.

"Really? When I was growing up, I was scared of Johnny Cash. He
had been to prison and all. I like him now. Maybe the stuff you're
scared of when you're a kid you chase when you're grown up."

Simone nodded, half listening. "Thanks for seeing me," she said.
Tony Orlando and Buddy Hackett stared down at us from the wall.
Simone wore a khaki shirt and denim pants. Light makeup. *Cash: "Some-
one to hear your prayers, someone who cares."*

"You sounded upset," I said. "What happened?"

She looked over her shoulder to make certain no one was listening.
"Gardner went ballistic on me. He said he couldn't see me until after
the election."

"I told him we met."

"Jonah, if he doesn't see me now, he won't see me after he wins."

"Simone, it's just not smart. Barri Embrey's poking around. What
happened after you and Re—him—talked?"

"We . . . you know." I couldn't decide whether to lean across the table
and chew on the corner of her mouth where she had an indentation, or
stab myself with a plastic fork. When a woman was beautiful the way
Simone Lava was, you hated her. The root of your rage was the knowledge that she's not yours, which is to say that you hate her because you
love her. It's a selfish sentiment, nevertheless, your anxieties, however

offensive, are rational: her freedom genuinely *is* a threat. If she's not caged, she will leave because that's what a wild bird does.

"He's not leaving you, Simone," I said, winging it.

"Do you want him to leave me, Jonah?"

Johnny: "I will deliver, you know I'm a forgiver."

"I can't make those decisions for him. I told him we met. I didn't give him an order. But you can understand why I had to find out. I need to protect him."

"I know you do."

"It's not you I'm worried about, it's Digby Stahl. It's Barri Embrey. This can get very nasty."

"I know. I know."

I hate it when the naïve claim to be seasoned. It wasn't one of those things reason could address. You just can't educate people beyond their life experience.

A sweet waitress named Holly came over and took our order. Holly had seen me here with Edie and the kids, and I could only imagine what she must have suspected. Then Simone opened the bomb bays and dropped it: "Maybe I should just go to Barri Embrey once and for all and tell her that Gardner and my life is none of her damned business—none of anybody's business."

J.C.: "Lift up the receiver, I'll make you a believer."

"I don't think you want to do that, Simone."

"Why shouldn't I? Look what she's doing to our love."

"If you did that, Rebound's wife would leave him in the middle of the election, a media shitstorm would follow, he'd lose the election, he'd blame you for ruining his life, and then where would everybody be?"

"Ugh!" Simone groaned. "I know. I guess."

"Be patient. Everything will be fine," I said, an efficient little lie.

Simone rested her chin in her hands, her elbows balanced on the table. "Jonah, you've had a lot of girlfriends, haven't you?" she asked. She propped up her sunglasses on her forehead and leaned her head in toward me.

"Why would you ask that?"

"You're a very sexual person."

I went cold. This was utterly untrue. Of any delusions I may have possessed, I have always seen myself as a very conventional man with the sexual ethics of a pilgrim. Even though sex was something that most adults had done at various points in their lives, seeing others do it, as I had in the photos of Rebound and Simone, conveyed a certain mammalian baseness, which reaffirmed for me that there was something more to sex that I just wasn't seeing.

"No, Simone, I am not," I said rather sternly. "But I suspect you have a reason for wanting me to believe that I am."

"The best men never see themselves the way women do."

"That may be true, but if women were that magnetically attracted to a man like me, it would have shown up before I hit middle age."

"You just have a bad self-image, Jonah."

"No, I don't. I think I'm pretty terrific. I'm really practical about these things. If I were that hot, my life would have taken a different course."

"You just don't send signals, that's all. Men like Rebound send signals, which is why they always pick something up."

"There may be something to that."

"You don't trust me."

"I'm a married man darting around in the shadows with a gorgeous woman half my age who happens to be the governor's mistress. Would *you* trust you?"

"I hate that word, *mistress*. It sounds so sleazy."

"How would you like it to sound, Simone?"

"I just have this vision I can't let go of."

"What's in the vision?"

"I see Gardner and me pulling up to a nursery school in Washington. We get out of the motorcade, and all of the children are waving, they're so excited to see us. There's a school orchestra, and they play 'Hail to the Chief.' Rebound stands back a little—you know how he is with children, a little nervous—but I hug them all and they're so happy. It's so sweet."

"Did you ever notice, Simone, that the dreams you have always have you and Rebound in front of an audience? It's always a coronation, not a marriage."

"I don't see it that way, Jonah."

"I know you don't, kiddo."

"I'm not *that* much younger than you."

"You're practically a fetus."

That broke Simone up, and I felt studly that I could make a girl this hot laugh. "You know, Simone, a lot of us come from places that aren't special."

Simone tilted her head to the side, real Jennifer Love Hewitt vulnerable. "What do you mean?" she said.

Holly the waitress came and set our subs before us. "It's just that you're very ambitious. That's okay. A lot of us who are ambitious need to think we came from somewhere exotic."

I thought my observation wasn't too bad, but Simone's face froze. I was cutting at something terribly raw. "Your grandfather was Mickey Price," she said.

"Can I tell you something, Simone? The great disenchantment of my life was realizing what my grandfather really was."

"A gangster?"

"It's more than that. No, actually, it's less than that. I needed to believe for a long time that Mickey was the leader of a vast underworld that ran everything. I saw *The Godfather* a million times. I needed to believe in the dignity, the conspiracy, the idea that men in the shadows were moving presidents around like chess pieces. Do you know what the mob really is? I mean, really?"

"What?"

"It's a loose collection of crooks. That's all. At one time they had power in some pretty big alleys, but they were a phenomenon, not a power."

"What's the difference?"

"Organized crime was a movement, like socialism or something. You had events happening in the world that made people think, okay, we all should get a piece of something. But it wasn't like one guy masterminded it. Mickey was one guy in a big organic movement."

"I always heard he was so powerful."

"Yeah, but power over what? A handful of thieves and gamblers?"

"Why did you believe he was so powerful?"

"Because I needed to. We were being chased all over the world by the cops. I was a kid. I had to believe that it was all about something important. I had myself a little cause, us against the big bad world. Because I lost my parents so young, and because I was running all over the world feeling like a nobody, I needed to believe Mickey was a great big somebody."

"You don't anymore?"

"I loved my grandfather, but he wasn't much. I guess that's why it's so important to me to create something. I don't know you very well, and I'm not sure why I'm telling you this stuff. I don't know where you come from," I said. "But I'd hate to see you spend your life trying to plan the perfect state dinner."

"I'm not doing that," Simone said firmly, articulating for me with a pout that certified what I had long suspected: *The most powerful drive in America is the desire to be recognized for who we are not.* I could also see that the sermon I had been rehearsing for decades had been for my own benefit.

I drove Simone back to the Celebrity Motel. She closed her eyes in a curious way, opened them slightly, and leaned toward me, kissing me full on the lips. To my horror, I did not push her away, but kissed her back, my right hand trembling on the Porsche's gearshift. *Reach out and touch faith.* The softness of her lips held me, but it was her intangible floral scent— she smelled like April in high school—that kept me kissing her back. Simone slowly pushed away from me, and I froze, speechless. I began to tally the crimes I had just committed, but I couldn't inventory them. Instead, I could only fathom myself against the backdrop of betrayal. I drove out of the Celebrity's lot much too quickly. I had had enough of Simone for one day. I had had enough of *myself* for one day, not to mention the metastasizing sense that the handler was being handled.

WHO KNOWS WHO KNOWS WHAT?

"How arrogant would I be to assume that no one could possibly know the muck of my own history?"

Chief Willie walked beside me along the boardwalk.

"Okay," Chief Willie said, "I got inside Simone's room. There are holes in the wall big enough for a lipstick camera and transmission wires under the molding."

"So, the cameras are gone?" I asked.

"Looks like it. But the placement was consistent with the photos we saw."

"Any sense of when they might have been taken out?" I asked.

"Nah," Chief Willie said. "The wallpaper where the camera was was newer than the paper on either side, but I can't date it on sight. With a blackmail op, it's best to get your dirt and dismantle the hardware quick. It's illegal, so if the target gets curious and finds something, you're in deep moose turds."

"But the thing was in there long enough to get Rebound," I said.

"Chief Joe of Nez Perce say, 'Injun must keep thing in long enough to cause trouble,'" the Chief said, giving me a bawdy elbow. "Ah, who knows who knows what?"

．　．　．

Who knows who knows what? That's the question that kept my breath shallow. I had the goods on Rebound, and he didn't know it. My dirt pile on Easy Veasey was growing steadily higher, and I wasn't sure if he knew how much I knew. Veasey had showed up with Mr. Unruh looking eminently confident. I shuddered. I glanced in my rearview mirror as I drove back to Cowtown, expecting I was being followed. My instincts told me that Barri Embrey had more than a journalistic interest in the governor. I had suspicions about the sexual designs of Score the Helper on my wife. If I had my quick grope with Simone, why would it be impossible for Edie to have one with Score? And how arrogant would I be to assume that no one could possibly know the muck of my own history, a catalyst for my anxiety that I hadn't shared with Jerry Cohen? Was I so much more clever than everyone else? The Pine Barrens were filled with the bones of men who thought that way. Including one that I had killed.

My killing happened shortly after Mickey died. A young Philly gangster named Noel had approached me searching for Mickey's millions. I didn't have any of Mickey's money, but Noel didn't believe me. He stalked me throughout the summer following Mickey's death while I advised his boss, Mario Vanni. Noel was a new breed of gangster, the kind of man for whom killing was sport, not a by-product of business. He wanted the money, sure, but for a beast like Noel, the money was a dividend of murder, his life's work.

Noel would not relent. It was his stalking of Edie that bypassed my superego and plugged me into my own beast, the creature to whom I had always felt so superior. Noel had frightened Edie, but he hadn't hurt her. I lied and told him I had the money. Irv the Curve had a shotgun rigged in the trunk of a car, and when I arrived at a clearing in the pines where we were to retrieve Mickey's stash, the shotgun blasted Noel as he sat stunned in the passenger seat. But he lived. He lived, that is, until I made my way from the driver's seat to where he sat, and I fired into his head as he leaned forward to retrieve his gun. One of Irv's men who was hiding in the woods also fired at Noel at the same time I did. I don't know whose bullet killed him, but I know that I had pulled my own trigger, and had gone willingly to a place where I knew a life would end.

Irv's men disposed of Noel and the bloody car, using whatever industrial methods such men have used since bootlegging sprung from that iron-rich soil. Irv knew I had fired. My Uncle Blue, who was there, knew. Mickey's associate, Carvin' Marvin, also knew. Fuzzy Marino was there. And I am so slick a killer, so universally feared, that no one ever talked or speculated? How does anybody know who says what over a scotch in a casino bar?

So, now we're on the record. I've got a killing under my belt. The knowledge that I had a secret of my own that may or may not be known by others made me wonder what Rebound had been alluding to when he conveyed that someone may have something from way *back*. When your past comes looking for you and that past is rotten like a corpse, you unravel. You send signals the way Rebound was sending them. The wicked can read one another, and I recognized Rebound's external panic because it resembled my inner version. It was not hackneyed guilt as much as it was the fear of being discovered. I jotted down my seventh revelation on a grocery store receipt:

You're not as impressive as you think you are.

VISITING THE DEAD

"Later he saw moral dimensions."

GOV. EYES BIG BUSTS

In his alcove at the Alter Kocker Arms, Freon Leon sat reading an item in the *Probe*. The one-paragraph "article" by Barium Enema read as follows:

> Governor Gardner Rothman met with South Jersey sculptor Christian Josi to discuss creating a large bronze bust of himself for the state capitol. Josi, who recently created the bust of Julius Ceasar at Ceasar's World casino in Atlantic City, told the *Probe* that he was "honored to be considered to create a bust of a great man" like Rothman. Josi acknowledged taking the governor through his Princeton studio, where Rothman studied the famed sculptor's many works.

Jesus Hortense Christ. This, in a nutshell, was why Rebound needed me: perspective. The more desperate he felt, the more grandiose he became. There was no use confronting Rebound about how this had happened; after all, he'd lie. Currier, on the other hand, would feign simpatico with me before he lied, a nuance I couldn't stomach. I rubbed my temples, feeling a deep loathing for my chosen career. This was Barium Enema's warning shot that she was growing impatient.

I knocked on the door of Irv the Curve's apartment. He opened it, more hunched than he had been when we last met. He looked at me curiously. "Who the hell are you?" he said.

"It's the Ghost of Yom Kippur Past."

"So that's supposed to scare me?"

I shrugged my shoulders.

We took Irv's Cadillac and drove to Murray's. I told him about Simone, but left out my little obsession.

"So, Jonah, you're guarding this broad of Rothman's?"

"In a manner, I guess."

"You cutting yourself a slice?"

"No," I said, quickly well aware that I was exploiting Irv's vaguely worded question. Kissing isn't sex, no? Stay with the technicalities.

"But you're thinking about it."

"Okay, yes."

"Leave her to me, I'm single," Irv winked.

"You still open for business?"

"Ahhh!" he swatted.

We sat down in Murray's, and an orange-haired waitress whom I had always called Dollsy took our order.

"I don't know why it is that God gives me chances with women now, but not when I was twenty-one. Why does He make things happen in the opposite order?"

"To remind you that you're not God. I'll tell you a story. There was this guy we knew, Heshie Ripnick. Heshie checks himself into Caesar's and orders up a hooker for himself through some service. Whatever. Heshie gets his knock on the hotel room door, he opens it up. The hooker's his daughter."

"My God."

"It gets better. Heshie has a heart attack. He gets home after the hospital in a cab, and the locks on his house are changed, and his wife has divorce papers taped to the door. The daughter talked."

"Obviously. So what's the message?"

"Some guys aren't good at *shtuppery*. I'm not talking about the act even, what you put where, but the procedural aspects. Screw the morality, it's the logistics that always perplexed me. I suppose that's one reason why I never got married."

After lunch, Irv asked that we go to the cemetery to "visit" my parents and grandparents. We set a stone on their graves in the Jewish tradition. Irv scratched his nose and pulled me over to a collection of empty grave plots. He pointed to them and looked at me sternly. "This'll be me here. Over there is Sharky, that's Dukey, and down a few is Nooky."

"What about the rest of the Seven Dwarfs?"

Irv ignored my wise remark. "Don't think I'm thrilled about being so close to Nooky Mendelson. Very large nostrils he had. Could suck in a small child. Whenever some poor mother would be looking for her kid on the beach we'd all say under our breath, 'Look in Nooky's nose.' I knew him seventy years and he nearly drove me to drink. Can you imagine what he'll do to me in eternity?"

"No, I can't."

"Nooky's wife, Doris. Gorgeous! Once you looked at her you'd slit your wrists. A real vulnerable type. Nooky cheated on her, too, and with a real ug."

Irv ordered me to put a stone on Doris's grave marker, so I did. "What about one for Nooky?" I asked.

"He can get his own damned stone, inhale one with those nostrils of his. You know, Jonah, I always thought Doris had a thing for me."

"Did you ever act on it?" I asked.

"Are you kidding? Your grandfather was like a cardinal with that stuff. If you weren't married you could do your nonsense, but not with the wife of one of ours. He said it was bad for business, and he was right."

"Would he have killed you?"

"Mickey wasn't kill-happy. Very reluctant with the bullets. Not so much when he was young as when he got older," Irv said, as if a softening of attitude toward murder with age was commonplace. "Later he saw moral dimensions, I guess when he wasn't so desperate. In Prohibition, he took out a few. My old boss, Dutch Schultz, for one. Then he got older—

about your age—and the blood wasn't so cute anymore. How are things with Rothman?"

"I can barely tolerate being in the same room with him," I said. "Even when he's not saying anything, I'm sure it's a lie. Even though I know about the girl, and he knows I know, he still seems scared."

Irv sucked on his upper lip, which made him look like a bulldog. "It all comes out in the washroom."

"You mean in the wash?"

"Whatever. Now calm down with everything, especially this girl. Trust me, she's quicksand. You know what your grandfather taught me? He said the next best thing to having a talent is knowing that you don't have it."

"How did that come up?"

"In the old days when we were having trouble with the Dutchman, I got brave and said I'd take him out myself. Mickey laughed at me, and, you know, he wasn't a big laugher. He said I wasn't a muscle guy, and when I acted like one, I looked like a schmuck. He said I should know what I am and stay with that. As for you, Jonah, my advice is if you need something new, take up golf."

"You know, I actually thought about golf once a few years ago, but dropped it after I tried it."

"Why?"

"I figured I don't need another thing in my life to be bad at."

"Christ, you're a pill."

CLOSE SHAVE

"Norah had plans to parlay her internship into a career in sports marketing."

"It all comes out in the washroom." This is what Irv the Curve had said. He glared at me when he said it, too, as if it had been no mistake.

Rebound was not only angry and afraid, he appeared to be angry and afraid of *me*. My thoughts drifted back to the first time I ever met him. I replayed the experience. They were in the Golden Prospect's laundry. Rebound was leaning against a washing machine. The laundry room was in the Golden Prospect's basement. They did not want to be seen or heard, and wouldn't be against the hydraulic wail of the motor.

Secrecy made sense. Rebound was a public figure, a basketball star who had been making political noises. Mickey and Irv were gangsters. Perhaps they were cutting a deal to throw basketball games? While Mickey was morally capable of such a swindle, he was known for his honesty in gambling circles, which made game-rigging bad business.

Mickey had glared at me as soon as I peeked in the door, so I left.

I subscribed to the LexisNexis news service, which I could access from my laptop, and called up media coverage from the spring of 1980 using the words "Sixers" and/or "Rebound Rothman" as keywords. The Sixers had been doing pretty well. It would be hard to make a case that Rebound was throwing games for the mob. Besides, could one player really be relied upon to throw games? I considered that he may have had accomplices, but figured if they had had any incentive to come forward, they certainly would have done so during Rebound's rise in politics.

News reports indicated that Rebound would retire from basketball in July 1980. That would have been a month or two after I had seen him meeting with Mickey and Irv. I came upon a handful of reports about him doing promotional work, pumping hands at car dealerships, and other such indignities. In September 1980, Rebound became engaged to Marsha Pinkus and announced his bid for the Atlantic City council.

I sat at my desk in the attic and keyed in "article summary," which retrieved only the headlines of stories that ran in regional newspapers in the Delaware Valley in the spring of 1980. There were hundreds of articles, including some that were offbeat and entertaining:

- ROTHMAN TO APPEAR ON "LOVE BOAT" EPISODE
- SIXERS MANAGER ANGRY ABOUT WARPED PRACTICE COURT
- 76ERS MOURN "SUNNY SMILE" OF INTERN
- WILL ROTHMAN SLAM DUNK HIS WAY TO WHITE HOUSE?
- NBA INQUIRY ON POINT SHAVING
- DR. J DIAGNOSES REBOUND OVERRATED

It was the SUNNY SMILE headline that hit me. I called up the small article, which appeared in the *Philadelphia Bulletin* shortly after Memorial Day 1980. It read:

76ERS MOURN "SUNNY SMILE" OF INTERN

Friends and family came by the hundreds to bid farewell to Philadelphia 76ers travel office intern Norah Kelley, 18, who died last week of a cerebral hemorrhage. A wake for Kelley, who lived in Maple Shade, New Jersey, was held at the Queen of Heaven Catholic Church in Cherry Hill.

Father Thomas Dixon of Queen of Heaven remembered Norah's sunny smile. A marketing student at La Salle College, Norah had plans to parlay her internship into a career in sports marketing. Accompanying her parents, Arthur and Kay Kelley, and her older sister, Barbara, were 76ers general manager Burton Perkins and team members Tom Barrett and Danny Corr.

I printed out the article and read it over again, searching for Rebound's name. It wasn't there.

I called up the article on the point-shaving inquiry. It was short and insipid. It appeared to be a feud among a few players who were trying to get each other in trouble. I wrote down the names of the players involved, and conducted a more detailed search. Nothing. The investigation had either been intentionally quashed, or it disintegrated due to a lack of evidence.

I felt my heart gallop in my chest as I read the article about Norah Kelley yet again. I drove to Margate. The Rothmans were out of town. A lone state trooper was parked in the driveway. I waved to him, and told him I had to pick up an envelope that Rebound had left for me at his front door.

I knelt down and examined the sandblasted negative of the graffiti on the front steps. The "Hore" vandalism. The *H* in "Hore" could have conceivably been an *N*, depending on how I tilted my head. The connecting line in the letter slanted a bit from northwest to southeast, as opposed to the horizontal line in a well-executed *H*. The *e* at the end of the word was also ambiguous, a possible effect of spray-painting something quickly. The *e* could have been an *a*, the vandal spelling "Nora," either misspelling it or getting chased off before he could write the *h* at the end.

I passed the trooper, and told him that Rebound must have forgotten to leave the envelope, and drove slowly away, breathing very shallow.

I called Torch Wyeth: "Can you pull an Internet trick for me?"

A WAKE-UP CALL

"This is a sign that the people feel no one is above judgment."

Releasing a statewide poll on morality in New Jersey was like dropping self-defense manuals on France—a prank worth entertaining.

The front group we cooked up to sponsor the poll was called the Garden State Values Council. The Council was headed by a Pennington minister whose Main Street church would soon sprout a new addition, thanks to the generosity of the Howard and Sylvia Pinkus Foundation.

I didn't want the minister to hold a press conference announcing the poll because that could trigger pain-in-the-ass reporters asking too many questions (such as "Who paid?"), so I simply had him issue a news release with the important statistics. The results of the Values Council poll were counterintuitive: People throughout New Jersey were intensely concerned about morality. On the surface, given what I knew about Rebound's personal conduct, this could have been a bad thing—*if* Rebound's private life were to become public. So far, we had kept his affair(s) under lock and key, so we were all right. Among the poll's conclusions were:

- 82% thought that overall morality had declined since the last election
- 79% felt they would evaluate candidates for office on personal conduct

- 77% said a candidate's religious beliefs were relevant to consider
- 66% would not vote for a candidate who had committed adultery
- 71% wanted to hear more from the candidates about their moral codes
- Only 14% supported the statement "Voters should not be judgmental"

The poll was picked up by Delaware Valley wire services and ran in a sidebar in virtually every daily newspaper in the state. Television news teams in Philadelphia, Trenton, Newark, and New York showed the poll results on slick screen fonts. Digby Stahl battled before the cameras to declare the poll "a wake-up call for those who believe that what's good and what's right is alive in New Jersey." He thundered:

"Elizabeth and I have brought God back into our lives."
"We act tough in New Jersey, but under it all, this is a God-fearing state."
"We've gone too long without asking hard questions of our leaders."
"This is a sign that the people feel no one is above judgment."

That evening I studied the videotape I had recorded of Digby's give and take with the press in slow motion. As his geyser of goodness saturated New Jersey, Digby's eyes closed just a little, his eyelids fluttered, and his upper lip retracted as if he had just skidded in donkey snot.

Rebound, of course, did not know we were behind the poll and that his in-laws' foundation had paid for it, so he called me in a panic when he saw the reports.

"What the hell am I supposed to do, given . . . you know?"

"Don't do anything." I said.

"Don't do anything?" he repeated. "This Digby prick is all over the news acting like the Pope, for chrissakes!"

"Let him."

"Let him!?"

"Trust me. Let him."

The following morning an article in the *Probe* examined the growth of Swedish industry in New Jersey. Among the facts reported were the 18 percent rise in Swedish imports this year in the state (the reporter overlooked that Italian imports were up 23 percent) and the expansion of Ikea stores into a greater number of affluent suburbs. A map helpfully denoted the Ikeas with dots (old stores) and triangles (new ones). KBRO-TV news reported new incidents of Judge!-related vandalism at Saab and Volvo dealerships in Merchantville and Tenafly, New Jersey, suburbs of Philadelphia and New York City respectively. In Paramus, a high school homecoming bonfire was filled with ABBA records. A Newark-based news anchor opened his broadcast somberly with the bonfire behind him: "Tonight, there is an evil moon over Paramus."

OLD CRIMES

"Governor, did you know this girl?"

The E-mail to Lucas Currier that one of Torch's assets sent from a Kinko's in Trenton was entitled "76ers Intern Death Case Reopened." I had Torch use a private e-mail address for Currier that only a handful of people knew about. It was a risk, but not a huge one. The attachment purported to be from a Web site we fabricated entitled "New Jersey Old Crimes Report," and it read:

> Maple Shade cops reopening an investigation into the death of a former Philadelphia 76ers intern, Norah Kelley. Kelley died under mysterious circumstances in 1980, and been known to associate with team stars like Danny Corr and Rebound Rothman.

I had it sent in the evening so Currier would have the information in time to share the 76ers tidbit with Rebound at the following morning's briefing. But he wouldn't have time to check the pedigree of the information. Nyuk nyuk nyuk. I got to Morven early and sat on one of Rebound's sofas after lying to his secretary that I had been asked to attend. Rebound strode in looking like a Ralph Lauren advertisement, his hair choreographed to be windblown just so.

"I didn't know you were going to be here today," he said.

"I had a voice mail telling me to come," I fibbed. I shared with Rebound an innocuous bit of polling information, which I pretended was vital. Currier, true to form, entered and shared his daily 76ers suckup: "Hey, Governor, Jonah," he said cheerily, ignoring my invasion. We bantered about the day's headlines until Currier said: "Governor, did you know this girl who was with the 76ers, the one this investigation's about?"

"What girl, athlete?" he asked nonchalantly, fixing his tie.

"Let me look," Currier said, opening his leather portfolio. "Norah Kelley."

Rebound stopped fixing his tie. "Who is she?" he asked.

"She was an intern who died in 1980," Currier said.

I shrugged my shoulders. I was like LaTrina—*I don't know nuthin'.* "The only thing I remember from back then was a bunch of kids in school talking about a point-shaving scheme," I said.

"Aw, that was total bullshit," Rebound said, coming alive. "It was just a rumor by some mope who got cut." The governor laughed, buoying himself.

"That's all I remember," I echoed. "But I never heard of this girl," I said. "Does she ring a bell with you, Governor?"

Rebound scrunched up his face. "Not really," he said, his head facing neither Currier nor me. Then I saw it. The subtle gesture where he made his lips get small. The prune face. The lying face. "I read in one of the damned papers that Digby's saying something about my kids," Rebound said angrily. "You guys better be damned sure that he knows there's a price to pay for that kind of bullshit. I'm gonna go through that bastard like shit through a goose!"

Sure you are, General Patton. Currier's eyes met mine. He had that what-the-hell-just-happened look. He knew Rebound's cycles—when he felt besieged, testosterone flooded his brain. Digby Stahl had no more attacked Rebound's children than Juliet Rothman was Cher. Ironically, in this case, Rebound's diversion may have helped deliver the truth: the man had known Norah Kelley.

A THOUSAND GHOSTS

"I bet he's been talking to that old lady down the shore."

Maple Shade was a good name for the small South Jersey community where Norah Kelley had been raised. There were maples, and there was shade, and probably had been since the town was established in the late 1600s. There was also a Main Street that boasted something called the Little Red Schoolhouse. According to one sign on Main Street, a recent community cleanup had been sponsored by the "I Luv Maple Shade Committee," a message so thoroughly, well, nice that I felt guilty about setting foot there as a spy. The houses were modest, many of them having been built during the first half of the twentieth century.

The house where Norah's parents, Arthur and Kay Kelley, still lived was on Euclid Avenue, which ran parallel to Main Street. The Kelleys were retired schoolteachers. Their large white two-story colonial with blue shutters appeared to have been freshly painted, judging by the way the shiny paint clotted in grooves along the shingles. It was the largest house on the street. A greenhouse filled with plants jutted out on the right. Old trees hung weeping above the structure, a light October breeze occasionally dragging the leaves mournfully across the roof.

I considered for a moment whether or not the Kelleys could recognize me. I had my gray goatee, which made me appear very different from how I used to look when I did TV appearances. Just to be sure, I popped out my contact lenses and put on a pair of round wire-rimmed glasses. I checked myself out in the mirror, and thought I looked like a college professor. Who just happened to be carrying a .357 Magnum.

I rang the doorbell. Mrs. Kelley came to the door. She was an attractive woman in her mid- to late sixties. She had blonde hair pulled back into a short ponytail. She also had a dimple in her chin that offset her schoolmarm demeanor with a hint that she had once been popular with the boys, perhaps at a dance held long ago in one of the proper brick schoolhouses that dotted towns like this, places that were comfortable existing in the shadow of Philadelphia's skyscrapers.

"May I help you?" she asked.

"Are you Mrs. Kelley?"

"Yes."

"Mrs. Kelley, my name is Ben Siegel. Was your daughter Norah?"

A thousand ghosts that had been resting behind her eyes came dancing out in a swirl around her head.

"Yes, why?"

"I'm an independent private investigator. I saw an item in a state bulletin about your daughter. It suggested that there was an investigation of some kind into her death. I hadn't been aware of any investigation, and wanted to ask you if you knew anything about it."

"It was . . . twenty-five years ago."

"I know, I know. That's why I'm confused. I have the article. Would you like to see it?"

Mr. Kelley appeared at the door. He looked me over, and asked his wife what was going on.

"This man said he saw something about an investigation about Norah," Mrs. Kelley said.

"About Norah?"

"Yes, Mr. Kelley." I took out the fabricated Internet article about the reopening of the investigation. I handed it to them, but remained outside.

"Who do you work for again?" Mr. Kelley, a slim man with salt-and-pepper hair, asked.

"I'm independent, sir. My clients don't like me to give out their names, and I'll understand if you find this peculiar. It's just that my client is interested in this case, and was surprised that someone was looking into it."

Mr. Kelley handed the article back to me. "We never heard of any investigation. This was a lifetime ago."

"I know it was, sir."

Mr. Kelley shot me a death glare, and I totally understood it. It was time for me to find another way into this.

"I completely understand your reaction—"

"Who do you work for, anyway?" Mr. Kelley said.

"I'm sorry, sir, I can't divulge that."

"Do you have any identification?"

I was the one with the gun, but I was scared of this old man. Morality had a certain force to it, and subterfuge an inherent fragility.

"Let me check here," I said, fumbling around my pockets. "No, not in there," I laughed nervously. "I may have left my ID in the car."

"What kind of investigator does that?" Mr. Kelley said to his wife. "I bet he's been talking to that old lady down the shore . . . making what happened sound all sordid. Now you listen to me, fella—"

I thought of the scenario: I'd run. I'd take off. The Kelleys would take down my license number. I'd be identified. Barri Frigging Embrey would run an article about how the governor sent a goon to silence the parents of a dead girl. What would Irv the Curve do? Irv would be cool. Irv would know that folks are prone to suggestion, feel guilty about things they shouldn't feel guilty about. Nervous laughter looks like guilt. Running seals it. No, I'd do just what I did to LaTrina—I'd push back. *"The old lady down the shore"? "What happened sound all sordid"?* These were openings.

I pulled off my glasses and could hardly see the two figures in the doorway. I squinted at them. "What are you worried about, Mr. Kelley?"

Mr. Kelley stepped back.

"I asked you a question," I followed up. "You wanna get a squad car down here now, and we'll hash things out about the old lady down the shore, what you know and what I know, and see what comes out."

"You get the hell out of here!" Mr. Kelley seethed.

I stood flat-footed. I raised my hands and said, "That'll be all for now. I'll call you if I have some more questions."

I turned and walked away as the poor Kelleys slammed the door on me. I fired up my Porsche, hung a U-turn, and cruised down Euclid Avenue. As soon as I got to Main Street I hauled ass back down the shore.

What was that line from *Hamlet?* "By indirections find directions out." The Kelleys inadvertently told me something that I hadn't known before: Norah had probably died at the beach in circumstances her parents found repulsive. And there was an old lady who knew about it.

Chief Willie answered his cell phone. "Geronimo!"

"Yo, it's me. You were right about the parents' address," I said.

"How'd you do with them?" Chief Willie asked.

"Bad and good. They knew I was hinky, but they're hiding something."

"It's a bad memory for them, man. Can you blame them?"

"No, I guess not. But they did let something slip out." I told Chief Willie about Mr. Kelley's rant.

"I can dig around a little with shore cops," Chief Willie said.

"While you're at it, dig around on the parents."

"What, you're pissed off that they rattled you?"

"No, it's not that. These Brady Bunch types make me squirrelly."

"You think everybody's a thug underneath, is that it?"

"Something like that."

REGIME CHANGE

"I've been stalking other women."

Effective political operatives have a tendency to die young because they worry. *We* worry. *I* worry. Simone was a loose cannon rolling around the deck of the HMS *Rebound*, firing on hormones rather than strategy, and this didn't make for good electoral navigating.

On the subject of hormones, mine were mounting a regime change, and the target of the coup was my ever-weakening brain. Yes, I wanted to see Simone in order to protect my professional investment in Rebound, but there was a Y chromosome in overdrive.

As the winking Celebrity Motel sign came into view, I was conscious that my visit had the whiff of a grainy porn movie from the 1970s:

CANDI: Look, Bambi, the pollster's here.
BAMBI: But, Candi, we don't have money to pay him.
CANDI: He's kind of cute.
BAMBI: Maybe he'll give us his poll for free. (they giggle)
(Music: *Waa waa, chick-a waa waa*) . . .

"Hey, Jonah, where ya been?" Simone asked, her voice raspy as she opened the door to her room. She was wearing a warm-up suit, as if she needed warming up. Her features were so naturally magnificent that I wanted to throw myself over the edge of the balcony. It's strange the way beauty physically hurts. The pulse of Johnny Cash's "Personal Jesus" was still with me: "Things on your chest, you need to confess."

"I don't know how to tell you this, but I've been stalking other women."

Simone laughed. "Why are you standing all the way over there?"

Because I made out with you for a second, which was frigging idiotic.

"Are you up for lunch?"

The boardwalk wasn't desolate, but it was close. A handful of dazed gamblers milled about wondering why they had exercised their free will to visit the seashore in October.

"What's on your mind, Jonah?" Simone asked as we walked. She had changed into a denim shirt and black jeans, and wore a wool sports jacket on top. She had on a khaki-colored baseball cap and her Jackie O sunglasses.

We stood in line in a café inside the Golden Prospect. A troll of a man waddled in behind us and pretended to spy out the wait. I knew this ploy to move to the front of the line. It was the tactic perfected by New Yorkers who thought God had created lines for others. The little son of a bitch was hoping no one would notice. When he got to the front of the line, he turned around to give his wife a visual update on his progress, but remained standing at the front of the line. A Midwestern couple (so they appeared) actually backed off from the troll, assuming that he must have known something that they didn't.

Normally, I reserved confrontation for important matters, but my reservoir of testosterone was overflowing. Besides, I was carrying a .357 Magnum, which gave me the kind of synthetic confidence that fueled gun control advocates everywhere. I told Simone to excuse me, and approached the troll, who was attempting to appear inconspicuous.

I nodded at the Midwestern couple, who were curious about my movement.

"Sir," I said to the troll, conjuring up my best tombstone eyes, "these nice people were ahead of you."

"I was just—" the troll said.

"You were just what?" I said.

The troll's eyes hardened. It was the look of man who had gotten away with this stunt for a lifetime and who viscerally resented being caught.

"Who the hell do you think you are?" he asked me. I was feeling uncharacteristically fearless, aloft even.

"Get to the back of the line, please."

"Son of a bitch," he said in a way that suggested generic anger, as opposed to *me* being the son of a bitch. He waddled off, motioning for his wife to join him. My hate-laden eyes followed them.

"It's a trigger point with me," I told Simone. "I can't explain it."

She nodded in a way that made me feel in charge.

"Gardner said you worked for President Reagan a long time ago," Simone said, playing with her salad. Sunlight ricocheted off the boardwalk's metal railings and found a resting place in the center of Simone's sunglasses, which were perched atop her hairline.

"I wasn't that much older than you are now," I said.

"What was President Reagan's Secret Service code name?"

"Rawhide. Has Rebound picked out his Secret Service name yet?"

"Probably," Simone snorted. "He thinks about stuff like that. He probably gave himself a name like . . . Stallion." I wanted to agree with her, but held back. "He's totally obsessed with the election. His election. His career. I'm supposed to sit in that birdcage and wait for him to grace me with his . . . you know."

What I wanted to say was: *Women like you thrive on abysmal treatment,* but I had been ranting on this subject since I was a teenager, and had grown tired of it. I kept my comment insipid: "You never know what makes people tick."

I chose a spot on the horizon and fixed on it. "What's wrong?" Simone asked.

"I had an argument with my wife," I said, because it was the first thing that came into my mind.

"About what?" Simone asked, her lips budding into a pouting rosebud.

"My work habits. I don't know, she wants me to be more useful around the house. Like a workman. She resents my career."

"It's not easy supporting a family on one income," Simone said.

Simone understands me.

"No, Simone, it's not."

"If she had any idea what you go through in a day, she'd understand."

"Well, she doesn't have any idea. She's very sheltered."

"She has you to shelter her."

"I'm happy to provide the shelter."

"But you resent it."

"Maybe a little."

"Things build up inside until they explode out." Simone sucked her thumb.

"Maybe she has things building up inside her, too," I said, scaring myself.

I took Simone back to the Celebrity, where she went into the bathroom to brush her teeth. My God, she's brushing her teeth, I thought. She wants her breath to smell good. Why? Was *it* about to happen? A possibility that I hadn't considered before crept into my head like a fugitive: perhaps my marriage was over; after all, things between Edie and me had been awful lately. Tears sprung from my eyes without attendant sobs, and I wiped my face with my hands. Simone was still in the bathroom brushing. Calm. Calm.

Wait a minute, if Edie and I were through, why was I in tears? Why did I want to go home to my family? With Rebound, I was feeling nothing except a desire to not see him, and I sensed resignation in his eyes whenever he saw me. Perhaps this was what was over, Rebound and me. As a broad conclusion, I felt I could make this lesson number eight of this affair:

Sometimes you outgrow people. Sometimes they outgrow you.

I wrote it down on the back of a Celebrity postcard. I saw that a cassette had fallen behind the boom box on Simone's dresser. I picked it up. *America's Best Marches.* "Hail to the Chief" was among them. She hadn't been kidding.

I heard her fiddle with the bathroom door. It's time to leave, Jonah. Once she's near you, you're horizontal and you know it.

"Hey, Simone, I just got an important call. I'll be in touch."

THOSE LOVABLE KELLEYS

"It means Norah died in Atlantic County, down the shore."

"Well, Mongoose, when you're right, you're right," Chief Willie began. We were in a booth at Sack-o's Subs on Ventnor Avenue.

"About what?"

"About the parents. The Kelleys. They paid off the mortgage on their house at the end of 1980 and retired in their midforties."

"People can do that," I said, a little skeptical.

"Only if they've made brilliant investments or inherited big wampum, which they didn't, according to estate records. Just think about it. These people were only a little bit older than you are now. There was a God-awful recession in 1980, and these two teachers retired. Talk about hinky."

"What about Norah?"

"The death records are in Cape May Courthouse."

"What does that mean, Chief?"

"It means Norah died in Atlantic County, down the shore."

UPPER

"These events tap into the deepest fears that the powers of this state cannot be trusted to take care of a diversifying population."

I once lost a friend, Billy Pearl, when I referred to his neighborhood on the west side of Cherry Hill as a "nice middle-class place." Color dropped from his face like a curtain would if the rod had snapped from the wall. We were at Johnny's Pizza on Kings Highway, which was a few blocks from his house in the Kingston Estates on the west side of town. After I made my faux pas following a game of tennis at his high school, he had only one retort: "Upper."

By *upper*, Billy Pearl had meant *upper-middle-class*. To me, the term "middle-class" was a neutral one, as I considered myself to be a member of this orbital system, albeit in that brown dwarf of organized crime. Billy and I were in college at the time, and I suppose that sensitivities about where we fit into the great food chain of life ran high.

Billy Pearl's self-assessment, however, wasn't altogether insane. After all, Cherry Hill was considered a wealthy community in many circles. But there's a catch: while the east side of Cherry Hill was populated by the McMansions of suburban Philadelphia professionals, the west side of town where Billy lived was characterized by very pleasant developments—some called "estates"—that contained well-kept but considerably smaller houses.

I never imagined at the time that this evaporated friendship would provide any practical utility, but two decades later, it did.

Today marked the homecoming football game between Cherry Hill East, the true Uppers, and the Middles of Billy Pearl's Cherry Hill West. When Torch Wyeth asked me if I had any recommendations for a South Jersey town with hair-trigger class sensitivities, Cherry Hill was the first place to come to mind.

The streets running from Cherry Hill West's tennis courts down to Jonas Morris Stadium were lined with cars. The grilles of the west side's heavy American vehicles appeared to sniff the rear ends of the east side's BMWs and Mercedes, which were being driven without self-consciousness by children.

Tension between the very affluent and the somewhat affluent is a different species from conventional class warfare. With ghetto children versus suburban kids, the hostility was out the open. The poor kids conveyed contempt, and the rich kids conveyed fear or, if they were jocks, synthetic machismo. As the two Cherry Hills came together, the warfare was chilly, not shooting hot. A marching band was playing in the distance, and teenagers milled into the stadium wearing school colors (purple and white for West, red and white for East).

Halftime. Marching bands stood poised at opposite ends of the gridiron. The occasional fart of a trumpet echoed against the metal bleachers.

Before the marching bands could take the field, a solemn military *prrrupp-prrrupp* of a snare drum captured the passive ears of the marching band and audience alike. The schools' bands appeared especially confused when it became evident that the drumming did not come from either of them.

The beat grew louder until a collection of twenty beefy Nordic young men of approximate high school age wearing mostly red, the wealthy East colors, followed their drummer onto the field marching in perfect cadence. When they reached the fifty-yard line, two boys, one at the front of the formation and another at the back, hoisted posts that carried a large white sheet. Painted on the sheet in blood-red glossy paint was the simple word:

JUDGE!   .

What does a full stadium do with such a provocation? While the word and its exclamation point had taken on a special subtext in recent weeks, the initial response to it was puzzlement.

As the ambiguous spectacle made its way toward the twenty-yard line, Torch's plants within the East bleachers began to applaud, whoop, and wave the Swedish flag, which caused the rest of the stadium to assume that the muscular boys with the Judge! flag were somehow tied to East. This, in turn, chafed the raw nerves of the West crowd, which began to boo. The thousands on hand knew neither why they were cheering nor why they were booing. Nevertheless, the spectacle was sufficiently optical that KBRO-TV shot it.

Later that day, King Carl XVI Gustaf of Sweden attempted to dedicate an Ikea in Secaucus, but the event was cancelled when his motorcade was pelted with Swedish meatballs. I saw on the television at a sports-themed restaurant in Cherry Hill someone fleetingly waving a placard painted with a red swastika and circle with a slash through it. The sensation of a ball-peen hammer struck me in the chest. I fumbled for my cell phone to call Torch. He wasn't in his office, and his cell phone didn't answer. I left him a frantic message. This was the goddamned problem with these campaigns—you couldn't control the path of the hurricane. Despite the technicality that the protestor was opposing Nazism, the swastika in any format was too damned charged. Never mind the historical technicality that the Swedes were *anti*-Nazi. Pray, Jonah.

I remained at the bar nursing a parade of club sodas and watching the coverage. Throughout the day, a rash of vandalism erupted throughout New Jersey, the familiar Judge! symbol appearing on shopping malls, places of worship, turnpike overpasses, courthouses and strategically located sidewalks (usually within a block of media outlets, thereby assuring coverage). "Smell My Volvo" was one of the more memorable works of painted literature. The Newark Police Department had to mobilize reinforcements when the city's already riot-prone population gazed skyward and were stabbed by a giant searchlight with the Judge! symbol beamed in blood red into the heavens. My cell phone rang. I answered it, running outside. Torch.

"God, no swastikas!" I said.

"What are you talking about?"

"I saw a guy waving a banner with a swastika and a slash going through it."

"Are you serious?"

"Yes!"

"But it had a slash going through it, right?"

"Yeah, but no swastikas! Not with slashes, nowhere, nohow. We want resentment, not genocide. And we don't want people thinking"—careful, Jonah, you're on a mobile line—"that people from . . . that country are Nazis! That ratchets the emotion up too fucking high!"

"Shit, I'll move on it."

The following morning, an editorial in the *Star-Ledger* ran with a piece called SAAB STORY, which attempted to examine the anti-Swedish sentiment with chin-scratching insight:

> What could this all possibly mean? Is it a reminder that New Jerseyans are being judged, and if so, by whom? Is the graffiti the work of supporters of gubernatorial candidate Judge Digby Stahl, who has always mused about his Swedish roots, or a protest against him? Is the vandalism a reaction to the recently reported growth of Swedish industry in the state? New Jersey has experienced a menu of intolerance in its history, but anti-Swedish sentiment is a first. That the behavior falls more into the category of chillingly comic than it does obviously malignant is all the reason for us to examine its origins.

The broadcast media was alight with trauma specialists, psychologists, "tolerance counselors," and urban legend authorities who attempted to put the weirdness into an explainable context. Some of the highest-profile pundits Torch and I could find offered assessments of the vandalism and ensuing unrest.

Rutgers sociology professor Diane Moody said on KBRO-TV: "New Jersey has always been a melting pot, and it appears that people believe there are dark forces that aren't too keen on any more melting."

Trenton psychiatrist Tom Marsh was quoted in the *Star-Ledger*: These events tap into the deepest fears that the powers of this state cannot be trusted to take care of a diversifying population. These anxieties seem to be personified in the form of Judge Stahl for some reason."

Sister Debra Hamilton of the Newark Diocese observed on the most popular drive-time radio program in North Jersey: "Those who attempt to use differences of faith and ethnicity to disrupt will ultimately find that it's our differences of faith and ethnicity that unite."

The events that followed the emergence of the vandalism weren't riots as much as they were intense protests against the influx of Swedish products into the region, which, of course, were said to be costing New Jerseyans jobs. There was no mention made of the guy who carried the swastika/slash placard. Thank God. How does an organizer of such skullduggery straddle the line between rowdiness and madness? The answer lies in the oldest phenomenon of New Jersey politics, "walking-around money."

Torch Wyeth's cash, liberally distributed to various ministers, priests, and rabbis, was sufficient to bring out vocal protestors who were compensated to get rowdy, but not too rowdy. After my reaming, Torch put the word out to throttle back. A quick call to the local media announcing the (convenient) location of a given protest was enough to convey the impression of a vast grassroots movement deeply concerned about the Judge! graffiti and all that it implied about the state's hypersensitive residents. One individual in each harassment cell was designated media spokesperson.

Jim McCarthy, an Irish contractor from Tenafly, said: "Now Judge Stahl knows what we think about his moral superiority."

Jane Mulcahy, an insurance saleswoman from New Brunswick,

huffed: "I don't approve of vandalism, but we don't like people talking down to us. I'm tired of hearing about Judge Stahl's great morals."

Bruce Ochsman, a store owner from Deptford, said: "I used to be a Democrat, but under the veneer, Stahl is made from the same stuff as the Republicans he has dinner with when the cameras aren't rolling."

GRACE UNDER PRESSURE

"When the going gets tough, Rebound's gone."

"Jesus God. Jesus God. Jesus God," Rebound shouted as I walked into the study off of his office in Morven. He was standing in front of the TV.

"What is it?" I asked, feigning utter calm.

Rebound winged his *InStyle* magazine featuring the legally mandated cover shot of Jennifer Aniston at me. The spine of the thick book hit my chest and hurt. For a nanosecond, I wished I had kissed Simone longer.

"What is it?" Rebound shouted. "Look!"

I glanced down at *InStyle* and read the headline: "JENNIFER ANISTON IS LOOKING GOOD ON TOP OF THE WORLD," I read.

"Not that, the TV, the vandalism!"

I nodded at the TV. "At least things are going well for Jennifer Aniston."

"Goddamn you, Jonah, look at this mess! Look at what you've done."

"Right on schedule."

"What the hell is going on?" Rebound demanded.

"There are protests in Cherry Hill. I suppose it's a reaction to Digby's being a judge and snotty."

"Lucas told me one guy had a swastika banner!"

"It was an anti-Nazi thing, not pro-Nazi."

"This thing can spin into disaster if you don't get your shit together!" Then he added, "I don't know what's going on!"

Rebound was partly right, but I couldn't validate his panic. I treated his concern as if he were just operating in one of his three staff modes: Evasion, Accusation, and Ignorance. Today, we'd begin with Ignorance.

"You wanted Digby stopped," I said.

"Of course, he's challenging me. But all these people," Rebound said, pointing to the screen. "Everybody's upset and rioting."

"They're protests, not riots. People get that way when they feel someone who dislikes them may be elected to the Senate. It's your job to reassure them now."

"Don't talk down to me," Rebound snapped. "What the hell have you been up to?"

"I've been putting the program in place to get you elected."

"While you're out spray-painting the state, I've got a country to run," Rebound said, gritting his teeth and holding his hands aloft like Yul Brynner in *The King and I*. His eyes swirled red and yellow. He began pacing the room, furiously stopping to evaluate each potential exit. The door to the garden was no good because there was a tour going on. The passageway to his office wasn't an option because his environmental staff was waiting for him. Then there was the bathroom. He stopped and considered it. Now there was an option—sitting down on His throne and heaving out a few mandates.

"*What?*" I asked. A *country* to run?

"These people need me," Rebound said.

Rebound took in a few more minutes of the news report. The Cherry Hill stadium stunt was on now. Lucas Currier entered. Rebound pointed at Currier, then at the screen, and uttered this twitter: "As governor of this state, you better be damned sure this is taken care of," Rebound thundered. He had just graduated from Ignorance to Accusation.

"Absolutely," Currier sucked.

"Governor," I said. "The point is that *you* be the one to take care of this."

"You and your genius schemes. When I get back from my swim, you had better damned well have dealt with this." And now we had reached our trifecta at Evasion. Protests engulfed the state and Rebound was going to stick his head underwater.

At what point in a man's life does he stop holding his tongue? At what point do the dividends of silence dry up, and his fear of The Consequences subside? What were The Consequences, anyway? No clients, and no ticket back to Washington, that's what. I felt myself aging.

Or was it something deeper with me? Was there something in my character that needed this and begged to be accused of letting Rebound down?

It is 1977. I get a B- in chemistry this semester in high school. Mickey, under indictment for a labor shakedown, barks at me. "So much for the Ivy League," he says. "Fine, sell beach umbrellas in Pleasantville." I am failing him. I am failing my dead parents. My B- isn't for a lack of trying; I'm awful at science. I look at the periodic chart of the elements and see a kaleidoscope of boron and manganese conspiring against me. There is no correlation between input in and output out, effort and achievement. I have hit the limits of my competence. I run as if the Cossacks are on my heels and make honors grades in my English and history classes, the "artsy-fartsy" classes, as Mickey calls them, as if I had taken to wearing dresses. The semesters steamroll on, and eventually the letter comes from Dartmouth. I'm in. "Look at the big genius," Mickey claps. "Don't forget your beat up old Pop-Pop now that you'll be with the cream-dealer-cream . . ."

"How long are you going to deny that you're the governor?" I asked.

Currier's jaw dropped open.

"I am the governor," Rebound said.

"You keep saying that as if you're not sure," I said.

"How many times do I have to remind you that I'm the governor?"

"Me? None," I said. "I know you're the governor. You know what your staff says: 'When the going gets tough, Rebound's gone.'"

"That's enough, Jonah," Currier said.

"And what will you advise Rebound, Lucas?" I asked.

"This isn't about me," Currier pointed.

"Exactly," I said. "The question on the table is, what is it about?"

"It's about getting out of this fucking jam," Currier said. "It's about leadership!"

Rebound stood up straight.

"Well," I said. "Let's go with that. It's interesting that every discussion we have about leadership begins and ends with some petty infraction committed by yours truly. I know how united you must feel, but we've got protests breaking out."

"Protests that you caused," Rebound said.

"Yes, right after I shot JFK. Now, Governor," I said, "how shall we quell these protests?"

"The people have to calm the hell down," Rebound said.

"Exactly. It should have never gotten to this. The people of New Jersey, despite divergent backgrounds, have always managed to make things work. They need a leader now, Governor. They need you to remind them that their pain is genuine, but that not even you, who benefits from the outrage against Digby, wanted it to come to this.

"Here is a speech I prepared. There is a recording studio in Trenton waiting. You can lay it down there. There's not a station in the state that won't run it. Lucas, alert the press that the governor will speak on radio at noon."

"Radio? Why not television?" Currier asked.

"Because when the governor is stressed, or speaking about something he's not comfortable with, it shows in his face and it upsets people," I confessed.

"That is not true!" Rebound bellowed. "I'm a very visual governor."

Screw it. "Not when you open your mouth. We can't have that."

"I do not lie!" Rebound shouted.

"This doesn't come through on radio?" Currier asked, ignoring Rebound.

"You believe *him?*" Rebound pressed.

Currier didn't answer. Instead, his eyes queried for my answer.

"Lucas, it doesn't convey in audio," I said.

"Which is why you've been keeping him away from TV on touchy speeches," Currier said, his jaw slack.

"That's right. But," I continued as if Rebound wasn't there, "he works well in still photos, which is why when he leaves the studio, a bunch of kids from Lawrenceville Progressive Elementary will hug him on the steps."

"You think I'm a liar, Jonah, don't you?" Rebound seethed.

"I think you have a veracity disability. You need to get familiar with this speech and get over to the studio right away if you want to win this election. Tomorrow, you'll *tape* a talk at an elementary school, but we'll get to send the version *we* like out."

Rebound's lips parted as if to insult me again, but I cut it off, deftly, I thought, with another pitch to Rebound's ego: "Lucas, a motorcycle escort—like the ones the Secret Service do for the president—would be appropriate. The more motorcycles the better."

"Right," Currier said. "But Jonah, how will we know if this worked?"

"Because the world will have declared one of the first great acts of peace in the twenty-first century."

"The *world?*" Rebound inquired.

"When the world applauds you," I said, "New Jersey will follow."

"Why will the world applaud me?" Rebound asked, calmer.

"Because of an award you'll be getting in Sweden next week."

"Sweden?" Rebound asked.

"Let's survive today first. Then we'll worry about Sweden. And by the way, I'm still out that twenty-five grand I personally paid to one of our operatives."

"We'll take care of it," Currier said.

A CURSED LITTLE HOUSE

"How many stories do houses like this inspire?"

"Here's the deal," Chief Willie began on the boardwalk. "I don't know much about any Whitey Leeds yet because I've been boring down on Miss Jugs Harbor Township, but a Leeds family does own some rural property. I'll keep digging. I did find out that our buddy Easy Veasey was a registered lobbyist for the Southern New Jersey Agricultural Disposal Cooperative in the eighties. It's a trade group that deals with farm waste disposal."

"My first career choice, but I flunked Goat Shit 101 in grad school."

"That's too bad, Mongoose. Some things they don't teach you in the Ivy League. See where I'm going with this, or do I have to rub some sticks together and light your ass on fire?"

"I get it. Veasey has some knowledge of how inconvenient problems are disposed of."

"Right. Some legislation was passed in the late eighties that liberalized how farm waste could be ditched. Since Veasey was the lobbyist, he'd probably know that the farmers wanted to save money on disposal by getting rid of stuff however was easiest. That would mean he could be familiar with how pigs could be used to eat through dead farm animals if nobody was looking."

"Which means Veasey might know Whitey Leeds."

"It's a good leap to make. You know Veasey ran cockfights, didn't you?"

"Yes, I knew that."

"Another hint that he knows the farm world. Now, Mongoose, before you go and see your little Ms. Lava, you want to see the house she grew up in?"

"Sure."

Chief Willie flipped me a photo of the most average of little houses, a ranch in Little Egg Harbor Township. It was gray with green shutters. It appeared pinkish in the sunlight, and I thought of that John Mellencamp song "Little Pink Houses": "There's winners and there's losers, but that ain't no big deal . . ." There was a carport on the right side of the house, and a picture window near the entryway, which presumably fronted a living room. Whoever first bought the structure had been proud; after all, home ownership was a shibboleth of arrival. Still, it was a cursed little house, I thought, not in that there was anything demonically wrong with it, but in its ordinariness. It was the kind of house you drive by or fly over a million times, remarking neither on its beauty nor its horror. It would never dawn on a person that anything at all went on inside such a place. How many stories do houses like these inspire? I didn't know, but I strongly suspected that such dwellings somehow connected the arcs of all my players.

THE WALL OF CHILDREN

"Eloquent in its simplicity."

Rebound sat on a chair at the head of the fifth-grade classroom at the Joyce Kilmer Elementary School on Chapel Avenue, which was a mile from Cherry Hill West where Torch Wyeth's Judge!-offensive had taken place two days before. Sitting behind the governor was a collection of beautiful children sitting on risers, as if the events of the past few days had been about some fanatical strain of evil sponsored by a foreign antichild terror cell.

The child prop was necessary because it allowed Rebound to take a defiant position that no one could quarrel with—that bigotry, judgmentalism, child molestation, chemical warfare, snot, whatever—must be confronted, and that Governor Gardner Rothman, candidate for the United States Senate, was just the leader to do it. A subject matter such as riot-quelling was also sufficiently unequivocal that I did not fear Rebound's lying facial tick betraying him: it was safe to assume that he truly *was* antiriot. The speech had to be sufficiently vague that everyone who heard it, from the three *I*s to New Jersey's befuddled Swedes, would think it was addressed to them.

No media were allowed in the classroom save our own camera crew.

With the wall of children behind him, the governor read our short state-ment in a soft voice into the TelePrompTers that were set up around the room to make it look as if he were imparting a bedtime fable to a class-room filled with children.

When you are young, you want people to be perfect. When you grow older, you find out they are not. When you do, you face a choice. Do you love people for who they are, or do you judge them to be less than you are because they are not perfect? We all think we are perfect for a long time, and gradually we find out we are not. Most people are doing their best. If they succeed, it's because they tried their best. But if they fail, it's not always because they weren't trying, or because someone else hurt them, it's because sometimes there was something invisible standing in their way. We can't always see what that barrier is, but we know that good people don't judge without knowing the answers, and that answers don't come by judging, they come by questioning.

When the taping was done, we transmitted Rebound's talk via satel-lite to broadcast media throughout the region. A teary-eyed school-teacher who had witnessed the talk commented for local media outside the school. "It was just what the children needed to hear in these turbu-lent times," Miss Byer said.

As Rebound's motorcade made its way slowly down Kings Highway, toward Route 70, the street was lined with grownups streaming from the office buildings and children trailing their teachers from the Cherry Hill Library. The large Chevy Suburban stopped in front of the library, and the crowd whooped when the rear door of the vehicle opened. Two po-lice cars swiftly pulled between the Suburban and the curb, the officers climbing out as Governor Rothman's size-thirteen Allen Edmonds shoe hit the blacktop. Onlookers grinned the grin of the starstruck as Rebound pumped random hands on the curb. He took special care not to miss any of the children. An orchestra of cameras popped and flashed until the late autumn air was a symphony of clicks and claps. We then had him stop at an Ikea and buy lawn chairs in order to pacify a shell group Torch formed at the last minute, Swedes for Peace in the Garden State, or SPIGS. As the acting chairman of SPIGS, Norbert Svensen denied to a reporter that the acronym of his group was a veiled anti-Hispanic slur, Rebound thundered before a gaggle of adoring Ikea employees his campaign's core civil rights message: "As long as I'm representing New Jersey, a person of any race, religion, or nationality can shop at Ikea whenever they darned well please!"

One of the best ways to position a situation as having been masterfully handled is to create the situation, then place pundits in the media to declare that its handling has been masterful. Which is why:

A professor of political science at Temple University called Rebound's Joyce Kilmer talk "masterful."

A lecturer at Rutgers said it was "poignant."

Graduate students at Princeton declared it "Kennedyesque."

A Democrat who owed me a favor said it was "eloquent in its simplicity."

The director of the Swedish Historical Society proclaimed it "A study in tolerance."

REBOUND THE SUN KING

"The light just loves the guy."

In response to Rebound's Joyce Kilmer speech and his quelling of the
protests, Digby Stahl did what any politician whose opponent was enjoy-
ing a fresh bounce would do: he wormishly attempted to disassociate
himself from his own earlier rhetoric, which was hard to do, considering
that the media were relentlessly juxtaposing his preriot judgmentalism
with his postriot tolerance. Now Digby, against the montage of protests
and the loaded word *Judge!* cancanning across television screens like
Third Reich chorus girls, was hocking up desperate chestnuts such as:

- "Nothing could be less moral than the passing of judgment in the absence of knowledge."
- "There is nothing more despicable than intolerance based on race, religion, or antique notions of social class."

I thought a campaign-season advertisement would nicely bolster our
ethnically sensitive imagery and further marginalize Digby Stahl. We
filmed the ad at an elementary school playground in Atlantic City on a
chilly late-October Thursday morning. The backdrop was visibly inner

city: a cracked asphalt basketball court with a backboard net made of chains; apartment buildings along the horizon and car horns in the distance reminding civilization that somebody had important places to be. Most of the children were black. Some were Hispanic, but a few were white. There was an even mixture of boys and girls.

When Rebound's Chevy Suburban pulled up behind a New Jersey state trooper's squad car shining impossibly bright, the children lined up on the court like pastel idols on a game board. Their eyes and mouths widened in wonderment when Rebound stepped from the vehicle, glowing in the warm local applause. *What must one achieve to travel in something so bright,* they wondered?

Rebound wore jeans and a 76ers T-shirt beneath his beloved bomber jacket. For some reason, he brought Dude, who slipped from the Suburban, reddish like a placenta. A dozen children, fourth-graders mostly, swarmed Rebound, who budded at the enthusiastic assault. When the cameras were operational, Rebound shed his bomber jacket to the applause of a gathering throng. With a high school kind of authority I hadn't been witness to in decades, Rebound divided up the boys and girls into two teams. He would play a few rounds on one team, and then switch to the other. Dude would be on one of the teams.

With two shoulder-mounted cameras following his every move, Rebound proceeded to miss most of the shots he fired. This was purposeful. He wanted the children to do better than he did, which, of course, they did. Rebound held his breath at his own failed arcs and feigned disappointment when the opposing team sank one.

Lucas Currier stood on the sideline and surrendered an admiring nod. In the most gorgeous moment of filming, Dude took a shot and Rebound, perhaps on purpose, lost his balance and fell back onto the asphalt as he attempted to block it. A Hispanic boy and a hauntingly beautiful mocha-skinned girl collapsed onto the governor. These fluid falls were greeted with cheers from onlookers, and a tender administration of noogies by Rebound to the Hispanic boy. The laughter was universal, and Rebound's conducting of the events confused me because no man can conjure such a scene from nothing. Without uttering a statement of policy or issue position, Rebound was the catalyst for this jumble of tiny humanity, which brought a reluctant sun from behind a cradle-shaped cumulus cloud. I declared victory to myself until Dude Rothman slinked into my line of vision. Dude, catching his breath from a recent sprint, lingered against a rusted chain-link fence, as expressionless as a knight as he watched his father's teeth glint while a handful of urban urchins secured a coveted sliver of Rebound Rothman. Dude's brown beagle eyes appeared to be asking what he did wrong. As he lingered alone, the advertising director tapped me on the shoulder, pointed to Rebound, and quipped, "The light just loves the guy."

When the filming was over, we retreated to an editing studio where we laid down the footage to Three Dog Night's early 1970s hit "Black and White."

A newly nervous Currier looked over my shoulder at the television monitor and remarked, "The Irish and Italians may not like it."

"True, but they won't publicly oppose it, now, will they?"

Currier, no political neophyte, had no choice but to bite his upper lip in concession. I took this opportunity to remind him yet again that I hadn't been reimbursed for Torch Wyeth's work, and owed Race Card Strategies another twenty-five grand. "Geez, I'm sorry," Currier said. "We'll cut you the whole thing tomorrow."

DISPOSITION

"How long does it take until a death certificate is issued?"

Chief Willie Thundercloud paid the Atlantic County Office of Vital Records a visit in search of Norah Kelley. He had been to Vital Records many times over the years, and like any good investigator, had his sources. Chief Willie had called ahead to let his contact there, Penny Solomon, know he was coming in. Penny was in her early thirties and conveyed the impression that she had just returned from Woodstock. Which would have been impossible because she hadn't been born until a decade later.

"Greetings, Sacajawea," Chief Willie said, handing Penny flowers.

"Aren't you far out?" said Penny. "What are you looking for, Big Feather?"

"Squaw. Norah Kelley. Young woman who died in the spring of 1980."

"How sad. Suspicious circumstances?"

"I think so, Penny, but I'm hoping you can shed some light."

"There's a sitting room with Atlantic County history down the hall."

"Our little love nest."

"Oh, Chief Willie . . . wait there, and I'll be back down in a few."

Penny returned fifteen minutes later with a folder containing a dozen or so papers of white, pink, green, and yellow. The forms one must fill out to die, Chief Willie thought. She handed them to him, pivoted, and returned upstairs.

Norah Kelley, age twenty, had died on May 12, 1980, in a home on Buffalo Avenue in Ventnor. The cause was listed as being a cerebral hemorrhage, consistent with the news reports we had read. An autopsy confirming the cause of death had taken place at Atlantic City General Hospital on May 13.

Chief Willie flipped further back in the file. A copy of the death certificate was in there. It had been signed by the Atlantic County coroner on June 16. June 16? That was more than a month after Norah died. That was unusual. Chief Willie summoned Penny.

"What is it, Chief Willie?" Penny asked.

"When somebody dies, how long does it take until a death certificate is issued?"

"Within a day or two. You need it for burial."

"Is there anything in here that indicates where Norah was buried?"

Penny took the file and rested it against a windowpane. She flipped to a section toward the back of the file and pointed to a lined box that read "Disposition."

"She wasn't buried, Chief. She was cremated. See this box that was checked?"

Chief Willie took back the file and studied the next few pages. Finding nothing else striking, he sat back down on a hard wooden chair, the kind that is designed to get you to stand up and leave as soon as possible.

"What's bothering you?" Penny asked.

"Help me here," Chief Willie said. "If you wanted a young woman to die, and you wanted it to look like an accident, a cerebral hemorrhage is as good as anything, right?"

"Or car accident."

"Not if you die in an house in Ventnor."

Chief Willie took a few notes and returned the file to Penny, slipping four fifty-dollar bills inside the folder. He then headed to Cowtown, where the two of us stood against the fence of the corral.

Chief Willie began to reason the whole thing through out loud: "You've been thinking about when you first met Rebound. You dig some more and you find that a young intern died in 1980, around the same time Rebound met Mickey and Irv. The girl dies of a cerebral hemorrhage. But the death certificate is filed a month later, which is unusual. Time enough for somebody to tamper with it after the fact. Why would you tamper with it? To change the cause of death. What about the body? Cremated. Also convenient."

"Or, Chief, maybe we're dreaming. What's the theory here, Rebound is a killer? That's a big leap from being a conceited bastard. He was a basketball star in the late seventies. He got engaged to Marsha in September 1980, but he'd been seeing her before then. Assuming he cheated on her, he could always lie. He didn't have to kill Norah," I said, "assuming he even knew her."

"He knew her, Jonah—stay with that—but why *would* he kill her?"

"I don't know, maybe it could have been one of those rough sex deals where something got out of hand. Terrible accident, stuff like that."

"But, Mongoose, why the death certificate mischief, why the cremation?"

"Maybe she wanted to be cremated. I think maybe we're turning a politically embarrassing boff session into a homicide."

"Maybe we are, Mongoose, but what if we're not?"

"Give me a theory, Chief Willie."

"Fine. In short . . . four words: Squaw got in way. Rebound feels responsible for that girl's death. Maybe it was an accident. Maybe it wasn't. He was involved with Norah. He was starting out in politics and he had her killed because she was getting in the way somehow. He went to the boys for help."

"Jesus. I'm not naïve about my grandfather, but killing some girl—"

"I know, I know—"

"Where's the address of the place in Ventnor where she died?"

Chief Willie handed me his notes. "I was going to check it out."

"See what you can find out about who owned the house back then. You've got the name of the coroner who signed the death certificate?"

"Yeah. O'Rourke."

"See if you can find out anything about him. Would he have been the kind of guy who would be inclined to reach the conclusions of his sponsors?"

PAY NO ATTENTION TO THE MAN
BEHIND THE CURTAIN

*"Sometimes I hear you say things to the governor on the phone
and then he says them on TV."*

Ricky and Lily sat on either side of me. *The Wizard of Oz* was on a cable channel. I hadn't seen the film in years, but remembered thinking it was scary, with the flying monkeys, the house landing on the Wicked Witch, and her green wart-laden sister melting into snot.

Lily's chipmunk voice asked, "Is this real?" The wizard's massive head smoked up the screen. The dog, Toto, opened the curtain to reveal the tiny old man working the levers that controlled the grand optics of the Wizard of Oz.

"Pay no attention to the man behind the curtain," the old man thundered.

I thought about answering in the negative—*"No, Lily, nothing like this could ever happen"*—but I didn't want her psychic foundation to be built on lies the way mine had been. *Pop Pop Mickey makes saltwater taffy, Jonah, and the police don't like him because of his religion . . ."*

"There's no such thing as men with big green heads," I said, which made her laugh. "But there are men who nobody knows who work behind curtains to . . . make movies and make it *seem* like there are men with big green heads."

"Sometimes I hear you say things to the governor on the phone and then he says them on TV," Ricky said.

"Well, yes, I'm kind of like the little man behind the curtain," I acknowledged.

"Can you make smoke?" Lily asked.

THE HOUSE ON BUFFALO AVENUE

"Who are you looking for?"

Chief Willie found out that the woman who had owned the Buffalo Avenue house where Norah Kelley died still owned it. Her name was Hannah Byrd, and according to Atlantic County tax records, she was seventy-six years old. She no longer rented out the ground-floor apartment where Norah had lived and died.

Hannah Byrd answered her front door, which I reached by climbing twelve wooden steps. She was a mild blue-haired woman with a hawk nose and little untrusting eyes that looked like accidents behind large red glasses. She wore a warm-up suit, the kind elderly people do because they are comfortable, not because they are warming up for anything.

"Yes?" she said.

"Mrs. Byrd, my name is Jonah Eastman. I am a pollster who is working on the upcoming elections. I was hoping that you would be nice enough to take a few moments to speak with me."

"I don't know about politics," she said.

"You don't need to, Mrs. Byrd. This isn't an official visit. I'm trying to learn about someone who used to live here."

Mrs. Byrd's eyes darted around like minnows.

"Who are you looking for?" she asked, still not opening the door much.

"I'm looking for Norah Kelley."

Mrs. Byrd's eyes stopped zipping around, the minnows frozen in an ancient winter pond.

"That was a sad story, Mr. Eastman. It was long ago."

"I'm not trying to hurt you. I'm not a reporter or anything."

"Then what do you want to know about her for?"

"You may have a hard time believing this, but I'm trying to understand what happened because it may relate to some people that I know, including her family. May I come in? Or if you'd feel more comfortable, you are welcome to walk with me outside."

"I've seen you before," she said.

"I'm on TV sometimes. I'm in politics. I also grew up around here." Time to whip out the big gun, the one that would make her reticent to slam the door on me. "You may remember my grandfather. Mickey Price."

"I didn't know him," she said. "I didn't believe everything I heard."

"You probably should have," I said with a vulnerable smirk.

Mrs. Byrd returned my smirk, and she opened the door wider. It was good to know that Mickey's name still had that effect on people.

Her house was furnished in *All in the Family* colonial. The carpeting was deep and the sofas were flowered. They had probably always been old. When my eyes rose, I noticed them: there were birdcages all around, but there were no birds inside them.

"Look at all of these birdcages," I said.

"Oh, yes, I collect them," Mrs. Byrd said. "Because of my name. Byrd. My late husband, Walter, thought it was our trademark."

"I see. You don't have any birds?"

"I used to. It became too much of a hassle to take care of them when I went away. Sometimes I go on cruises with my sister. She lives in Blackwood."

"Oh, Blackwood. Sure."

Mrs. Byrd gestured for me to sit down on one of her sofas. I sat and felt as if I might sink down to Beijing.

"Norah. I found her, you know. A beautiful girl."

"I didn't know that you found her. That must have been horrible."

"Walter had died the year before. I felt like God was ganging up on me."

"I lost both of my parents a few years before that, and had to live with my grandparents. We were chased all over the world by the cops. Sounds like it was a nasty time for both of us."

"Poor thing, yeah."

"Did Norah like your birds?"

"She was crazy about the birds. I let her take some of the birdcages down to her studio."

"I'm sorry to ask this, but when you found her, Mrs. Byrd, where was she?"

Mrs. Byrd sighed. She looked upward, presumably for divine guidance. God didn't answer. "Her radio was on. It was always on. She was lying down between two of the bigger birdcages. Like she was crawling out."

"Did Norah have a roommate?"

"She had a sister who stayed with her sometimes. She stayed with Norah on the weekends, but had a job in Trenton or somewheres. The place is too small to rent it out to more than one person full time. I stopped renting it a few years ago. Too much hassle. You know how kids are today."

"Kids could be pretty rowdy in 1980, Mrs. Byrd. I was one of 'em."

"Oh yes, but nothing like today."

"Was Norah rowdy?"

"Not a loud girl, no. Very respectful, but the boys did love her, and did they ever come around." Mrs. Byrd smiled and winked. "Sometimes I would ask her to turn the music down, but it was never a problem."

"Did she have a boyfriend she liked in particular?"

"Why do you ask?" she said, the minnows dispersing behind her glasses.

"My grandfather was friendly with a man who you may also recognize, because I have reason to believe he visited Norah here. Gardner Rothman."

Mrs. Byrd's head fell. "These things were so long ago. She had many visitors, a pretty young girl like that."

"I don't suspect you of doing anything wrong, Mrs. Byrd. Did Gardner Rothman visit Norah Kelley?"

"Norah worked for the basketball team. She dreamed such dreams, loved being with the stars."

"Yes, Mrs. Byrd, I know. Did Gardner Rothman visit Norah Kelley?"

"She was very popular. Lots of boys came by."

Evasion. Mrs. Byrd was afraid. I didn't want it to seem like I was interrogating her, because I had no legal authority. Tread lightly, Jonah. She can throw you right out on your ass if she'd like. Try a different scheme. Lie.

"I know Rothman dated Norah."

"She thought they would get married," Mrs. Byrd conceded after a beat. "She knew he would go into politics. She thought he would be the president."

"Did Norah and Rothman ever fight?" I asked.

"Not that I heard." A stray tear fell from Mrs. Byrd's eyes. "They laughed a lot. Those were different times. Parties, parties. I think some of them may have, you know, smoked a little."

"Do you mean smoke marijuana?"

"Yes. I told Norah that I'd have none of that nonsense, but she said it was a friend doing it, not her. I never had a problem with her again."

"That's good," I said, my mind beginning to whir. "When did Rothman and Norah stop laughing, Mrs. Byrd?"

A frightened lip-pursing from Mrs. Byrd. "When Norah got sick," she answered matter-of-factly.

"How was she sick?"

"Throwing up. Things got very quiet down there."

Mrs. Byrd covered her face with her hands. "I thought this all died," she cried. I saw another tear escape beneath her cupped hands.

"I'm sorry, but you thought what died?"

"This. All of this. It just stopped right away after Norah's funeral."

"Maybe somebody made it stop," I said, assuming that "it" referred to hard questions. "Do you know what kind of sickness Norah had, Mrs. Byrd?"

She laughed. "Do you have a wife, Mr. Eastman?"

"Yes, I do."

"Do you have children?"

"Yes, I do."

"How did your wife feel when she became pregnant?" she asked me as if I were the biggest idiot on earth.

A DEMON ON WHEELS

"What the hell was I capable of?"

Norah Kelley had been pregnant, I ruminated as I pulled my Porsche out of the little space on Buffalo Avenue. Then she died. Of a cerebral hemorrhage. Perhaps it was the same kind of hemorrhage that President Lincoln had at Ford's Theater, or the one O. J. Simpson's beautiful ex-wife Nicole had. I felt a murderous rage swell behind my eyes. The sense was so powerful that I contemplated the wisdom of carrying a gun. What the hell was I capable of? And whom would I shoot? But I knew the answer, and part of my rage derived from guilt because I had, once again in my life, found myself allied with a murderer.

Calm, Jonah. You don't know that Rebound killed her, you just don't know. This man who gave you a break, Jonah. He gave you a shot at a respectable client— him—when nobody else would touch you, and now you're the moral conscience of the universe?

But I *did* know. You didn't have to know something to *know* something. I knew who and what Rebound Rothman was beneath the glittering veneer, and I hadn't wanted to see it for so long. Hell, I couldn't see it—I made my living off the man. I felt around my side. My gun was there.

Suddenly the gearshift began to rattle, and my hand automatically abandoned the gun in order to bring the damned Porsche under control. No matter how I shifted it, the car wouldn't respond. I tried thinking badass thoughts—the theme to my favorite 1960s cartoon, *Speed Racer*. "Here he comes / Here comes Speed Racer / He's a demon on wheels." The car began to coast in neutral as I maneuvered it onto the shoulder of the road. Normally this type of thing would provoke a tantrum, but it didn't today. God had finally registered with me that taming complex beasts was not always noble, and misery was not always character-building. I was tired of reading books that I was supposed to read, but found boring. I didn't want to ride thoroughbreds that fought me every inch of a trail ride. I didn't want to have lunch with insufferable people just because it was polite. This Porsche had been exquisite purgatory, but I was finished with it, thus glorious lesson number nine of the course, which I wrote down on the car's registration:

Avoid things that piss you off.

BOOK IV

FAMILY STATE. FAMILY MAN.

"People in Washington say it's not the initial offense that gets you into trouble, it's the cover-up. They say you should admit what you did, get the story out and move on. What this overlooks is the fact that most of the time the cover-up works just fine, and nobody finds out a thing."

—George Carlin

THE WRONG MAN

"He's not big on consequences."

It's the dreams that get to me. I know they're not supposed to mean anything, and I hope they don't, but they rev me up without taking me anywhere.

Simone is reclining in a stuffed chair in Dartmouth's Sanborn Library, one of the smaller buildings on the campus. Sanborn has a reading room where tea is served in mismatched cups and saucers in the late afternoon. I am sitting in a study carrel directly across from Simone watching a parade of alpha men (and more than a few betas) drop by on bended knee to present the Shakespearean coquette with a verbal hors d'oeuvre: Do you want some tea? What are you doing for Green Key Weekend? Check out the dude with the Mohawk. *All of these customs were preferable to the carnal truth:* Get naked, wench.

Uncharacteristically confident, I set aside Philip Roth's Goodbye, Columbus, *and approach Simone. Upon seeing me, she places Budd Schulberg's* The Disenchanted *back on the shelf and presses her head back into the great beige pillow that envelopes her head like a satellite dish. She may be dressed like Cleopatra. She may also be pregnant. I lay down beside her and cradle the back of her head with my hand, her hair entangling between my fingers. The moment my lips, which are chapped from the dry winter, brush against hers, an odd series of staccato tickles flit across my skin. I assume them to be long fingernails, which they are, however, I raise my head to see that I am kissing my grandmother, Deedee, who says, "THIS is what you climb on?" She then smacks my forehead with her palm and reminds me that she had warned me about "this." I shout as I run from the library with all of the alpha and beta males squinting at me in disbelief. I see from the lawn outside the library that they have lined up to comfort Simone. One Euro-looking boy—man, I guess—spots me out the window and shakes his head in a way that suggests I am crazy.*

When I saw Edie's face resting against her pillow, I exhaled very slowly as I mouthed a blessing I learned when I was a boy.

I was hitting the flippers on a pinball machine at Popeye's arcade while I waited for Chief Willie. I was the only one there save Popeye, who lingered on the boardwalk taking in the suckers in pursuit of an oxygen fix. I stopped as three high-as-a-kite mooks wearing doo-rags approached me. The tallest one, an Eminem wannabe, kept his hand in a fat pocket and asked, "You got any spare change, bitch?"

I'm always so tough in front of the mirror in my bathroom, but it didn't convey to the boardwalk. I was scared despite my gun.

"Pardon me?" I asked, trying to affect a coarse expression.

"I want some change. I wanna play some games," Eminem said.

"I can't help you," I said, looking for a way to distract the trio. *Now would be a good time to use the gun, pinhead,* I thought. Yes, Jonah, but what will you do once you whip it out? Are you going to just start shooting? After all, this dirtbag appears to be carrying. Why not just give him some money and be done with it?

"Oh, we need your help bad, bitch," Eminem said.

I felt my bladder twitch when the Lord God smiled upon me in the form of Chief Willie Thundercloud, who entered the arcade. He was wearing a Western hat with an eagle feather, Western boots with silver tips, a suede jacket with tassels streaming urgently from every edge, and enough turquoise on his hands and wrists to make him look like a map of the Caribbean.

"Witch doctor says, 'Go to jail. Go directly to jail. Do not pass Go. Do not collect two hundred dollars,'" Chief Willie said, Injun-style.

With the Chief here, my fear dissipated, and I felt like Rambo.

"How 'bout you, Tonto?" the second thug, Puberty Mustache, asked, cocky. "You got any change?"

Chief Willie looked at the trio quizzically. "Are you fucking shitting me?" he asked, his eyes flat and economical.

Now, this was a scenario the boys hadn't anticipated. Three blitzed muggers go after a victim, and the victim asks, "Are you fucking shitting me?" It was a poetic moment when all of the lessons of human physics appear onstage for their statuette and give a little speech: *Yes, this is how the world works, nimrods—objective reality, none of this it-depends-on-your-point-of-view crap.*

Eminem looked at his colleagues for a reaction. They in turn looked back at him. As the cross-glancing was in play, Chief Willie's Sig Sauer P232 appeared in one liquid motion, pointing it toward Puberty Mustache's nose. The other two thuglets stepped back, and Chief Willie began to sing a song of rage by local lady Patti Smith:

> Baby was a black sheep. Baby was a whore.
> Baby got big and baby get biggah.

It was actually frightening, the brutal boomerang dipping into the smoky basement of South Jersey culture to chasten lads who would become murderers soon enough, but not on principle.

I took a loan from Chief Willie's courage and pulled my revolver, which genuinely appeared to frighten the little gang. I pointed it at a stunned Eminem. Chief Willie stepped forward and removed a small revolver from Puberty Mustache's pocket. He then backed up, pointed his Sig in the direction of the two sidekicks with his right hand, and aimed the revolver with his left at Puberty Mustache's head.

"Hey there, Mongoose," Chief Willie said, alternating his focus between Puberty Mustache and his sidekicks. "You know why I aim at the nose?"

"No, educate me."

"You hit the nose, you blow out the medulla oblongata in the brain. He dies before he hits the ground. And with hollow-points, well, let's just say there's no open casket."

"Good to know," I said nervously. "You like the Sig, huh?"

"Yeah, I do," Chief Willie said with conviction. "The older you get, the less burden you want. My old Beretta would take a guy's head off, but c'mon, who needs it? The Sig fits real sweet in a kidney holster and doesn't fuck up my Armani. Now, the three-fifty-seven you've got with hollow-points . . . that's a closed casket for sure."

"I've never seen 'em open a casket for one of my masterpieces."

"Okay, boys," Chief Willie said, "Get down on the ground and pour yourselves a hot cup-a prison cornholing." Two of the boys complied, their lips Arctic blue and rubbery, but a stubby one remained defiant, testing out a cinematic diss: "That little pistol you got's for pussies."

Chief Willie frowned briefly, and then grazed the stubby punk's inner thigh with a gunshot—right up near his crotch, too. Stubby collapsed onto the ground more in shock than pain as Popeye crossed himself in the archway.

"Sitting Bull say, 'When woodpecker shoot off mouth, bigger bird shoot off pecker,'" Chief Willie said, adding, "As General Custer learned at Crow's Nest . . . Mongoose, pat down Mr. Weak-ass Lip Fuzz, and get his wallet, while I talk to his associates about married life in prison." I complied. Chief Willie fired once in the air, which caused me to jump. Puberty Mustache broke into tears. The one who Chief Willie shot at was rocking back and forth, wailing at the minuscule amount of blood on his thigh. Chief Willie retrieved a .45-caliber Glock from Stubby's pants. "Popeye, call ACPD," Chief Willie shouted.

"Oh my heaven," Popeye said, coming alive and fumbling around beneath a counter for a telephone.

"You think this pond scum here works for your lobbyist friend, trying to shake you up, or worse?" the Chief asked.

"That was my thought, yeah."

Picture this: Chief Willie and I are collectively kneeling down over three thugs, patting them down for weapons and identification while Chief Willie begins to engage me in business matters as if we were sharing a milkshake. "You know your friends in Maple Shade?" he asked. "Mom and Dad. Well, they make a lot of calls to one of your favorite periodicals. *Probe*."

"No shit?"

"No shit. The extension of your favorite reporter."

"The Enema?" I said.

"That's the one."

"What do they want with each other?"

"Beats me."

The ACPD entered in a triad of shoulders. "Hey, Chief Willie," one of the officers said.

"What's up, Dale?" Chief Willie said. He explained to Officer Dale and his partner what had gone down, adding that he thought Stubby was reaching for his gun. Ignoring the fact that an unknown man (me) had a .357 Magnum pointed at Puberty Mustache's head, they proceeded to cuff the young men, whose lives were effectively over. A twinge of sympathy lingered in my conscience as I imagined these gutter creatures as someone's children.

"You know who you tried to hold up, dumbass?" Officer Dale asked Puberty Mustache.

Puberty Mustache nodded in the negative.

"The wrong man."

Chief Willie smirked. The police escorted the ruined boys out.

"We can't spy on the Enema, but I say the two retired schoolteachers are fair game," I said. "Now, my turn. I went to see this Mrs. Byrd. Guess what she has all over her house?"

"Sculptures of Rebound's package?"

"Close. Birdcages."

"So?"

"I'm just getting started. She admitted Rebound came there to see Norah. It was all hot and heavy until Norah got pregnant."

"Mother-a-God."

"Now, Mrs. Byrd never had evidence Norah was pregnant, but she said she had morning sickness, and that's when it went south with Rebound."

"Didn't you say he met Marsha around then?"

"He met Marsha earlier, but got engaged to her in September."

"A baby would have ended that engagement pretty quick."

"Right. Rebound's political career began around then. Pinkus money has been paying his way for a quarter century."

"No marriage, no money."

"Right. Norah was a Catholic," I said. "So we can guess where she may have stood on abortion."

"So, what, Rebound just whacks her after he knocks her up? Sounds pretty speculative."

"It is, Chief. I'm not saying any of this would hold up in a court, but it would be deadly speculation on *Election Throb* or in *Vanity Fair*. And it takes us further from coincidences and closer to Rebound being a bigger shit than we ever thought he was. When you start throwing in all the hocus-pocus around the death certificate stuff, the mosaic comes together."

"You know him better than I do. Is Rebound the kind of guy who would kill her in cold blood?"

"That would be too equivocal for him. Rebound wouldn't want to deal with the blood, the sound of bone snapping . . . sensory stuff. He couldn't handle seeing evidence of what he had done. He's not big on consequences."

"The girl managed to die somehow, Mongoose."

"Something Mrs. Byrd said gave me another possibility. She said that those were big party days."

"You saying drugs?"

"A death by drugs could go any number of ways, you know? Did you find anything out about that coroner, O'Rourke?"

"Just atmospherics. He hung with the kind of nobility that could doctor a death certificate. He was an operator in Mayor Barton's crew." Barton had been mayor of Atlantic City in the late 1970s and early 1980s. He had been convicted for a role in the ABSCAM scandal.

"Where's O'Rourke now?"

"Died in 1998. But here's the thing, Mongoose: if O'Rourke was linked to Mayor Barton, it meant he was a guy who could be gotten to by the right guys, guys in your grandpop's crew, sorry to say. O'Rourke could have fudged the death certificate. He traveled in those circles. We can't prove—"

"But it's enough to make Rebound paranoid as hell," I said. "Now, what you have to figure is that Norah's parents must have known that something was up. I mean, a young girl dies like that . . . don't they have questions?"

"Maybe they just wanted it to go away, especially if she was pregnant and drugs may have been involved," Chief Willie said. "Maybe they were bought off."

"Maybe that's what Barium Enema is onto." I rubbed my stomach.

"What's wrong, Mongoose?"

I told him about the graffiti on Rebound's steps. He said nothing, just shook his head. "Chief, maybe you should go and see your girlfriend at Vital Records?"

THE MATTER OF REIMBURSEMENT

"In the end, they were all on the same side."

I had a vital statistic of my own to deal with: money. I had paid Torch Wyeth twenty-five thousand dollars out of my own bank account to get the Judge! program up and running, and despite assurances from Currier that I'd be paid back quickly, not one dime had entered my account. I had been logging onto my account every hour from my laptop to see if the transfer had landed, but the balance was still tipping with spare change just north of four grand. Four thousand and three dollars and twenty-four cents, to be exact. There's something about being a tiny bit over a round number that reminds you how close you are to collapsing.

Irv the Curve drove so little anymore that he agreed to let me use his Cadillac. After I picked it up, I drove down to the Rothman's house in Margate to have a talk with Marsha. Her invitation to sit down was perfunctory. There was no banter, no rebellious references to Rebound, just a well-to-do housewife who was being as polite as she had to, but no more.

"What's up?" she asked.

"Marsha, I hate to be mercenary, but I paid one of Rebound's political vendors twenty-five grand out of my pocket. I was supposed to get a check a few weeks ago, and now I owe the guy another twenty-five. Can you do anything through the foundation to expedite this?"

Marsha appeared perplexed. "What vendor?" I felt my heart stop.

"It's a company called R.C.S."

"I never heard anything about it."

"You haven't?" I envisioned myself roasting on a spit, alternating between the heat of the fire and the comparative cool of the sky.

"No, Jonah, honestly. Why don't you ask Lucas?"

"I have."

"And what does he say?"

"That it's being processed."

"Huh. I'll ask Lucas when I see him," Marsha said, as if she were a fembot whose battery had run low.

I analyzed her face closely for any betrayal of strategy. I believed that Marsha truly may not have heard about the initial request, but also didn't believe she would ask Rebound or Currier about intervening. In the end, they were all on the same side, and I had learned, however slowly, that the rich didn't get that way by paying their bills; they got rich by cultivating sycophants for whom the privilege of serving them was payment enough. When I inspected Marsha's eyes, I saw neither malice nor guile. This was just how she had always done things. I drove Irv's Cadillac away feeling an uncharacteristic contempt for the rich, not to mention the impulse of vendetta that I had always viewed as being beneath me. Not anymore. It was time for reimbursement.

CHIEF WILLIE GOES IN

"It's easy to think you're morally clean if you're physically distant."

"Yeah," I said, answering my mobile phone in my attic study.

"It's me," Me said. It was Chief Willie. "I'll talk vague. It's about Lois Lane." Barium Enema. "Here's what you ought to know. Lois stopped off to see the nice couple in Maple Shade."

"Well, we knew that she knew them."

"She hugged them hello and good-bye. Kind of a strange relationship between a beat reporter and a source, huh?"

I went through my files about Norah Kelley again, hoping for a Lt. Columbo moment, the one where he scratches his head like a big dummy and tells the guilty suspect what he suddenly "realized." That realization, of course, would send the perp to prison. I was no Columbo, and couldn't find anything in the articles about Norah's death that jumped out at me. There was one possibility, however, that had begun to haunt me as I studied the articles written at the time of Norah's death.

I met Chief Willie at the Steel Pier and told him that while I had succeeded in getting near the Kelleys' house, I hadn't succeeded in getting inside.

"What are you looking for?" Chief Willie asked. "Jewels, a high-definition TV?"

When I told Chief Willie what I wanted to see, he studied the sun for a moment. "I can bogart a photo, sure."

I can understand why my grandfather never saw himself as a murderer; after all, his hands were never bloody. The rough stuff always happened somewhere else, and it's easy to think you're morally clean if you're physically distant.

I was a good forty miles away from the break-in in Maple Shade, but Chief Willie and the Viking broke it down for me when we met that evening at the food court in the Cherry Hill Mall.

The Kelleys got into their Audi at six o'clock. Chief Willie was watching from his utility vehicle, and dispatched another car waiting on Main Street to tail the couple. Ten minutes later, when the Audi had made its way onto Route 70, Chief Willie pulled his van up to the house that was directly behind the Kelleys. The Viking got out and crept quietly across the lawn to the greenhouse addition on the side of the residence. These were always easy to penetrate; after all, what kind of loser would risk prison to steal a cactus?

But it wasn't a plant the Viking wanted.

The Kelleys had a small round table in the greenhouse where they presumably enjoyed coffee, or something other than a full meal, which would require room to spread out. There was a small, rectangular wicker table adjacent to the round one that held a collage of photos. When Chief Willie and the Viking had cased the residence earlier, they considered taking a zoom-lens photo of the collage, but there was one problem: A large, weeping plant was draped above it, and the heat vent below it would blow the leaves in front of the picture frame at inconvenient moments.

The Viking crouched down beside the greenhouse door awaiting his *go* command. The light in the kitchen, which was adjacent to the greenhouse, spilled into the room, making it a tad too bright for an ideal break-in. Nevertheless, the windows themselves didn't rise directly from the floor; rather, they were mounted on a brick foundation that was about three feet high. In other words, the Viking could slither on the floor undetected until he got to the photo.

A voice echoed in the Viking's earpiece. "They're heading for Medford," Chief Willie said. "Looks like they're going for dinner. You're cool for a while."

Greenhouse doors were notoriously flimsy. First the Viking, gloved, of course, attempted to open it. It was better just to enter than to *break* and enter. Nah, the Kelleys weren't that dumb. It was locked. Well, gotta try. Next, he slid a container the size of a calculator out of his pocket. He removed a device containing two parallel strips of metal. One piece went inside the lock, the other the Viking manually manipulated. Click.

The Viking pressed the Start button on his stopwatch and entered, closing the door behind him. He crawled on his belly across the tile over to the wicker table, which was pressed against the wall. He reached up with his latex glove and pulled down the picture frame. The Viking studied the collage with his flashlight to determine which photo he wanted. Then he flipped the frame downward so that the photos faced the tile floor. He pried loose the back of the frame and removed the small picture that he had targeted, being careful not to disturb the other ones. *This is the one.* He slipped the photo into his backpack, placed the frame back on the credenza, and crawled out of the greenhouse. The operation took ninety seconds.

Within ten minutes, the Viking and Chief Willie were at the Cherry Hill Mall with the photo. Chief Willie stood beside me. The Viking held the photo up. Staccato breaths and a little dizziness. The Viking began to sing impishly: "That's the way we became the Brady Bunch."

THE (COVETED) HOLLEWMUN PRIZE

"I referred to this practice as 'trophy laundering.'"

I had located a community north of Stockholm, Sweden, called Uppsala. Uppsala had a community service award named after a twentieth-century Good Samaritan named Thorsten Hollewmun. One week before Election Day, the good people of Uppsala gathered in a schoolhouse amidst the lush, rolling hills and presented local do-gooders with a gold-plated medallion signifying their contributions to the community.

In exchange for a new Uppsala recreation center donated by the ubiquitous Pinkus Foundation, the chairman of the award committee agreed to award New Jersey Governor Gardner Rothman the coveted Hollewmun Prize for his humanitarian efforts to quell the unrest that had recently taken place throughout New Jersey.

Beyond coming up with the idea and handling the arrangements, I had no desire to see Rebound get his award. I was afraid I might strangle him with his medallion. I was able to capture it on the news. Jersey's *Graftnet* featured complete coverage, from Rebound arriving in Stockholm with Marsha to his procession to the white brick schoolhouse in Uppsala, where the flag of New Jersey was hoisted beside the Swedish flag.

The ceremony was brief, with a presiding official (whose name sounded like Vyerten Dyerten) inside the solemn blond wood library stating in broken English:

> *Governor Gardner Rothman, yes, of the American village of New Jersey, brought together the good people of his village after a time, yes, of much difficulty. Today, yes, after his speech to bring reassurance back to the village where people had risen up against each other, now they are in harmony with people of all religions, races and tolerations. For this, it is with prideful . . . pride that we, the citizens of Uppsala, present Governor Gardner Rothman of the American village of New Jersey with our greatest honor for duty, the coveted Hollewmun Prize.*

The small audience of Uppsalians and New Jersey journalists applauded as Vyerten Dyerten placed the gold medallion around Rebound's neck. Rebound turned and stood for the multiple pops of cameras. I had told him not to speak.

The following morning, voters in New Jersey rose to find that every daily newspaper in the state had run with a photo on the front page of Rebound stooping knightly before Vyerten Dyerten to receive his medal.

I referred to this practice as "trophy laundering." It consisted of receiving an award from a foreign entity when people back home thought you were a real shit. The logic here was that if you brought a coveted prize from abroad back to the United States, it would get people who either disrespected you or took you for granted to rethink their earlier assessments. After all, people who live far away must know what they're doing, especially the Swedes.

I accompanied Rebound from the charter section of Atlantic City International Airport to his house. A separate car took Marsha wherever. When she saw me, she nodded, but didn't say hello. The look on Rebound's face was one of relief, not joy. I understood the dynamics of this less-than-euphoric reaction . . .

Rebound was part of a tiny class of people who lived in a parallel universe where reality is managed by professional realists like me. Top politicians, like royals and celebrities, flitted about inside of a bubble within this parallel universe where they only saw smiling faces, accommodating staffs, and vehicles that arrived and departed on a narrow schedule: theirs. It becomes impossible not to conclude while in this bubble that God created heaven and earth for your personal comfort. You can come to believe that if doors open for you, private planes fly for you, and humankind is your bellboy, that your marriages will work, your ventures will pay dividends, *and that there's no way god will let you get caught being blown by an intern because you are YOU.*

I could see the strain not so much on Rebound's face but in his hands, which were chafed from toying with putty that he was presently grinding into a knuckle, and examining its imprint. I speculated that his strain came from his realization—so late in life—that God could pop that bubble at His pleasure. And if He chose to do so, Rebound would be relying upon compensated mortals to reassemble what God shattered. We mortals would inevitably fail. It reminds me of what Mickey said after John F. Kennedy Jr.'s plane went down. The flight experts on TV were speculating about what caused the crash, and Mickey barked, "I'll tell you what caused it: the poor schmuck thought he could fly!"

"Congratulations on the award," I said.

"It was quite a ceremony, athlete. Thanks for your efforts," he said perfunctorily. We rode in virtual silence back to Margate, where I had left Irv's car. Then I drove home, my utility far behind me.

HAVING A GOVERNOR

"What is it that you suspect, Jonah?"

Barri was waiting for me in a booth at Olga's Diner in Cherry Hill, unsmiling.

"You look tense, Barri," I said, sliding into the booth facing Route 73.

She was expressionless for a moment. "Just a little out of sorts."

"About what?

"You."

"Me? Why?"

"To be honest with you, I would have thought you would have gotten things out of your system before you got married. I know you've been trolling around with Lava."

I shook my head in the negative. "You're making an assumption that's understandable, mein sleuth, but it's wrong—as is your theory about getting things out of your system."

"I assume we're talking about sex, and what I gather is your noble effort to distract your client from himself."

"We are, in part."

"You may just be a man of Herculean self-discipline . . . So, Jonah, lay your theory on me."

I dug in to share with Barri the tenth lesson of the affair I had labeled in my mind "Shakedown Beach":

You don't get stuff "out of your system."

"See, Barri, people who screw around a lot before they're married tend to screw around a lot *after* they're married. People who tend to be monogamous before they get married tend to be monogamous afterward. It's a personality type, it's not a threshold that's saturated. It's how you're wired."

I sensed Barri was evaluating whether or not to believe me by the way her face let go of some of its tension. Truth was, I was trying to determine whether or not I should believe myself.

"Darwinian theory suggests that the male instinct is to get his genes into the next generation," Barri said, flipping on her glasses in a way that made me want to throw them off.

"No doubt about it," I said, trying not to look at the freckles that dotted her neckline like little arrows pointing south. "And I'm not exempt from Darwin. It's just that the animal can do battle with the man."

"And what did the man tell you, Jonah?"

"If I told you the truth, I'd be telling a reporter something deeply personal, and not self-flattering."

"We're off the record."

"I suspect that sex leads to trouble, Barri."

Barri recoiled. "I see," she blinked. "Why did you trust me with this?"

"Because sex isn't the only thing a person doesn't get out of their system."

"What's another thing?"

"Vengeance. That desire throbs like a sex drive. It's a passion that leads to trouble because it must end in a climax. It eats up good people."

"How do you stop it?" she asked plaintively.

"Some people have . . . a governor, for lack of a better term—something that keeps them in line, something that regulates an animal drive. Others don't. Do you have a governor, Barri?"

When Barri spoke again, her face was strained, the way a face looks when it's choking back tears. She was on the verge of a confession, and

I knew I had been wrong about my earlier suspicion that she had been a woman scorned by Rebound. Barri shifted her position, which put her in an unflattering light in the brightness of the autumn sun. "I'd like to think I do," she said. "What about you, Jonah?"

"I do, more than most. I suppose it has to do with how we deal with losing what we think we should still have."

Barri breathed in deeply. Her eyes went hard, and then melted. "I know what you think about my interest in Rebound, and I'm insulted. What is it about the male ego that makes you think it's always about a woman who's been rejected?"

"You were the one who thought I was banging Simone. Besides, that's not my theory."

"What is? Stop the striptease."

"My striptease stops with Norah Kelley," I said.

Barri's eyes flooded, but the moisture froze the moment she detected that I could see it. Her jaw thrust forward in a primate signal of attack.

"It is a horrible, horrible story, Barri. I know now that Norah's older sister roomed with her in the spring of 1980. I know Barbara and Norah had high hopes for the summer that followed. I remember those times, since we're about the same age. I can tell you every Top Forty song from that time. I met a girl myself that spring, and I remember that Linda Ronstadt's "How Do I Make You" was playing on the radio when we met.

"I also know that Norah's sister Barbara goes by Barri, and that you married and divorced a Hammonton contractor named Michael Embrey. And I suspect you hold Rothman responsible for Norah's death. You're probably right to hold him responsible, but I also suspect that it won't do you much good. This guy's not destined to go to jail." I laughed involuntarily, the way dorks do when they subconsciously recognize that they don't have enough social grace to transition to another moment. Truth was, I didn't want him to go to jail. Tomorrow was Election Day. A victory was in my self-interest. Barri's bloodlust would have to wait.

"Norah was pregnant. Given your family's religion, abortion wasn't an option. Then she died. We both suspect that it's more than coincidence. We're probably right, Barri, but being right and getting justice are two different things."

"It was *you*, then. You went to my parents' house."

"I didn't know they were your parents. You know I wouldn't investigate a reporter."

Barri sighed. I could tell she wanted to rip into me, but she wasn't pure in this, and she knew it.

What I didn't tell her was that I had ordered a break-in at her childhood home to "bogart" a photograph. That photograph featured two stunning young women standing in between their parents at a high school graduation—Norah's graduation, her golden tassel mimicking the color of her long late-1970s hair. Barbara and Norah looked alike, not exactly, but the resemblance was close enough that a parent could easily see the dreams of one in the other's eyes. Barbara must have seen her sister's snuffed ambitions in her own eyes every time the makeup artist at *Election Throb* forced her to stare in the mirror while blemishes were covered, shines were powdered down, and the bronze of long-ago summers was artificially restored.

Barri's eyes remained frozen. They looked like Cooper River in early March when skaters would nervously test the ice trying to determine if it had gone soft in anticipation of spring. Even when the ice appeared safe, the skaters never glided in complete comfort, knowing that the ice possessed a fickle hardness that represented the illusion of strength.

"You know how she died, don't you, Jonah?"

"I think so."

"You owe me the truth."

"No, I owe you a news story, but it may not be the climax you wanted."

"Don't negotiate with me."

"I need more time to get your story. Then we'll talk about Norah."

THE OFFICIAL GENIUS

"Maybe you'd be happier with Score the Helper."

I rose early on Election Day, really relaxed. The big day, after all, was an anticlimax. I drove the kids to school and went on an hour-long run around a nearby high school track. The track was rubberized, which was a benefit to my increasingly rickety knees. As I ran, I considered that I should be doing something . . . official, useful. But the election was truly out of my hands. I couldn't even vote, my registration only being good in the People's Republic of the District of Columbia, where my business was technically based.

By the time I completed my run and contacted one of my exit-poll guys, it was abundantly clear that Rebound was going to the Senate. Seven out of ten people polled outside random voting locations indicated support for Rebound. I had been through enough of these circuses to know where events were leading. Even if Digby gained some ground, there was little chance with this skew that he would overtake Rebound.

I drove home and turned on Fox TV. It was too early for *The Throb*, so I flipped through cable channels until I came upon the fusilli head of the Antichrist filling the screen. Abel Petz was the guest on the Fox News Channel.

"You've got quite a track record, Abel," Shep the host said. "Would you say your polling strategy clinched the election for Rothman?"

"Well, Shep, it's not about polls, it's about goals," Petz said.

I envisioned myself pumping a .357 round in Petz's groin, a shot that would take awhile to be lethal, but would hurt beyond any human expression. What pun would the Petzer come up with at that point?: *"It's not about getting shot down low, Shep, it's about keeping your head held high . . ."*

"Governor Rothman has always had a clear sense of purpose," Petz said. "Digby Stahl was just saying the same old things. The voters of New Jersey want leaders, not repeaters."

"As always, Abel, you're the man," Shep said.

Petz averted his beagle eyes and swatted away Shep's latest certification of his zenlike control over time and space.

I had revised my thinking. I wouldn't fire a .357 round into Petz's groin, I'd buy a little .22 revolver, lock him in one of the barn stalls at our place in Cowtown, and pop him in various nonlethal locations over a period of a day or so. Drag it out.

I wondered what Edie would think of me if she knew I had thoughts like this. I calmed down when I acknowledged to myself that Petz had not badmouthed me, he had just taken credit for Rebound's victory. It wasn't very nice, but it was within the confines of the Geneva Convention rules of electoral war: the first consultant on the air explaining why his guy won was the Official Genius.

Edie, who had maintained her New Jersey voter registration, came home and informed me that she had voted for Digby Stahl, which didn't surprise me. I was glad she had. I had the conviction it would keep our homestead pure.

That afternoon, after the kids got home from school, KBRO declared the election for Rebound. No sooner than Digby conceded did our home phone ring. Edie answered. "Can I tell him who's calling?" she asked sternly. "Simone?" Edie said with a question mark in her voice, handing me the phone. I had, of course, told her about Simone. Not my erotic obsession with her, but the political problem that she posed for Rebound. The partial confession relieved the tension of my makeout sin for about five minutes until I realized I was spinning my wife.

Simone was hysterical. "Gardner hasn't called me all day," she cried. "And he won. He won, and I'm all alone."

"Calm down," I said, "calm down. I'll be there. I'll come over." I hung up.

This exchange went over like a whale turd in a goldfish bowl with Edie.

"Where did you do your graduate work in bimbo-sitting?" Edie asked.

"C'mon, Edie, this race is still alive."

"Of course it is. When will your work for that man be done?"

"She's going nuts," I tried to explain feebly. "If she goes public before the win is declared, we're screwed."

"Yes, Jonah, *we're* always screwed, aren't *we?*"

"No, we're not, Ede. We're almost done, I promise. I just have to calm her down before she sets off a shitstorm."

"What about the shitstorm in our house, what about that?"

My ears began to roar. I felt as if the disruptions caused by my career were all that Edie and I spoke about anymore, and I had burned out on the subject. Yes, my hours had been weird. No, I hadn't been myself. Yes, Rebound was disruptive. But this is how I made my living. After all, the fabled millions of Mickey Price had yet to materialize in my account at Merrill Lynch. I decided to be a prick, so I told Edie the truth: "I was flat broke before the Rothmans hired me. Broke. I was this close"—I held up my hands in a pinching gesture—"to asking to move in with your parents. Maybe you'd be happier with Score the Helper, if I'm such a disappointment."

Thus Jonah Eastman, the Ike Turner of South Jersey, the worst husband ever, left his family, climbed into an old gangster's Cadillac DeVille and raced to the sanctuary of Miss Little Egg Harbor. Who would understand me.

PROM NIGHT, TAKE II

"I noticed her address—firstlady@barrens.net."

Simone's door opened, and she pulled me in so that I almost lost my balance. She was wearing a peculiar, glossy, low-cut dress, which, after squinting at her for a second, I recognized as the same one she wore in her Little Miss Egg Harbor Township photo. It occurred to me that she might be insane.

"Oh, Jonah, I don't know what to do," she cried. Simone took a few steps back and sat on a warped little motel room chair just outside the birdcage. She leaned over and cradled her head in her hands, her breasts nearly spilling out of her dress.

I backed up until I was standing against the motel room door. Fifteen feet away, Simone rose silently. Her expression was a combination of lost and sensuous, like a very naughty babysitter trying to see how much she could get away with with a boy only a couple of years her junior. Simone backed into the birdcage, and she let her dress fall into a formation that resembled the peeled rinds of a fruit that grew somewhere I had never been, like Macedonia.

"C'mon," she said, motioning me toward the birdcage.

I froze. I had a phobia about that birdcage. And fucking up my entire life.

"No, you c'mon," I said.

Simone huffed, but she stepped out of the birdcage and stepped across the floor toward me, her toes gripping the carpet. "Are you threatened by a sexually independent woman?" she asked.

"Yes!" I said, quite candidly.

As my two hands reached out toward her breasts, a questioned stabbed me: what does *she* want with *me?*

And then I gagged and threw up on Simone's spectacular 1970s *Playboy* magazine breasts. Well, not right away. First, I got shooting pains in my chest and arms.

Simone went into the bathroom to shower off, not an irresponsible reaction to having just been vomited upon by a man who had just beheld her body. I felt it was safe to assume that this had been a first for her.

The laptop on her desk was on. As soon as I heard the spigot, I peered at the screen. Her name was swirling around on her designated screen saver. I fingered the mouse pad. Her e-mail was up, as was a state government Web site, which made sense because she was a state intern. I noticed her address—firstlady@barrens.net. Barrens was a local Internet provider, unaffiliated with the state government. In other words, a private account. Hmm.

I wasn't handy enough with computers to play around with it. Besides, I heard the water in Simone's shower throttle off. In full private dick mode, I scanned the room for signs of private dick stuff. The only thing that appeared out of place (with the exception of the giant fornicating birdcage) was a strip of wallpaper that appeared to have been re-pasted.

I walked over and felt along the wall. My fingers rose over what felt like a tiny marble, or a glass contact lens. I quickly turned on the lamp that sat on the night table directly across from the birdcage. I saw that the little convex protrusion glinted in the light.

A tiny camera lens. It had been reinstalled. I removed a small penknife from my pocket and pried the lens from the wall, as if this would some-how reverse any capture of my reaching out for Simone. But wait a minute. Could this device have picked up my aborted boob grab, which had taken place a dozen feet to the left of the lens, which seemed to be trained on the birdcage? I pocketed the little lens and shut off the lamp in time for the luminescent post-puke prom queen to reemerge in a too-small Celebrity towel.

"Are you okay?" Simone asked.

"I guess it comes down to what Jerry Seinfeld said: 'You can't have sex with someone you admire—there's no depravity.'"

Simone executed a one-eighth grin. I hovered by the door, but thought it would appear suspicious if I just slipped out without saying good-bye to her.

"Don't leave, Jonah. I need you," Simone said.

"No, you don't." I laughed when I said this.

"If I don't need you, Jonah, what do I need?"

"Trouble. Just consider me your knowledge partner."

Simone saw that her screen saver was not on. In other words, she knew I had checked out her laptop. Her jaw shifted out and her mouth opened. Her teeth appeared small and sharp like a hyena's. She was ac-tually ugly. Whether it was my ostensible rejection of her or her specula-tion about what I might have seen on her laptop, she said, "I have never known anyone to despise another person the way Gardner despises you."

I nodded, conveying genuine sorrow. "I know that now, Simone."

Then I left the Celebrity Motel feeling strangely holy.

POST-HURL REVELATION

"We're in that place."

I called Chief Willie, who roared down to the Celebrity in his black Trans Am. It was about five o'clock, and the sun had long since retreated west. Chief Willie pulled his TransAm into an alley, which startled me. I got in the car and confessed to him what had happened with Simone. He nodded as if he had heard this kind of thing before, which of course he had.

I simpered to Chief Willie: "I always had this notion in my head that I'd have these . . . Frank Sinatra years. You know, the variety. Never happened."

"You know, Mongoose, Springsteen was fulla shit on that point. Remember he said, 'We're gonna get to that place?' Well, no, we won't. We're *in* that place, you and me."

"I know."

"Reminds me, I had a cousin once who went to Colorado to find herself . . . she wasn't there. Now, show me the bogart from Simone's wall."

"It's a lens, all right," Chief Willie said, examining what I had pilfered.

"She wanted me to . . . do it with her in the birdcage, and she seemed pissed when I didn't walk over to her."

"You think that the camera only covers the birdcage?"

"Probably. Which means my little titty-grab and hurl-o-rama probably didn't make the shot."

"I think it may be time to go in. I want to dismantle the thing and see where the photos or films are stored."

"I need you to do something else," I said.

"What?"

"Bogart her laptop," I said.

"I think I'll pull a terror deal, set off a loud but harmless device, and clear the place out. Then I'll go in wearing some kind of uniform when people run out."

I ignored the tactical description. "She wanted to trap me, Chief," I said. "And who the hell am I?"

"A married man, for one thing, Mongoose. What did she say when she called you to come over?"

"She was a basket case. She said she hadn't heard from Rebound all day, since he won."

Chief Willie sucked on his upper lip and broke into a grin, which appeared sinister under the lonely alley light.

"What is it?" I asked.

"It's Election Day, Mongoose. She thought she was going to Washington with him. That's what this prick promised her. He won, thanks to you. He's waving to the crowd on TV with his wife. With his wife who owns him. You see? Rebound's on his way to Washington, and she's stuck at the tollbooth at the Egg Harbor exit of the Atlantic City Expressway. She sees the whole gig coming apart, so she wants to trap you last minute, so you'll weigh in for her."

"I think this thing runs deeper than we ever knew."

Chief Willie pulled out of the alley. He would drive me to my car—Irv's car—a few blocks away. Who but Fatima the Netherworld Hell-Bitch walked toward us? She was not in her Hell-Bitch getup, however. She was wearing a hippie-style sundress, and was carrying a poodle.

"Hey there, Fatty," I said out the window.

"I'm not Fatima anymore," she said matter-of-factly.

"No?"

"No, I'm Indra the Pet Psychic," she said.

This got Chief Willie's attention. "So, sweetheart," Chief Willie said, "what does a pet psychic do?"

"I predict your pet's future."

"What," Chief Willie said, "like Fluffy's gonna shit on the rug at six o'clock?"

"More spiritual than that," "Indra" said.

"All right, Fluffy's gonna shit on the rug, die, and go to heaven?" Chief Willie retorted.

"Closer," Indra said.

As Indra walked off with her new identity in tow, Chief Willie concluded, "See, Jonah, we all can change."

EVERYBODY LETS YOU DOWN

"Did you find yourself a stripper who holds the answer to your life?"

"I've known you to nap, but not lay in a hammock on a November night in New Jersey staring at wood planks," Edie said.

I faced Edie so that we were nose-to-nose. Even the slightest shift in position caused the hammock to swing off-balance. Edie and I held each other still and waited until the hammock centered itself in a gentle sway. "You caught me in the middle of an epiphany," I said.

"People don't have epiphanies; they suddenly decide to admit what they've long thought. So what's the epiphany? Did you find yourself a stripper who holds the answer to your life?"

I took her question calmly because we had had discussions with this subtext before. "She's not a stripper," I deadpanned. "She's an apparel removal technician."

I kissed her nose where it turned up at the end. I did not tell her about how I threw up on Simone Lava. While confessions have great symbolic utility, in my case, I couldn't envision the right spin. *Edie, I went to the Hosebag Motel hoping to boff the governor's psychotic tart, but then I puked on her . . .* That my failure to consummate the boff may have been anchored in my fidelity was not exactly a negotiating point in my favor.

Edie then buried her face in her hands and began to sob. She was not a big crier, so it really threw me off. What did she know? I panicked.

"What's wrong?"

"I just feel so sad for you," she said, catching her breath. "Everybody lets you down. Any man you try to lean on attacks you or deserts you. No father. Mickey ranted at you when you began to make it. Rebound attacks you. It's just so sad."

"I have Irv," I said, trying to calm her down.

"A wonderful role model," Edie laughed through her tears.

"I don't know, kiddo, I guess it's just in fairy tales that we get role models. Maybe . . . maybe it's actually a good thing."

"All that betrayal? How?"

"Because it gives me a mission. To never let you and the kids down," I said.

Edie considered this. "You wouldn't have let us down even if you had had better characters to teach you. It's who you are."

"You don't know that. Maybe I wouldn't be who I am if I hadn't been shaped by these characters."

Edie's doe eyes were liquid innocence. I could tell that she didn't buy my premise, but that was all right. I suppose that if I had wanted to marry a hard street operator I would have tried harder with girls like Simone who were all backseat knowledge and no faith. As much as Edie's obliviousness to life's sharper edges was a source of friction, I decided that it must have been a brand of friction that agreed with me, that I had sought. And for all of her protests, there must have been something inside Edie that drove her toward a rapscallion like me.

"Look how thin you are." Edie said. "Your beard is coming in so gray. It's time to get him out of our lives."

"I know," I said.

Ricky motioned for me to come inside quickly as he held the telephone. It was Atlantic City Hospital. Irv the Curve was in intensive care.

SUNSET INSIGHT

"You can't fence redemption."

If the smoking gun of symbolism were ever needed to certify that a certain type of man was dying off, this was the mother lode: Irv the Curve was scheming death in the Frank Sinatra Wing of Atlantic City Hospital. Friends who aren't from Jersey couldn't believe it when I told them that there really is a Frank Sinatra Wing, but they inevitably looked into the matter and found out that I wasn't lying.

So here it was, under the hepcat gaze of Ol' Blue Eyes, that God chose to have Irving Aronson face the final curtain. Fittingly, the lobby had a giant photo of Frank, probably taken in the late 1970s. He was grinning broadly in his dinner jacket and holding his hands out as if he were telling the cops, "Nothing goin' on in here, gents . . ."

The Geater with the Heater was evangelizing doo-wop from a radio playing at a nurses' station. I passed two dozen or so rooms before finding Irv's. Most of the women who were dying inside these rooms were wearing makeup and had cosmetics set out on the little tables that swung over their beds. One is never so sick in Atlantic City that one can't look smokin' hot. My grandmother, Deedee, was like this. She died in this hospital of Alzheimer's disease, which may have stripped away her dignity, but it didn't lay a hand on her vanity. I was with her when she died. She was lying back, her flame-red hair cascading over the pillow, when a nurse came in and tried to take her lipstick off the table. Deedee gripped the nurse's wrist and said, "Fuck off, sweetheart, can't you see I've got a man in here?" I adored her. Her last words were "night-night," which is what she used to say to me when she tucked me in when I was little.

The old men who were dying in the Frank Sinatra Wing were here in part because they thought cholesterol was a concept invented by feminists to pussify them, and they weren't going to let that happen even if it killed them, which it would.

These men ate red meat and, for exercise, extended a finger and asked their best friend to pull on it. The resulting cocktail of flatulence and laughter was psychotherapy and a workout rolled into one.

The men dying here today "took" massages because they felt good, not because they improved circulation.

The only thing they opposed about the war on Iraq was that it didn't happen sooner, and that it was too polite.

You were either a friend or an enemy, a sissy or a stand-up guy, and they took their caps off even in the most casual beach restaurants.

They were a touch bigoted, but knew it was wrong, and wrestled with how to rise above it, especially since many of the health care workers now tending to them in their final moments were variations of darker shades.

These men cheated on their taxes, but had served honorably in the military.

They disapproved of Bill Clinton, but had the integrity to admit why: they were jealous *they* weren't getting blown by a peer of their granddaughters.

They liked the Three Stooges, were perplexed by the popularity of Woody Allen, and thought Nixon got screwed.

To these men, the Mafia was a belief system, not a criminal organization, and they had probably led people to believe they had ties to the rackets when most of them didn't.

Not one of them had ever logged onto the Internet, and they didn't feel they had missed anything.

They secretly sobbed when their first grandchild was born.

They were perfectly comfortable with sweeping generalizations because they were confident in their abilities to make exceptions, if necessary.

These were my people. I disapproved of them as a teenager, but I loved them now. I was genuinely frightened that they were leaving me alone with Barbra Streisand, whose albums they had once purchased, but had disposed of when she forgot who had been in her audience for all of those decades, and why they had been listening.

Irv was sitting up. The right side of his face was slightly twisted, but he looked better than I had anticipated. He winked at me above his reading glasses.

"They said it was a small stroke, but I'm older than Methuselah, so how could anything be that small? But all professionals have to lie, don't they?"

Irv reached for the night table and pulled out a folded piece of paper. "I carry this poem, Jonah. It gets to something we talked about. It's Yeats. Listen," he said, reading:

> I heard an old religious man
> But yesternight declare
> That he had found a text to prove
> That only God, my dear
> Could love you for yourself alone
> And not your yellow hair.

Irv closed the book, and then he closed his eyes.

"That's nice," I said. "It makes me think of a girl I knew when I was little. She had blonde hair like the girl in your poem. The thing I remember most about her is the way she always squinted when she looked at me. I used to stay up at night trying to figure out what she meant, or if she meant anything at all. I would spy on her on the playground to see if she squinted at anyone else, or just me."

"Did you ever find out?"

"No. She may have looked at other people that way, but I always thought with me . . . she knew something about me that I didn't know about myself. I haven't seen her for thirty years—she moved away—but sometimes I still think about what she knows."

Irv rubbed his eyes. "Do you know why I carry that poem?"

"I guess so. We feel what we feel, don't we? It's the way she looks, it can be the way she squints her eyes, the expression she makes when she reads . . . any of these can do the trick."

"How can something so shallow hit us so deep?" the old man asked the middle-aged man.

"Maybe it's not so shallow. Maybe the way we respond to raw beauty is deep in some way that God understands but that we don't."

"Mmm. What have you decided to do about Rothman?"

"I feel like releasing the photos of him and Miss Turbo Tits to the *Probe*."

"And what would that get you?"

"I don't know, I'm just venting. I'm tired of his venom," I said.

"Your grandfather did that to you, you know? Ranted at you. Reminded you of your gritty roots so that you wouldn't get above yourself. That's what Rothman does—reminds you of a low time in your life to keep you in his service. You don't have to go to that dance anymore, Jonah."

"It'll be nice to be free of him and his delusions."

Irv sat up a little. He looked annoyed. Or maybe pained. "Listen to me, son. Let me explain it to you. See, Rothman is in his fifties. His best days are back there." Irv pointed with his thumb behind him. To a lime-green wall. "He's not gonna be president any more than the Puerto Rican girl who takes my bedpan's gonna be president. There's two ways Rothman can go. He can go with fantasies about his future, or he can accept what he is and what he's going to be. Now he lives in his head with his fantasies. It's a better place to be. But deep down, the man he really is is coming for his reckoning and there is a . . . contradiction . . . that's at the root of men like Rothman. My old boss, the Dutchman, had it, too. These men must believe in their hugeness to scam against what that demon inside them is whispering: 'You're nobody.' Every time you show your face, you remind him of what he is, and he hates you for it. When you're young, you're fighting to get ahead. When you're old, you're fighting to hang on. It doesn't make it right, the things people do. But it's good to know about."

A pregnant pause took the hospital room hostage. There was no appropriate moment to spring what I had to spring.

"What about your own reckoning, Irv?"

"What?"

"You're defending Rebound. The things you're saying make sense. I understand the things that men do to hang on better than you think. Do you know what I didn't understand until now?"

"What's that?"

"Why you let me go through this whole search, leading me along bit by bit, instead of telling me the whole story from the top."

" 'The truth must dazzle gradually or every man be blind.' Emily Dickinson," Irv said.

"I figured out that you had a secret, too. A secret you were hiding. Something worse than buying off a dirty politician, which was routine. I think you did something that even violated your standard."

"So, son," Irv continued, "do you think I diddled Doris Mendelson even though her husband was one of ours?"

"No, Irv, I do not."

"Then what did I do?"

I formally accused Irv of what I had concluded over the course of the summer: Irv had been complicit in the death of Norah Kelley. Dispassionately, he unfolded the mechanics of the tragedy. When he was done, I followed Irv's line of vision toward the sea. He was expressionless, and for a moment I thought perhaps he had died with his eyes open. Until he blinked.

"You can't fence redemption," I said softly, thinking of the components of this shocking narrative that I would convey to Barri Embrey. "If Rebound's so weak, he's been pretty good at getting strong men to do his dirty work," I said. "I have a daughter, Irv."

"I know you do."

"Do you know her name?"

"Lily, of course. As you judge, son, remember that men like Rebound need fixers like you and me. You also have advanced his cause, Jonah. That statewide poll of yours. On morality? That didn't sound like the Jersey I've lived in for almost a century."

I sighed. "I did it in Tennessee. It was statewide *down there*. I just didn't specify in Jersey that 'statewide' meant Tennessee."

"So, you, too, confess what's convenient."

"I know, Irv, but—"

"Right, Jonah, wickedness has degrees. This is understood. So what are you gonna do about Rothman? If you give those pictures to the newspaper, you've performed a therapeutic act, but not a strategic one."

"What do you mean?"

"I've never gotten any satisfaction trying to vanquish an enemy. Maybe I wasn't a very good vanquisher. You want a reckoning, not revenge. You want to get him out of your life in a way that serves you. Don't look to vanquish him. If you want satisfaction, go ride horses with your kids. The moment those pictures get out, you gain nothing. Think practical, not vengeful. What you did years ago to that beast, Noel, you had to do. It was practical, not vengeful."

While my feet were parked firmly on the floor, the accelerator in my brain was whirring at a million revolutions a minute to no particular end.

So I just stroked Irv's hand as if I were beginning the process of becoming as smart as he was.

"Oh, Jonah, that Doris Mendelson was something else!"

THE TRUST

"You know. I know. God knows. Amen."

Driving home from the hospital, my cell phone rang. "Do you know what cookies are?" Chief Willie's voice asked.

"Computer cookies?"

"Yeah."

"They're footprints that show where somebody's been on their computer."

Chief Willie nodded and read a printout of cookies denoting in stark digital terms how the former Miss Little Egg Harbor Township had been spending her time during the past six months. He began digging around with some cybersleuths after I gave him Simone's private e-mail address.

"Mongoose, you thought she had a grade-A rack from day one. What you didn't know was that her brains were in the same league."

"She may never be first lady, Chief Willie, but she may be chairman of the Fed someday."

"No shit. And you should remember, Mongoose, that the key to happiness is knowing what will make you unhappy. That motel, son, is not a happy place."

. . .

Edie met me at the door of our cottage after she heard me close the door of Irv's Cadillac, and she said, in classic Edie simplicity, "The hospital called. Irv died."

The service was at Glick's Funeral Home in Atlantic City the following day. There were no women in the small sanctuary, just familiar old *shtarkers* like Mort the Snort and Darth Schnader. Rabbi Wald presided and recited *Yizkor*, the Hebrew prayer for the dead, in addition to a few prayers in English. In lieu of a formal eulogy, Rabbi Wald told a simple story:

"Dudley Moore once asked Peter Cook if he had learned from his mistakes. Peter Cook answered, 'I think I have, yes, and I think I can repeat them almost perfectly.'" The rabbi paused for knowing chortles. He concluded with all of seven words: "You know. I know. God knows. Amen."

Outside of the funeral home, a meticulous little cotton-haired man approached me. He looked a little like Mickey, but his eyes were gentler. He extended his hand, "I'm Doc Rose, Jonah. Irv's lawyer. Can we talk alone?"

Doc Rose gestured to a bench. It was an unseasonably warm November day, so I didn't mind sitting outside.

"Irv named you the executor of his will," Doc said.

"He left a will?"

"That surprises you?"

"A little. My grandfather didn't."

"The bosses always die with the least. They can't own anything. They stash it with their friends and family. There's irony in here somewhere."

"So, you knew Mickey?"

"Of course."

"You know, Mickey didn't give me anything to stash."

"That wouldn't have been his way. A man like Mickey knew what money does to fine young people."

"And what is that, Mr. Rose?"

"Turns them into pudding."

"I see. Why are we talking?"

"Because, Jonah, of what has to be executed."

Doc Rose held a document in his hand. As a rule, I don't understand anything that lawyers write. I don't speak Latin, and I am convinced that the appearance of foreign words indicates that somebody's up to no good. What I did understand, even at first glance, was that there was something very unusual about Irv's will: aliases.

Your beloved, Irving Jacob Aronson, also known as Mr. Fenwick, Swarthmore Louie, and Tommy Carnation.

"Okay. What is there to execute?" I asked, not knowing what else to say.

"A trust is the sole beneficiary of all Irv's assets. It was established ages ago, 1980 to be exact. Every dime goes toward a congregation he wanted to establish for, you know, guys like him."

"Gangsters," I said, clinically.

"Let's just say it's for people who couldn't get into a normal congregation."

"All right. We can say that. Where will this congregation be housed, in a room somewhere?"

"Oh, no, he wanted you to build it."

"Build it? From scratch?"

"Not yourself. With architects, contractors, and the like. It won't have just one religion, he wants it to be interfaith, but he'd like Rabbi Wald to run it."

"All right. Mr. Rose——"

"Doc."

"Doc, I'm sorry to be crude, but how much money exactly did he leave for this congregation?"

"About fifteen million."

I looked flatly at Doc Rose and deadpanned, "Fifteen million."

"Yes, plus the land in Margate across from Lucy the Elephant. Irv bought it around the time he made the will. Could have sold it for a fortune but he wouldn't do it. He said it could only be used for this purpose. I'll contact you about the transfer of funds for building purposes. He anticipated you would commission the architect and all of that."

"You know, Doc, I don't have much experience with religion myself. I'm not sure how to even get started on an interfaith congregation."

"I don't know myself, Jonah. The only specifics he gave me were the rabbi and the name of the place."

"Don't tell me, *Vilda Chaya* Reform?" I said.

Doc Rose laughed. "That would be a good name, I suppose, but no, he said it should be named for some woman."

"Doris Mendelson?" I asked, sure of myself.

Doc nodded. "I knew Doris. Good-looking broad. How she ended up with Nooky I'll never know. He had a peculiar nose, but who know what makes things work?" Doc removed a folded copy of Irv's will from his coat pocket. The document had been signed in December 1980. "See here, the Doris Mendelson Interfaith Chapel and Community Center.

"Now there's a scholarship fund, too," Doc said. "Do you know a Norah Kelley?"

"I knew who she was," I said softly, everything Irv had confessed to me completing the horrible events of so long ago.

"The scholarship—about a million dollars, by the way—is set up in trust for women who excel at this particular high school, let's see here—"

"Maple Shade High School," I said.

"Yes, that's right." Doc Rose was a man too smart to ask follow-up questions. Whereas the manifestation of Irv's guilt was cataclysmic to me, Doc Rose had spent a lifetime swimming through the filters of men's souls, and was long past eager analysis of the residue he had found.

"Oh, and one more thing," Doc said. "Irv left you his Caddy. You'll get the title in the mail."

THE LINE OF DEPARTURE

"At what point do we call it even?"

Senator-elect Rothman was aping JFK on the rear deck of his beach house. He was wearing his leather bomber jacket, the one he had used during his Russell Crowe period. Rebound had an unlit cigar in his mouth.

"Scoping out the New Frontier?" I asked him.

"The sea relaxes me," he said. *Ask not . . .*

"I went to see Simone. I tried to calm her down. She's inconsolable."

"Didja get any at least, athlete?" he said with a smirk.

I wanted to ram his cigar down his throat.

"No, I actually got sick in her room, if you want to know the truth."

"No kidding? Not all guys are cut out for thoroughbreds, Jonah. You know that, riding horses and all."

I tried to process his statement. Was it an insult, a neutral quip? My self-doubt had long since run dry. Rebound continued to face the ocean, his back to me. *Pay any price, bear any burden . . .*

"Are you sure the name Norah Kelley doesn't ring a bell?" I asked.

"No."

"Strange."

"What?"

"This Norah Kelley thing."

"Oh, right, from that old news story."

"A reporter asked me if I knew why her body was being exhumed."

"Exhumed?"

"Yes. From her grave."

Color fell from the governor's face. He shook his head quickly like a man with Alzheimer's who was a fatty cell away from forgetting his name for good. "She was cremated," Rebound told a cloud.

"Oh. How would you know the disposition in death of someone you didn't know in life?"

Rebound snapped back to the present. "Norah Kelley?" he asked.

"Yes."

"Oh. Oh, right. I was thinking of someone named Laura Kelley."

"Well, whoever the hell she was, she wasn't cremated. Look at this bulletin from the State Police."

I handed Rebound the printed version of a genuine e-mail from Penny Solomon, Chief Willie's friend at the Vital Records office, to a nonexistent contact at the State Police. It read:

> TO: tm@njsp.gov
> FR: psolomon@njbvr.ac.gov
> RE: Norah Kelley Disposition
> Ted, I have received your request for the exhumation of Norah Kelley. She was interred at Pine Ridge Memorial Ground in Audubon. There seems to have been some confusion as to her disposition. One set of records indicates cremation, but this is not the case after all. Let me know how I can help.

"I guess they've got some new DNA technology that can test out the remains of unborn babies," I said. "I don't know why the press is bothering me with this."

"I don't know either. I've got to catch up with Lucas, Jonah."

"Family State. Family Man," I said, crossing the line of departure. This brought Rebound around, which accomplished my objective of getting him angry.

"I took you when no one would touch you!" Rebound jabbed expectedly. But it still stung.

"And I took you from obscurity to the political playoffs. At what point do we call it even? At what point do we say we advanced each other's causes?"

Rebound turned toward the ocean. His back was to me. "Everybody said you were damaged goods. Between your grandfather, those stunts you pulled for Mario Vanni—"

"What else do you have to offer, Governor, than a rehash of scars from my past?"

"You're going back to nowhere, Jonah."

Rebound glared daggers at me, his bag of tricks having run down to the kind of pulpy remnants you get at the bottom of a cereal box. "I trusted you," he said, reaching for humanity.

"For good reason. I was loyal. What made me untrustworthy? That I know what you are? That I'm tapped out? My debt to you was sufficient to demote me from consultant to slave. I paid for some of these stunts personally and didn't get paid back."

"You know I don't handle the money!"

"You never handle the dirty work, do you, Rebound?"

"I honestly don't know what you're talking about."

"Yes, you do, but you've let everybody bury the bodies for so long that you mistake not having dirt on your hands for being clean."

"You're all ego," Rebound said to me.

"Well, Governor, if you have to overdose on something, it might as well be ego," I said.

Rebound's eyes went black. It was a scientific to-the-core reaction. He couldn't spin his way out of this one: it was goddamned elemental. For the first time, I saw a murderer in his eyes.

"What the hell does that mean?" Rebound whispered.

"It means something that Mario Vanni once told me: 'Sometimes the dead talk the loudest.' "

The governor's eyes withdrew into his skull. The witchy darkness in his face did not make him appear menacing despite his size. His eyes were frog's eyes, scared little eyes bugging out in fear. Come to think of it, Rebound's size was a liability here. There was something about a lame giant that made you want to kick him and put him out of his misery. He tossed his cigar away and withdrew putty from his pocket, kneaded it for a second, and threw it into the sand.

I walked off the deck and saw Rebound's eyes in the massive, but very thin, glass wall that separated the residence from the elements. Eyes can form sentences and convey trenchant realizations such as the one I was reading in the glass:

You have the pictures, don't you, Jonah? What else do you have? Who knows what they've got from back . . .

LIVE FROM MARGATE

"We can't just dig up a body."

In law enforcement they call it "tickling the wire." It means to rattle the suspect, and then see what he does. Before I provoked Rebound, I left a mobile phone on the dish where the Grapes of Rothman spilled from their bowl, which obscured the device. The phone had been programmed not to ring out loud when called, just to begin receiving sound. Soon after I departed, Currier joined Rebound. Chief Willie called my strategically abandoned device from his car. Chief Willie's phone was hooked up to a recorder, which captured Rebound's frantic discussion with Currier. Chief Willie played me the tape at his house:

"Damned Jonah!" Rebound said.

"What now?" Lucas asked.

"One of his press worms is telling him they're going to dig up Norah."

"I thought you said she was cremated."

"Yeah, but I told him I didn't know who the hell she was, and then I said she was cremated after he pressed me, so he knows I know who she was."

"Goddamn it! She was cremated, wasn't she?"

"Maybe not. That's what that prick said. They can test DNA on bodies, even figure out pregnancies."

"Shit. You shouldn't have hidden this from me until now. Christ."

"We've got to get to that body first—"

"We can't just dig up a body." Currier laughed desperately.

"We've got to do something. Go to that gangster over there. Tappo. Make him some kind of frigging deal. You greased him to snatch the roofers' union from Digby, so you can have him handle this. Have him dig her up, replace her, whatever the hell they do. Something."

"What's the worst they can find? I've got to know, Rebound."

"They can find that she had enough coke in her to kill an elephant."

"Where did the drugs come from?"

"From one of Mickey Price's guys. He slipped it to me."

"Why the hell did you involve Mickey Price?"

"I wanted him to take care of the girl. He wouldn't. I told one of his boys that I needed some coke. I didn't tell him why. He thought it was party crap, so he gave it to me. She wasn't supposed to die, goddamn it!" Rebound shouted like Charles Manson. *"Just the fucking baby! I thought it would just get rid of the baby!"*

Rebound began to sob. *"She was another lay, for Christ's sake. That's all she was. Another lay! Was I supposed to give up everything for a piece of ass, the kind of thing everybody back then was doing?"*

Live from Margate, a manslaughter confession.

PORTFOLIO

"Every guy who says he's in the CIA turns out to be a complete poodle fart."

I had promised Barri Embrey a story and now it was time to deliver it to her. The exchange would take place at our favorite spot, the Short Hills Deli in Cherry Hill. My paranoia was cresting, and I had decided to bring protection with me today in addition to my .357. Chief Willie Thundercloud was sitting beside me in Irv's Caddy, his headdress resplendent. I retrieved the manila envelope with the goodies for Barium Enema. Chief Willie and I made our way toward the deli. The moment we set foot onto the sidewalk, a sun-weathered Mr. Unruh stepped from beside a van and stood in our path. His hand was in his jacket, where a firearm almost certainly was. Chief Willie reached in and prepared to liberate his Sig.

"What, we're gonna have a shootout in broad daylight in suburbia?" Chief Willie said to Mr. Unruh. "Shoppers everywhere and all. Or is that lipstick you're reaching for?"

Mr. Unruh stood in his leather jacket and khakis, thinking it over. He slowly withdrew his empty hand from his coat. He grinned artificially and crouched into a martial-arts stance. "The package," was all Mr. Unruh said.

"When were you with the CIA?" Chief Willie asked.

"Nobody talks about the Agency," Mr. Unruh replied.

"The Agency?" Chief Willie repeated to me, loud enough for Mr. Unruh to hear. "This guy is a bigger slab of pimento loaf than I thought he was."

Mr. Unruh crouched into another position and hissed "Sssssaaaaah," which prompted Chief Willie to spit on him.

Mr. Unruh blinked, momentarily stunned, and then advanced on Chief Willie, tilting back on one leg in preparation for some kind of kick. Simultaneously, Chief Willie withdrew his Sig and pointed it at Mr. Unruh's crotch. I took a few steps back, deciding that I offered little value added in a match between a half-crazy pro wrestler and a purported CIA wet boy. Mr. Unruh blinked and Chief Willie lunged at him shouting, "Yaah!" Mr. Unruh stepped backward. Chief Willie switched his Sig from his right hand to his left. As the spook followed Chief Willie's shift, Chief Willie punched him in the nose with a very short right. As Mr. Unruh stumbled back, Chief Willie stuck one foot behind him and slammed him until he fell over.

Mr. Unruh was flat on his back now. Chief Willie fell onto the super-secret CIA agent, knee-first into the poor bastard's groin. Mr. Unruh emitted a shrill *oof,* an expression one step beyond a registration of pain. Chief Willie placed the barrel of his gun into Mr. Unruh's mouth.

"What would Sitting Bull say, Chief?" I asked as Mr. Unruh's eyes reddened pleadingly.

"Dunno. But Chief Willie say, 'Ferret who thinks he is grizzly bear ends up in grizzly bear's shit.' You know, I've been in a lot of fights, and I've lost a few," Chief Willie told Mr. Unruh philosophically. "But every guy who says he's with the CIA turns out to be a complete poodle fart. That means one of two things: Either the U.S. is totally screwed or your ass wasn't with the CIA."

Chief Willie turned to me. I had my envelope in my left hand and my right around the grip of my holstered gun. Two business-casual dudes stepped onto the pavement and recoiled when they saw Mr. Unruh, gun in mouth, wetting his khakis. "You go do your meeting, Jonah," Chief

Willie said. "I'm taking Steven Seagal here into the Pine Barrens and chopping him up." Chief Willie pointed with his chin to the two business-casual dudes. "You two! You see anything here?"

The men held up their hands and backed away. Chief Willie winked at me. As I approached the restaurant, Sheik Abu Heinous backed up an ancient Lincoln Mark IV, popped the trunk, and he and Chief Willie threw Mr. Unruh into the back. The thug's head hit the back of the trunk, hard. The half-dozen witnesses on hand didn't see anything because this was Jersey.

I studied Mr. Unruh as he rolled his eyes, half-conscious.

"Nice work, Chief Willie," I said.

"You gotta love what you do, Jonah."

Barri arrived at the restaurant five minutes after I did. I slid the package across the table. She felt it without opening it up.

"It's a cassette, photographs, and a short narrative that explains everything," I said.

"I'll study it. Thanks."

"Be careful, Barri. Violent men have gone to great lengths to get it. I wouldn't bring it home."

"I'll work on it at the office."

"That's smart. I need you to include a particular fact in your story, and I assure you that it's totally true. It involves a thug that Veasey sent after me, a pig farmer named Whitey Leeds."

"Never heard of him. What did he do?"

"He's a giant piney. He shot out my tires until I drove off the road in the Pine Barrens. He tied me up, but I escaped before he came back. It was the day before I met with you a few months ago when I started growing this goatee to cover up where I banged my chin in the back of his truck. It's completely accurate to say you have a source who was kidnapped by a giant South Jersey pig farmer. It's also accurate to say that the man who was kidnapped is cooperating with authorities as they attempt to link him to Veasey's scheme. Some big people will go down here, Barri."

She nodded and tentatively prepared to ask her next question: "Is one of those big people Rothman, Jonah?"

"He was the target of a scheme, but there's no proof of any kind that he was successfully blackmailed."

"Shit."

"I do have another story for you, Barri, but it's not one for the paper. It's one between you and me."

"It's about Norah, isn't it?"

"Yes, Barri, it is."

Barri exhaled, which I interpreted as a signal for me to go: "I make my living working with clients in trouble. It's been two decades. One thing I've noticed is that when a man steps over the line, he's a dude just being a dude. When a woman misbehaves, she's unstable. You've got a great career and now you've got a great scoop. If you try to take Rebound down, you'll be known everywhere as a bitter woman, scorned in a desperate attempt to avenge the death of her young sister with exotic hearsay."

I told Barri what Irv the Curve had told me on his deathbed.

"Do you remember 1980, Jonah?" Irv had begun. *"They killed Angelo Bruno in March. The old guys were dropping like maggots when the new blood moved in. We were all running for cover. The FBI was cracking down. The big hotel companies were muscling us out of the casinos. And our friends in politics . . ."* Irv laughed, which degenerated into a cough. *"They nailed 'em in AB-SCAM. From city councils in South Jersey all the way up to the Senate. Senator Williams—gone!*

"In my business, Jonah, we don't retire with a pension. Our pension is our last hustle because we have to move the money we make around to keep everybody happy or they turn on us. I was seventy years old. I needed to produce or I'd be next. I needed to hang on.

"This kid Rothman comes along. He could have fallen under the thumb of the Italians. He could have gone with the unions. This is Jersey. He's a weak one, that Rothman, like clay. You can do whatever you want with him once he's in your hands. So I cultivated him. Mickey and I went thumbs down on offing that girl. Rothman

comes to me—me alone—after we turn him down on the hit. He says he's got this girl
with delusions of grandeur. He wanted a lay; she wanted a prince. Men behave as
well as their options. Rothman was a star. Stars have endless options. He says he needs
some, you know, the drugs. He wanted to make this girl happy and try to persuade her
to get rid of the baby. Keep them partying as usual. He said his usual sources had been
busted and he couldn't go trolling down Atlantic Avenue, what with his fame. So I got
him what he needed. It takes a certain type of hombre to know when his jig is up. I
knew my run was over, which is why I did what I did. Never messed with drugs in my
life. I didn't know he was gonna kill that girl.

"*I sent Freon Leon to paint her name on Rothman's house when I heard ram-*
blings that Veasey was up to something. Leon said he got nervous when he heard
something, and fucked up the job somehow. He didn't explain himself. Later, I sent
him to your in-laws' place to take up that proverb, let you know you were going in the
right direction."

Cornpone Norah Kelly had gotten herself filled with a billion little
Rebound tadpoles that swam upstream and fertilized another generation of also-rans. And then Marsha Pinkus entered the great showroom
of Rebound's psychodrama to provide the missing ingredient in his ambition concoction: world-class cash.

Mickey and Irv, while brutal men, were not the worst of brutes.
When the request to kill Norah Kelly outright was denied, Rebound had
gotten to work. But Rebound *did what was best for him,* the motto of his
era. After all, it was the Age of Aquarius. It was the Age of Mickey Price.

"Jonah?" Barri asked.

"Yes?"

"I know I can't use any of this . . . about Norah. . . for all of the reasons you've said, and more. The confession of a dying gangster . . . Jesus,
I'd be a joke. But if Rothman won't be punished, what will become of
him?"

Barri appeared resigned and disinclined to litigate the matter further
with me. I leaned in closely toward her. Despite the crow's feet deepening
around her eyes, I decided that they didn't neutralize her looks. I kind of
liked older broads, I decided.

"He will be sentenced to a life of mediocre whoredom."

"Who will sentence him, Jonah?"

"I will."

'Tell me you're through with him, Jonah."

"I'm through with him, Barri."

VEASEY SPINS

"He's no Greg Louganis."

I followed Barri Embrey in her BMW to the Island House condo in Margate. The Viking had been tailing him and said that he was home, intelligence that was shared with me, and that I in turn shared with Barri.

Barri intended to ambush Veasey with the information that I had given her. I called Chief Willie and told him what was about to go down. Forever searching for more of the mosaic, Chief Willie had a proposal: "Let's see where he goes after she leaves."

Chief Willie and I sat on a set of bleachers that abutted Lucy the Elephant. From this vantage point, we had a good eye on where Veasey parked his Mercedes. Chief Willie told me that Sheik Abu Heinous had driven Mr. Unruh to a regional sewage plant for a dip and, hopefully, a confession.

We heard the shattering of glass, which rained down from a fourteenth-floor balcony, followed by a spinning pink man hurtling toward the earth. I turned away. Chief Willie didn't.

The sound Veasey made when he hit the pavement was not what I would have expected. Veasey popped like a water balloon, and his finely woven suit contained the devastation of his organs for the short term.

"He's no Greg Louganis," Chief Willie observed dryly.

The small bronze face of Barri Embrey appeared on Veasey's balcony. She was covering her mouth with her hand.

Chief Willie flipped a toothpick in his mouth and put his arm around me. "We learned something here, witch doctor."

"What's that, Chief?"

"Pigs can't fly."

"Instructive."

"And another thing, Jonah," Chief Willie said, with a hint of the father he never was in his eye: "War is not a means to an end. Wars are fought because men like them. We get to see who the enemy is and we get to see who we are."

With that, the great Chief Willie Thundercloud, the most perversely grounded man in South Jersey, plucked an eagle feather from his hat, placed it in my hand, and drove into the shore mist. I climbed into Irv's Cadillac and pulled away, the weary expression of Lucy the Elephant receding in my mirror.

THE PROPERTY

"I want to present you with the chance to buy a rare property."

I met Vadim Pokolov at a picnic table in a small park in Buena Vista Township. It was a rural community near Vineland. Many of the homes that dotted the road were old; some of them dated from the mid-1800s. I got lost on the way, and an elderly gentleman who worked at a gas station corrected me when I pronounced the town's name "BWAY-nuh." It was "BYOO-nuh," he told me, as if my having gotten lost was tied to my mispronunciation.

I wore a suit beneath my overcoat, which may have been excessive, but I wanted to underscore my seriousness. I set down this morning's *Probe*, which featured Barri Embrey's big story. The headline read:

CASINO LOBBYIST HAD SCHEME TO BLACKMAIL ROTHMAN IN SUPPORT OF RIVERBOAT GAMING PROPOSAL
by Barri Embrey
A *Probe* Exclusive

Vadim appeared, slipping from a navy-blue Cadillac wearing a black sports jacket, black shirt with a white tie, and canary-yellow pants. Despite the November chill, he wore no overcoat. There was still the gulag cut-throat in his walk.

We shook hands and sat across from each other at the park bench. I set my laptop on the table. He placed a box of cigars beside my laptop.

"You don't mind the cold?" I asked him.

"This is like heat wave in Moscow. You like Cuban cigars?" he said, his eyes twinkling like a troll.

"I do sometimes, yes," I said.

"These are Davidoff."

"That wasn't necessary, but thank you. Sometimes I like to take walks in the woods and have a cigar."

"Yes, but be sure to put out. Smokey Bear says, 'Only you prevent forest fires.'" Vadim laughed deeply from his gut.

"I see you know American advertisements," I said, none too sharply.

"America is wonderful place. Many bears. I like Smokey Bear. I like Yogi Bear. I got for my daughter teddy bear. I like also how animals talk in your cartoons."

"I did, too, growing up. I still watch cartoons with my kids, but I like the old ones better than the new ones."

"I must agree with this. SpongeBob makes no sense to me. Animals are like people. You look at animal and know he thinks things. But sponge? How could sponge have thoughts?"

"At the very least, Mr. Pokolov, we've agreed today on American cartoons."

"Yes, we agree. I am Vadim to you. I was happy to see you. Doc says nice things. I have study your grandfather. And Irv. I express sorrow for Irv's loss."

While Vadim's English was imperfect, there was an intangible quality about his eyes that hinted at a cold and flawless mind. But his organization would not have a man like him scoping out properties if he were entirely without emotion; after all, no one wants to to tip their hand to an icicle. Vadim knew American cartoons. I was duly disarmed.

"Thank you. Irv thought a lot of you. I want to present you with the chance to buy a rare property. You should feel no obligation to me to accept it because of Doc or Irv, and you have my word that I won't discuss our talk with others if you do not have an interest."

"Thank you for discreet words."

"Vadim, while I don't know the extent of your business interests, I would think that for someone expanding his investments in America, it would help to have a friend in national politics. There is a new United States Senator from New Jersey, of course."

"Yes. Rothman. He is, how as you say in America, 'going to places.'"

"That's true. How and where he goes will depend a lot on the people who influence him. Rothman will not only be able to vote on legislation, he will be able to introduce it, provide a platform for issues, he will be able to have influence over regulatory bodies, perhaps affect the outcome of judicial inquiries, that type of thing. With immigration crackdowns, a senator can stop a deportation with a phone call. I understand that it's next to impossible to get a work permit these days. Whatever business plans you have, Vadim, they will not be possible if your colleagues are not able to get into the country. The victims of prejudice, be they Russian or black or whatever, have always needed advocates in public life. Rothman's value to you is hard to measure, but it could ultimately be in the hundreds of millions or billions depending upon how far he goes. I have a chance for you and your interests to influence him more than any other party."

"Attractive idea. But why would he be influenced by a foreign enterprise that is not constituent? Rothman does not strike me as man in need of wealth."

"That's true, but Vadim, I am a man in need of wealth, and I have items in my possession that I would be willing to sell to you and only you that would give you influence over Rothman."

I opened my laptop and remotely accessed a series of photographs. I wanted Vadim to see that the photos were not on my hard drive in the event anyone else was watching and thought they could simply steal my computer. Vadim put on his glasses and studied the photographs without expression. I then told him how I had "tickled the wire"—conned Rebound into thinking Norah Kelley was going to be exhumed, which caused him to mobilize Lucas Currier to do his dirty work. And I played for Vadim Rebound's confession, the confession I recorded when I had my final visit with him.

When I was done displaying the contents, he leaned back and removed his glasses. I shut down my laptop.

"These photographs . . . quite damaging to man who runs on family values," Vadim said. "And the confession on the voice tape? Heaven be helping him. The American media holds different standards of conviction than courts. That is where this information would be most threatening, no?"

"You've learned a lot about this country for a man who has not been here long, Vadim."

"Outsiders are the best observers. Outsiders know people as they are, Jonah. Insiders only know people as they want them to be. You have got my attention. I am not the only acquirer of assets for my business, you understand."

"I understand. I should be clear, though, Vadim, that it is in my interest to transfer these assets quickly, before Rebound takes office. I believe what I have is most valuable on, ah, the ground floor, as we say."

"Tell me, Jonah, is there really a body to dig up?"

"No, sir. The senator-elect will discover that soon enough. But I got what I wanted."

"Yes, yes. It occurs to me that a man like you would not want to live like grandfather with money hidden everywhere. Many times, my business buys assets in ways that are hidden and that may not be comfortable to you. You are not man who wants to live as fugitive."

"That's true. I want to sleep at night."

"What kind of life do you want to live, Jonah?"

"A modest life. One where I can pick and choose clients. I might want to do some teaching."

"Admirable goals. How might you achieve them?"

"I bought some land a few years ago in a suburb of Washington. I was going to build a house there someday, but it seems we'll be here in New Jersey for a while. It's good land that has appreciated over the years. If I were to sell it at a great profit, there would be nothing illegal in that. How could I help it if a naïve buyer, perhaps one from another country, paid far more for it than he should have?"

"You could not help it at all," said Vadim. "It would be lucky investment for you. You pay your tax on the profit and invest the money as you wish. Such naïve foreigners like myself not doing homework on land purchase! What kind of annual income would you need to live this life you wanted?"

"I have no ambitions to live like a king, but comfort is important. If I had conservative investments that paid me $250,000 per year, plus other income for teaching and consulting, that would suit me just fine."

"To do that, a portfolio of about four million American dollars would be needed," Vadim said.

"I was thinking five."

"I am an uneducated peasant. Foolish enough to be taken in by your extravagant promises."

"Plus, Vadim, as a finder's fee to you personally, I would throw in a Porsche Carrera."

"That is very expensive car," Vadim said, his eyes widening.

"It's too temperamental for my taste. I never got adjusted to the shifting."

"Shifting is headache. I myself do not enjoy shifting and am not one to attract attention to myself, but there are those who could appreciate fast car."

"If you decide to go ahead with this exchange, I'll leave my keys in a safe deposit box along with the proof of everything I just told you. I can hand over the key to the box to you or someone you designate."

I must have betrayed some emotion at this exchange, because Vadim folded his hands together as a clergyman might. "I want you to think about this fact, Jonah."

"What fact?" I asked, perhaps more jumpily than I should have.

"This man you sell . . . if *he* were selling *you* there would be no agony, just transaction." Vadim swept his hands together as if he were wiping off sand.

NIGHT-NIGHT

"Is it the bad man?"

The sun melted beyond the tree line to the west. The early stages of the sunset caused the green of the pines to reflect against the white paint on the Morrises' coral fence. It took about forty minutes from this point until sunset.

Lily and Ricky sat in their pajamas-with-feet putting Legos together. Ricky wanted to stick with the blueprints, but Lily had no patience for the manufacturer's prescription, and wanted to assemble the rainbow of blocks into a free-form mutation of her own imagining.

As I rose to mediate, three raps fell against the door. It was Score the Helper. I felt the muscles in my lower back tighten, fearing that he was about to impart some practical household wisdom that would cause my defects to magnify in Edie's eyes.

"Can you come out on the porch?" Score asked.

"What's up?" I asked, stepping out.

"I just came back from the Wawa, picking up some milk," Score said, then stopped. "There's a brown Ford pickup parked out on the west side of the property."

Edie stepped out onto the porch. "What's happening?"

I told her. The muscles in Edie's face tightened.

"Okay," I said. "Did you see anyone near the truck?"

"Nah, man, I didn't see nothing," Score said. I was secretly thrilled by his lousy grammar. Edie would tire of this rube pretty fast, I thought.

"You have a shotgun, right?" I asked.

"Right," Score said. "It's in my truck. Should I call the police?"

"Yes," I demanded. "Edie, walk the kids over to your parents right now."

"What are you going to do?" she asked.

"I'm going to go out there and find somebody," I said.

"You're not going alone," Edie ordered.

"You take the kids right now to your parents. Score will stay with you and watch the house. Your dad has a gun, too," I said.

"What is this, a *Die Hard* sequel?" Edie huffed. "This is insane."

"You've got fifteen seconds to offer a better idea, Edie," I snapped. "There's a hired killer in those woods."

"We'll take the kids to my parents," Edie said. "Score will stay outside. My parents will stay inside with the kids and call the police. I'll go out with you."

"Are you senile?" I said, taking hold of Edie's wrist. "I only have one gun."

"Let's get the kids," she demanded.

We hustled Ricky and Lily across the gravel road to my in-laws, who were finishing dinner.

"Why are we going out?" Ricky asked.

"It's just for a little while," Edie explained. "Daddy has to go out for a bit."

"Is it the bad man?" Lily asked.

"I don't think so, kiddo," I lied.

"It *is* the bad man," Lily cried. How did she even know there *was* a bad man, I wondered. The same way I had always known there were bad men . . .

"Don't be goofy," I said.

Lily was not appeased.

I explained the situation to Bob Morris, who snarled, turned, and headed upstairs surprisingly fast to load up. Elaine shuffled the kids upstairs, too, enthusiastically suggesting something about building a house of cards.

Back at our cottage, I retrieved my .357 from the lockbox, and stuffed a box of bullets from a separate closet into my jacket pocket. I tacked up a quarter horse named Money (because nobody rode her for free), and set about into the woods. Money decided to relieve herself, and sprayed the earth with whatever had been a beverage earlier. Kicking her didn't help, so I waited out her bodily function while a murderer—one whom I had intentionally baited through a newspaper article—came for me.

Think Clint Eastwood here, Jonah. Whitey is coming, but you knew he's coming. Act like you're just going for a late-afternoon trail ride. Keep your hands on the reins as if everything's cool, but keep your gun's grip wedged into the top of the saddle for easy grabbing.

I listened for footsteps, but heard none. In ten minutes or so the woods would be dark. There was no way that I'd stay out there after it got dark. It would be smarter to head back home and wait for the bastard there. I figured I could wade in a little deeper before being blinded.

The problem with trying to think like Clint Eastwood was that I wasn't Clint Eastwood. Who knew, maybe Clint Eastwood wasn't even Clint Eastwood. My chest began to tighten and my stomach convulsed. Maybe I had judged Money harshly before for relieving herself so violently. Maybe she couldn't control herself, as I feared I was struggling against the same weakness.

A branch on a large pine moved unnaturally. It appeared to jerk from behind the tree. I pulled back on the horse's reins to slow him down. Then I saw that awful floppy hat, which managed to be doofy and menacing at the same time. Whitey Leeds was holding the big branch, and before I could stop, he stepped further out from the tree, which spooked the horse, and as I tried to regain control, the branch hit me in the chest and I fell, grabbing the revolver from the saddle on my way down.

My hand was obscured in a clump of foliage, but I began to find my grip. Whitey didn't let go of the branch as he stood astride a few yards from me. Keep him talking. Make him think I'm helpless. I pretended to be breathing heavily. I scanned him up and down for a weapon, but didn't see one other than his branch. My grip on the gun wasn't certain. The moisture from the leaves kept it sliding.

"You're aggravatin' me already."

"You persist in using that word incorrectly. I believe I'm *irritating* you, not *aggravating* you. There's a subtle difference, but if we're to progress here, it's important that we establish what it is that I'm doing."

"What the hell are you talkin' about?"

Piss him off, Jonah. Act in a way that he won't understand. Go outside his experience.

"You're a big dumbass inbred retard," I said, looking over his shoulder, forcing a laugh.

"Keep talkin', dead man. That's what you told that newspaper lady. If I'm so dumb, why's your ass on the ground?"

"Because the authorities have your truck and are going to be all over you in a minute."

"You're a big liar, boy, just like that fib you told about the camera in your car," Whitey said, pulling a Colt from his pants.

I swallowed hard. "You broke my arm," I huffed. My grip on my gun became adequate, but no better, beneath the leaves.

Whitey fired the Colt to the side of my head. The earth shook where the bullet smashed into the ground.

"Go back to the house, Vinnie!" I shouted off to the side, a desperate attempt to make Whitey believe that we weren't alone. "The retard's got me. Watch out for my kids."

"That's gonna be the last time you talk to me that way, greaser. You think you can bluff me again like—"

Greaser?

"They're out there."

"Who's out there?"

I hadn't seen the force of a ballistic projectile against a human being since I shot Noel in the Pine Barrens a few years ago. The movies don't capture it correctly. Hollywood portrays bullets as small objects boring through flesh and bone, but in reality, it's more like a weather force, a phenomenon of physics that is so powerful it moves the entire target in time and space. In the movies, a man can get shot and think afterward—reload, wince a little, shoot. When a real man is shot, it so annihilates his conception of gravity that thinking becomes impossible because thought is of this world, while a missile knocks you into another plane of physics.

Chunks of Whitey Leeds's stomach landed on me at precisely the same moment I heard the blast. When he fell, Edie came into view from beside Squaw, her horse. She was holding a shotgun.

Whitey was still alive, slowly propping himself up, studying his wounds in an existential way. He was about six feet from me, and his Colt was between us.

Edie was breathing heavily. "Please turn around for a second," I told her. Surprisingly, she complied.

I pulled my revolver from the foliage, and turned to Whitey Leeds, whose eyes were filled with surprise, as if this was an ending he couldn't have fathomed, when to me it was such a logical outcome.

"Please, God almighty," Whitey said.

"You see God around here, asshole?" I shouted.

A hollow-point .357 has a way of introducing an odd rainbow of colors and textures into nature. As Whitey began to gag, his senses throbbed into full alert in total recognition of his pain, his fate, and his executioner. This was my objective with the throat shot. I wanted him fully aware of who was killing him. Then, as he fell back, I blew off the top of his head with another shot, which fertilized the pines with an explosion of brain, bone, blood, and suede from that damned hat. I stood and studied the remnants of Whitey Leeds, and determined there must have been something gravely wrong with me because I found the sight oddly calming. "Night-night."

I stepped over Whitey to Edie. She fell into me, and turned her head slightly to make sure Whitey was dead. I stopped her from making the full turn. "He aggravated me," I told her. "Now, where did you get that shotgun?"

"When this all began, you said I didn't know what went on in this real world of yours," Edie said. "I married a man who has been chased by ghouls for forty-some-odd years. Those ghouls don't die easily. I bought it when we moved up here. I keep it in a locked panel in our bedroom. You went out to the woods like you've done this before," Edie said, looking straight ahead.

"I have, Edie." I glanced over at her and waited until she met my eye. "I have gone into the woods to kill a man."

Edie's face tightened, expressionless. Then she recovered. "That gangster? Before we got married?" she said.

Edie examined my face to determine whether or not it was the face of a killer. I preempted any question that she was inclined to ask with a defensive rationalization: "He threatened you, and then he came, armed, to kill me, and I killed him."

"When?"

"A few weeks before we got married."

"Why didn't you tell me?"

"It's not the kind of thing you tell your new bride."

Edie and I mounted our horses and rode back to the cottage.

"What did you do with him?"

"Irv and Mickey's boys took care of it."

"Do you have any other secrets, Jonah?"

"Probably."

"Do any of them involve Rebound's little girlfriend?"

"She made a move and I threw up on her."

Edie laughed through her nose. "Smooth. Sounds like you."

"I know."

"Are you telling me these things to make me feel better about shooting that giant?"

"No, to make me feel better about it. Do you know what's bothered me all these years? That I *don't* feel worse about killing Noel. I don't feel good about it, but I was more concerned about you knowing than I was about having done it."

"He was going to kill you, Jonah. Like that man out there was."

"How could I love you and the kids so much and feel nothing for men I killed? It's like I'm a time bomb who's a decent guy on the surface but a sociopath underneath."

Edie tilted her head to the side in disbelief. "You never throw up. What made you throw up on Rebound's girlfriend?"

"I got sick all of a sudden."

Edie's eyes widened as she stood and kissed my nose. "You're not a sociopath, Jonah."

Police cars flooded the driveway as we dismounted back at the cottage. I imparted to Edie lesson eleven:

When you turn the other cheek, you get bitten in the ass.

TUNNEL OF LOVE

"If you can't kill the devil you know, kill the devil you can."

The next morning, I was watching *Action News* as Senator-elect Rothman dedicated a new Russian-language school. "Our Russian friends have a home in New Jersey," Rebound declared. A burly man who was wearing a black suit and a dark gray shirt opened at the collar stood rapaciously behind Rebound. For Rebound, it was now A Time to Squeal. Or maybe not. Perhaps he felt no surrender, just inconvenience; Rebound, after all, could always ladle up some rationale from his pot of grandiosity. Let God handle it, Jonah.

Two days before Thanksgiving, Dude Rothman was arrested in Somers Point for possession of marijuana with the intent to distribute. According to the *Probe*, the police had been alerted to a stash by a tipster. I had a gut feeling about where the tip had come from: a renegade deep in the bowels of Digby's campaign had his big dreams shattered with the Election Day loss. One day visions of a Capitol Hill apartment danced in the operative's kaleidoscopic mind, the next day his meal ticket was confetti.

Dude got out on bail fast. A haggard Marsha Rothman was at his side with a top-flight Atlantic City defense attorney who specialized in springing affluent brats from shore scrapes. The expression of Dude's televised face was ghostly shock. His outlaw fantasies had been a hell of a lot more fun than outlaw realities. During his night in the pokey, he had found the ambience to be remarkably different from that of his plush Margate beach house. In the end, it was hard to decide which grandfather had done more damage to his offspring, my grandfather the hoodlum or Dude's, the liberal progenitor of Pinkus Automotive.

Senator-elect Rothman's office issued a brief statement acknowledging that this "was one of those things families go through," and expressed hope that the situation could be handled privately. It was a good response, but I knew down deep that Dude Rothman would forever remain that unique breed of American lost soul, ricocheting between his gratuitous rebellion and the trust fund that financed it.

I love Thanksgiving. It's a perfectly American holiday where people of conflicting religions can all agree that eating is the answer. Edie played a Springsteen song, "Tunnel of Love," on her guitar. She was doing it ostensibly for Ricky and Lily, but I got the message: "You've got to learn to live with what you can't rise above."

I blew her a kiss. Then I rubbed my jaw where it hurt from whoever it was who had decked me outside of Shekels Bank the night before.

The Age of Aquarius taught my generation that perpetual euphoria was a reasonable goal. Edie and I were as compatible as two people could possibly be, but compatibility and euphoria were not one and the same. I know that as I dust off the photograph of Mickey and Deedee that's on a shelf beside Irv the Curve's old copy of *The Disenchanted,* another morsel of my inheritance. It was taken during the 1950s when they were in Venice. Their heads are leaning in toward each other. Deedee's eyes are closed blissfully, and Mickey appears to be either suppressing a smirk or trying to conjure up a pleasant expression after having been forced into the frame against his will. As a boy, my mother kept this photograph on her dresser. I passed it all the time, taking it in passively, at face value, as a child would: A happy couple suspended in upbeat inevitability.

I hold the photograph today and no longer see it as being one-dimensional. Mickey and Deedee are fluid, and I can sense the tremors beneath the surface: the aging cigarette girl desperate to obtain evidence that she had been to Venice; the elusive criminal straining to balance a Darwinian aversion to any record of his whereabouts with the pleas of his firecracker wife for just one picture. Some kind of deal had been struck, but only God and two bickering ghosts were aware of the contents of the arrangement.

Deedee's long-ago prediction that I would "make up" for a lost boyhood turned out to be false, or perhaps I had just interpreted it in the self-absorbed way that an American teenager at the Bicentennial would: that God owed me a debt that would inevitably be forgiven. Or it's possible that Deedee had been correct, and that by "make up" she meant that I would fabricate an adolescent drama with someone like Simone at an unknown point way in the future.

At dinner, a jiggle of cranberry Jell-O slid through me. Warmth in the belly was not a familiar sensation, but I was feeling it, at least for the moment, and I enjoyed an epiphany, which became the twelfth lesson of my saga, which I'd write down somewhere and eventually present to Ricky and Lily:

Happiness is relief.

Along with the photographs and tape recordings of Rebound and Simone, I provided Vadim with a detailed narrative of everything that I knew about Rebound and Norah Kelly. I had sold our property in Poolesville, Maryland, for $5.2 million to the Trans-Baltic Aluminum Company, which was controlled by Vadim's syndicate. Its real value was probably $800,000. After paying Torch Wyeth the remaining twenty five thousand dollars he was owed (for which the Rothmans had also stiffed me), Chief Willie and the Dames, then taxes, it left me with somewhat less than I fantasized about, but enough to throw off the kind of income that I needed to slow down and take only the projects that I wanted.

In the beginning, I thought Rebound had set me on a simple diversionary campaign to attack Digby in order to keep negative scrutiny away from him. What I did not know at first was that the engine that drove Rebound's obsession with destroying Digby was a secret that served as the very foundation of his political career. If you can't kill the devil you *know*, kill the devil you *can*.

The thing that makes me believe that Rebound killed Norah was how Irv the Curve used her death as the fulcrum for his own repentance. Irv, like Mickey, came from a time when there were still standards, however warped. He had been complicit in murders, but would never step outside without a jacket and tie. Not an admirable standard, but a standard still. Irv had wanted Doris Mendelson, but suppressed his temptation because there was a larger order to be preserved.

As for Simone, her true love was stardom and its attendant melodrama. In a sense she and Rebound were briefly married, united by their vulgar sense of destiny. What neither of these idol worshippers would ever understand is that for some of us, everydayness, the absence of chaos, was a good thing.

Simone had been behind it all. Her improvised charade with me had been engineered to keep me as her loyal servant as her campaign to win Rebound deteriorated. Like Rebound, when Simone was in doubt, she did what she knew. The "cookies" on her computer had demonstrated that she had been studying gaming legislation for about a year. In short, it was a too-clever-by-half attempt to catalyze Rebound into accepting her inevitability in his life, dumping Marsha, and getting on with Operation First Lady.

If Simone's thought process was hallucinogenic, her methodology had been keen: She had tipped Veasey off about her affair with Rebound and then filmed them together in flagrante delicto. She gave the film to Veasey, who began blackmailing Rebound into lobbying for riverboat gambling. Rebound, in turn, dropped hints that he would support the riverboat bill. Veasey, whose billings from his regular clients had dried up, went back to them with a lucrative proposal to kill the riverboat bill he had covertly sponsored with a bribe to Assemblyman Harris.

Simone did not scurry into oblivion. She confessed on-the-record to Barri Embrey that she had been the intern who had sparked all of the chatter about A Time to Kneel. She got her own gossip radio program on a little station in Margate called *Hot Lava*.

Rebound, through Currier, declared the latest allegation against his meal ticket to be "sheer fantasy." It was the word of a chippie against that of a regional icon, so the story ebbed away. When Simone's version first broke in the press, Rebound was conveniently hospitalized for food poisoning. This approach would appeal to Marsha's nurturing instincts. Besides, it wouldn't require an empirical diagnosis—he could recover as soon as he was out of the shithouse.

I used to think self-delusion was a malignant tick of personality, but now believe that it has a purpose in nature. It gets us through things that hurt. Somewhere deep within Rebound's psyche must have been implicit knowledge that he was a man of limited skills who had once had a moment around the Bicentennial. In that moment, as the nation lay constipated in a Grand Funk Railroad kind of averageness, Rebound had displayed a flash of what resembled brilliance, but was really just a beguiling shadow, like the Man in the Moon. In subsequent years, the further Rebound fell short of some competence, the more deeply he retreated into a cinematic projection of himself. His energy for playing the role of Rebound Rothman was boundless, but perhaps it had to be. If Rebound couldn't play Rebound, who would he play, what would he do?

Ricky and Lily decided they wanted to sleep with Edie and me that evening. Before we closed our eyes, Edie whispered atop the two bundles between us and said, "Strip away your hoodlum affections, Jonah, and you're a very quaint man. That's your secret."

As dry snow tickled the windowpane, I saw a dreamlike rendering of myself in the glass holding aloft the Grapes of Rothman, the fruits of my freedom from Rebound. My sense of triumph deflated when I realized that I was just holding my sweat socks. Somewhere in the night, the primordial voice of the Geater with the Heater incants gospel about the soul that I'm still trying to reckon with. And who in hell was it that knocked me to the ground as I handed over the key to the safe deposit box to Vadim's man? The answers dwell where Rebound and I were conceived, in the shadows of the South Jersey pines.

Acknowledgments

My wife, Donna, and my kids, Stuart and Eliza, accept my literary antics with grace. Hopefully, Eliza, one of these books will pay for that horse.

Every writer should be fortunate enough to have an editor like Sean Desmond, who provided vital guidance at all stages of this book. My agent, Kris Dahl, has been a stalwart advocate, as have my other friends at ICM, Catherine Brackey, Alan Rautbort, and Teri Tobias. Thanks also to Bob Stein and Karen Robson at Pryor Cashman for their legal wisdom.

My business partner, John Weber, and my colleague, Maya Shackley, provided unwavering support during one of the most challenging chapters of my life.

My father, Jay Dezenhall, to whom this book is dedicated, offered critical insights on how the world works that impacted how this book turned out. My sister, Susan, never fails to provide the requisite cheerleading.

Judi Dranoff Malove liberated the spirit of a blonde girl who squinted at me during the bus ride from Jamaica Drive to Coles School in 1970. I vaguely recall owning a leather wristband with an embossed peace symbol during this period. If that's what spiked the affair, it would make sense. Also, thanks to Penny Solomon for allowing me to borrow her name for a character that doesn't remotely resemble her.

Nina Zucker has been brilliant in generating media attention for my books. Thanks also to Linda McFall and Rachel Eckstrom at St. Martin's, and Sandi Mendelson, Judy Hilsinger, and Nancy Friend for the heightened profile.

Mr. and Mrs. Joseph Truitt of Cherry Hill West—why am I still trying to impress you after all these years? Fred Squires, there is something very wrong with you, but your support is coveted.

Steven Schlein and Jim McQueeny provided great information on the nuances of New Jersey politics. Marc Wassermann never fails me on South Jerseyana.

As for the gang at Dezenhall Resources whom I've abused for literary purposes: I am grateful to Marty Kramer for his sportsmanship and enthusiasm for Chief Willie Thundercloud, and to the media team, including Mark Pankowski and Diana Mohoreanu. Christian Josi offered insights into firearms and overall matters of suaveness. Malinda Waughtal keeps my engine from overheating.

Michael Johnson, whose diabolical mind suggested the idea for "Race Card Strategies," the fictional consulting firm, must be praised for the kind of thinking that makes for fun writing (not to mention the overall decay of society).

Mickey Chucas's wisdom continues to astonish.